S0-BAG-080

*Praise for*

# THE CLOCKWORK VAMPIRE CHRONICLES

"I dived straight in, emerging a couple of days later – with a grin on my face… an engaging, fast paced cocktail of violence and intrigue that grabs you right from the outset and doesn't let go until you run out of pages."

*My Favourite Books*

"*Kell's Legend* is a roller coaster ride of a book that grabbed me right from the first page and tore off at a rate of knots like I hadn't seen in a long time."

*Graeme's Fantasy Book Review*

"*Soul Stealers* is fast, brutal and above all unmissable, there is quite simply nothing out there that can currently compare to Andy Remic's unrelenting, unforgiving and unflinching style. The new King of Heroic Fantasy has arrived. 5\*\*\*\*\*"

*SFBook.com*

"Add to the mix a good dollop of battlefield humour… backed up with a stark descriptiveness and it's a tale that gives Remic a firm footing within the genre."

*Falcata Times*

"A rip-roaring beast of a novel, a whirlwind of frantic battles and fraught relationships against a bleak background of invasion and enslavement. In other words, it takes all the vital ingredients for a good heroic fantasy novel and turns out something very pleasing indeed."

*Speculative Horizons*

"A fun ride… I give it four bloody axes out of five."

*Gnostalgia*

# ANDY REMIC

# *Vampire Warlords*

## BOOK THREE OF THE CLOCKWORK VAMPIRE CHRONICLES

**ANGRY ROBOT**

**ANGRY ROBOT**
A member of the Osprey Group

Midland House, West Way
Botley, Oxford
OX2 0PH
UK

www.angryrobotbooks.com
Gears of war

Originally published in the UK by Angry Robot 2011
First American paperback printing 2011

Cover art by Adrian Smith.
Set in Meridien by THL Design.

Distributed in the United States by Random House, Inc., New York.

ISBN: 978-0-85766-106-7
eBook ISBN: 978-0-85766-107-4

Printed in the United States of America

9 8 7 6 5 4 3 2 1

# PROLOGUE
## *Portal*

The wind howled like a spear-stuck pig. Black snow peppered the mountains. Ice blew like ash confetti at a corpse wedding. The Black Pike Mountains seemed to *sigh*, languorously, as the sky turned black, the stars spluttered out, and the world ceased its endless turn on a corrupted axis. And then the Chaos Halls *flickered* into existence like an extinguished candle in reverse.

A sour wind blew, a death-kiss from beyond the world of men and gods and liars, and smoke swirled like acid through the sky, black and grey, infused with ancient symbols and curling snakes and stinging insects. The smoke drifted down, almost casually, to Helltop at the summit of the great mountain Skaringa Dak. The Granite Thrones, empty for a thousand years, were filled again with substance. With flesh.

The three Vampire Warlords, as old as the world, as twisted as chaos, formed against the Granite Thrones where they were summoned. *Almost*. Their figures were tall, bodies narrow shanks, limbs long and spindly and disjointed, elbows and knees working the wrong way. Their faces were blank plates on a tombstone, eyes an

7

evil dark slash of red like fresh-spilled arterial gore, and yet their worst feature, their most unsettling feature, was in their complete physical entirety. For in appearing, they did not settle. Did not solidify. Their nakedness, if that was what it was for the Vampire Warlords wore no clothing, was a diffusion of blacks and greys, a million tiny greasy smoke coils constantly twisting and writhing like an orgy of corpse lovers entwined, cancerous entrails like black snakes, unwound spools of necrotic bowel, and their flesh relentlessly moved, shifted, coalesced, squirmed as if seeking to strip itself free of a steel endoskeleton forged from pure hate. Their skin coagulated into strange symbols, ancient artefacts, snakes and spiders and cockroaches and all manner of stinging biting slashing chaos welcomed into this, The Whole. They were not mortal. They were not gods. They were something in-between, and oozed a lazy power, terrible and delinquent, and none could look upon that writhing flesh and wish to be a part of this abomination. Their skin and muscle and tendon and bones were a distillation of entrapped demons, an absorption of evil souls, an essence of corrupt matter which formed a paved avenue all the way back to the shimmering decadence of the vanishing Chaos Halls.

The Vampire Warlords turned their heads, as one, and stared down at the two men... the two *vachine*, who had summoned them, released them, cast them into ice and freedom.

And the Vampire Warlords laughed, voices high-pitched and surreal, the laughter of the insane but *more*, the laughter of insanity linked to a binary intelligence, a two-state recognition of good and bad, order and chaos, pandemonium and... lawlessness.

"You," said Kuradek, and this was Kuradek the Unholy, and his skin squirmed with dark religious symbols, with flowing doctrine oozing like pus, with a bare essence of hatred for anything which preached the word of God upon this decadent and putrefying world. In the history books, the text claimed Kuradek had burned churches, raped entire nunneries, sent monasteries insane so that monk slew monk with bone knives fashioned from the flesh-stripped limbs of their slaughtered companions. Kuradek's arm lifted, now, so incredibly long and finished in fingers like talons, like blood-spattered razors. General Graal, mouth hung open in shock and disbelief, hand pressed against his face where Kell's axe had opened his cheek like a ripe plum, nodded eagerly as if frightened to offend. Fearful not just of death, but of an eternity of writhing and oblivion in a tank of acrid oil.

"Yes, Warlord?" Barely more than a whisper. Graal bent his head, and stared in relief at the frozen mountain plateau beneath his boots. Anything was better than looking into those eyes. Anything was better than observing that succulent flesh.

"Come here, slave."

"Yes, Warlord."

General Graal straightened his back, a new anger forcing him ramrod stiff and his eyes narrowed and he stepped up onto the low plinth where the Granite Thrones squatted like black poisonous toads. Kuradek was standing, and the other Warlords, Meshwar the Violent and Bhu Vanesh, the Eater in the Dark, were seated, gore eyes glittering with an ancient, malign intelligence.

"You sought to control us, just as the Keepers controlled us," said Kuradek.

Silence flooded the plateau, and all present lowered heads, averted eyes, as a wind of desolation blew across the space, chilling souls. Graal, teeth gritted, did well to maintain that gaze. Now he was close, he could make out finer details. The skin, the flesh of coiling smoke, of writhing symbols, of constantly changing twisted imagery, was glossy – as if wet. As if *oiled*. And now he could see the Vampire Warlords' vampire *fangs*. Short, and black, like necrotic bone. Not shimmering in gold and silver like the vanity of the vachine. Graal ground his teeth. Oh how they must have laughed at the narcissism of the vachine sub-species. How they must now be revelling in such petty beauties the vachine had heaped upon themselves.

"No, I…"

Graal stopped. Kuradek was staring at him. Foolish. He could *read Graal's mind*. Kuradek made a lazy gesture, and for a moment his entire being seemed to glow, the smoke swirling faster within the confines of its trapped cell, Kuradek's living flesh. General Graal, commander of the Army of Iron, was punched in an acceleration of flailing limbs across the granite plateau. He screamed, a short sharp noise, then was silent as he hit the ground and rolled fast, limbs flailing, to slap to a halt in a puddle of melted snow. He did not move. Kuradek turned to Kradek-ka, who half-turned, as if to run. He was picked up, tossed away like a broken spine, limbs thrashing as he connected with a rearing wall of savage rock. He tumbled to the ground, face a bloody, smashed mask, and was still.

Now, the other Warlords stood. They moved easily, fluid, with a sense of great physical power held in reserve. All three gazed up as the Chaos Halls gradually

10

faded and the stars blinked back into existence, one by one. Now, the wind dropped. Total silence covered the Black Pike Mountains like a veil of ash.

"We are here," growled Meshwar, and as he spoke tiny trickles of smoke oozed around his vampire fangs, like the souls of the slain attempting escape.

"Yes," said Bhu Vanesh. Also known as the Eater in the Dark, Bhu Vanesh was a terrible and terrifying hunter. Whereas Meshwar simply revelled in open raw violence, in pain for the sake of pain, in punishment without crime, in murder over forgiveness, Bhu Vanesh was more complex, esoteric, subtle and devastating. Before his imprisonment, Bhu Vanesh had prided himself on being the greatest vampire hunter; he would and could hunt anything, up to and including other Vampire Warlords. Before their chains in the Chaos Halls, Bhu Vanesh had sought out the greatest natural hunters in the world and let them free in forests and mountain landscapes, using himself as bait, himself as hunter. When the hunt was done, with his captured victims staked out, he would gradually strip out their spines disc by disc, popping free of torn muscle and skin and tendons, and he would sit by the camp fire as his hunted victims screamed, or sobbed, or simply watched with stunned eyes as Bhu Vanesh savoured his trophy, licked the gristle from the spine in his fist, sucking free the cerebrospinal fluid with great slurps of pleasure. Bhu Vanesh was the most feral of the three Vampire Warlords. He was the most deadly. An unappointed leader…

Bhu Vanesh was the *Prime*.

Meshwar pointed to an albino soldier. "You. Soldier. Get Graal." The man gave a curt nod, and crossed to the General, helping him wearily, painfully, to his feet. Graal leant on the albino soldier, panting, blood and snot and drool pooling from his smashed mouth, his battered face. His pale vachine skin was marked as if beaten by a hammer.

Kuradek strolled across the clearing, and a cool wind blew in as the world was restored to normality, as blood-oil magick eased from the mountains like a back-door thief slinking into the night. Kuradek climbed up a rocky wall, his thin limbs and talons scarring the rock. Pebbles rattled down in the wake of his climb. Then he stood, on a narrow pinnacle of iced slate, and gazed out over Silva Valley, once home to the vachine civilisation, now flooded, thousands of vachine drowned to seal the magick that would return the Vampire Warlords to the mortal realm.

Shortly, his brothers joined him, and the three tall, spindly creatures, their shapes a mockery of human physiology, their flesh constantly shifting in chameleonic phases of smoke and symbols, stood tall and proud and surveyed the world like newborns.

"The vachine are dead," said Kuradek.

"Mostly," observed Meshwar.

"Those that live need to be hunted," said Bhu Vanesh, a smoke tongue like a rattlesnake's tail licking over black fangs. He anticipated the hunt in all things. It was what gave his existence simple meaning.

"Not yet," said Kuradek. "We are new again to this world. We are weak from escape and birth. We need strength. We need to build the vampire clans. Like ancient times, my friends. Like the bad old days."

"Suggestions?" Meshwar turned to Kuradek, narrow red eyes glowing with malevolence.

"I remember this country," said Kuradek, looking back over hundreds of years, his mind dizzy with the passage of time, coalescing with images of so many people and places and murders. "This is the homeland of the Ankarok."

Bhu Vanesh made a low, hissing sound.

"They were imprisoned," said Meshwar. "Just as we."

"Yes. We must watch. Be careful. But until then, I feel a stench in the air. It is an unclear stench. It is the stench of people, of men and women and children, *meat*, unhealthy and unclean, with no pride or power or natural dignity. We must separate, my brothers, we must head out into the world and," he licked his black fangs, eyes glinting by the light of the innocent moon, "we must *repopulate*."

"So we go to war?" said Meshwar, and his voice held excitement, anticipation and... something else. It took little for Meshwar to become aroused.

"Yes. War. Against all those deviants, lacking in vampire purity!"

# CHAPTER 1
## *Underwurlde*

Events were a blur for Saark, the rich dandy, the flamboyant womaniser, for all that interested him in life was fine wine and raucous sex, silver platters of finely carved pig-meat, juicy eyeballs soaked in thin apple sauce from the figarall fish caught in iron traps under the Salarl Ocean. He was obsessed with pleasure, with joy, his own unstoppable and unquenchable *lust*; Saark was a hedonist, a narcissist, a nihilist, and unashamed of his open succulent fire. And yet now, now it was a blur. His life was a blur, and everything in it filled with a dreamlike quality, a haze of misunderstanding, of confusion – and more importantly, of–

Pain.

The knife cut into his chest and he may have screamed, his kicking limbs lurching in epileptic spasms. The knife was burning hot then ice cold, burning, burning as the tip skewered his skin, and his muscle, and sawed rhythmically and with razor-eagerness through his breast-bone leaving him gasping, teeth clacking repeatedly, fingers flexing as he begged *begged* to make it stop make it stop, but the face over him was hard and brutal, the face of the vachine Watchmaker, Kradek-ka and Saark's blood flushed down his chest, his belly, and he felt something removed from him.

Saark lay there, gasping, flopped like a fish on the Granite Throne and black snow fell and a cold wind whistled, disturbing his long black curls. The wind smelled good, smelled of ice and freedom beyond the mountains, beyond this imprisonment of the blade which had sundered his pale weak brittle flesh. The mountains. The Black Pike Mountains. Skaringa Dak. Helltop.

These names were distant, now, tails of smoke, and his blood pounded in his veins and he was different. Saark had been infected by the bite of the Soul Stealer, her venom pumping round his veins and infusing him with the *toxin* of the vachine, the vampires, a second-rate disease for a second-rate hero... Saark laughed. Blood bubbled around his lips from punctured lungs. He felt like he was dying. And he knew: surely he was.

Saark could ascertain noises, shouting, the clash of weapons, but they were all gone and lost to him. Consciousness fled like a startled kitten, and when he awoke the cool granite of Helltop was pressing his face like a lover. He heard more shouts, and sobbing, and one eye could see the dark sky filled with a *portal* into the Chaos Halls, the Blood Void, the Bone Graveyard, and a fist of fear punched through Saark as he listened to the steady *thump thump* of his heart, open to the world, and slowly his hand crawled across the ground. His fingers crawled across his own slick flesh, slick and cold, drenched in iced blood, and he found a hole gaping over his heart, and his fingers could feel the trembling of his *heart* within because he was open to the world, carved up like a pig on a slab, and that was so sweet, so ironic, so frightening.

A hand soothed his brow. Beyond, he could feel a terrible presence, of death and hatred and omniscient rage. The Vampire Warlords had arrived. And Saark, even in his disorientated state, knew desolation.

"It will be all right," soothed a voice in his ear, and he recognised Nienna and he smiled, and her hands were stroking his face. He could see fear in her eyes, though, and knew then he would die. What could she see? How could she save him?

Saark tried to speak, but could not.

Saark tried to move, but could not.

Distantly, through a mesh of fractured thoughts, words came to him, all tangled, interlaced, like the stranded threads of cotton his mother used to repair his trews. *We must go. We must! We cannot! He's dead. Bring Saark. Bring Saark. He's dead.* They echoed backwards and forwards, reverberating as if they were a drunk's uneven song in the bottom of a sediment-layered tankard. *Bring Saark! Bring him!* A woman's shriek. Oh how he longed for a woman's shriek, but that was a different world, a different age.

Movement. Ice. Cold. Wind. And then–

Plummeting. A feeling of weightlessness. And Saark remembered no more.

On the icy plateau of Helltop, with the Vampire Warlords solid and real behind him, newborn demons and dark gods and *vampires* from the Chaos Halls, Kell, with Saark over one shoulder and dragging Nienna behind him, his mighty axe *Ilanna* in one huge fist and rage and fear pumping through his breast like molten hate, Kell leapt for the hole in the mountain's summit, leapt for the vertical-tunnel so recently brimming with waters which spilled out, were *forced out* under awesome pressure to flood Silva Valley and drown the vachine living within…

Kell's logic was simple. Leap down the vertical tunnel. *Escape!* It had water, down there, somewhere, spoke his desperate mind; and that would cushion their fall. If not? Well, a grim side of Kell's soul decided, if *not* then sudden impact, sudden death, it would be better than living as slaves to the vampires.

Kell blinked. General Graal was in his way.

Nothing stood in Kell's way.

In reflex, Ilanna flashed up, smashing Graal's sword aside as if wielded by a tottering toddler, and in the same movement singing blades sliced Graal's left cheek apart as if paring tender braised beef from bone. Graal stumbled back with a shriek, and Kell and Saark and Nienna tumbled into the hole, into the ancient tunnel worn through rock by a million years of probing meltwater. In that instant, Kell glimpsed three figures on the Granite Thrones. They were fashioned from black smoke. Their eyes were blood red. And they were watching him.

Gravity caught Kell in its fist and pulled him downwards, separating him from his companions. All thoughts and fear were smashed aside like a blow from a helve. Acceleration became his mistress, fear glued his teeth shut, and Kell fell into a headlong dive that seemed to last forever…

The tunnel was long. White. Images flashed and blurred before Kell's eyes. He tumbled occasionally, hitting the sides of the vast tunnel wall but they were smooth, worn by floods and ice and a raging torrent. His hair and beard streamed behind him. Tears eased from old eyes. He dragged Ilanna, his axe, his sweet-heart, to his chest and lowered his chin and waited for a terrible impact…

It never came. Gently, the tunnel curved and Kell was sliding, then free again and falling, diving, and he heard a distant scream but could do nothing. He glanced back, and saw only darkness. Again, he was cradled by a curve in the tunnel, and friction slowed him, burning the flesh of his hands and he yelped, in surprise, in shock at sudden raw agony but it told him one thing, one certainty: it hurt like a bastard, and that meant he was alive. This was no dream. Kell narrowed his eyes and gritted his teeth and fell through Skaringa Dak – dived, through the heart of the mountain.

Tunnels flashed past. Some lit with mineral deposits. Some were huge, caverns dissecting the tunnel through which Kell fell and he thought, *where is all the water?* And he realised, *a flood, a flood of magick, drowning Silva Valley, drowning the vachine civilisation*… and then he hit another curve, which slowed him, and he was sent tumbling through air and darkness and plunged into water so cold he gasped, ice-needles driving through his eyeballs and brain and numbing him. He was deep under, and he clung to Ilanna. *I will not let you go, I will not lose you, my love*. With a sudden spurt of anger Kell punched upwards, powerful legs kicking, and he broke the surface with a splutter and desperate intake of air. He went under again, but fought upwards and as he gasped and breathed, he saw the nearby glow and kicked out for it, his strokes urgent, cold battering through his old bones.

It was a beach, of sorts. Kell kicked and struggled, then flopped uselessly onto his back, great chest heaving. Kell had never been one for swimming, and he hated the water with a vengeance.

Pain and fear ran rampant through his blood, and Kell pushed himself to an upright position and cleared his nostrils with snorts, head spinning. He heard something then, a crying, a thrashing in the underground lake. *Nienna!*

Dropping his axe, Kell surged back towards the freezing lake. "Nienna!" he boomed, and his voice reverberated back a hundred times more powerful, a cackling of demons.

"Grandfather!" shrieked the young woman, "I've got Saark, help, he's dragging me under!"

Kell kicked off his boots, muttering darkly, and with the surreal and ghostly glow behind, leapt back in to the freezing waters, powering over to Nienna and taking the dead-weight of Saark's body from struggling hands. Kell struck back for the shore, Nienna following, and they lay there on the black sand panting, exhausted, shivering with core-biting cold, and Kell rolled Saark to one side and growled and said, "You should have let him sink. What sense, Nienna, in rescuing a corpse?"

"He's not dead," panted Nienna.

"I watched them carve out his heart!" snapped Kell, weary now, and crawled and stood, and rubbed his hands together. "Of course he's dead! Now we need a fire, girl, or we'll also die in but a few short hours."

"But…"

"Nienna! Stand up! Get moving. Keep moving."

She stood, and they looked around. The shore of the vast underground lake seemed to stretch off for eternity. The cavern was vast, endless, and the glow came from eerie stalactites and stalagmites which sat cloaked in some kind of fungus. Kell moved to one, and peeled back a little. He sniffed it. He touched it to his tongue. "I hope it burns. Because," he gazed around, long grey hair plastered to his shivering scalp, "if it doesn't, we're going to die down here."

The beach was littered with stones and rocks, of a million different descriptions, all washed up over millennia. Kell set Nienna to gathering the glowing fungi, and he found several rocks, striking them together until he found a combination that gave a spark. Back from the water, near a cluster of flowstone and stalagmites, Nienna piled the scraped fungus and Kell knelt, feeling foolish, shivering violently. He struck sparks in the fungus, and on the fourth attempt it glowed, and flames flickered. An odd-smelling smoke rose and heat blossomed from glowing flame-petals. Kell glanced up. "Get more," he said.

"Bring Saark to the fire," said Nienna.

Kell ground his teeth in annoyance, but gave a nod. He moved back down to the lapping shore. He bent, and lifted the dandy, and retrieved his axe. He carried both back to this odd subterranean campsite and threw down the axe. He laid Saark out. Saark's eyes opened.

"Thanks, old man," he said, voice a hoarse whisper. "Thought you were going to leave me out there to die."

"Saark! Gods, man! You tough little cockroach!" Kell moved Saark closer to the flames, and stared in awe at the savage chest wound. He could see Saark's heart beating within, pulsating with very, very slow thumps. Kell shivered. Saark was a hair's-breadth from death.

Nienna returned, and they piled more fungus on the fire. Flames roared and within minutes steam was rising from their sodden clothes. Saark's eyes had closed, and Kell gestured to Nienna. They stepped away from the fire.

"There is nothing I can do for him," he said, sadness buried in his eyes, in his voice. "I wish there was, Nienna, truly I do. It is a miracle he has lasted this long. He must have lost a lot of blood."

"Can you not stitch him? I've seen you sew wounds before!"

"No, Little One. It is too wide. It's straight through the bone. We must… sit with him. But when it is time to move on, well…" Kell gripped his axe tight, trying to convey understanding through gesture.

Nienna understood clearly, and she punched Kell on the arm. "No!" she hissed. "You're not going to kill him! I won't let you."

"We cannot take him with us, girl. Look around you! I doubt very much we will survive. How foolish, to try and drag a guaranteed corpse."

"He may be a guaranteed corpse to you," said Nienna, eyes cold, voice in the tombworld, "but he's a fine friend to me, and I will not leave him. You go if you wish, *grandfather*. But I will find a way to get Saark back to the sunshine."

Kell sighed, and watched Nienna return to Saark. He ground his teeth, and rubbed at his temples, and moved back to the fire as the chill of the underground cavern bit him with tiny fangs. *She has the stubbornness of her mother in her*, he thought bitterly, but that only led to further painful memories, of ancient days, and Sara, and Kell closed that door with a violent shove.

Saark moaned, and his eyes fluttered open. "Where am I?" he murmured.

"You should be dead," growled Kell.

"Nice to see you, too, you old bastard."

"I'm simply being honest," prickled the aged axeman.

Saark coughed, and Kell rubbed at his beard. "I reckon we'll need to be moving soon. Don't want those Vampire Warlords ramming claws up my arse."

"How long have we been stranded?"

"A day, maybe."

"If they wanted us, they would have found us," said Saark, voice a croak, eyes watering. "Is there anything to eat?"

"No."

"Anything to drink?"

"Just brackish, oily water. At least the lake will sustain us."

Saark laughed, then grimaced in pain. "You bring me to the finest places, Kell."

"Yeah, well, we ain't married yet, are we?"

"At least you acknowledge there might still be time. Ha!"

"Not whilst I'm breathing, lad."

"Where's Nienna?"

"Gathering more fungus. It burns well, but with a strange smell."

"I recognise that smell, Kell. It's drugsmoke. You're keeping us all high. Well done, that man. I thought my pain had receded; it's because I've been inhaling a natural narcotic for the last few hours. Don't you feel the buzz?"

Kell bared his teeth, face eerie by the light of the fire and the glowing, fungus-covered stalagmites. "Yes. But what you're feeling – that may be the smoke, I agree, or it could just be the vachine blood which now runs through your veins in a torrent."

There was an awkward silence.

"Listen," said Saark, finally, eyes shifting uneasily.

Kell placed his hand on Saark's, and patted him. "Don't you worry, lad. I know you think I'm an insane vachine killer… well, I *am* an insane vachine killer, but you're one of us. You're a friend. I promise to you, here and now, on my honour, on my blood, on my axe, that I *will not* kill you – vachine, or no vachine. That settle you?"

Saark coughed. Blood rimed his lips. "Thank you. But you do not know what you promise. You do not know how it feels."

"Explain it to me."

"Wait. Somebody's coming."

"How can…"

Saark grinned. "*Vachine* senses. They are good, Kell. Very good."

Kell rose, Ilanna in his great fists, and scanned the black shoreline with narrowed eyes. If it was the Vampire Warlords, immortal deities or no, Kell would give them a taste of his axe they'd never damn well forget!

And if it was General Graal come sniffing around after blood and violence? Kell smiled, a nasty smile on such a wise, old, ravaged face. Well, Graal had it coming from a long way off.

A figure picked its way carefully along the shoreline, gradually materialising into a woman. She was tall, limbs wiry and strong, but whereas once she had sported short, cropped black hair, now it was long, gently curled, and luscious like the pelt of a panther. Whereas once her features were gaunt, ravaged by cancer, sunken eyes and narrow bloodless lips, her flesh stretched like ancient, oil-stained parchment, now her skin was smooth and pale like marble, her face proud with high cheekbones and glittering dark eyes. She was a striking figure. A beautiful woman. She had the tiny, pointed teeth of the vachine. The gentle, slow *tick tick tick* of the machine vampire. A clockwork vampire.

"Myriam!" snarled Kell, and readied himself for battle.

Myriam approached, warily, both hands held wide to show open palms, no weapons. Her eyes met Kell's, and she knew there was death waiting there; but then her eyes met Saark's, and a smile touched her lips.

"He is still alive," she said, voice no longer the croak of the dying.

"No thanks to you, vachine bitch. Arm yourself, Myriam, because by all the gods I'll cut you from head to quim, whether armed or no."

"I have not come to fight," she said, stopping, boots crunching on the stones of the dark beach. "If I'd wanted you dead, I could have picked you off from five hundred paces with my bow. And you know that's true, old man."

Kell grinned. "Yeah. Well. I don't die easy." He moved forward, lowering his head, face full of rage and thunder, Ilanna lifting a little and seeming to *glow* black in anticipation of battle. Myriam had betrayed them, allowed Kell and Saark and Nienna to be caught by the Soul Stealers, *aided* in their capture by the Soul Stealers and delivered to General Graal trussed up like festival turkeys for summary execution. She was the enemy, through and through. She was a vachine contortion. A puppet. She must die.

"No!" screeched Nienna, dropping her armfuls of fungus and racing across the beach to stand before Kell. She held her arms wide. "No, Kell, no! Don't do this."

"Get out of my way, child, or you'll feel the back of my hand."

"Hard brave words from the Black Axeman of Drennach!" she sneered. "Such heroic spit to threaten a little girl."

Kell focused on Nienna for the first time. "She will betray us. She is the enemy. She must die. Have you forgotten so easily what happened on the bridge? I have not."

"Hear her out, grandfather." Nienna's voice softened. "*Please? She has her bow. I've seen how incredible she is with that weapon – devastating! She could have easily killed us from afar – all of us.*"

"Girl, you are fast becoming a thorn in my side!" Kell snapped, but lowered his axe, aware he was putty in her fingers, and knowing deep in his soul he would regret allowing Myriam to live.

"Yes, but surely I'm a thorn on a rose?" she said sweetly, and turned to Myriam. There were tears in Nienna's eyes. "Myriam? You have come to help?"

"Yes, child," said Myriam, and smiled, and there was love in her eyes. "Kell released me. From imprisonment. From thrall. From slavery."

"Explain," growled Kell.

"When you killed the Soul Stealers, Kell. They infected me with their blood-oil, their disease, and used clockwork to change me into a full vachine. I was theirs to command, not just through words or gratitude, but by – it is *hard* to explain. They took a part of my soul, and I took theirs. We were joined. I could not refuse them; Shanna and Tashmaniok were a drug for me. I was their marionette. But when you killed them, I was dazed for a while, and then their essence faded back to the Chaos Halls and I was set free. And then I saw the Vampire Warlords, I listened to their words, and I was filled with an absolute terror. I ran, Kell. I was frightened. I slipped away from Helltop and came looking for you. Believe it or not, you people are the only family I have."

Kell grunted, and slumped down beside Saark, who was panting heavily. "Well, you've found us in a sorry mess. I hope those bastard vampires don't come after us, for we are in no real state to defend."

Myriam moved forward, keeping a wary eye on Kell and his axe. "May I examine Saark's wound?"

"Go ahead. The lad will be dead by tomorrow." He fixed a beady eye on Myriam. "And you had a great part to play in that, girl."

Myriam knelt, and peeled back the torn linen pad which Kell had placed over the wound. "It has begun to heal," said Myriam.

"Nonsense," snapped Kell. "And even if the flesh healed, I've seen wounds like that before on the battle-field; he'll surely be riddled with infection. Gangrene will set in turning his flesh into a stinking putty. He will die, horribly, there is no doubt. And in a great amount of pain."

"Kell, shut up!" breathed Saark, scowling. His eyes fixed on Myriam's. "What's happening to me?"

"It is the vachine blood-oil in your veins. You have changed, Saark. You already know this. You now possess accelerated healing powers, and no infection will touch your tainted blood." She glanced at Kell. "The old man is wrong. There will be no gangrene for you; no maggot-filled infections. Your flesh is clean, because no bacteria can face the vampire parasite."

"Why so?" asked Kell, intrigued.

Myriam gave a small smile. "His flesh is cursed. No

26

infection will touch him. Nienna! Bring me some of the fungus; the more yellow, the better."

Nienna carried some to the hunter and knelt by her side, watching carefully. "Can you help save him?" she said, voice soft, eyes wide. Nienna was in a permanent state of shock; she had seen too much death. Her childhood had been stripped away like bark from a tree, leaving her scarred and naked.

"Watch." Myriam tore the fungus into pieces, and taking a flat rock, began to crumble it between her brass vachine claws. "Mulgeth weed, it also grows in the Stone Lion Woods – in the cold, dark, damp places. It has many precious properties for those who live in the wilds."

"It burns well," said Kell, "although I wouldn't smoke it in a pipe, that's for sure."

"Some physicians use it," said Myriam. She opened her pack, now at her side, and removed a tin cup. "Nienna, run down and gather water from the lake," she said, handing the cup. She turned back to Kell. "Mulgeth weed removes pain, aids in healing, and yes, we can even eat it. But if one was to use it for too long, it would destroy a person's brain from the inside out; it delivers a slack jaw and permanent yellow drool. Soon, any such over-indulging individual would be down the Shit Pits at the docks shovelling fish-heads for a living."

Kell leaned close to Saark. "Hear that, lad? No downsides for you, then."

"Kiss my rosy arse, Kell," he coughed, wincing in agony.

Nienna returned, and dripping water into the crushed Mulgeth weed, Myriam kneaded it into a thick paste. Then, she leant forward and packed the hole in Saark's chest with gentle fingers. He groaned, a low sound of agony, and once Myriam had filled the hole she covered the wound with a bandage taken from her pack. She took another pouch, and from this a small, brown glass vial. She unstoppered it, and dripped a single drop of clear liquid into Saark's open mouth. Within seconds, he was snoring.

Myriam turned to Kell. "Now we must discuss Falanor. We must stop these Vampire Warlords."

Kell snorted. "We are trapped under the mountains, lass. What would you have me do? Topple the damn peaks on their heads?" Then his eyes turned dark. "And your words are fine and brave, coming from one who fled the enemy. Fled from them, yes, or maybe, instead, you are still in league with Graal and his bastards?"

"No," said Myriam. "The Vampire Warlords, they are terrible indeed. Dark creatures from the Chaos Halls. They were banished there once before, but Graal and Kradek-ka brought them back using blood-oil magick to open a portal! But I know their plans, Kell. I heard enough, before I was able to slip out down the passages into Skaringa Dak. I heard enough to bring the information to you!"

"Go on," said Kell, listening, brow furrowed. "But that part of your story where the mighty Kell saves Falanor and rides home on the arse-flanks of a pig carrying the severed heads of three Vampire Warlords in a tattered old onion sack, and sucking on the honeyed teat of a rescued virgin, well it needs to be excised right at the start."

"Grandfather, listen to her," said Nienna, sitting cross-legged on a stone. "What have you got to lose?"

"All our lives?" suggested Kell, but muttered something unheard and scratched his beard. At least the oily lake had sluiced him clear of blood, gore and vachine

28

brains, vachine clockwork. He was feeling barely human, for a change. "Go on girl, let's hear it. Then I'll focus on getting my granddaughter clear of this unholy shit-hole, and back to some semblance of sanity."

"Not in Falanor, you won't," said Myriam, voice soft. She glanced down at Saark, face now relaxed in peace, then back to the old, grizzled warrior. "There are three of them. Kuradek the Unholy, with a passionate hatred for all human religions. His favourite pastime was slaughtering monks and ladies of the cloth; or even worse, changing them into vampires and letting them loose on their colleagues. He burned churches and temples to the ground, then would eat their ashes, laughing that his shit would be baptised in holy fire. Now, he intends to return to the northern city of Jalder. He will control the northern half of Falanor, and build up his army of albinos and… and *vampires*."

"They killed everybody in Jalder," said Kell, voice cold and hard. "I was there. I saw it."

"No, Kell. They killed *many* in Jalder. But men are more resilient than you give them credit. They hid. In cellars and attics and warehouses. In the sewer systems, in the shit cauldrons of the tanneries. Kell, many survived, trust me. Kuradek knows this, and he will hunt them down, turn them into his vampire slaves. Into parasitical puppets he can control."

Kell took a deep breath. He thought of his few friends in Jalder, old men, old warriors from back at Crake's Wall, Jangir Field, the Siege of Drennach, and the Battle of Valantrium Moor. If any could have survived the ice-smoke, then surely these were the men?

"I don't know," said Kell, slowly. "It was a miracle I survived the invasion. If it had not been for Ilanna…"

"This is what Graal told Kuradek. This is what I heard."

Kell nodded. "And what of the other two bastards? They going to set up a nursery and wean baby vampires with bottles of blood?"

"No, Kell. Meshwar the Violent will head south, rule Falanor's capital, the city of Vor. There, Graal believes even more rebels survived the ice-smoke invasion. There are thousands of tunnels beneath the city, a huge and sprawling complex. When Graal's invasion began, many fled into the tunnel and sewer network. Many hid. And Vor is vast, as you well know. It is Meshwar's job to hunt down these people, weed them out, turn them into his vampire horde."

"And the third?"

"Bhu Vanesh. The Eater in the Dark. He is a hunter, from the old days," said Myriam, and she rubbed at her eyes, weary now despite her vachine blood. Terror edged her words, and Kell noticed a slight tremor to her hand. If she was faking her fear, then she was a very good actress. But then, Kell had met many a good actress in his years of battle across Falanor. He'd killed a few, as well; on stage, and off.

"And what is his wonderful plan?"

"He will seek to take control of the Port of Gollothrim."

"Ship building?" said Kell darkly, brow furrowed. "He would seek to expand their dirty little empire west? He wants transport for his army, doesn't he, Myriam?"

"Yes. His albino slaves and vampires will take the existing navy, and also build him an extended fleet of ships. With this new, mammoth navy they will head west across the Salarl Ocean – expand their Vampire Dominion across the world!"

"What of Graal?"

"He will go with Bhu Vanesh. Oversee the ship-building. One could say he has been... demoted. Graal thought he could control the Vampire Warlords. But they are all-powerful. They have other plans."

"Graal always was an arrogant bastard. And I didn't get to carve my name on his arse with my axe. Not yet, anyways. Still, l at least carved him a new cheek flap."

"Graal was less than complimentary about that," said Myriam, flashing a dark smile. Her eyes met Kell's. "You understand what all this means, axeman? You *do* understand?"

Kell sighed. It was a sigh from deep down in a dark place weary of carrying the weight of the world. "I'm a retired soldier," he said. "I'm a simple man, a man of bread and cheese, of coarse wine and nostalgic memories of battle. It was never meant to be this way. I was supposed to live out my final years in Jalder, see this young lady through university, maybe travel the Black Pikes one last time before dotage crushed my rotten teeth in his fist, and watched my mind dribble out my ears."

"We have to stop them," said Nienna, who had been listening, quietly, head to one side. Her eyes flashed dark.

"We cannot," said Kell.

"You can!" snapped Nienna. "If anybody can halt this madness, Kell the Legend can!" Hope was bright in her eyes. Her hands and lips trembled. Her focus was complete.

Kell shook his head. "I'm an old man, Nienna," he said gently. "My back hurts in the cold. My knees hurt on stairs. My shoulder is an agony every time I lift the damned axe. And, and this will amuse you, Myriam, for it is your damn fault... the *poison* is still in my bloodstream. The poison *you* put there. Lingering, like a maggot under a rock."

"I gave you the antidote," said Myriam, her lips narrowing.

"Which does not always work?" Kell raised his eyebrows. Myriam remained silent, chewing her lip. "I thought not. With your eagerness to become a vachine, you killed me, woman, as sure as putting a dagger through my heart. Your antidote bought me time. But the evil liquor is still there: in my veins, in my organs, in my bones. I can feel it. Eating me, slow and hot, like an apothecary's acid."

"I am so, so sorry about that," said Myriam, but knew her words meant nothing. She had been dying, from a cancer riddling her every bone. To coerce Kell into helping her, she poisoned him with a rare toxin from a breed of *Trickla* flowers found far out west beyond the Salarl Ocean. Her antidote, however, had not been enough; or maybe the poison had been rampant in Kell's system for too long. What did he have now? Weeks? Months? A year? By saving herself, Myriam had effectively condemned Falanor's greatest hope. Falanor's last true hero. Myriam felt this irony slide through her like honey through a sponge, and she smiled a dry smile, a bitter smile. By her actions, Myriam may have condemned the world.

"I do not believe it," said Nienna finally, placing hands on hips. Her eyes were narrowed, brows dark with thunder. "Are you sure, grandfather? Sure about all this? I watched you fight those Soul Stealers. You killed them! Like they were children!"

Kell laughed sharply. "Oh, how the young do so romanticise. They almost had me, girl; if it had not been for Skanda's help, I would be slaughtered horse-meat on a butcher's worn wooden slab." His gaze transferred to Myriam. "You came here for help. To help yourself, yes, through fear of your new masters; but to help Falanor was an after-thought. I am sorry, Myriam. Battle weighs heavy on my old body, and my twisted mind. There is nothing I can do. For once, Falanor must help Herself."

Myriam bowed her head. Tears lay like silk on her cheeks. "So be it, Kell," she whispered.

They travelled for hours down narrow tunnels barely wide enough to accommodate Nienna. Eventually, when exhaustion crept upon Myriam, the hardy and seemingly tireless vachine, and Nienna was like the walking dead, they called a stop in a small alcove. It was cold, and damp, but then so were all the tunnels under Skaringa Dak.

Nienna lay, wrapped in a thin blanket, her finger stump throbbing. After an albino soldier amputated her finger in retaliation for Kell's defiance after they had been taken prisoner, events had moved so fast, so frantic, she had barely a moment to consider her new severance. But now. Now, despite her exhaustion, sleep would not come. Her eyes moved through the darkness lit by strange mineral lodes, and came to rest first on Kell, snoring, lost in the realms of distant dreams and memories and battles; then on to Myriam, breath hissing past her small, pointed fangs. Vampire fangs. *Vachine* fangs. Nienna rubbed at her finger, and winced as pain flared up her hand, up her arm. Kell had expertly stitched the wound, the *amputation*, slicing a flap of skin and pulling it over the neatly cut bone. He had tears in his eyes. Tears of sorrow, but also of guilt. He blamed himself. He felt completely responsible. And Nienna supposed he was, to a large extent; but then, if he was to blame for the loss of Nienna's little finger, he was also to blame for saving her life time after time after time. She could forgive him one small mistake, if mistake it was. She grimaced. In war, they all had to make sacrifices. And at least she was still alive.

Nienna rubbed her finger. It had been the most painful moment of her life, and the act of butchery, the look on the albino soldier's face – well, it was something she would never forget. Just like Kat's murder was something she would never forget. The vachine, the cankers, the soldiers, the battles – her grandfather striding with axe in hand, with *Ilanna* in hand, and turning from an affectionate old soldier, a retired old soldier, white-haired, funny, loving, ruffling her hair, cooking vegetable soup, polishing her boots with spit and polish and hard elbow grease, chastising her for neglecting her studies, nagging at her to smarten up her clothes, eat better food, be nice to her mother even when her mother shouted at her, neglected her, allowed her to starve. Nienna laughed bitterly. Oh yes. Her mother. A good strong woman, everybody said. A religious woman. Pious. When she died, she had earned a place in the Bright Halls. But Nienna remembered a different aspect to her character. Nienna's mother, Kell's daughter – Sara, the daughter who had disowned Kell and swore never to speak to him again. Well, to Nienna she was a cold woman. A hard woman. A woman of iron principles. A woman who made Nienna's flesh creep, made her hackles rise, a woman who'd made her life a misery with constant religious studies, muttered prayers and the eternal, submissive worshipping of the bloody gods!

Damn the gods, thought Nienna.

Let them burn in the furnaces of the Blood Void!

Let them rot in the Chaos Halls!

Yes. Kell might be a hard man, a drinker of whiskey, a pugilist, he might be a butcher and all the other things people called him – and what she had seen. But he had a core of goodness, Nienna knew. He had a kind heart. A kinder soul. And to her, no matter how others tried to deviate matters, he was still a hero. He was Kell. Kell, the Legend.

Sleep finally came.

And with it came a dream, a dark dream, a dream in which Bhu Vanesh hunted her, panting and giggling through a dark, deserted city, through empty streets and temples and cathedrals, running over slick greasy cobbles. And as he caught her, his fangs gleamed and he reached for her succulent throat...

As Nienna tossed and turned in her sleep, so Myriam's eyes flickered open. She uncurled, like a snake unfurling from the base of an apple tree. Myriam stood, and stretched, revelling in the feel of new muscles, new bones, and the death of the cancer within. How could cancer survive in a being which was itself a predator? A cancer on civilisation? How could cancer cells eat her own, when her new vachine cells were far more aggressive and vicious and violent than anything *Nature* could possibly conjure? Where Nature had failed, man had stepped forward. Myriam's eyes narrowed. In her opinion, the vachine were the pinnacle of evolution. It could get no better than this.

Gently, she reached down. Beneath Kell's arm was sheathed his Svian, his reserve blade for when Ilanna was lost. It was also, according to ancient, esoteric legends

(although Kell would never admit it as such), a ritual sui-
cide blade. For when times got bad. Real bad.

Myriam withdrew the Svian. The pattern of Kell's
snoring altered, then he snorted and relaxed again, and
she toyed with the blade for a few moments, running
her finger up and down the razor edge. A bead of blood
appeared on her pale white finger. She licked it clear,
tongue stained berry-red for just an instant. Then it was
gone, the blood-oil was gone, and she gave a little shiver.

Inside Myriam, something went *click*. She felt the
rhythm of springs and counter-weights. She felt the spin
of gears. She felt the stepping of advanced clockwork
mechanisms, entwined with her flesh, her bones, her
organs. And Myriam revelled in her *advanced evolution*.

Could she let anything get in the way of her vachine
existence?

Could she let *Kell* get in the way?

Of course not.

And something pulsed deep in her mind. In her
heart. In her *clockwork*.

She felt the need growing. Growing strong. And Myriam did so need to feed. It burned her, like a brand. Like
birth. Like death. Like existence. *Existence*.

Myriam lifted the Svian blade. It glinted in the reflected luminescence of the mineral-layered walls.

Her eyes shifted to Kell.

And her smile was a cruel, bloodless slit...

## CHAPTER 2
# Warlords

General Graal was sucked through the blood-magick lines, and it felt like dying, and felt like being born, and eventually he was lying on a cold tile floor in a kitchen, staring up at the smoke-stained, wood-beamed ceiling in the High Fortress at Port of Gollothrim. The *High Fortress*. He smiled a sickly smile. It was also known locally as *Warlord's Tower*.

The world was a blur for Graal. First, he could smell woodsmoke. Then he could smell the sea, a distant tang of salt, the taste of fresh sea breeze. Stunned, for the blood-oil magick *sending* was like being punched into the earth by the fist of a giant, Graal gradually fought for his senses to return. He heard distraught sobbing. He breathed, breathed deep, and inside him clockwork went *tick, tick, tick*.

Graal moved his head to the left. Kradek-ka lay unconscious, blood leaking from his eyes. His flesh was pale and waxen, and at first Graal thought he was dead – until he heard a tiny stepping of gears, witnessed the gentle rising of Kradek-ka's chest. Then Graal looked right, and jumped at the savagery of the sight...

Bhu Vanesh was there, seven feet tall, narrow, smoke-filled, long arms and legs crooked. One hand held a limp figure, a plump woman bent over backwards, blood dripping freely from where her throat had been entirely ripped out. Her eyes, dead glass eyes, were staring straight at Graal. He shivered. Bhu Vanesh turned a little, as if sensing Graal's return to consciousness. Blood-slit eyes regarded him, but Bhu Vanesh did not break from his task: the task of feeding. His second hand held another woman, this time slim, petite almost, and wearing the white apron of a kitchen attendant. She had long blonde hair, very fine, like silk, which spilled back from her tight entrapment revealing her throat, pale and punctured and quivering.

As Bhu Vanesh sucked vigorously on the plump woman, his eyes watched Graal. Graal stared back. Then Graal's gaze shifted to the slim blonde woman's eyes, and they were frightened, face contorted in pain. Her hands were clenching and unclenching, and for a moment Graal felt sympathy which was instantly dashed against the jagged towering shoreline of his cruelty.

Graal stood, and watched, and knew with a malicious joy that Bhu Vanesh was weak. Weak from the Chaos Halls. Weak from travelling the lines of blood-oil magick; the Lines of the Land.

Eventually, the plump woman closed her eyes. She shuddered. She died. Bhu Vanesh withdrew his fangs with squelches, and dropping the plump kitchen woman with a newly slashed throat, he lay the blonde on the kitchen tiles, and slit his own wrist with a talon. The black and grey smoke coiled back, and a thick syrup oozed free. He allowed this to drop into the slim blonde's mouth, and then knelt back on haunches and watched. Graal said nothing. There was nothing to say.

The blonde started to writhe and contort, her body spasming, trembling, muscles growing taut then slack, taut then slack. Black oil seemed to bubble at her mouth, then flowed out of her eyes and ears and quim, staining her white uniform and pooling under her body.

Graal looked left, out through a narrow window. He was uncomfortable watching the vampire change. It reminded him too much of his youth, and some very bad times. Bad times which had been excised from his memories – until now.

Graal observed the dawn, a wintry grey-blue sky. Distantly, he could make out the sea, and a phalanx of seagulls crying as they swept past his vision. Gollothrim. The Port of Gollothrim. The Fortress. Was it still occupied? Graal shivered. They'd soon find out…

Returning his gaze, he saw the transformation was complete. The blonde woman stood, and seemed uneasy in her shell. Her eyes were now black – jet black, and unnaturally glossy as if filled with a cankerous honey. This, this was the sign of a Vampire Warlord's servant. Graal remembered, now, his thoughts flowing back through a long history, a longer deviation.

"You." Graal was snapped back to the living, the present, and realised Bhu Vanesh was pointing at him. Graal stared for a moment, then glanced at the woman. She was smiling, showing her own vampire fangs. Dead, but alive. The undead. Not like the sophisticated clockwork vachine at all…

"Yes?" snapped Graal, anger flooding him. Anger, and bitterness, and regret. What had he done? He glanced down at the waxen figure of Kradek-ka. What had *they* done?

"Take Lorna to the Division General's quarters. He is here. I can smell his fear. Lorna will begin my recruitment. She is the First."

"Yes."

"And Graal?" Bhu Vanesh's voice was a low, low rumble. Those red eyes cut through Graal's nerve like an assassin's garrotte.

"Yes, Warlord?"

"Forget your manners again, and I will cut off your head and suck out your brains."

Graal paled. He bowed his head a fraction. "Yes, Warlord."

A winter sea breeze caressed the stone corridors of Port Gollothrim's High Fortress as Graal led Lorna, this newly baptised and transformed vampire, towards the central control point of this south-western Falanor city. Prior to the Vampire Warlords' resurrection, Graal's Army of Iron had not made it this far; which meant, in theory, the population of the city was sound. Those, that is, who had not fled after Vor was sundered.

Graal paused, and stared from a high window. Below, the city appeared deserted. And then he saw them, a group of rough-looking men down by the seafront. Huge walls lined the front, presumably to halt high tides or violent storms. Graal's eyes strayed, and he saw a woman, further down. She carried a babe in her arms, and walked quickly, nervously, looking often over her shoulder. She reached a small line of cottages and ducked quickly into a doorway. So. Port Gollothrim was still home to… Graal smiled. Fresh meat. Templates. Vampire templates. But where were the soldiers? Called away to fight his Army of Iron, in Vor? Possibly.

Graal rubbed his chin. His torn cheek was stinging, but

even now he could feel accelerated vachine flesh knitting together. He would be healed by the next morning.

He felt Lorna's eyes on him. He turned. "What are you looking at?"

"A nervous man."

Graal stared, hard, then smiled a cold thin-lipped smile. "So, Lorna, bitch, Bhu Vanesh's First, born straight into our world of horror by simply being in the wrong place at the wrong time. You think you are so powerful? Let us see you perform. Perform, like a dancing monkey jerking on the puppeteer's strings."

Lorna's head tilted, and she observed Graal, and he felt the clockwork of his heart accelerate a little. Then she turned, and Graal led her no more. She moved fast, bare feet padding the cold stone flags, white kitchen apron stained with blood and the black gore from Bhu Vanesh's veins. Her neck showed the twin bites of the vampire. Her skin glowed in an ironic mockery of life.

Now, Graal followed. Lorna needed no guidance.

She accelerated, and Graal had to jog to keep up. Down long corridors, up steps, until they burst into the Division General's chambers and surprised the five men there. Division General Dekull stood beside a large polished oak table, with four other men; all wore military uniforms of black and silver bearing the Falanor crest. The table was filled with maps, and several glasses of half-drained wine.

Dekull, a large man with bull-neck and over-red complexion, thinning brown hair and large hands, stared for a moment in abject confusion. "Who the hell are you?" he growled, red-face forming into the frown of a man who did not take interruptions lightly. Then Lorna squealed in sudden bloodlust, real *blood* lust, and a burst

41

of energy fired her and leapt at him, fastening arms and legs around him, teeth lusting for his jugular. He staggered back, knocking the table over. Wine spilled across maps. He tried to grapple with the newborn vampire, but there came a sudden *crack* as she snapped his arm like tinder, and Division General Dekull screamed, high-pitched and animal, and this slammed the other men into action. They drew swords and charged as Graal watched impassively from the doorway.

Four swords slashed at Lorna in quick succession, as her knees came up, bare feet on Dekull's chest and she kicked up and backwards, through a somersault, landing behind one soldier. Swords clanged together in discord. Lorna's fist punched into one man, and *through* him, bursting free of his chest in a splatter of blood. She stood, holding his jiggling body upright, then let him fall as the three remaining men leapt back, faces uncertain, eyes narrowed. Lorna took a long lick of slick blood from her elbow to her still-clenched fist. Her black eyes gleamed.

"Come on," she growled, voice feral and husky.

One man screamed and charged, and she deflected his sword blow on her left arm where the razor-edge peeled her skin back like flesh from soft-braised pork. Her right hand dropped, grabbed his crotch, and ripped back hard detaching chainmail trews, penis and testes in one mangled lump. The other two men edged towards the door, then one, Command Sergeant Wood, turned and kicked his way savagely through the leaded window. He climbed out onto a high ledge and disappeared from view. The final man dropped his sword with a clatter. Division General Dekull was kneeling, blood pooled around him, nursing his broken arm.

Bone protruded from flesh, a savage break, a sharp stick pointing at the roof.

Lorna strode to the surrendered soldier, and knelt before him. She seemed almost tender. The man, a young commissioned officer named Shurin, trembled as urine leaked down his legs and pooled around his feet. It stank bad.

"I didn't mean it," Shurin whispered, eyes imploring. "I beg forgiveness."

"There is no forgiveness," said Lorna, and he was on his knees before her and she took his face in her hands, a palm against each cheek and she was smiling and Shurin's piss gurgled as it swilled around them, and she pulled his face towards her, as if they were parted lovers returned for a final kiss; then she lowered her fangs, and they sank into his flesh, and he screamed and began to kick, to struggle savagely in the nature of any trapped beast and the piss-stink of the coward. Lorna sucked Shurin, and drank him hard, and left his deflated corpse like a limp doll on the flagstones.

Lorna stood. She licked blood from her lips. She radiated power.

Graal was examining his fingernails, his air one of debonair cool, his eyes detached from the bloody scene before him. He knew the situation; understood it inherently. Until Lorna killed, and fed, she was not true vampire. Now, with this fresh intake of blood, she was almost there. Almost. Now, in the same way the vachine used clockwork to finalise their victims' transformation to vachine, Lorna had to make her own slave; her own *ghoul*. It was the Law of the Vampire. One of the Old Laws. For the vampires were a race of the enslaved...

Lorna was advancing on the barely conscious figure of Division General Dekull. His broken arm cast odd shadows against the wall. Outside, the winter sun was a copper pan pushed into the sky.

"You missed one."

"What?" Lorna's head snapped round.

Graal looked up. Gestured to the window. "You missed one. Sloppy."

"I saw no help from *you*," she snarled, blood still slick on her fangs and causing her frail blonde hair to clump in rat tails around her face.

"This is not my freakshow," smiled Graal, coolly, and turned his back, departing the chamber to look for Kradek-ka. Behind him, he heard Lorna's soothing words. First, he heard the *crack* as Lorna put Dekull's arm back in line. His scream shook the rafters. Then she fed, and fed him her blood, and in so doing spread the black blood of Bhu Vanesh, from killer to victim. She spread the disease. Spread the curse.

It was night.

Graal sat in his large, almost regal sleeping chambers, nursing a glass of port at a smooth-waxed redwood table. Across from him sat Kradek-ka, face still battered from his collision with a jagged mountain wall. He looked far from his usual composed, serene self.

Outside, a large pale moon hung in the sky like a pancreas cut free by a drunk surgeon. Yellow light filtered into the sleeping chamber, and tumbled lazily across Graal and Kradek-ka's sombre features.

"So it is done," said Kradek-ka, and took a drink from his glass. Graal nodded, and rubbed his eyes. Bhu Vanesh's vampiric plague had swept through the High

Fortress in less than a day. Now, he had a hundred and fifty vampire slaves, a jagged hierarchy ruled over by Lorna and Division General Dekull. Dekull had shown himself to be a formidable taker to the cause; and of course, once he was under Bhu Vanesh's control, the Vampire Warlord instantly had access to Dekull's emotions, his thoughts and, more importantly, memories. The instant Bhu Vanesh's blood was in Dekull's veins, they shared a hive mind. Bhu Vanesh knew the layout of the High Fortress, the Port of Gollothrim, the details of Falanor army units, and everything else of military interest. He had absorbed the Division General's mind. This was one of his *talents*.

And now, night had come.

Bhu Vanesh lifted the portcullis, and with the baleful yellow moon glaring down like a disapproving eye of the gods, had pointed out into the city. Before him, arranged on a cobbled courtyard, were a hundred and fifty vampires. They were soldiers, stablehands, cooks and cleaners. Each wore twin marks at their throat. Each had gloss black eyes. Each could smell fresh blood. Out there, in the city, in the world…

"Expand my slaves," said Bhu Vanesh, stalking back from the portcullis, head bobbing a little, legs working with curious joints and making him even less than human. Not that it took much imagination. In the gloom, the flowing smoke of his flesh was even more pronounced.

Silently, the flood of newborn vampires headed into the night, spreading out, disseminating, each on a personal mission of feeding and violent coercion.

"It's done," agreed Graal. Bitterness was in his mind, on his tongue, in his soul. He licked his own vampire fangs. The feeling from Bhu Vanesh was tangible. He hated not just humans, but the albinos *and* the vachine. His arrogance was total. To Bhu Vanesh, everything that walked or crawled was inferior. A slave. There to be used, toyed with, and ultimately consumed as food.

"We must take him. Take them all! Send them back to the Chaos Halls!" Kradek-ka had the light of madness in his dark vachine eyes. He was a Watchmaker! A Royal Engineer of Silva Valley! He was not used to being a slave...

"Sh!" snapped Graal. He glanced around the chamber. He gave a narrow smile. "I think our elite brethren are the kind to employ many, many ears. Let us just say I understand your frustration, and I agree with your train of thought. What we must do is strike when he is at his weakest."

"With each new slave, he grows stronger. With each drop of fresh blood, he grows more ferocious! You know the legends as well as I, Graal. What I want to know is why the magick failed us? Why, by all the gods, did we lose control?"

Graal shook his head. "It was a cheap dice-trick. A card con, like the sailors pull down on the docks. Who wrote the ancient texts? The servants of the Warlords. They wove betrayal into the narrative, after all, who would summon them back without believing in their own mastery? What incentive in being a slave? A puppet? We were cheated, Kradek-ka. And our arrogance, and greed, allowed us to be cheated. Without our efforts, without our lust for power, the vachine would have remained in Silva Valley. We were kings of a small pond; now we are fucking slaves, just like the rest of them."

" '*Thus how thee mightye are crushed lyke shelles againste thyr throynes,*'" misquoted Kradek-ka, and poured

46

himself another glass from the crystal decanter. The port glimmered, like blood, in his glass. Somewhere, out in the city, a human gave a terrible scream. Several cracking sounds followed. Then a deep silence flooded back in.

Graal and Kradek-ka's eyes met.

"How do we solve this, and still remain dominant?" said Kradek-ka.

"Our first step is to kill Bhu Vanesh."

Kradek-ka nodded, and nursed his drink, and listened to the vicious hunting far out in the darkness.

Command Sergeant Wood sat on the roof of the High Fortress, the Warlord's Tower, and brooded. His short sword sat across his knees, and he squatted, huddled beneath his thick army shirt, shivering uncontrollably. Not just from the cold, the wind, the ice, but from everything he had witnessed. And more. The things he could see unfolding in the city beneath him. Horrible things. Nightmare things.

King Leanoric was dead. That was news he handled well. Even the invasion, the Army of Iron – unbeatable, invincible! – as a soldier, this was information which he could grit his teeth and try to plan for. Blood-oil magick. Ice smoke. Cankers. All these things Command Sergeant Wood had witnessed, and fought, and after Leanoric was smashed at the Battle of Old Skulkra, Command Sergeant Wood – with several platoons of elite men – had headed south to warn his superiors. But their way south had been blocked by hundreds of cankers, snarling, roaming free. It took Wood and his men three days to circle the beasts, and they had two encounters which lost Wood six men. It had been a grim time. But still, a time Wood could fight with fist and sword and mace. But now? Now this… *abomination*.

Command Sergeant Wood observed the city below. The Port of Gollothrim. The city of his childhood. A city he loved with all his heart, all his soul. As a boy he had run riot through the narrow cobbled streets, stealing from market traders, organising other orphans and vagabonds into a tight unit that preyed on rich merchants and dealers in silks, spices and diamonds. He was caught at the age of sixteen after robbing a spice magnate, who died from a heart attack during the robbery, and Wood was sentenced to hang. But he'd been rescued from the gallows by a kindly old Captain, Captain Brook, and afterwards joined Brook's Company as a helper, sharpening swords, oiling armour, cooking for the men. Now, here, Command Sergeant Wood had risen as far through the non-commissioned ranks as a soldier could go. He was tough as an old boot left for months in the desert sun, harder than the thick steel nails which held together the Falanor Royal Fleet. But Wood had a soft spot for his men, and even more so, his *city*. The Port of Gollothrim. *His fucking city!* Which was under attack from within…

Command Sergeant Wood had fought cankers and vachine, so he was not averse to surprises. The speed with which the High Fortress was taken was hard for Wood to comprehend, and to *accept*. But even more so, was the changing of people into these… *creatures*.

Wood spat on the high roof, and his eyes tracked a vampire through the distant streets below. There came a tinkling, the smash of glass, and the vampire entered through the window. Wood heard screams. He shook in rage, his fists clenched, eyes narrowed. Then, silence flooded up to him through the icy darkness.

"You were a hard one to find," said Lorna, and Wood uncurled smoothly from his crouch on the edge of the High Fortress roof. His eyes moved beyond her, but she was alone.

Despite his size, his barrel chest, his large hands powerful enough to crush the spine of any man he'd fought, Wood leapt nimbly down to the flat roof, slick with damp and ice, and slashed his sword several times through the air.

"You come here for me to teach you a lesson, girl?"

She laughed at that. A pretty, tinkling sound. She ran a hand through her fine blonde hair, and her claws lengthened, her fangs gleaming under the baleful yellow moon.

"I think it's the other way round, Command Sergeant *Wood*."

"So you know my name."

"You will make an extremely useful addition to our ranks. After I play with you. After I *suck you*." She grinned at him, eyes mischievous, and he reddened. Wood was not a man comfortable with sex. Never had been, never would be.

He smiled grimly. *Join your ranks? I'd rather die first. Rather cut my own throat with a rusty fucking razor. Rather string myself up by the balls! But… Hopefully, it wouldn't come to that.*

She attacked, fast, in the blink of an eye – and came up short, almost impaling herself on the point of Wood's sword. She back-flipped way, then moved sideways, and Wood tracked her.

"You move fast for a fat man," she said.

"Come closer, girl. I'll show you a little bit more."

She snarled, and her gloss black eyes narrowed. Then she charged, in a series of bounds, and leapt ducking under Wood's slashing sword, but he slammed a left hook that pounded her head, knocking her sideways into a straight right that spread her nose across her face. Wood's boot smashed her head, and even as she hit the stone he stamped on her chest, then her face. She lay stunned, and Wood moved swiftly, picking her lithe, seemingly frail body up and lifting it high above his head. He leapt onto the battlements edging the roof of the High Fortress, and gazed down to the distant cobbles of the courtyard.

"Bhu Vanesh will kill you for this!" Lorna mumbled through broken teeth. Her shattered, swollen cheeks changed the shape of her face. Wood gave a short nod.

"He should come find me himself, then," snapped the old soldier, in the same military bark that had sent hundreds of men scuttling across many a desolate parade ground. His powerful shoulders bunched and he launched Lorna into the air. He watched her fall with interest, and when she hit the cobbles it was with a sickening crack. Wood fetched his sword, then returned to the edge of the roof. Glancing down, he watched Lorna start to move, her broken, snapped shape starting to writhe, beginning to squirm. Somebody ran to her, and she gradually climbed disjointedly to her feet and glared up at him.

"Hell's balls!" Wood snapped, and ran for the far end of the roof. Here, he knew, there was a tunnel he could use to escape. But what to do? Where to go? How could he fight such creatures? How could they *die?*

And it came, in a flash of brilliance. Of inspiration.

He would travel the city, and gather to him those who still lived. The criminals, the smiths, the soldiers, the market traders. And they would arm themselves.

And they would fight this scourge.

With a new objective, a *military objective*, Command Sergeant Wood loped off into the darkness.

Jalder was Falanor's major northern city and once a trading post connecting east, south and west military supply routes, known as the Northern T. Sitting just south of the formidable Black Pike Mountains, and separated by the Iron Forest, Jalder had been the first city hit when the vachine invaded south from the mountains and their stronghold, Silva Valley, and using their albino ranks, the Army of Iron.

Since that invasion, where General Graal had used a mixture of blood-oil magick and cunning, first to take out the northern scouts and guards, then to infiltrate Jalder's Northern Garrison and slay the entire regiment based there with not a single loss of life to his own army – *since* those days, months earlier, since the flooding of magick summoned *ice-smoke* which chilled and killed, and allowed soldiers to run riot capturing and murdering the vast majority of Jalder citizens – well, for those that remained, life had been unbearably hard.

It could have been expected that all would die, such was the hardship in Jalder. The ice-smoke froze people in their beds, froze traders selling wares at market stalls, murdered children playing in the street. And those not killed had been rounded up by the Army of Iron, and even worse, many were eaten when a unit of rogue cankers broke free and rampaged through the streets, ripping out throats and snapping off heads.

The Army of Iron had moved south, leaving behind a token garrison of three hundred albino warriors and five ethereal, ghostly Harvesters in order to patrol the deserted city of Jalder, mopping up stragglers and warning Graal of any military activity behind his advancing lines.

Twelve weeks had passed.

And incredibly, some people had survived.

They lived in sewers, and attics, in the tanneries and deserted fish-stores, they scuttled like cockroaches beneath the floorboards of once-rich, proud dwellings, they hid in the towers of Jalder University, in the dungeons of Jalder's Marble Palace, in the Dazoon Clocktower and the old guild spice-houses. They scrabbled for food like vermin, dressed in rags, their weapons rusted. But they survived. They *existed*. And slowly, warily, they began to fight back.

The resistance was led by a small, narrow-faced man known simply as Ferret. He was slim, wiry, but incredibly strong for his size after a life of hardship as a thief, a pit-fighter, and later in His Majesty's Prisons, including a stint in the terribly harsh *Black Pike Mines*. What Ferret lacked in brawn he made up for with speed and accuracy, dirty-fighting and the ability to use his mind. In those first days when the ice-smoke rolled through Jalder, he had been safe in the dungeons – until two albino soldiers went through the cells systematically killing all prisoners. When they came to Ferret, he'd been curled in a ball in the corner of his cell, crying, begging for his life, covered in snot and sores. The two soldiers opened the cell, and one studied his nails whilst the second moved in for the kill – gurgling as Ferret leapt forward, out-stretched fingers punching through and *into* the soldier's throat. He took the dying warrior's sword, hefted it thoughtfully, and split the second albino's skull straight down the middle with a single blow. Turning back to the first man, with finger-holes through his oesophagus pouring white blood, Ferret took hold of his hair and hacked free his head.

Three months ago.

Three months!

How things had changed. How life in Jalder had changed for those poor unfortunates still left. The Harvesters roamed the streets, directing the patrols. Many of the humans remaining were soon killed... killed and *harvested*. The old, frail, weak, scared. The children had proved resilient; good at hiding, and learning quickly to kill in packs with youthful ferocity, and without remorse.

And gradually, they had all come to Ferret. This small man, this skinny man, with his lank brown hair and pockmarked features like the arse of a pig. He was one of the downtrodden, one of the underdogs. But hell, Ferret had come good. Ferret had shown that it was all about *the mind*. All about planning, and thinking, and instruction. Not simply violence, but the *planning* of violence.

Ferret gathered those stray and directionless men and women and children to him; he organised them into groups, the children into food foraging parties, the woman into units who practised with swords and bows during the day, and mended armour and fashioned arrows by night. They discovered underground tunnels near the river, and set nets to catch fish thus providing fresh food and protein. They used the old furnace chambers of the tanneries to cook their food, so that smoke and fumes would be carried up high brick chimneys and away on distant winds. They slept, huddled together under old furs and blankets the children found in rich merchants' houses, and always with weapons to hand. Once, a unit of five albino soldiers found a sleeping pit – the battle had been fierce, but short, with twenty people slaughtered including one of Ferret's trusted "Generals", as he liked to call those he promoted and put in charge.

In those first days, the resistance had numbered maybe five hundred: the strays in the sewers, those hiding in attics and cellars, shivering in the cold dark places. Now, they were no more than two hundred. Slowly, systematically, they had been rooted out and killed. It depressed Ferret more than he could ever admit, and now, as he sat in his little control centre deep within an old tannery building, cold, silent, the huge cauldrons empty, the fires gone out, he waited with three of his Generals for his best weapon, his most trusted ally, his most vicious soldier – a twelve year-old girl they called Rose. Beautiful on the outside, but sharp with thorns beneath.

Rose was a slim, quiet thing. But she had proved herself time and again as the most capable *soldier* in Ferret's resistance. She was superb at gathering intelligence: where albino soldiers would patrol, if there would be Harvesters, what was happening in the outside world. She had her own routes through the city, and Ferret did not ask. Her results were what counted, and Ferret did not need to know the details.

All he knew about Rose was that her parents had been killed when she was young, maybe four or five years, and she had survived in the city from that early age on her wits and intelligence and intuition. She was a born killer, despite her angelic appearance. She was dangerous beyond compare.

Her tiny bare feet pattered down the corridor, and Rose glided into view; warily, for she was always wary;

but with an easy and confident manner. She was a girl in tune with this odd underground environment.

"Hello, Rose."

"Ferret," she said, her dark eyes glancing to the Generals, then around the room. "Nice hideout."

"You have information?"

"Of course. You have payment?"

"Yes." Ferret smiled, his narrow face breaking into genuine humour. *Never trust anybody who did something for free*, he thought. With Rose, he had to buy her information. Usually with precious stones, which he had children through the city scouring rich merchants' deserted houses to find so he could keep this particular human gem in active service.

Ferret tossed her a small velvet bag of rubies. "Here you go."

Rose snatched the bag from the air, and looked around suspiciously. She frowned, then seemed to relax. Ferret tuned in to her senses; he had never seen her frown. Was there something wrong? Had she seen, or sensed, something he had not?

Ferret felt his alertness kick up a few degrees. He loosened his sword and knife at his belt, but kept the smile on his face for Rose. He glanced to the three Generals; all huge men and proven warriors, despite their soiled garb. It was hard to keep clean fighting from the sewers. They stunk like three-week-dead dogs. All except Rose, that is. She was perfectly clean, her simple black clothes fresh as virgin snowfall, her shoulder-length black hair neatly brushed. Nothing about her indicated a covert lifestyle of information gathering, and the secret murder of albino soldiers.

Rose tipped the rubies onto her small, white hand.

They looked wrong, somehow, sitting there in the girl's palm. Then, in one swift movement she ate them, swallowing with a grimace, and glancing up to Ferret. She allowed the velvet bag to drop to the stone floor.

"The albinos know where you are," said Rose.

Ferret felt a thrill of fear course through him, tugging his senses like drugsmoke, pounding through his head, flowing like molten lead through his veins.

"What? This place? They know about *this place*?"

"Yes," said Rose, and glanced around. As if nervous. Ferret had never seen her do that before; never seen her portray anything but the utmost calm, secure in her knowledge that she was unobserved, had not been followed. Now. Now she was different. She was out of character. Ferret grimaced, as he realised the emotion she carried like raw guilt. Rose was *scared*. "They are coming for you," she added, almost as an afterthought.

"Tonight?"

"No. Now. *Now!*"

Even as the words brushed past her lips on a warm exhalation of air, so there came a scream of bricks and torn steel, and a shower of rubble cascaded into the underground chamber. Bricks clattered in the control centre, dust billowed, and Ferret and his generals had drawn weapons, were standing ready, as one *of the vampires* leapt snarling from the dust, so fast it was a blur, hitting one general in the chest and bearing him to the ground with talons slashing open his throat. The large man convulsed, started to thrash, choking on his own blood, on geysers of blood as he flopped around, arms and legs kicking, but pinioned to the ground as if the vampire was a heavy weight.

Ferret licked dust-rimed lips. The vampire was tall, thin, with white skin and a near-bald head. Long ears swept back, and it turned a narrow, elongated face towards him, eyes red, fangs poking over its lips and with a start, with a *jump* that nearly kicked his balls through his belly, Ferret realised this was Old Terrag, once a butcher down on the markets by the Selenau River, an expert with a cleaver by all accounts, and now an integral part of the resistance in Jalder. Old Terrag was one of Ferret's most trusted men. Now, he had changed...

The vampire snarled, lowering its head as the cut-open general slowly ceased his thrashing, blood dropping from fountain to bubbling brook, and with a blink the huge war hammer hit the vampire in the face, sending it catapulting in a flurry of limbs across the room. Ferret glanced at Blaker, and gave a nod. The huge general had kept his wits about him and crept through the billowing dust. Even when Ferret had not. *Shit. That won't happen again. Well, over my dead body. Especially over my dead body!*

Ferret glanced back to Rose, but the young girl had gone. "Damn," he snarled, as the vampire hit him in the back and his face smacked the stone floor, hard. Stars flashed through his skull, and he was blinded. He could hear scuffling, hissing, snarling, and Ferret jacked himself up and began to crawl. There came a *crack*, like wood breaking, and a terrible scream. This was finished off with a gurgle. Ferret searched around for his sword, and as his vision cleared his fingers curled around the short, sturdy blade. He found a wall, and realised most of the lanterns had gone out. Smashed. Only one weak flame burned, and Ferret scrambled around until his back was to the wall, and he crouched there, sword touching the ground, looking, listening. *Use your brain, damn you! Think!*

Three generals. Two definitely dead. And a hammer blow to the face for the attacking bastard. A blow which should have cracked the vampire's skull in two like a fruit on a chopping block, had simply stalled it for seconds. *What have they done to you, Old Terrag? What did they make you?* But Ferret knew. He'd read the stories. He'd heard the old tales, warped and twisted fantasies passed down through generations. Old Terrag was a *vampire*. And much, much stronger than the albino soldiers who patrolled the streets of Jalder making Ferret's life miserable.

There came a roar, and Dandig attacked with his axe. Ferret squinted, saw something squirm through the dust and still spilling rubble from the hole in the roof. The two figures clashed, one a huge bear of a man, his neck as wide as Ferret's thigh, his biceps not much thinner, a black-hearted bastard of a killer who only obeyed Ferret because he didn't know where the gold was kept – or in fact, that there was no gold at all. The axe swept for Old Terrag, who swayed back, changing direction, leaping, bouncing from the wall and launching at Dandig from above. Clawed hands took hold of Dandig's head, as the axe on its return sweep made a *humming* noise lashing under Old Terrag's elongated, stretched out body. And whilst still airborne, the vampire twisted Dandig's head, and Ferret waited for the *snap* of breaking neck but it was worse, much worse as the vampire kept on twisting and tendons crackled and popped and the head *came clean off*. Blood fountained. Dandig's confused body collapsed like a sack of sloppy shit.

Ferret tried to lick his lips, but could not. Fear had drained him of spit.

Old Terrag straightened, *damn, he'd always been a tall bastard,* and stared for a while at the pumping body on the floor. The head had rolled off into the shadows, and Ferret knew the man would have been completely pissed off. Dandig wasn't a man used to losing.

Ferret fought down the urge to splutter a histrionic giggle.

Old Terrag turned that blood gaze on Ferret and his balls retracted to pips. "Your turn, Ferret," hissed the vampire and Ferret was frozen, a statue, a carving from ice, and the vampire launched at him and he wanted to scream and curl up in a ball, to crawl away to some dark recess and lie there until he decomposed. *There there, Fador, soothed his mother and tucked him under the thick sheep-wool blanket but the dark was all around, those tales from Uncle Grimmer still vivid and bright in his child's colourful imagination, the clockwork vampires and clockwork werebeasts creeping through the dark with talons longer than a man's forearm... prowling... ready to strike...*

He blinked, and Old Terrag was on him, flying at him, arms outstretched and he jerked up his sword in sheer panic, no timing, no skill, just a flurry of scrabbling and movement and the blade flashed and Old Terrag impaled himself on the blade. Ferret heard steel bite through flesh, through bone, through muscle, sliding through Old Terrag's chest, through his heart, to exit on shards of spine.

They squatted there, together, like lovers, and Old Terrag's outstretched clawed fingers took hold of Ferret's face and their eyes met. Ferret licked his lips. The vampire was shivering on the sword, impaled, and Ferret could see the tip of his blade on the other side of the vampire's body. Old Terrag trembled, and hatred etched the drawn back skin of his face, *its face*. Ferret thought he was dead, then. It still had the strength to twist off his head. Like it did with Dandig. Shit.

Then Old Terrag closed his eyes, and smiled, and died.

Ferret waited for a minute, waited to see what would happen. Then he scrambled from underneath the body and put his boot on the vampire's chest, withdrawing the short sword. Its heart. He had pierced its heart!

He leant against the wall for a few moments, breathing heavily, then wiped sweat mixed with brick-dust from his brow, leaving a muddy red smear on his sleeve.

"You can cut off their heads, as well," came the gentle voice of Rose, as she emerged from the dust.

Ferret coughed, and snorted snot to the ground. "You've seen them killed?"

"A few," she said. "The eastern quarter of the city is all but overrun. All your rebels." She smiled, sadly. "All of them... *changed*."

"How are they changed? With magick?"

"With a bite. To the neck. Then they seem to die, and they come back to life and are quick, and strong, and hard to kill. As you saw." She glanced at the three twisted corpses of Ferret's Generals; three hardy men, grim men, men who had slaughtered albino soldiers for fun. But one vampire had killed all three. And would have killed Ferret, if not for a twist of fate. Of luck.

"Shit. We have gone to the Bone Graveyard!"

"No. We are in Jalder. You must tell your people. They will listen to you. You must tell them how to fight. How to kill..." She glanced at the corpse of Old Terrag. Already, it had gone black, crinkled as if cooked, and the stench was unbearable. "How to kill these creatures."

"I will," said Ferret. "Come with me, Rose."

"No."

"It's death out there!"

"I know." She smiled. "But I have things I must do."


His name was Vishniriak. He was a Harvester. He was a leader amongst the Harvesters. He came from under the Black Pike Mountains and was tall, wearing thin white robes embroidered with gold religious symbols and threads. His face was flat and oval, his head hairless, his nose tiny slits which hissed when he breathed. And eyes... small black eyes without emotion, but glittering with a feral intelligence.

He stood on the battlements overlooking the city of Jalder, and the wind howled, and his robes flapped and whipped, snapping viciously. He turned to his left, and stared at Kuradek the Vampire Warlord with tiny black eyes.

Hate flowed through him.

Vishniriak, and the Harvesters, hated the Vampire Warlords. But he knew they were tools. And a good workman uses the best of tools.

To the Harvesters, the Vampire Warlords were the best of tools.

"Send them," said Kuradek, his flesh swirling, flowing, and Vishniriak knew that one day there would be a reckoning, and one day they would fight; but now. Now they were allies. With a single goal.

Vishniriak looked down into the courtyard, the same place where months earlier a flood of albino soldiers, the Army of Iron, had marched down into the city of Jalder under cover of ice-smoke and slaughtered most of the population, corpses ready for the *Harvest*.

Now, there were nearly a hundred vampires, pickings from the hardiest men and women and children who had stood against the albino soldiers still active in the city. But not now. Not now.

It had been fascinating for Vishniriak to watch, and no matter how much he hated the vampires in principle the domino effect of their transformation had been stunning and swift. Kuradek had found three humans, infecting them, making them his primaries, his ghouls, then sent them out to find and infect others. Like a plague they swept through the eastern quarter of Jalder. Until none were left.

It had taken two nights.

Now, they would ease out into the city like a brass medical needle penetrating a succulent vein.

And they would hunt. They would convert. They would feed.

Until no humans remained.

# CHAPTER 3
## *Zone*

"I hope you're not going to use that?" Nienna's voice was gentle. And very, very close.

Myriam started, and turned, her movement reflected in the Svian blade. "Child. You move quiet for a... mortal." She smiled. The irony was not lost on Nienna. Myriam glanced down at Kell, snoring gently, face relaxed in sleep, just another old man. Another retired soldier. How easy it was to be deceived, for Myriam knew he was the greatest killer on the continent. She moved to replace the knife in Kell's under-arm sheath, and with a *slap* her wrist was enclosed in Kell's mighty fist. Despite her accelerated vachine strength, the power of the clockwork, Kell's grip was like a steel shackle and she could not move. He opened one eye.

"Finished your game?" he growled.

"No game," said Myriam.

"I wondered if you'd try."

"Maybe I'm not that foolish," she said, and winced as the grip tightened, forcing her to drop the blade – which Kell took from her, neatly, and sheathed it with a whisper of oiled steel on leather.

"Maybe you are," he said, sitting up and releasing her. She rubbed her pale flesh, glancing at the angry-red welts where his fingers had crushed her.

"You're still strong, for an old man."

"Better believe it," he grunted, and stood. He kicked Saark, who opened an eye to observe Kell like a lizard from a hot rock.

"Come on, dandy," he growled. "We're moving out."

"You could have just told me."

"I find a boot up the arse infinitely more persuasive."

"I was having such sweet dreams, of a buxom young tavern wench I once entertained. She could do amazing things with fresh cream and cracked eggs. You should have seen the foam!"

Kell stared at him. "So then, even your new vachine blood has done nothing to kill your wayward libido?"

"If anything, Kell, it has made me more rampant!" Saark stood, and smiled, and stretched himself, muscles aching from an uncomfortable, cramping sleep. But at least he could stand. At least he could stretch. "Now, my old and bedraggled friend, I can do it all night." He touched his chest, tenderly, remembering the savage wound and his near-death experience. He cast it from his mind. It no longer mattered; he was not dead. He was alive. And he was going to drink deep from the cup of hedonistic fulfilment.

"Yes." Kell coughed. "Well. Be careful where you stick it. You've gotten in enough bloody trouble already."

"Like I always prophesied," announced Saark, brightly, "you are the miserable, moaning voice of doom! You should learn to lighten up, Kell. Look at me, heroically skipping along the jaws of death and you don't hear me whining like a little girl with a broke skipping rope. But you, Kell, Kell the mighty Legend, after all we've been through and lived and endured, still you're bleating like a lamb on a cliff ledge without its mama. It's like adventuring with my fucking grandma. What next? A stick? Incontinence trews? Senility? Oh, but you're already holding hands with *that* old goat." He winked.

Kell snorted, and scowled, but did not reply. Saark was right, but Kell could not help but have dark thoughts. It was simply the way he was built. With age came great wisdom. It also came with a great amount of moaning. Kell snorted again, and cursed the day he'd met the dandy.

Nienna moved to Saark, and touched his breast lightly. "How do you feel? How's the wound now?"

"Healing," said Saark, and pressed his own hand to the chest-wound. "Myriam's drugs helped me sleep." His eyes moved to the now-beautiful vachine, with her long dark curls and flashing, dangerous eyes. She stepped out into the tunnel, surveying the route ahead. Her hips were wide, legs powerful, waist narrow, breasts full beneath a tight leather jerkin. Saark licked his lips. "I had very sweet dreams," he said, finger lifting to touch his tongue, and then dropping to touch his chest unconsciously.

Nienna saw the look and gesture, and said nothing, but frowned, and turned away. Back to Kell. "Do you trust Myriam?" Her voice was quiet, and she watched Saark move down the tunnel towards the newly changed vachine. She felt a sudden bitterness then, for they had a connection now; a bonding. They were both newly changed, both a *different* breed to the human. Myriam and Saark were vachine. Whereas she, Nienna, was human. Human, and young, and weak. Too young for Saark. Her eyes narrowed again. For a fleeting moment she wished Shanna and Tashmaniok, the Soul Stealers, had bitten *her*, changed *her* into vachine. Shared their blood-oil. Shared their clockwork. Infected her with their disease. *Then* Saark would have shared with her. He would have looked at her in a different light. Nienna's eyes gleamed.

Kell rubbed his neck, and rolled his shoulders, then his hips, groaning as he worked at the stiffness which came after sleep. "I trust her as much as I've always trusted the conniving bitch. Which is to say, not at all. But what option do we have? She says she can guide us from this place. If she lies, well then, I'll cut her head from her vachine shoulders and we'll make our own way out."

"That would be… interesting," said Nienna.

"So you want her dead, now?"

"Not dead. Just out of the picture." Nienna crossed to Saark, and touched his arm. He turned to her, lightly, a laugh on his handsome face. The gaunt look of the near-dead was fading. His accelerated vachine healing was kicking in fast. He no longer looked like a walking corpse; health and strength had returned. He took Nienna's hand, but was still talking to Myriam.

Kell watched all this, and growled a low growl as realisation struck him. There was something there, between Nienna and Saark. Or at least, there was something there from Nienna. Previously, Kell had always focused on the dandy and his machinations towards Kat, Nienna's older friend, for that had been the obvious flirtation. It had taken his eye from the more subtle approaches of his granddaughter.

"Horse shit," said Kell, and spat on the tunnel floor. "Come on!" His voice was loud and brash. "Let's get moving. You sure it's this way, Myriam, my sweet little angel?"

Myriam gave him a strange look. Her lips curled into half-smile, half-grimace. There was a question in her eyes but Kell stared back, a hard look, a dark look. The same look Dake the Axeman got shortly before his head was cut from his mighty, heroic shoulders.

Myriam shrugged. "Yes. Two days, by my reckoning. Although I'm not sure what we'll do when we get there, the river is too fast to swim, although there are some albino storerooms nearby. Let's hope they're not full of soldiers, hey?"

"Makes no odds to me," grunted Kell. "One way or another, we'll be passing through." He lifted Ilanna, and his meaning was obvious. Myriam did not miss the inherent threat.

"Let's move, then," she said.

When they stopped for the night, it was warmer, and Myriam found some shards of crate for a fire. "It'll be smelt for miles around," muttered Kell unhelpfully, but did not stop her lighting it. They all needed heat. More. They needed the light and morale-boost of a good fire. There was something about the tunnels which invaded a person, chewed its way down into a person's internals... and sucked out their life and guts and soul. The tunnels, indeed, Skaringa Dak itself, was a huge tomb. Being inside the mountain was like being buried alive. Being inside the mountain was like being *dead and buried*.

Nienna found herself a quiet corner, and using a thin blanket given to her by Myriam, tried as best she could to make herself comfortable. Saark approached and knelt beside her, offering her a cup of water. "Myriam found it, down yonder. A pool which doesn't taste of sulphur and shit. It's fresh. Try it!"

"Such small pleasures in life," said Nienna, "that we are reduced to this. Thankful and rejoicing for a simple taste of fresh water."

"Yes, hardly beats the honeyed wine and whore-houses of Vor!" grinned Saark, then looked immediately contrite. He glanced at Kell. "Sorry," he said. "I was forgetting your youth. And my big mouth."

Nienna touched his arm. "I'm not as young as you think," she said.

Saark's eyes glittered. They were dark and entrancing, and Nienna gazed into their rich depths. "Too young, my sweetness, I think," he said with an easy, disarming, friendly smile. And under his breath, "Far too *dangerous*."

"I'm only a few months younger than Katrina," pointed out Nienna. "And her youth wasn't a problem for you."

"Yes. And look how that ended!" snapped Saark, the smile falling from his face. He sighed, and rubbed at tired eyes. "Sorry. Again. I'll not forget what that bastard Styx did. Such a waste. Such a sorrow."

"Yes." Saark pulled gently away from Nienna, and she lay under her blanket, looking at him. His hair was long and black and curled. Even without oils and perfume, he was a picture of masculine beauty. Well balanced. Perfectly formed. Yes, he *had* been through the wars, but recent travel, exercise and constant battle had simply enhanced his athleticism, making him even more of a naturally powerful warrior than when they'd first met. That, and the vachine enhancements... His skin now glowed. His eyes glittered like jewels. He was like... a *god*.

"I'm cold," said Nienna.

Saark gave a long, lazy pause, eyes locked to hers. "That's a shame. That's what it's like, down here in this wasteland." He glanced to Kell again, then back to Nienna meaningfully. "I, too, miss warm and cosy beds, and the easy living. Maybe one day, I'll be able to warm you. But not tonight, my precious." And then he was gone, and Nienna could smell his natural perfume, and she bit her lips and rubbed her eyes and stared at her grandfather. Saark's fear of the old man was palpable. Nienna scrunched herself under her blanket, and tried to think pleasant thoughts. Instead, she dreamed of Bhu Vanesh, hunting her, hunting her through dark citadels... and nobody could hear her screams. Nobody could ever hear her screams...

For three days they journeyed through narrow, winding, underground tunnels. Sometimes they had to climb across savage vertical drops, and on several occasions they came to guard outposts: small wooden buildings, usually empty of everything except wooden cots without bedding. At least this meant they had firewood, and Kell broke up the cots and they burned them at night, as much for the comfort of living flames as for any real heat they produced.

On the fourth day, Kell stopped and tilted his head. Then looked to Saark. "You hear it?"

"Yes. You have exquisite hearing for a human," smiled Saark.

"Helps me to kill," grunted Kell, and carried on.

"What can you hear?" asked Nienna.

"Water. A river."

They continued for another hour, until the tunnel spat them out on a gentle rocky slope. It was littered with rubble, and a sloping shingle bank led gently into a wide, fast flowing and *very* deep underground torrent. Back by the tunnel entrance there was another guard outpost, which Kell approached warily, Ilanna ready in huge fists, and down along the shingle black moss grew, and black vines twisted and turned amongst the stones like narrow, skeletal fingers.

"I'm amazed anything grows down here," said Nienna, crunching down to the water's edge.

"Don't go too close," said Myriam, and placed her hand on Nienna's shoulder. "To fall in, that would be to die. The cold and ice would chill you in minutes."

Nienna twisted away from Myriam's grip. "I don't need your advice. I'm not stupid."

Myriam looked to Saark, who shrugged.

"It's empty," called Kell from the guard hut, then stepped inside. He emerged after a few minutes. "There are some supplies. A sack of grain and weapons."

"Swords?" said Saark.

"Aye," nodded Kell, and threw Saark a thin military rapier.

Saark caught the weapon, and swished it through the air several times. "Well balanced. Good steel." He lifted eyes and met Kell's gaze. "Maybe our luck is improving?"

"Yeah, well don't get too horny. This place is a dead end." He nodded to the river.

Saark glanced up and down the shingle slope, and saw Kell was right. The only access was via the river. Then he noticed a short jetty, in black wood, half rotten and listing to one side. It had been repaired with old rope, but threatened at any moment to crash into the river.

"I get the impression this place isn't used often," said Saark.

"I think the damn albinos have more things to worry about than us, lad. You remember back on Skaringa Dak? The sky going out like a candle? The appearance of those pretty boys, those Vampire Warlords?"

"I remember," said Saark. He glanced up and down the river, and shivered. Then he looked over to Myriam, then back to the thickly churning waters. He could see lumps of ice. "I know what you're going to suggest."

"You do?" Kell looked impressed.

"We have only one option."

"Which is?"

"The river." Saark's eyes were dark. "If we don't build it right, we'll drown, Kell."

"I know that, lad. But if we stay here, we'll either freeze or meet another group of Graal's arse-kissing gigolos. It's one of those risks we'll have to take."

"I'm not a boat-builder," said Saark, eyes narrowed, voice suddenly wary with suspicion. "What do you want *me* to do?"

"Go and cut that rope free from the old jetty. We'll need it for bindings. And I'll sort out some timber."

"What will I cut it with?"

"There's knives in the hut."

"Are they sharp?"

Kell stared at Saark. "I *don't know*, lad. Go and have a bloody look."

Muttering, Saark moved to the guard shack and peered in. It was dark, and damp, wood mouldering, the sack of grain rotten. Saark curled his lips into a sneer, and crept in as if afraid to touch anything. He found one of the knives, blade rusted, hilt unravelling, and stepped back out to the shingle. "This knife is rusty," he said.

Kell looked up. He sighed. "Just do your best, lad."

Saark moved to the jetty, muttering again about being rich, and honoured, and noble, and how manual labour was a disgrace to his ancestors and so far beneath Saark he should live on a mountaintop. He stopped and peered warily at the treacherous footing. Water gushed around the jetty with gusto, bubbling and churning. Reaching out, Saark touched the wood with a grimace, and it was slick with mould. The whole structure shifted under his touch, shuddering.

"Great," he said, hefting the rusted knife and starting to saw at one piece of rope.

Back at the shack, Kell pried free several planks using the tip of Ilanna's butterfly blade, whilst whispering an apology to the axe. She was a killing weapon. A weapon of death. To use her for simple carpentry was total sacrilege.

Myriam built a small fire, and with Nienna's help cooked thin soup. They used a little of the grain, and watched in amusement as Saark fought with the rope, the rusted knife, and even the whole shaking jetty. Despite his usual visual elegance, his élan and poise and balance, the minute he touched any form of menial task it was as if Saark's thumbs had been severed. He growled and cursed, and finally cut free a length of rope, arms waving for a moment as he fought not to fall into the river. Myriam leapt forward, grabbing the back of his shirt and hauling him back.

"Thanks," he said.

"You dance a jig like a criminal in a noose."

"The only crime here," he said, smoothing his neat moustache, "is having to perform basic peasant labour." He stopped. He was close to Myriam, and her hand had slipped from a handful of shirt to the base of his spine. It was as if she held him. Close. Like a lover. He turned, into her, and breathed in her natural perfume. She was sweet like summer trees. Ripe like strawberries. As dangerous and tempting as any honeyed poison.

Myriam was as tall as him, and their eyes met only inches away, and their lips were close. Myriam licked hers, leaving a wetness that glistened. Saark stepped back, breathing out deeply, and saw that both Nienna and Kell were watching them.

"What's the matter?" he growled. "Never seen an artist wrestle with a rope before?"

"A piss-artist, maybe. Let Myriam do it," said Kell. "That way you won't bloody drown."

"The cheek of it!" But Saark handed Myriam the dagger, and retired to the fire. He watched her move elegantly, and climb out onto the jetty to the far end. It trembled and he felt his heart in his mouth. Swiftly, she made a cut and began uncoiling the old, blackened rope. To the left, Kell was gathering a formidable supply of planks, at the expense of the shack's rear-end wall where the wood was more sound.

Saark looked back to Nienna, and was surprised to find her glaring at him.

"Something the matter, little monkey?"

"I'm not your fucking little monkey," she snarled, and Saark lifted his hands, palms out, and shook his head a little, face confused. Nienna calmed, and gazed into the fire. Then she snapped back to Saark. "You enjoy touching her, did you?"

"You have nothing to worry about," said Saark. "You forget, easily, how this was the woman who stabbed a knife between my ribs. I do not forgive, nor forget. Not as easy as you, it would seem."

"Back then she was dying, she was a husk," snapped Nienna. "Now she is… pretty. Beautiful! Her skin glows. She is strong, and the picture of health. And you are both now…"

"Vachine?" Saark laughed. "I've yet to discover if that is a curse I will soon regret. Yes, it has healed me. Yes, my eyesight is a thousand times better, and I do not tire like once I did. But there is a price, I can feel it; there is always a price."

"Bite me," said Nienna.

"What?"

"Make me like you."

"No." Saark frowned. "This is madness. If Kell heard you speak thus…"

"What would he do? He's a grumpy old man. A fucking *has-been*. Bite me, Saark, then take me with you. When we get out of the mountains, we can flee together!"

"Whoa!" Saark leant back, and saw that Nienna's eyes were gleaming, almost with fever. Gently, he leaned towards her and put his hand on her knee. "What's going on inside your pretty head, Little One?"

"Stop treating me like a damn child!" she hissed. "You know what I want!"

Saark laughed easily. "Yes, I am predictable, am I not? But what you ask will get me killed. You know it, and I know it. If we are together, how long before Kell comes hunting us down? How long before sweet

Ilanna cleaves through my skull? Where then your childish love?"

"Childish love? How *dare* you!"

"I dare much, little girl," said Saark, and smiled easily, eyes glowing. "If you simply want a quick session with your legs wide, any soldier in the barracks will accommodate you. I can arrange it, if you like. But if you want prime steak, if you want to *feel* Saark's superior touch and skill and expertise, well, you'll have to wait until you're a little older. I'm not the same as the perfumed absinthe drinkers in Vor who seek out little boys and girls for their fun. That is a practice I helped stamp out."

Nienna, with eyes wide, stood and stalked off, just as Myriam arrived and dumped a large coil of rope beside the fire. She sat, and looked at Saark. "You know I heard most of that?"

"I know."

"Do you think it'll work?"

"I hope so. Much as I'd like to taste her youthful sweetness, I'm sure the price would be too high." He glanced again at Kell. "Far too high."

"There is a price for everything in life," said Myriam, giving him a dazzling smile.

"I'd noticed," muttered Saark.

They ate in a tired and weary silence, the gloom and cold getting to them despite their meagre fire. After three hours of grunting and hard work, stomping around in the shingle, Kell had finally fashioned a raft.

They stood, staring at the vessel, and Saark wore a frown like a deviated ballroom mask from the *Black Plague Tribute*, an illegal and anti-royal piece by one of Falanor's most twisted playwrights.

"So, what's that look mean, then?" said Kell, scowling.

"Nothing! Nothing. I mean, is it supposed to look like that?"

"Like what?"

"Like *that*. I mean, all twisted and uneven. I swear by all that's unholy, Kell, you're no bloody carpenter."

"I know I'm not a carpenter," snapped Kell. His eyes blazed with anger. "That's the whole damn point! This is a life and death situation; we must make do with what we have; work with our limited tools. Which means *none*. This is about *escape*, Saark, not pissing carpentry."

"Still." He pursed his lips. "She hardly looks seaworthy."

"*She* is *not* a bloody galleon," snarled Kell, hands on hips, his fury still rising.

"And *I* can bloody see that!" said Saark. "To be honest, I think I might take my chances with the soldiers and demons. If we try and ride the river on *that thing*, we are sure to die."

Kell stared at him for a moment, then shrugged. "Suit yourself. You coming, Myriam?"

"I'm coming," said Myriam, flashing Saark a weak smile. She grabbed one edge, and with Kell they dragged the makeshift raft down to the water's edge, where the water tugged eagerly.

Saark shuffled after them, and stopped, shifting from one foot to the other. "This is starting to feel like a military training camp," he muttered, as he watched Kell making last minute adjustments, pulling several of the binding ropes tight. The timber creaked in protest under Kell's exerted pressure.

"Meaning?"

"Well, we did all sorts of horse shit like this during training. Carry rocks and logs, build rafts, work as a team to get across the river, make stepping stones, swing from high trees, climb like monkeys up pointless walls of rock, run through the mountains, navigate blizzards, that sort of thing. Hah! What a chamber pot of rotting turds that whole thing turned out to be!"

"So, you've built a raft before?" Kell glanced up as he worked.

"Sort of."

"How can you 'sort of' build a raft? You either do or you don't."

"I directed their actions, like a good captain should."

"You mean you let others do the real graft, whilst you sat on your arse thinking about women?"

"Of course," smirked Saark, failing to grasp even the subtlest strand of sarcasm. "That's the way it should be. Royalty and people of breeding doing the commanding, whilst, ahem, no offence meant, but peasants work their fingers to the bone."

"So I'm a peasant, eh lad?" Kell straightened, and rubbed his hands on his jerkin. The skin of his hands was ingrained with dirt. His fingernails were mostly black from impacts during battle. His huge hands wore the hardy skin of sixty years of toil.

"Of course you are!" said Saark brightly. He grinned, and slapped Kell on the back. "But don't worry, old horse! I won't hold it against you! As you say, I've worked with worse tools."

Kell lifted Nienna onto the bobbing wooden raft, and then held out his hand for Myriam, who stepped lightly aboard. The raft bobbed. It looked far from safe. Kell glanced at Saark's beaming face, then stepped on himself. It took his weight, and he placed a hand on the low, makeshift tiller he'd fashioned from the lid of an old cherrywood chest. The raft began to drift from the shore.

"Hey, what about me?" snapped Saark, suddenly. His eyes went wide.

"Better jump for it, laddie."

"Hey, wait, I thought, I mean…"

"Didn't think you'd want to touch my dirty peasant's paws," grinned Kell. The gap was two feet distant now, and the current started to turn the raft. "Better be quick, when the current gets us you'll never make it."

Saark took a step back, and with an inelegant squawk, leapt for the raft. He hit the edge, and scrabbled for a moment, one leg sinking into the ice-chilled waters to the thigh. Then Myriam grabbed him, and hauled him onto the rough-lashed planks where he lay, gazing up, panting.

"You would have left me," he said.

"Don't be silly," smiled Kell.

"You would. I know you would."

"Well, maybe one day you'll learn your lesson," said Kell.

Saark pushed himself up. "And what lesson's that?"

"You never bite the hand that feeds."

The current caught the raft, and with a rapid acceleration they were slammed along the cavern and disappeared rapidly into a narrow, blackened tunnel. To Saark, it felt as though they were being sucked down into the Chaos Halls themselves…

Cold air hit them. They were plunged into total darkness. The raft moved forward swiftly, rocking occasionally, and Saark found himself sitting very, very still. Fear of water was not something that had ever really occurred to him; he had only ever *really* been on the Royal Barge on Lake Katashinka, and even then he'd always been drunk. Now, however, a cold sobriety had him in its fist and every little rock, or shift, every turn and dip and rise made his stomach flip over, and injected him with a sudden nausea and need to be sick. A white pallor invaded his face, but because of the gloom nobody realised his fear.

They seemed to slow for a while, travelling down narrow tunnels, and then emerged into a huge cavern. Fluorescent lodes glinted in the walls, lighting their way, and ice gleamed on rocks and stalagmites.

They plunged into darkness again.

"Does anybody feel sick?" said Saark in a small voice.

"You big girl," snapped Kell. He was concentrating hard, attempting to *feel* the flow of the river, to anticipate – in the Stygian black – whether they were being pulled toward the rows of harsh, jagged rocks, like gnashing teeth, which lined the way.

"No, no, really, I feel incredibly queasy."

"It'll be your wound," said Myriam, not unkindly. She crossed to Saark, and took his hands. "Here. Let me soothe you."

"Yeah, I bet you will," said Nienna, voice small.

"No, honestly, I feel really..." Saark scrambled to the edge of the raft, and threw up noisily over the side. He vomited for a while, and there was an embarrassed silence, and finally Saark sat up.

"How you feeling?" growled Kell.

"That was your fault."

"*My fault?* How, in the name of Bhu Vanesh's *bollocks*, did you come to that conclusion?"

"It's your boat control, isn't it? You're all over the place, man!" He turned to Nienna and Myriam, little more than ethereal white blobs in the dark. "I'm sorry, ladies, to lose my equilibrium in such a way. I'm sure you must feel queasy as well."

"Not I," said Myriam.

"Nor I," said Nienna, eyes flashing daggers. "Maybe you've been sucking on something you shouldn't?" She flashed a glance to Myriam, but it was lost in the gloom, in the surge and sway of the raft.

"Something's coming," said Kell.

"What do you mean, 'something's coming'? What can possibly 'be coming' out here?" But even as Saark was spouting his vomit-stinking words, they hit a sudden dip and the raft fell several feet, splashing with a slap onto a swirl of churning water; Kell fought with the makeshift tiller, which gave a *crack* and came off in his hands. He stared at Myriam.

"That's not good," she said.

"You idiot!" screamed Saark. "You're supposed to be steering the damn thing! Now you've broken it! You bloody idiot! What the hell are you doing?"

"I'm not doing anything," snapped Kell. "This whole game is out of my damn control. But I'll tell you what I *will* do if you keep blaming me for freaks of nature, you freak of nature, I'll be steering your big fat stupid face into the current of my fucking *fist*."

"No need to be like that," said Saark primly – as they hit another sudden dip, and the raft tipped madly and Saark rolled towards the edge, squawking like an infant. "Wah!" he screamed, and Myriam launched after him, grabbing hold and dragging him back without ceremony.

"Get hold of something!" she hissed, and retracted her claws. Then the pain hit Saark, as he realised her *vachine claws* had saved him by hooking into his thigh muscle.

He screamed again. "You punctured me! You grabbed my bloody *muscle!* Are you addled on *Fisher's Weed?* Devoid of your better judgement? Are you insane? Look, I'm bleeding, I've got blood all over my pants, there's blood everywhere, on my pants, and everything!"

"There'll be more soon," muttered Kell. But they hit another drop, and as water washed over them and they clung to the raft for dear life, so it began to turn and rock, and drop into choppy troughs flecked white with foam. A roaring came to their senses. It was loud, and vicious sounding.

"That sounds like a waterfall," said Saark, carefully.

"So it does, lad," snapped Kell.

"You know that shack back there? You remember how it was never used?"

"I suppose I understand, now," said Kell.

Saark turned his moaning on Myriam. "I thought *you* said you *knew* this path?"

"No. I said I could guide us out."

"What, and dropping us off an underground waterfall is getting us out, is it? Am I truly surrounded by idiots?"

Myriam gripped him. Her vachine fangs flashed. "Listen, Saark, I never said I'd been this way before. Only that I knew of tunnels which led out from the Black Pike Mountains. If you're so damn perfect, you paddle us back up the fucking river!"

"Wait," said Nienna, and her voice was soft. She held up a hand. "Listen."

They listened, and heard the roar of fast-approaching falls.

"I hear my imminent death approaching," whimpered Saark, eventually.

"Can't you hear the cracking?"

"Great! A rock-fall as well! Wonders will never cease!"

"No. It's ice," said Nienna.

"Well," beamed Saark, "that's just fine and dandy. Helps us out of our predicament nicely, and with all manner of– HOLY JANGIR FIELDS LOOK AT THAT BASTARD!" It was a black band of nothing and it was scrolling swiftly towards the adventurers on the raft, rimed with an edge of sparkling white ice and dropping *dropping* into a cold vast nothingness filled with blackness and steam...

# CHAPTER 4
## *Wildlands*

Kell fell, air rushed past him, and he prayed the hefty raft didn't hit him in the back of the skull. Rocks smashed to his left and right, and clutching Ilanna to his chest he managed to angle his body into a dive. He dreaded the impact with ice-chill water, dreaded that harsh impact slam to face and body and soul. He knew it was enough to kill a man, and he knew armour and weapons could drag a man to his death – he'd seen it before, several times, watched warships settle into the ocean like dying dragons, watched men flail and scream, panic invading them as quickly as any ice waters, only to be sucked under heaving green waves and never return. But Kell would never give up Ilanna. He would never give up the Sister of his Soul. Not even if his life depended on it...

Saark screamed like a woman, flapped like a chicken, and did not care that the world could and would mock him. He hit the water with a gasp, went under deep and surfaced flailing like a man on the end of a swinging noose – only to see something huge and black and terribly ominous tumbling toward him – and he realised in the blink of an eye it was the raft *the fucking raft* and he leapt back and twisted, swimming down, *down*, and something made a deep sonic *thump* above and Saark *knew* the bastard would hit him, push him down, drown him without any emotion and he swam, bitterly, secure in the knowledge that he was cursed and he was a pawn and the whole bloody world was an evil game-board designed *just* for him. Bubbles scattered around like black petals, and eventually, as pain lacerated his lungs and bright lights danced like flitting fish, he struck for the surface, gasping as he emerged in a burst. He bobbed there for a while, in the gloom, listening to the roar of the waterfall, and then his eyes adjusted and he saw Kell, Myriam and Nienna on the raft, dripping, frowning, and staring at him. He scowled.

"Come on, lad," urged Kell. "What you waiting for?"

"What happened, did you all nail yourselves to the bastard thing?" spat Saark, and struck out through the undulating water.

"No," said Kell, taking Saark's wrist and hauling the man onto the raft, which bobbed violently. "*You* simply spent too much time paddling down there with the fairies. What were you doing, man? We thought you'd drowned!"

"Hah. I was simply counting my money." Saark looked up. They'd fallen a considerable way, and behind them the base of the waterfall churned. Steam rose, and ice crackled on rocks. Saark shivered, and then realised he wasn't dying from the cold. "Wait. Something's wrong," he said.

"It's a geyser," said Myriam. "The water here is heated from thermal springs deep below Skaringa Dak."

Saark scowled. "It smells odd."

"Sulphur," said Kell. "You should be thankful for the bath, mate. You were beginning to stink."

"Amusing, Kell. If you didn't have that big axe I'd put you across my knee and spank you. And we all know how you'd enjoy that!"

Kell stared at him. Hard.

"I take it back," said Saark, and watched Kell deflate. "Was only a little joke. At least we're not dead." He brightened. "So many women! And so few days left on this world!"

Kell handed him a broken plank. Saark stared at it.

"What's this?"

"I meant to say. Don't get too happy. It's time to paddle."

"You want me to paddle?"

"Yes, Saark. Paddle. Before we get sucked back into the waterfall's undertow, and dragged down to a real watery grave."

Swallowing, Saark began to paddle. His efforts did not draw comment, although they probably should have.

They sailed through more darkness, a deep and velvet black that brought back childhood nightmares of vulnerability and despair; and the tunnels soon turned chill again, making all four shiver and regret leaving the warmth of the underground spring. After more peaks and troughs, the sailing started to become rough.

"We're vibrating," said Saark. "What's that supposed to mean?"

There was ambient light again from mineral deposits, and it outlined Saark in stark silver making him appear as a ghost. He was shivering uncontrollably, thin clothing sticking to him like a second skin.

"It means we're in for a rough ride," said Kell. "Get a good hold onto something. And for your own sake, Saark, do not let go."

In the eerie silver light, the river became more and more choppy. Occasionally, they saw rocks appear like shark fins and glide past. Another roaring came to their ears, a gradual escalation of chattering sound as of a thousand insects, and the raft started to rock wildly. Kell clung on grimly, and Saark, with a start, ejected brass claws and stared at them in horror.

"Welcome to the world of the vachine," said Myriam, with a smile, and dug her own claws into the lashed timber planks. Saark stuck his claws into the wood, and hung on grimly, looking sick, looking miserable.

The raft slammed onwards… and the river suddenly dipped, into a vast slope with twists and turns, and Saark was screaming and Nienna clung to Kell whose face was grim and scowling, and they flowed past rocks, and chunks of ice, and the river suddenly widened and hit wild swirling pools, gulleys and troughs, and they were pulled first one way, then another, water splashing over them, drenching them to the bone with freezing ice needles and Nienna screamed. They were spun around again, almost capsized, then accelerated down a wide tunnel past sharp rocks and Saark felt as if he was falling, falling down an endless tunnel of vertical water streams and he knew he would die there, knew he would die after all the pain and suffering he'd been through and it felt bitter on his tongue, wildfire in his mind and he was scowling and shouting and clinging on for life and then –

Then it was calm.

They flowed out into cold winter light. The river swirled through a forest of towering conifers, hundreds of feet high and suffocated by snow. An icy wind bit their cold wet bodies.

Kell laughed, a deep rolling rumble. "We're out!" he breathed, and hugged Nienna, and gazed around, a man filled with wonder, a man seeing daylight for the very first time. He glanced at Myriam. "Well done, girl. You were right! You did well."

Myriam seemed to glow under the praise, and Saark looked down at his damp clothing, ragged, torn, mud- and blood-stained, and then he looked up at the sun. "Are we... safe, in the sunlight?"

"Hardly sunlight, Saark."

"I thought vachine..."

Myriam shook her head. "No. A fiction. The brightest of sunlight might cause you pain in your transformed state, but that is all." Myriam leant closer. "What you have to worry about, Saark, my sweetness, is the fact that you have blood-oil flushing round your veins, but no real clockwork to control it."

Saark gave a swift nod, and wary glance at Kell. "The Big Man said as much. Said I would need to bind with clockwork, although I do not know how such a thing will be achieved. Or, even if I'd want such a thing." He shuddered, and flexed his brass claws.

"You have no choice," said Myriam. "Without clock- work integration, without the skills of the Engineers, you will die."

"Thanks for that," scowled Saark.

The raft swept downriver, and Kell ripped free a plank from the edge of the ragged platform and used it to guide them to the shore, huge neck and shoulder muscles bulging as he fought the heavy flow.

Saark grinned, breathing deep the fresh cold air. After

what felt like an eternity in the tunnels under Skaringa Dak, it was good to be free of them again; good to be free of the Black Pike Mountains. Good to be back in Falanor. Good to be *alive*.

"'Kell stared melancholy into great rolling waves of a Dark Green World, and knew he could blame no other but himself for The long Days of Blood…'" Kell turned sharply, scowling at Saark.

Myriam tilted her head. "The poem?"

"Aye," said Saark, and as the raft grounded on a bank of snow, he leapt from it and stared back, as if it was some great sea beast recently slaughtered. "Thank the Halls I'm on stable land!" He placed hands on hips, and watched Kell step from the raft with Nienna clinging to one arm. She looked frail and weak, and his heart went out to her at that moment.

"We need a fire. Food. Shelter," said Kell, matter-of-factly. His eyes were burning. "Or we will die."

"I like a man who doesn't mince his words," said Saark.

"And I like a man who fucking pulls his weight! Now get out there and find us firewood, and find us a shelter, or I swear Saark, you'll be wearing another wide and gaping smile on your belly before the sun is down."

"Fine, fine, a simple 'please' would have sufficed." Saark turned to hunt for firewood, a dandy in rags, but the look on Kell's face halted him. He frowned, turning back. "Yes, old man? Is there something else? Maybe I should stick a brush up my arse and sweep the floor whilst I'm at it?"

"One more thing. No more poetry. Or I'll cut out your cursed tongue, and be glad I done it."

Saark snorted, and headed into the gloom-shadowed forest, muttering, "All these threats of violence are *so* low born, lacking in nobility, so uncouth and raw. Threats truly are the language of the peasant."

Moving into the forest, they found a natural shelter from the wind, and in a small alcove surrounded by holly trees and ancient, moss-covered rocks, built a fire. Myriam was gone for two hours, and returned with a dead fox brought down by a single arrow from her bow. As she went about skinning and gutting the creature, Saark stripped off his wet shirt and laid it on a rock by the fire to dry. He flexed his fast-repairing body, and Kell looked up from where he was sharpening Ilanna's blades with a small whetstone.

"You're repairing well, lad," he said, eyes fixed on the chest-wound cut from above Saark's heart by Kradek-ka on the plateau of Helltop. "I still find it hard to believe you carried that Soul Gem inside you for so long – and realised nothing."

"I was bewitched. Once. And only once." Saark sighed, and stretched out, like a cat in the sun, and ran his hands up and down his arms and flanks, checking himself. "It'll never happen again, I promise you that! And by all the gods, I've taken a battering since I met you." His eyes sparkled with good humour. His pain had obviously receded, and he was more his old self. "Look at all these new scars! Incredible. One would have thought keeping company with *The Legend* would have brought me nothing but women, fine honey-wine, rich meats and incredible fame. But now? *Now*, I'm stuck in a forest after the, quite frankly, most abominable adventures of my entire life, I'm riddled with bruises and scars, been beaten more times than a whore's had hot fishermen, stabbed, burned, chastised and abused, and to top it all the only company I get is that of a grumpy old bastard who should be crossbow whipped in the face for his taste in clothes, whiskey and women." Saark sighed.

Kell looked up. "Shut up," he said.

"See? Where's the witty banter? The dazzling repartee? I wish to discuss literature, philosophy and women. Instead, I get to grub in the woods for mushrooms and onions, dirty my nails like the lowest working man instead of being ridden like a donkey by a buxom farm lass!"

Kell sighed. And looked to Myriam. "Is the meat ready? The stew's bubbling."

Myriam crossed to him carrying a thin metal plate, and scraped a pile of fox meat into the pan. "I'll dry the rest, roll it in salt. We can take it with us."

"Good girl," said Kell, nodding his approval. Saark scowled, and started to remove his trews. "And what are you doing?" snapped Kell.

Saark, half bent, glanced up. "I'm sick of wearing wet clothes."

"You're not removing your stinking trews here, lad. Get out into the forest."

"But it's cold in the forest."

"I am *not* staring at your hairy arse whilst I cook," said Kell, face like thunder. "I, also, have been through much recently. And it's bad enough seeing your homeland torn asunder and your friends murdered by ice-smoke magick and insect-born albino soldiers, without some tart wishing to dangle his tackle over my fox stew. So get out into the forest, and try not to sit in the pine needles. They sting, you know."

Saark stared hard at Kell. "Kell, you're worse than any old fish wife," he snapped, but pulled his trews up and sauntered away from their makeshift camp, swaying his hips provocatively, just to annoy the old warrior.

An hour later, with the winter sun dying in the sky and pink tendrils creeping over the horizon chased by sombre, snow-filled storm clouds, Kell sat back with hands on his belly, and closed his eyes.

Saark was mending his torn shirt with needle and thread supplied by Myriam's comprehensive pack; a woman used to living in the wilds for weeks at a time, the provisions she carried were lightweight but necessary. Salt, arrows, thread, various herbs, and several spare bowstrings. As she pointed out, her bow was her life. It was her means to a regular food supply, and with fox stew in their bellies, it was hard for anybody to disagree.

Nienna was staring into the fire, lost in thought, holding the binding on her severed finger. Myriam moved and sat beside her. "Do you want me to look at that? It should be ready for a fresh dressing."

Nienna sighed, and nodded. "Yes. Thank you."

As Myriam unwound the bandage from Nienna's hand, examined the stitched flesh above the cut finger, and applied fresh herbs to the wound, Nienna found herself looking away, face stony.

The albino soldier under Skaringa Dak had taken her finger to punish Kell for an escape attempt. Now, she felt she was less than a full woman. No longer beautiful. No longer whole. Nienna looked down, and flexed her hand, wincing as pain shot up the edge of her hand and arm.

"Still hurts, yes?" smiled Myriam.

"Like a bitch," said Nienna.

"And you've met a few of those, right?"

Nienna laughed. "I didn't mean you."

"I did," said Myriam. She sighed. "I've done... questionable things." She stroked her own cheek, then rubbed at her eyes. "I'm tired of doing bad things. I have been given a gift. A second chance. I am strong now, and fit, and although in the eyes of the people of Falanor I am..."

"Outcast?" said Kell, softly.

They looked up. He was reclined, his body a shadowy bulk in the gloom of fast approaching night. Firelight glinted in his beard, in his glittering eyes. He may have looked like a big friendly bear, ensconced as he was in his tatty battered tufted old jerkin, but this was a big friendly bear that could turn nasty and insane in the blink of an eye.

"Yes. An outcast. Alien. The enemy." Myriam smiled at Kell, and shrugged. She turned back to Nienna. "Once this is all done, once this game is played out, I will be hunted to my death in Falanor. By every man with a bow or knife. The vachine are seen as evil. I cannot change that."

"They drink the blood of others," said Kell, voice still soft.

"And you eat the flesh of beasts," said Myriam.

"Not human flesh," said Kell.

"To the east, past Valantrium Moor, past Drennach, past the Tetragim Marshes, there are tribes who eat the flesh of men. They see it as no different to cow, or dog, or pig. It's just meat."

"They, too, are evil."

"Why so?"

"It goes against the teachings of the Church. Human flesh is sacred."

Myriam shrugged. "So you mean to tell me if you were ever put in a position where you were going to

92

die of starvation, and human flesh was on the menu, you absolutely would not eat? Not even to save your own life? To save the lives of your children?"

"I would not," lied Kell, throat dry, remembering the Days of Blood, where he had indeed eaten human flesh, and much more, and much worse. "I would rather die," he said, voice husky, eyes hidden.

"Well that's where we differ, then," snapped Myriam, voice hard. "But you should not judge so readily, Kell. I guided you and Nienna and Saark out from that bastard mountain; I saved your lives. This time."

"Lucky for us," nodded Kell, dark eyes glinting in the firelight. And now he didn't look like such a friendly bear. Now he looked far more dangerous. "But enough talk. What are your plans now, Myriam?"

"I will attempt to kill the Vampire Warlords."

This was met with momentary silence. The wind hissed through the trees, and it sounded like the roll of the ocean against a beach. It was hypnotic. Somewhere, snow clumped from high branches. Conifers creaked and sighed.

"Why?" said Kell, eventually, head tilted to one side. It was such a simple question, Myriam was speechless for a few moments as she composed her thoughts.

"It is the right thing to do," she said, eventually, and looked into the fire, refusing to meet his gaze.

"You will die, then," he said.

"So be it."

Kell growled. "This thing is too big for you," he snapped. Graal's Army of Iron is invincible; you know how they took Jalder, and Vor, and the gods only know which other Falanor cities. And I was there at Old Skulkra when the Army of Iron came from the Great

93

North Road, came from Vorgeth Forest like ghosts." He spat, and rubbed his beard viciously, as if angry with himself. "Those bastard Harvesters cast their ice-smoke magick. No soldier could stand against them!"

"But you still live," said Myriam, softly.

"I am different," snapped Kell.

"Yes, you have your magick axe," she said, half-mocking.

"There is nothing magick about this axe. And before you say it, no, she is possessed by no demon; let us just say Ilanna has an attribute none of you could ever guess."

"So you will not help?"

"I cannot fight Falanor's battles forever," he said.

"It looks like you've stopped fighting full stop," said Saark.

Kell looked at him, and pointed with a powerful finger. "Don't you bloody start," he said.

"Well," scoffed Saark, "look at you, look at everything we've been through, all the fights and the murder and the bloodshed. And the mighty Kell would turn his back *now*? Just as things got worse? The time he is needed the *most*!"

"That's the point, lad. We made things worse. Don't you see? We're pawns in another man's game. Every step we've taken since meeting up in Jalder in that cursed tannery has seen us step closer and closer to the resurrection of the Vampire Warlords. We made it happen, Saark. We fucking made it happen."

Saark shook his head. "That's so much horse shit Kell, and you know it. If it hadn't happened the way it did, it would have occurred another way. Yes, maybe we were set up to some extent – because Alloria had that Soul Gem implanted near my heart by the dark gods only *know* what deep and ancient magick. But the outcome was always written in stone, written in blood. Now we have to stop it."

"No." Kell ground his teeth.

"Why not?" said Saark. "I don't believe the mighty Kell has given up. Or maybe he's just turned soft, heart turned to butter, muscles to jellied jam, maybe the mighty Kell's dick has finally gone limp and he can no longer fuck young boys. But you still suck, don't you Kell?" Saark stood. Kell's head was down. "Is that all you want from life now, you dirty old bastard? To suck horse dick and bury your head in the ground? Wallow in self pity?" Saark sang, and his voice was a beautiful, haunting lullaby:

> *"He dreamt of the slaughter at Valantrium Moor,*
> *A thousand dead foes, there could not be a cure*
> *Of low evil ways and bright terrible deeds,*
> *Of men turned bad, he'd harvest the weeds,*
> *His mighty axe hummed, Ilanna by name,*
> *Twin sharp blades of steel, without any shame*
> *For the deeds she did do, the men she did slay,*
> *Every living bright–eyed creature was legitimate prey."*

Saark laughed then. His eyes glittered like jewels in the gloom of the snow-enslaved forest. "What a load of old donkey shit. You should complain. You've been misrepresented in *legend…*"

Kell slowly stood, boots crunching old pine needles. His eyes burned with fury. With killing rage. His fingers were curled around Ilanna's steel shaft and he lifted her, almost imperceptibly. "You better be careful what you spout, laddie," he growled, and he was gone from the world of humans, he was teetering along a razor blade looking down into a valley of madness. "Somebody might just cut out your tongue."

"What? For speaking the truth? If you don't help us, Kell, if you leave us to face the Vampire Warlords alone, then we will die. And the problem still remains."

"I SAID NO!" thundered the old warrior.

"ARE YOU MAD YET?" screamed Saark suddenly, stepping forward.

Ilanna swept up, a blur, and stopped a hair's breadth under Saark's chin. The dandy grinned. "You good and mad now, old bear?" he said, voice a little calmer.

"Yeah, I'm fucking mad," snarled Kell.

"Then let's go and kill these Vampire Warlords before they do any more damage!"

Kell stared into Saark's eyes for a long minute. Then he seemed to deflate a little. "I will not put Nienna at risk," he said.

"What, I am the reason for all of this?" snapped Nienna. The stump of her finger had been neatly bound, and she was sat, rubbing it thoughtfully. "You wish to protect me? Well, you'd better come with us then. Because I'm going with Saark."

"No, you are not," growled Kell.

"Yes, I bloody *am*. I am a woman. I have my own mind. You do not control me. Or is that what this is all about? It's not about me. Now, I'm your surrogate daughter... but you couldn't control your *real* daughter, oh no, and she went wild and now you seek to pass off your impotence and lack of control and lack of *fatherhood* on me. Well, I won't have it, grandfather. I am my own person, and to stop me you'll have to kill me."

Kell sat down by the fire, and stared into the flames,

chin on his fist. Firelight glittered in his eyes and Myriam, Saark and Nienna exchanged glances.

Finally, Kell looked up, and stared at each of his companions in turn. Slowly, one by one, he met their gazes, and they stared back, defiant, heads high, proud. "I simply want to save Nienna," he said.

Nienna knelt by his side. "To do that, grandfather, you'll have to help us. This thing is wrong, and you know it. We have to do the right thing. We have to kill this evil. I was there, on Helltop; I saw them brought back from the Chaos Halls, just like you, and the terror nearly ripped me in two. These Warlords have not come to Falanor so they can go sleep in comfy beds and have sweet sugary dreams. They are here for blood and death."

"Just like the vachine," said Kell, sharply.

"Yes," said Saark. "Just like the vachine. But I fear we are in the middle of something far more complex than we could ever understand; we are in the middle of some ancient feud. Unfortunately, we're the bastards being persecuted, used as pawns, and I cannot sit by and watch good people slaughtered."

"It will be a hard fight," said Kell, looking around at their faces.

"Is there any other kind?" grinned Saark.

"We may all die," said Kell.

"As I pointed out, you're ever the happy face of optimism. But we're used to you now, Kell. We can put up with your strange ways."

"You'll have to do what you're told, lad," Kell snapped, pointing with a stubby rough finger. "You hear me?"

Saark spread his hands, face filled with pain and hurt. "Do I ever do anything else?"

"Hmph," said Kell, and rubbed his beard, then his eyes, then the back of his neck. "I will regret this. I know it. But if you want to bring down the Vampire Warlords, if you want to spread their ashes to the wind, all of you," again he fixed Saark, Myriam and finally Nienna, with a little shake of his head, fixed them all with a deadly stare, "all of you must do exactly what I say."

Saark shrugged. "Whatever you say, old horse. You have something in mind, then?"

Kell stared at him. And he gave an evil smile which had nothing to do with humour. "Yes. I have a plan," he said.

They rode for two days, both Kell and Myriam realising that they had emerged northeast of Jalder, quite close to the huge dark woodland known as the Iron Forest. The Iron Forest was a natural northern barrier which separated Jalder from the Black Pike Mountains, and rife with stories of rogue Blacklippers, evil brigands and ghosts. Kell waved this idea aside when Saark brought it up one evening, just before dusk.

"Pah," said Kell, the skinning knife between his teeth as he ripped flesh from a hare brought down by the skill of Myriam's archery. Now, as a vachine, she was even more deadly accurate with the weapon. What the cancer had taken away, vachine technology had improved with clockwork. "There's nothing as dangerous in the Iron Forest as me, lad. So stop quivering like a lost little girl who's pissed in her pants."

"Little girl? Piss? Me?" Saark placed a hand to his chest, and winced a little. The wound from Helltop at the hands of Kradek-ka, now nearly fully healed, still stung him occasionally. "I think you'll find that when brigands avoid you, it's nothing to do with your notoriety, nor your mythical axe. It's to do with the great stench of your unwashed armpits which precedes you."

"Boys, boys," said Myriam, holding up her hand. "Please. Stop. Enough." Nienna giggled. Since the pain in her hand had receded, partially due to the natural healing process, partially due to herbs which Myriam mixed into a creamy broth every night and which eased pain and gave sweet, beautiful dreams filled with vivid colours, she had found herself mellowing incredibly. Imminent danger was far ahead, the travelling not so hectic, and she found she was a far different girl from the slightly plump and naive creature who'd been about to enter the academic world of Jalder University. Now, Nienna's muscles had hardened, toned from weeks of marching and climbing, even fighting; her hands were calloused from chopping wood and gathering branches, and there was a toughness about her eyes. This was a girl who had witnessed death, observed horrors beyond the ken of most Falanor nobility. The experiences had strengthened her. Built her in character and resolve. Turned her from girl, to woman.

Kell snorted. "You're a dandy peacock bastard."

"You're a stinking old goat with a prolapse." Saark laughed, his laughter the decadent peal of raucous enjoyment found at any hedonistic Palace Feast.

Myriam shook her head again, somewhat in despair. "Saark! Stop! Listen, we passed some wild mushrooms back down the trail. Please please please, stop arguing, go back there and collect them for me. It would add a great deal to the meal."

Saark sighed. "Well, that depends on my reward." He winked.

Myriam tilted her head. Her eyes shone, but before she could answer Kell butted in, voice harsh. "You'll get the back of my hand if you don't, lad," he growled.

"Ahh, but I know you love me truly," smiled Saark, making Kell's scowl deepen further. Grabbing his sheathed rapier, he trotted off down the fast darkening path. "How far?" he shouted back.

"Ten minutes' walk," replied Myriam.

Saark nodded, and was gone. A ghost, vanished into the angular, bent trunks of the Iron Forest.

"Will he be all right?" said Nienna, face a mask of worry.

"The glib fool can look after himself," snorted Kell, returning to skinning the hare.

Saark trotted along, quite happy, vachine eyesight vivid in the darkness. He pondered the gift of the bite from Shanna, one of the Soul Stealers sent, not to kill him, as he had at first thought, but to bring him to Skaringa Dak for the resurrection – or *summoning* – of the Vampire Warlords. What had Myriam said? He'd been injected with blood-oil, which partially turned him into a vampire. Gave him many of the benefits, but without clockwork to make him truly vachine, then he would die. Saark snorted. He felt far from dead. In fact, he felt more alive than ever! Stronger, faster, tougher, with a higher tolerance to pain and an amazing rate of healing. Saark wondered what sort of match he would be for somebody like… Kell.

He grinned. No. Kell would still kick him down into the Bone Graveyard. After all, Kell was something *special*.

Saark stopped. He'd wandered a little off the trail, and rotated himself, eyes narrowing. There it was. In his meandering thoughts, he'd started through the twisted trunks of the Iron Forest.

"Damn."

The Iron Forest sprawled for perhaps ten or fifteen leagues, a haunted barrier between Jalder and the Black Pikes. This reputedly haunted stretch of woods was made up from ancient towering conifers, spruce and red pine, birch and blue sarl, and huge sprawls dominated by even more ancient oaks, perhaps five or six hundred years old, crooked and black as if their ancient trunks had been burned in savage forest fires. But the trees still managed to live on, in twisted blackened husks.

This woodland was the reason Jalder's walls had never spread far north. And it had also been one reason the Army of Iron, led by General Graal, had managed to covertly approach the city's northern defences without detection.

Saark shivered, suddenly looking around. It was a damned creepy place.

Even though the winter sky was still filled with witch-light, the forest was black. Long shadows and branch-filtered gloom did little to brighten the path. Saark shivered again, picking his way to the trail from which he had so foolishly strayed. He hated forests. And he especially hated forests at night. Saark was a creature of Palace Courts, of feasts and banquets, of jesters and music, laughing and dancing, long silk clothes and powdered wigs, thick white make-up, rouged lips, pungent perfume and slick eager quims. Saark's world was one of money and liquor, and endless long nights of drunken debauchery. Woods were for woodsmen. Forests were for peasants. The whole of the outdoors, in fact, the more Saark considered it, were a peasant's playground. How could one enjoy life grubbing for potatoes? Chopping wood? Slaughtering chickens? He shivered. Surely, that was a life worse than death? But here he was, ironically, stinking like a pauper and probably looking as bad as any vagrant who wandered the back-street gutters of Vor. Saark didn't dare look in a reflective pool; he was afraid of what he might see. Afraid of how far he'd fallen.

Reaching the path, Saark stopped. To his left, he heard a *crack*. He froze.

Horse shit, he thought. There's something there!

An animal? Or a man? He gave a little involuntary shiver, which tickled up and down his spine. He drew his rapier, and the steel shone cold in what trickles of light leaked through the forest canopy.

Saark breathed, a stream of chilled smoke.

Or... was it something worse?

A soldier. An *albino* soldier. Or maybe even a vachine. *Maybe* even a canker.

"Double horse shit," he muttered, his own unexpected utterance startling him. To his right, a clump of snow fell from slumped branches. It crunched through the woods in a subdued way, echoes bouncing back and forth from ancient gnarled trunks.

Saark swished his blade. Well, whatever it was, it'd better stay away from *him!* He'd gut it like a fish! Carve it like a duckling!

Saark looked left, and right. He decided wild mushrooms weren't such a culinary necessity after all, and what he really needed to do *right at this moment in time* was hurry back to the security and *light* of the campfire.

Above, snow started to fall.

Darkness finally drew a veil across the sky.

"You old bastard," he muttered, and began to pick his way back down the trail. Something moved, in the undergrowth to his right. It was something large, ponderous, and as Saark stopped, so the *thing* stopped.

It has to be a canker, thought Saark. His imagination flitted back, to those towering, powerful, snarling evil creatures, huge huge wounds in their flanks showing the twisted corrupted clockwork of their deviant manufacture. Kell had killed a fair few, the mighty Ilanna ripping through towering flesh and muscle and gears and cogs. But Saark? With his pretty little rapier? Against such a creature he was less than effective.

Saark began to creep. In the darkness, something stomped and changed direction, heading for the path. With a start of horror Saark realised it would cut him off. He broke into a panicked run, but ahead something huge loomed out of the darkness, stepping menacingly onto the trail, and its bulk was terrifying, its eyes demonic orbs in the gloom, a swathe of black fur running across its shadowed equine flanks, and Saark screamed, turning, slipping suddenly on iced roots and hitting the ground hard with his elbow, then his skull. Dazed for a moment, he realised he'd dropped his rapier and his right hand scrabbled blindly for the weapon as the great beast moved up the path towards him, looming over him like a terrible huge smoky demon, and Saark opened his mouth to scream as terrifying huge fangs descended for his throat…

"Eeyore," said the demon, and a long hairy muzzle dropped and nuzzled against Saark's chin, leaving a long slimy path of hot saliva across his stubble and well-groomed moustache. Donkey breath washed over him. The donkey stepped back, and there came an unmistakable and unterrifying *clop* of donkey hooves.

"I... I just don't bloody believe it!"

Saark sat back on his arse, found his rapier, and with shaking fingers levered himself up from the icy trail. He stood, and stared at the donkey in the gloom.

"Eeyore," brayed the donkey.

Saark squinted. Then he rubbed his chin. Then he squinted again. He moved alongside the affable beast, and looked at the basket on its back. He rubbed his chin again. "And now I just don't *bloody* believe it! Mary! It's you, Mary! You came back over the mountains! It's me, Saark, your faithful owner, oh I'm *so* pleased to see you, *so* pleased you got away from those cankers and Soul Stealers, you must have come back through the Cailleach Fortress, then headed south down through the Iron Forest, following the trails until, by sheer coincidence, we were reunited! Joy!"

Saark stopped. He realised he was standing in the woods, talking to a donkey.

He rubbed her snout, and Mary nuzzled him. "Still. It's damn good to see you again, old friend." He grinned, and taking her loose dangling rope, led her on the trail back towards the adventurers' makeshift camp.

Stew was bubbling over the fire when Saark stepped triumphantly from the tunnel of trees. "Look, everyone!" he cried. "I found Mary in the woods! My faithful old donkey! She's come back to me from over the mountains! What a coincidence! It's a miracle!"

He beamed around, and Kell, glancing up, continued to sharpen Ilanna. "Good. Get her killed and gutted and skinned; we can put some donkey hooves in the stew."

"Ha ha," said Saark, smile wooden.

Kell stopped his honing and stared. "I'm serious. We're at risk of starving out here. As I've always maintained in the past, there's good eating on a donkey."

Mary brayed, nostrils flaring.

"You jest, surely?" said Saark.

"Leave him be," said Myriam, moving to examine the animal. It was indeed Mary, donkey, beast of burden, and Saark's honourable equine friend. She nuzzled Myriam's hand in a friendly fashion. "Are there any supplies still left in the basket?"

Saark rummaged around, and triumphantly produced dried beef, salt, sugar, coffee, arrows and blankets. "See, Kell, no need to kill my special friend. She has brought us much needed supplies! What a brave donkey. Yes you are, a brave donkey." He rubbed her snout.

Kell grunted.

Nienna moved close, and stroked Mary's muzzle. "I can't believe she found her way back. All that way!"

"Ahh, well," Saark stroked his neat moustache, "a clever creature, is your average donkey. You may think they're stubborn, and a bit docile, but I guarantee they have more brains than the majority of idiots you find in any smalltown tavern." He gave a meaningful glance to Kell, who was studiously ignoring both Saark and the donkey.

"Still. An incredible journey for a donkey," said Nienna. "Admirable. And that she managed to find you in the woods? What a stroke of luck!"

"She could smell his awful perfume," muttered Kell.

"You be quiet, old man," snapped Saark, bottom lip quivering a little, "just because you don't have a donkey of your own."

Kell stood, and stretched his back. He stared at Saark, a broad smile on his rough, bearded features. "Well lad," he grinned, and rubbed at his beard, and ran a hand through his shaggy, grey-streaked hair, and knuckled at weary eyes, then winked, "at least you'll have something to keep you warm under your blankets tonight, eh?"

And with that, he sauntered into the woods for a piss.

# CHAPTER 5
## *Regular As Clockwork*

Dawn was bright and crisp and cold. Snow clung to bare, angular branches, and in the magenta glow of a new morning the trees did indeed appear to be cast from iron. Most were huge, gaunt, stark against a brittle sky. Saark yawned, stretching, and opened his eyes to see Nienna sat by the fire, to which she'd added fuel and stoked it into life.

Saark rolled from under his blanket and shivered. "By the gods, it's cold out here."

"Did you sleep well, Saark?" Nienna didn't look up, but continued to prod the fire. Her voice was soft, lilting, like a delivery of fine soothing birdsong. Saark swallowed, and breathed deep.

"Yes, my sweet," he said.

She looked up then, and their eyes met, and Kell's snore interrupted the moment like a burst of crossbow quarrels. Saark glanced over to the old warrior, who had turned over in his slumber, boots poking from beneath his blanket. It was as if he was mocking Saark, even in sleep. *I am watching you, boy*, the sleeping warrior seemed to say. *Touch my granddaughter and I'll carve you a second arsehole.*

Saark crossed and sat opposite Nienna. He watched her for a while, her delicate movements, and with a start he realised... On their long journey, she had changed – from child, to adult. From girl, to woman. She was harder, leaner, fitter. Her eyes were creased, and her face, on the one hand weary from endless travelling and the threat of being hunted, was also *radiant* with a new, inner strength. This was a woman who had stared into the Abyss, and come back from the brink.

"How are you feeling?" asked Saark.

Nienna tilted her head, giving a half shrug. "Tired. What I'd give for a hot bath."

"Me too." Saark coughed. "I mean, on my own, not, not with... you." He stumbled to a halt. Flames crackled. Wood spat. In the Iron Forest, snow fell from branches. Mary's hooves crunched snow.

"Am I so hard to look at?" said Nienna, suddenly, tears in her eyes. "Am I so ugly?"

"No! No, of course not." Saark moved around the fire, and placed his arm around her shoulders. He gave her a gentle squeeze. "You are beautiful," he said.

She looked up into his face. Tears stained her pink cheeks. "You mean that?"

"Of course!" said Saark. "It's just, well, Kell, and that axe, and, well..."

"You always say that," snapped Nienna, and rubbed viciously at her tears, heaving Saark's arm from her shoulders. "I think, for you Saark, it is a convenient excuse."

"That's not true," said Saark, and placed his arm back over Nienna's shoulder. "Come here, Little One. And before you bite off my head with that savage snapping tongue, it's a term of affection, not condescension." Saark hugged Nienna for a while, and rocked her, and she placed her head against his chest – so recently violated, now repaired with advanced vachine healing.

Nienna could hear Saark's heartbeat. It was strong. Like him. And she could smell his natural scent, and it made her head spin and her mouth dry. She could see stars. She could look into heaven and taste the ambrosia of a distant, fleeting promise.

Kell coughed. "Sleep well, did you?"

Saark eased his arm from Nienna's shoulders. "Don't be getting any wrong ideas, old man."

Kell leered at him from the dawn gloom. "*I* wasn't," he said, almost cryptically, and disappeared into the woodland for a piss. Saark glanced at Nienna, as if to say, *See? My guardian devil*, but she was looking at him strangely and he didn't like that look. He knew exactly what that look meant. It was a look a thousand women had given him over the years, and Saark knew about such things, because he was a beautiful man. But worse. He was a beautiful man without morals.

He shivered, in anticipation, as a ghost walked over his soul...

They ate a swift breakfast of dried beef, and set off through the Iron Woods, Saark leading Mary by a short length of frayed rope. The walking was hard; sometimes there were narrow trails to follow, but more often than not these petered out and they had to travel cross-country, Kell leading the way and cursing as he fought the clawed fingers of the trees and tramped heavy boots through snow and tangled dead undergrowth.

After a few hours of walking and cursing, they stopped for a break. Or in the case of Saark, for a moan.

"My feet are frozen! We should build a fire."

"We haven't got the time," said Kell, face sour.

"Yes, but if my toes freeze solid I won't be able to walk. Even worse, I saw one man once, used to work over near Moonlake when we had those real bad falls a few years back. He was stranded, out on the Iopian Plains, out there for days he was. His toes went black and fell off!"

"They fell off?" said Nienna, aghast.

"I've seen this also. In the army," said Kell, removing his own boots and rubbing his toes. "The trick," he gave Saark a full teeth-grin, "is to keep moving. Keep the hot blood flowing. When you languish on your arse like a drunken dandy, that's when you get into trouble."

Saark ignored the insult, and gazed around. "But it is pretty," he announced. "Reminds me of a poem…"

"Don't start," snapped Kell. "I fucking despise poets."

"But look, old man! Look at the beauty! Look at the majesty of Nature!"

"The majesty of Nature?" spluttered Kell, and his face turned dark. "Where we're headed, boy, there's little majesty and lots of death."

Saark considered this, as Mary nuzzled his hand. "And where is that?" he said, finally, when Kell ignored the hint to continue.

"Balaglass Lake," said Kell.

"You're insane," said Myriam. "We can't travel there; it's poisoned land!"

"Whoa," said Saark, holding up a hand. "Poisoned? As in, gets into our bodies and chokes us, kind of poison?"

"Balaglass Lake is frozen," said Myriam. "But not with ice, with toxins. Even in high summer it remains solid, but as unwary travellers wander across its seemingly solid surface, then a pool will suddenly open up and eat them. I saw it, once. Near the edge. Man fell in, up to his knees; over the next few days, the… water, or whatever it is, ate the flesh from his bones. We strapped him down, used tourniquets, a leather strap between his teeth. He screamed for three nights until we could bear it no more and put him out of his misery." Myriam faltered, and was silent.

"A happy tale," snapped Saark. "Thank you so much for lifting my mood!"

"We need to cross it," said Kell. "It's the quickest way."

"Where to?" said Saark, face a frown.

"To the Black Pike Mines," said Kell.

They stood by the shores of Balaglass Lake, but there was nothing to see except a perfectly flat platter of snow. A wind sighed from the edge of the Iron Forest, ruffling Kell's beard as his dark eyes swept the flat plateau.

"You see?" pointed Myriam, behind her. They looked at the animal tracks. "Nothing heads out onto the frozen lake; it's as if the animals *know* it's evil and will suck them down."

"What freezes it, if not the ice?" said Saark, rubbing his chin.

Myriam shrugged. "Who knows? It has always been thus. Styx said his father, and his father's father, had both always known it as such a place. And that only the foolhardy attempted to cross."

"How big is it?" said Saark, peering out across the desolate flat plain.

"Big enough," laughed Kell, and stepped out onto the frozen surface. "See. Solid as a rock."

Saark stared at him. "It's when you say things like that the ground normally opens up and swallows you!

You should not tempt the Fates, Kell. Their sense of humour is more corrupt than a canker's brain."

"Ah, bollocks," said Kell. "Come on ladies, we have a mission. You want to save Falanor? Well it won't happen if you all stand there picking your noses."

"I do so under protest," said Myriam, and warily tested the surface with her boot. "Seeing a man scream with only bone sticks as legs taught me never to chance my luck here." Even so, she stepped onto the frozen lake and stood beside Kell. Then Nienna stepped out, and lifted her head proudly, turning to meet Saark's gaze.

Saark stepped from one boot to the other. "You sure there's no way round?" he whined.

"Get out here!" thundered Kell, and turning, stalked off across the plate of ice.

Warily, Saark followed, leading Mary who shied away, trying to pull back. "Shh!" soothed Saark, and slowly, gently, coaxed the donkey out onto the frozen surface.

Myriam, who was twenty paces ahead, turned. "See. Animals can sense it. Sense the death."

"Will you fucking shut up!" shouted Saark, irate now as he fought with the donkey. "Shh, girl, come on, girl, it won't hurt you, girl, please come on, trust me, it won't hurt."

"Is that how you coax all the ladies?" grinned Myriam.

Saark considered this, and frowned. "That's just a damn and dirty misrepresentation," he said. Then smiled. "Although I have to admit, it works sometimes."

Kell and Nienna were ahead, Kell striding through the powdered snow without a backward glance, the mighty Ilanna in one fist, his other clenched tight.

Nienna trotted by his side, and glancing back, she saw Saark and Myriam following.

"Does this lake really swallow people, grandfather?" she asked, staring down at her boots. She had come to trust the ground, and the thought of walking on thin ice filled her with a consummate fear.

"Old wives' tales," said Kell, without looking at her. His gaze was focused on the distant line of trees, a swathe of iron-black trunks no bigger than his thumbnails. Half a league, he reckoned. That was a long way to walk on treacherous, thin ice.

Behind, Saark and Myriam were making small-talk.

"Tell me more about the clockwork," said Saark, the rope from a disobedient donkey cutting into his hand and making him wince.

"What do you need to know?"

"You think I will die? Without it, I mean?"

"That is what Tashmaniok and Shanna advised. They may have been lying, though." She peered at Saark. "Why? How do you feel?"

"Wonderful! Powerful, strong, at the peak of my prowess! All pain is gone, my wounds have healed except for the odd twinge; I'm thinking maybe this clockwork vampire thing isn't so bad after all. I am faster, stronger, my eyesight more acute; my stamina rarely leaves me, and I have greater resistance to heat and cold."

"And yet you still moan about your cold toes," observed Myriam.

"That's because the moaning bastard will whine about anything!" shouted back Kell.

"By the gods, he has good hearing for a human," frowned Saark.

"Better watch him, then, when you're sat under the blankets cuddling Nienna."

Saark stared long and hard at Myriam. "I was simply offering warmth and friendship," he said.

"Yes," snorted Myriam. "I've seen that sort of friendship a lot during my short, bitter lifetime!"

Saark's eyes went wide. "Me? Really? You think I'd... " He considered this. "Actually, yes, of course you're right. I would. But you're missing the point. With that huge ugly axe hanging like a pendulum over the back of my skull, well, somehow I seem to lose that all-important *urge*." He grinned, but watched Myriam's face descend into pain. "Are you well?"

"Yes! No. It's just, well, I don't want to talk about it."

Saark replayed the conversation in his mind. Something had upset Myriam. What had it been? With his big flapping lips, he'd managed to put his damn soldier's boot in the horse shit again. Saark frowned, then stopped walking, placing his hands on his hips. Mary clacked to a halt behind him, and Myriam turned, a question in her eyes.

Saark moved to her, and he was close, and he could smell her scent, a natural wood-smoke, a musky heady aroma mixed with sweat and Myriam's natural perfume. It made him a little dizzy. It made his mouth dry.

"Yes?" she said.

"Nothing," he smiled, and leant in close, lips almost touching hers, and he paused, and felt her inch towards him, her body shifting, in acceptance, in readiness, in subtle longing; and this was his permission to continue and he brushed her lips with his, a delicate gesture as if touching the petals of a rose and he felt her *sigh*. He eased closer, pressed his body against hers, and they kissed, and she was warm and firm under his gently supporting hands, her body taut, muscular, stronger than any woman he'd held before. He heard her groan, and her kiss became more passionate and Saark understood now, *understood* with the clarity of blood on snow. She had been eaten by the parasite cancer, and retreated like a snail into its shell. Myriam had repressed her lust, her longing, her desires, and it had been a long time since she'd had a real man; a long time since she'd had *any* man. Saark grinned to himself. *I'll show her what a real man is all about,* and he kissed her with passion, with delicacy, with an understanding of exactly what women want, how to bring them out, how to allow them to enjoy themselves – and more importantly, enjoy themselves with *him*.

She pulled back. "You're a dirty scoundrel," she laughed. "Kiss me again."

She kissed him again, with an urgency now that was suddenly interrupted as Mary shoved her muzzle into Saark's cheek and flapped her lips with a "hrrpphhhhh" of splattered donkey saliva. Saark made a croaking sound, taking a step back, and Myriam laughed a laugh which was a tinkling of gentle chimes.

"I think she's jealous," smirked Myriam.

"I think you're right," agreed Saark. "Go on! Shoo! Bloody donkey! Bugger off!"

Myriam touched Saark's cheek. "I'll be waiting for you. Tonight."

Saark gave a single nod. "I know, my sweetness."

The Iron Forest shifted slowly back into view, but Kell had stopped up ahead. The travellers had become strung out, Kell in the lead, followed by a sullen Nienna walking alone, then Saark and Myriam trotting across the flat lake side by side, their faces awash with laughter and good humour. After a few minutes they caught up to Kell, whose dark eyes were surveying the black, seemingly impenetrable mass of the Iron Forest. It was dark, daunting, huge angular trunks and branches like broken claws. A dull silence seemed to ooze from the forest like an invisible smoke. No birds sang. No sounds came to the group, except for...

"Was that a cracking sound?" said Saark, going suddenly very still.

"Shh," said Kell.

They listened. Beneath, somewhere seemingly *deep* beneath, there came another series of tiny, gentle cracks. The noises were unmistakable, and this time in a quick-fire succession like a volley of crossbow bolts from battlements under siege.

"Should we run?" said Saark.

"A very bad idea," said Kell, softly. "We need to walk. Quickly. And I think we should spread out. Distribute the weight."

"I knew this was a bad idea," said Myriam, ice in her voice.

"Hold your tongue, woman! It's saved us three days' travel, and every day matters with those bastard vampires out there; or had you forgotten our purpose, so busy were you sticking your tongue into the dandy's foul mouth?"

"Let's just move," said Saark, holding his hands out.

They spread out, to a retort of more *crackles* from under the frozen surface of Balaglass Lake. This time, the sounds were nearer the surface; not deep down, like before.

"I'm frightened," said Nienna.

Kell said nothing.

They moved towards the iron-black trees, spreading apart, listening to the cracking sounds. Some were quiet, distant, deep below the surface; but some were loud, rising in volume suddenly until they made Kell's ears hurt. He increased his pace.

Saark was jogging, with Kell to his left, Myriam and Nienna to his right. Mary's hooves clumped the ice behind him, and he stopped, suddenly. He felt the ice beneath his boots *shudder*. Could the impact of Mary's hooves be making it worse? After all, there was some pressure there. Saark turned and stared at the donkey. Mary eyed him warily, and brayed, stamping her hooves as if to ward off cold.

"Whoa!" said Saark. "Don't do that, girl!"

"Eeyore," brayed Mary, as if sensing something beneath the surface of the snow, something like a predator closing in on them fast. Saark glanced up. Kell had made the bank, closely followed by Nienna. The bank was a muddy, root-entwined step, maybe waist height. Kell reached down, and hauled Nienna up to safety.

Saark started to run, then stopped as a crack opened in the surface before him. "Ahh!" he said, more an exhalation of horror than a word, and he took a step back. An evil, sulphurous aroma rose from the crack which zig-zagged before him. It shuddered, the whole toxic frozen lake seemed to shudder, and the crack grew yet wider. Saark ran right, where the crack petered out, and around it with Mary in tow still stamping those heavy hooves. Saark looked up, saw Myriam had reached the bank and Kell hauled her up a lower, ramped section. Her boots scrabbled and slid in the frozen mud. There!

Mary would get up that! *How did I get so damned far behind? What happened there? Are the gods mocking me again?*

He ran for it. Kell grew closer, beard rimed with ice, face screwed into a mask of concern.

"Come *on*, Saark!" hissed Myriam.

More cracks rang out, like ballistae from siege engines; Saark pumped his arms, and Mary trotted obediently after him – and suddenly stopped, hauling back on the rope, rear haunches dropping, a strangled bray renting the air. Saark was jerked back, nearly pulled off his feet, and he whirled, scowling. "Stupid Mary!" he snapped. "Come on! Come on, damn donkey, or I'll leave you out here to sink!"

Mary shook her head, braying, and a shower of spit hit Saark like a wet fish. Saark moved behind the donkey, and slapped her rump as hard as he could. Mary coughed, shook her head again, and launched ahead with hooves flying over the ice. Saark ran after her, saw her scramble up the slope, just as the ice opened up before him and his boots sank in up to the knees. He screamed, flailing forwards, stumbling, fingers brushing the bank. And Kell was there, leaning forward, and their hands touched and eyes met. "Oh no!" whispered Saark.

Kell turned, fumbled with Ilanna. "Grab the axe, lad," he shouted, leaning out. But another crack rent the air, and Saark went under, and was gone beneath the surface of the frozen lake.

"No!" screamed Myriam, but Kell grabbed her jerkin.

"Whoa lass, you can't go in there!"

Chunks of ice bobbed, and Mary brayed forlornly. Snow began to fall from a bleak pastel sky, and they stood there on the bank, watching the chunks of ice, listening to more cracking sounds and praying for Saark. Kell grimaced. What had Myriam said? That the man's legs had eaten away after the toxins of the lake came into contact with his flesh? *But maybe Saark will be lucky*, thought Kell. *Maybe he'll drown.*

Myriam strained again, and Kell picked her bodily up, and moved her away from the edge of Balaglass Lake, her legs kicking, eyes furious. "Put me *down!*" she hissed.

Kell dropped her on the frozen forest floor.

"I'm sorry, lass." Kell shook his head sadly. "He's gone. He's dead."

There came a surge from the lake, and Saark appeared gasping and spluttering, kicking and struggling. "I'm not fucking gone!" he screamed. "Help me out! Now! This shit! It tastes like shit!"

Kell sprinted back to the slope, and lying full length reached out with Ilanna. Saark grabbed the blades, careful not to sever his own fingers, and Kell hauled him onto the sloped bank where he rolled, coughing and choking. Saark was covered in what appeared a thick, oily, black green sludge, and he coughed up some huge chunks which sat, quivering on the frozen mud.

"Fucking horrible! It was fucking disgusting!" He struggled, fighting with his wet clothes until he stood, naked and shivering on the icy bank. He looked at everyone. "What? *What?* Come on, get me some fresh clothes, will you? Out of Mary's basket."

Myriam found fresh clothes, and Kell grabbed handfuls of snow, scrubbing Saark's violently shivering body free of the lake's sludge. When he came to Saark's groin, he handed him a snowball. "Here you go, lad. A man's cock is his own business."

"Myriam," said Kell. "Build a fire. I'll find some water, we need to get the lad cleaned off. And Nienna, can you get some firewood? Good girl." He turned back to Saark, struggling into thick woollens, his fingers almost blue. "What the hell were you doing, lad, putting that damn donkey before yourself?"

"I couldn't leave her!" snapped Saark.

"Well, I hope she was worth it," said Kell with a scowl.

"She is. She is."

"We'll see if you still think that when your flesh is peeling off your bones."

"I'd forgotten that," shivered Saark miserably, and stared forlornly at his boots. They were leaking black dye onto the snow. "The whoresons! Those boots cost a pretty penny."

"I think you've got bigger problems than that," snapped Kell.

Soon they had a reasonably large fire burning, despite Kell muttering about visibility and smoke and announcing their location to every damn soldier, brigand, Blacklipper and cut-throat for a two league circle. Kell found a frozen pool, and cracking it with his axe, bid Saark undress once more and jump into the ice-chilled water.

"But why?" he whined, kicking off his trews.

"Get that shit off your skin. And out of your hair. Don't want to go bald, do you?"

Saark looked at Kell in absolute horror, and undressed with acceleration. However, it took a prod from Ilanna to get a squawking, flapping, *very* unhappy Saark into the frozen pool and he went under, and spluttered up, and scowled and cursed, swore and chattered. He scrubbed at his hair, muttering obscenities to Kell, to

Mary and to the world in general. Then Kell hauled him out, wrapped him in a blanket and supported the shivering man to the fire, laying his clothes next to him.

"It's like having a baby again," muttered Kell.

"Well, if you hadn't dragged us across that bloody lake in the first place, I wouldn't be sat here with balls the size of acorns."

"So, nothing's changed, eh lad?" grinned Kell.

Saark was shivering too much to reply.

Myriam and Nienna got a large pan of broth cooking, and Kell disappeared into the Iron Forest searching for bad people to dismember. He returned after an hour, shaking his head, to find Saark slurping his third bowl of soup and in much better humour.

"See?" beamed Saark. "Nothing wrong with me! Nothing at all! I think all these stories about toxic lakes that eat men whole are nothing but horse-shit ghost stories spewed by cranky old woodsmen around their inbred fires." He gave a meaningful glance at Myriam, and then sat back, opening his blanket a little to allow more warmth in.

"By all the gods lad, put it away!" boomed Kell. "We don't want to be looking at that whilst we eat our soup!"

"What's the matter, never seen such an example of prime steak before?"

"I've never seen such a little tiddler!" roared Kell, good humour suddenly returned. "You make the sausages at the butchers seem quite majestic! Now put your clothes on, we've wasted enough time messing around here. We should get moving."

"I have barely recovered from my near death incident," whined Saark, pulling his blankets tighter with a scowl. "The least you could do is have some compassion!"

"I'll have some compassion when you're dead. Get your trews on, I found soldiers out in the forest. *Lots* of soldiers. Enough soldiers to, for example, give us a real bad day."

Myriam stamped out the fire, and they were ready to move in a few minutes, Saark complaining about his wet boots and how he was chilled to the bone.

Snow started to fall heavy, and clung to the angular branches of trees like a white parasite. They trudged through the silent forest, leaving a narrow trail and cutting randomly between the trees in case the soldiers had seen their fire, and came to investigate.

The sky was streaked with ice.

And through this frozen forest world, they moved.

They came upon a deserted farmhouse, a leaning, ramshackle affair with no obvious trails leading to it, or from it. It must have been deserted for years, and the woodland had slowly reclaimed the land, the road and the stables. It still maintained a roof, and that was something, for the snow was coming down thick. Kell was thankful for this; as he pointed out, it would cover their tracks.

Kell allowed them a fire, for without fire, he said, they may die; and to hell with the soldiers.

"If they do come," he grunted, "I'll teach them something new about cold. The cold of an early grave."

With a fire burning in the old kitchen fireplace, and the sky dark outside, the enclosing forest blocked out ambient light and gradually piled high with the fresh fall.

Myriam disappeared into the woods, returning with wild mushrooms and berries from which she made a stew, and Saark busied himself in the stables making sure Mary the donkey had a thick blanket over her back, and was not subjected to too many draughts.

Saark patted her muzzle. "I'd have you in the house with us, but you know what Kell's like. Grumpy old bastard. Soon as eat you as look at you."

"Talking to your donkey again?" said Myriam, almost in his ear, and he jumped.

"By the Chaos Halls, you move quiet, Myriam."

"Just one of my many talents."

She moved in front of him, and draped her hands over his shoulders. She leant forward and they kissed, and despite the cold and the snow, despite the darkness and the distant nagging fear of their mission, of the vampires, of the state of Falanor, here and now they were enclosed in a shield of warmth and desire.

"You coming to my bed tonight?" she whispered, husky, pulling away but not letting go. She was in control now, she was the dominant one, her confidence returned tenfold, her eyes bright and eager. Saark enjoyed this. Enjoyed the reversal. It was stimulating.

"Yes," said Saark, seeing no need at coyness. His hands moved down her back, onto her buttocks, and he pulled her to him so their hips touched. He was hard against her, and he grinned because he knew that she knew; and she knew he knew she knew. They kissed again. "I'm going to treat you so fine, Myriam," he said.

"I know," she smiled.

"Where's that firewood?" came Kell's coarse shout.

"Coming, Legend," grinned Myriam, and filled her arms with chunks from beside the leaning, rickety stables. "And then we'll have some poetry! We'll have some hero-song!"

"Not from me you won't," growled Kell, and slammed the door.

• • • •

The fire had burned low. They had arranged blankets before the flames, Nienna close beside Kell – *presumably so the old goat can keep an eye on me and her*, mused Saark. But as embers glittered, so too did Myriam's eyes and she rose, taking her blankets with her, and moved to the nearest bedroom. Saark followed, and stepping into the small room, he closed the door.

Myriam moved and opened the shutters. The snow had stopped, and eerie moonlight filtered in at an angle, highlighting her face, her high cheekbones, her smooth, pale skin. Her hair caught the moonlight, and shone like liquid silver shot through with strands of ebony. Slowly, she trailed to the bed and laid out her blankets. In silence, Saark did the same, and then they stood there for a while, staring at one another, like virgins on a first date, simply watching, not rushing, as if not quite sure what to do. Saark moved first, fired by lust and kneeling on the bed, and Myriam came from the opposite side to meet him. He touched her shoulders, and ran his hands down her arms, then leant in close and kissed her neck, and breathed in that musky scent. She groaned, a low, low animal sound from the pit of her stomach, and in that groan Saark sensed years of frustration, of longing, of need, and he caught sight of his own fingers in the moonlight and was shocked to see them shaking. *What's this? Saark, the greatest of lovers, the most incredible seducer in the whole of Falanor, shaking like a child at his first sniff of an eager quim?* He smiled, and enjoyed the sensation, and his hands took Myriam's head and his fingers ran through her hair. It was luscious, a pelt, and he kissed her and their tongues mated, and as they kissed they undressed one another, one item of clothing at a time, their hands that little bit too eager, a little bit too quick with excitement and the promise of what was to come. Saark touched Myriam's naked shoulder, as her hand slipped between his legs and took hold of his throbbing, eager cock. "A better performance than this morning," she purred, and bit his ear. He gave a little jump and grinned, face outlined by moonlight.

"You'd better believe it," he said, and his tongue left a slick trail down her jaw, then down her throat, and he took her left breast in his mouth, pulling slowly at the nipple between his teeth and holding it there as he felt himself *pulsing* in her hands and his own hand dropped between her legs. She was warm there, and wet, so wet, and Saark breathed in her scent and tickled her, slowly, teasing her with two fingers and her back arched and she reclined back on the bed, and Saark lowered his mouth to her cunt, and he played with her and she moaned, and his tongue teased and he nibbled and inside that dark sweet hole he could feel it, *feel* the *rhythm* of ticking clockwork and Myriam was groaning, writhing, and she could take no more and she pulled at him, her fingers eager and grasping, her nails leaving long red grooves down Saark's ribs and hips and he straddled her. Saark looked down. Myriam's face was bathed in moonlight, but more, she was lost, lost in an ecstasy and lost in the moment. She was so beautiful it that writhing, spellbound zone, and it was timeless, and endless, and she took his cock with both hands, pulling him urgently, guiding him into her and he fell, fell down a huge well of honey and spiralling scents, fell into a world of crazy colours which absorbed him, cushioned him, exploded him, and they fucked on the blankets in the moonlight, and it was slow, and beautiful, and sensuous, and Myriam clawed his back and Saark bit her neck, drawing a little blood with his vachine fangs but this made Myriam more wild, and she bucked, writhed, with him entrapped, unable to let go. It was magick, but a magick deeper than anything cast by the so-called magickers in their long silver robes back in Vor. This was a magick of Nature, a magick of the beast, and it was completely natural, a need, a lust, and they came together in a vortex of pleasure and fell down a long black well to the infinite realms of contented sleep.

It was morning. Early morning. A cool wind drifted in through shutters. Somewhere, a bird gave a splutter of song and Saark opened his eyes, looking up into Myriam's face. She rested her head on one hand, raised on her elbow, and she was staring down at him. She smiled, and he saw her vampire fangs, complete with traces of blood. His blood. But he did not mind. In fact, it excited him rather a lot and she noticed this with a purr of appreciation. "Again," she said, a growl, a simple command, and Saark gave a nod, and within seconds they were fucking only *this time* this time it was different and Myriam was more wild, far more feral and something had changed something had *gone* and they kissed and he thrust into her, thrust deep into her so hard he thought he would tear himself apart and they worked together, in perfect rhythm, and sweat was dripping from her face into his and as he rose frantically to an uncontrolled and uncontrollable orgasm so the clockwork went *click* and the brass wires and gold wires threaded from inside Myriam, and the clockwork seemed to *know* Saark was blood-oil infected, and they were needed, and the machines came through Myriam, through her womb and into Saark and he felt a scream well as he came, and in the moment of greatest pleasure, his moment of greatest *vulnerability* so the clockwork burned through him, entered him, and he writhed around and would have yelled and screamed but Myriam's hand clamped over his mouth and her incredibly strong body pinned him, rigid, locked down to the bed as the clockwork inside her *split* and *multiplied* and her eyes glistened and she understood.

Myriam stood, and watched Saark writhing on the bed, his eyes rolled back and white, froth at his lips.

Kell burst in, Ilanna in his great fist, eyes roving. "What's happened? Shit, Saark? Saark?" and he rushed to the bed and Myriam stood back. Saark thrashed, in agony, his body rolling and bucking and a smile was on her lips. Slowly, she dressed.

Kell turned on her. "What did you do to him?"

"I saved his life," she said.

"He doesn't look very well to me!"

"Listen. He was bit. By Shanna. You know how it works, Kell; I know you do. If he didn't get the clockwork, eventually the blood-oil would poison him; like the Blacklippers, but worse, for with them it's not in their bloodstream, only in their flesh. Here, he would have been dead within a week, no matter how strong he said he felt."

"Clockwork? But, how? How did you... " Kell's voice trailed off.

"Use your imagination, old man," said Myriam, and pushed past him, but he grabbed her upper arm. She struggled for a moment, but even despite her *vachine* strength, Kell was stronger. His grip was an iron shackle, his thunderous face doom.

"If you have hurt him..."

"Yes, I know, you'll plant that huge fucking axe in my skull. But just remember your complete lack of trust in a couple of hours when he comes round, and feels better than ever. Just you wait, Kell! I look forward to your apology. I look forward to that stupid pig look on your stupid flat face!" She shook off his hand and stalked from the farmhouse, looking for somewhere to wash. Her anger was tangible. Like blood mist.

"I don't understand," said Nienna, as Kell pulled blankets over Saark's naked body. "She said she gave him… clockwork? So that means now he's a full vachine? How did she do it?"

"I'll explain later," muttered Kell, and checked Saark's pulse. He had settled down, was still, although his eyes were still rolled back in his skull. His breathing was regular. Kell placed his hand on Saark's chest. Within, he could feel a heartbeat, but also a steady *ticking*; like a clock.

"Is he well?"

"Shit," muttered Kell and left the room.

Nienna moved to the edge of the bed, and sat beside Saark. She stared down at his face, and her hand moved, tracing down his beautiful features and coming to rest on his naked chest. She gave a shiver. And then she realised, both he and Myriam had been in here together. Naked. Now everything clicked into place. Now everything fit together.

Nienna's face changed, and the vision that swam across her young, pretty features turned her ugly for just a moment.

Composing herself, and biting her lip, and pushing away images of violence, Nienna stood and left the bedroom.

• • • •

Myriam sat by a bubbling stream. Ice froze the edges, but it flowed down the centre, pure and fresh and ice-cold. Small blue flowers grew along one bank, where the snow had been held at bay by a line of dark green pine. Her gaze followed the trees up, up to distant heights; she reckoned them to be a couple of hundred years old. Magnificent. Kings of the forest.

She sighed, and dipped her hand in the stream, thinking back to the night, and their love-making, and the absolute total pleasure. Then her eyes grew bright, and she thought now of the clockwork, and Saark's acceptance of the clockwork – for she knew, if it did not work his death would have been instant. He would have died inside her. But that had not happened, and Saark was, now, for the very first time, true vachine.

"'A creature of blood-oil and clockwork,'" she quoted. "'A child of the Oak Testament.'" She had spent precious little time with Shanna, and Tashmaniok, the Soul Stealers who had turned her into vachine – and so robbed the parasitic cancer which riddled her of another dark victory. But during that short time, she had learned from them.

And the rest – well, Myriam smiled. The rest was *instinct*.

A hand touched her shoulder. She had not heard him approach, and she turned, and smiled up at him, and winter sunlight highlighted her hair and her smile.

"Myriam," said Saark, and crouched down. Now, his skin was more radiant. Now, he was at the peak of physical strength; of fitness; of *clockwork* enhanced life.

"You feel well?"

"Incredible," he said. And inside Saark, something went *tick tick tick*. His eyes glowed. He reached down and kissed Myriam, and they stayed there for a while, kissing, holding hands, listening to the burbling of the stream.

"We should leave soon," said Myriam. "In case more soldiers come."

"Of course. Kell will be shitting buckets."

"Did I do the right thing?"

"You did the right thing," said Saark, and he could feel it, he knew, inside himself, that without the clockwork he would have died; and it would not have been a good death. What Myriam had done was save him. She had given him a part of her own clockwork engine. Her own machine had divided, and grown, and become a part of Saark, golden wires and brass gears worming into him, meshing with his flesh, building him into full vachine. Real vachine.

"I love you," said Myriam.

"And I love you," said Saark, amazed at himself how easy the words came; although, in all fairness, he'd spoken the words a thousand times to a thousand different ladies. This time, did he mean it? Saark filed that away for later analysis.

"Now, you will never die," said Myriam. "And we will live together, be strong together, forever."

Saark frowned, but Myriam was looking across the stream. She did not catch his face.

"Just think," she continued, eyes distant, "we are so strong, we are like royalty, Saark! We could have anything we wanted! Gold, jewels, land, titles, we could *take* anything our hearts desired!"

"Wait," said Saark, his voice soft. But Myriam continued, pushing on, unheeding of the tone of Saark's voice...

"If we conquered the Vampire Warlords, just think what we could do with their power, Saark?" She turned and looked up at him, and misread the confusion in his face. "We could use Kell, get to the Warlords, slaughter them. We could absorb their power, or use their legions – for that is what they will be doing, right now, as we sit here by this stream. They are creating vampires, creating armies! But we are superior, Saark, we are *vachine* and we could rule the world together!"

"Wait," snapped Saark, pushing back from Myriam and standing. She followed him up, and now it was her face that held confusion. "What the hell are you talking about? Taking anything we want? Ruling the Vampire Warlords? What kind of horse shit is this?"

"We are all-powerful *vachine*, can't you see? Together, we can do anything!" said Myriam, and he caught a glimpse of her brass fangs. They had slid out a little. And he knew; that was a sign – of attack.

"I think you get ahead of yourself, Myriam."

"You said you loved me."

"And I do. But I didn't realise that meant ruling the whole fucking world with you." There was heavy sarcasm in his voice, and Myriam's face flushed with anger.

"Don't turn against me now!" she hissed.

Saark held up his hands. "Whoa! Hold on. We had some great sex last night, and I like you, Myriam, really I do, but I didn't realise I was signing a contract! I didn't think we were becoming partners in the destruction of Falanor!"

"What's that supposed to mean? We'd save Falanor!"

"What, and rule in the place of the King?"

"The King is dead!" snapped Myriam.

"Yes, and we are not able to take his place. What's got into you, girl? What the hell is this madness?"

"It's not madness," she hissed, eyes flashing dangerous, "it's *ambition*. All my life I have been looked down upon, spat at, sneered at, misjudged, pitied, and then the cancer sought to end it all with a mocking final dark salute. But the vachine saved me. And with that salvation, I realised I'd been given a gift. And so have you. And we can use that gift to ascend in power. And to rule."

"I don't want to rule," said Saark, voice quiet.

"I thought we were in this together," said Myriam.

"You mean you thought I was a tactical manoeuvre?" snapped Saark, his own anger rising. "Is that what happened last night, Myriam? Was I just a fuck to get the clockwork inside me, so you claim the credit and use me to do your bidding? I've seen women like you, at court, thinking all men are weak-minded and easily controlled with their cocks. You think you can control us, and get absolutely anything you want. And yes, many times we are; we are weak, and gullible, and we think with our dicks and not our brains. But I tell you something now, Myriam, and you listen to me, and heed my words. I am not weak-minded. And greater than *you* have tried to turn me against Falanor; but I love my country more than I love life, and I will give my last breath to *save* this place, not condemn it; and certainly not to place some second-rate vachine *Queen* on the fucking throne!"

Myriam snarled, and leapt at Saark with claws out, slashing for his throat. He side-stepped, back-handed her across the face and knocked her to the frozen soil.

Myriam wiped her mouth, looked at blood-oil on the back of her hand, and snarled up at Saark.

"You'll regret that," she hissed.

"Show me," he said.

She leapt, and Saark punched her but she bore him to the ground, where he hit hard, grunted, and they both rolled down the bank and into the stream, crushing the swathe of little blue flowers. Myriam's claws slashed for Saark's face, and he caught her hands but one razor tip cut a neat line from his temple to his jaw. "I'm going to slice you open, a flap at a time!" she raged, struggling.

"How quickly love turns to hate," mocked Saark, and kicked her between the legs. She grunted, and Saark's elbow slammed her face, but failed to dislodge her; instead, her hand shot out and thumped Saark's face under the water.

Myriam shifted her body forward, and put her full weight on Saark's face. He struggled, kicking, bubbles erupting in a stream through the ice-cold waters. Myriam smiled, applying as much pressure as she could muster, and she watched him squirm as if through frosted glass, face distorted by the water, and by his struggles, and by his furious anger. He spluttered, and bubbled, and Myriam wondered how long it would take to drown a *vachine*…

"Up you get, lass." The voice was Kell's, and it was colder than an ice-filled tomb. Myriam leapt backwards, twisting into a somersault to land nimbly on the opposite bank of the stream. She glared at Kell, and her eyes dropped perceptibly to the matt black Ilanna nestling in huge bear paws. Kell smiled, and gave a narrow-lipped grimace. "Why don't you come over here," he said. "I have a gift for you."

"Fuck you!" snarled Myriam, and for a second her eyes moved from Nienna, standing pale and shocked, hands clasped before her, eyes wide, to Saark, glaring up at her from the stream and coughing up lungfuls of water. Then back to Kell.

He could see the fear in her eyes. A fear of the axe.

Then she was gone, sprinting through the Iron Forest, and in the blink of an eye she'd vanished through the trees.

Kell jumped down into the stream and Saark took his proffered hand, wrist to wrist in the warrior's grip, and was hauled to his feet. He brushed water off his jerkin.

"If I'd been quicker, I would have said I already had," said Saark, with a painful grimace.

"What? Fucked her?" Kell fixed him with a beady eye. "Lad, it's you who got a good fucking, that's for sure." Kell scratched his beard. "What, in the name of the Seven Gods and the Blood Void, was that all about?"

"A power trip, I think," said Saark, and stumbled up the slippery bank where Nienna reached out and helped him up. He smiled into her face, but she did not return the expression.

"Thank you, Little One."

Nienna scowled, turned, and disappeared through the forest.

Saark lifted his hands in the air. "What? *What?* Why are women so bloody complex? And what did I do to deserve *all of this?*"

Kell whacked him on the shoulder as he came past, and gave a bitter laugh. "You know *exactly* what you did, lad. And there's a hundred pregnant wives across the whole of bloody Falanor to bear witness to that one! However, we have more serious matters at hand."

"More serious than getting drowned?" mumbled Saark.

"Better come pack your stuff," Kell said, and his voice was serious. "There's soldiers out in the woods. Lots of soldiers. I reckon they're looking for something."

"Like us?"

"Yeah, lad. Like us."

## CHAPTER 6
## *Vampire Plague*

Command Sergeant Wood sat on the rooftop, hidden by a chimney, and watched the vampires drifting through the mist-tinged streets below. There were eight of them, a mixture of men and women, and one young girl who reminded him so much of his own dead daughter it brought tears to his eyes. She had long, golden curls, but only the pale face and blood eyes brought Wood crashing back to the present and the world and *reality*. She was a child no longer. No, she was a killer!

Watch. Think. Learn. *Act!*

*In the army thirty damn years. Never seen nothing like this. Give me a man with a sword any day! Give me a stinking Blacklipper with a rusted axe, give me a raw recruit with anger in his eyes, spit in his mouth and a dagger in his fist 'cos he thinks I'm a bastard on the parade ground! But this? This... abomination?*

Wood considered himself a religious man. He had always thought of the gods as higher beings in control of his life, and always done his utmost never to piss them off, well, as best he could. Wood tried his utmost to be a fair and honourable man, sometimes in battle he slashed his sword across the back of an enemy's neck, maybe stabbed a few through the back of the kidneys as well, but in the scheme of things he didn't lie, cheat, rape or murder. And this was despite being dealt a rough hand in the game of life. For the grey plague to take his wife had been painful beyond bearing; hanging on to her withered hand, weeping, not caring if he died by her side and went down the long grey path to the black waters of the Chaos Halls. No. He'd been ready for that. Sort of. Could bear it. Just. But for his nine-year-old daughter to follow two weeks later... it had been too much to bear. Three days after Sazah's death, Wood tried to take his own life. Tried to hang himself from the polished oak banister of a house now devoid of life and warmth, and love and laughter... and stinking that plague stink, with two corpses filling the beds.

Wood took a length of old rope, and with hands frighteningly steady, formed it into a noose. He tied it with a blood-knot he'd learned when fishing with his brother as a boy; a good, strong knot, not likely to fail. Then he dragged a heavy chair from the bedroom, his daughter's corpse nagging at the edge of his vision, and tied the remaining end to the banister. He stood on the chair, then climbed up onto the banister, one hand against the wall to steady himself. He looked down, to the polished terracotta tiles, and it looked a long way down, looked a long way down into the welcoming well of his own death.

No fear. He smiled. *No fear.*

He would join Tahlan, and Sazah, and they would be together and that would be the end of it. Wood smiled, nodding to himself. He felt himself shift on the chair, and he passed the noose over his neck. The rope had been coarse on his skin, chafing him a little, irritating him – he was a man of small irritations, as his army recruits knew all too well. But this time he did his best to ignore it. After all, he was about to make that final leap...

Then, the door to his house opened, and a wizened old man stepped across the threshold. He was stooped, wearing brown robes and carrying a gnarled, polished walking stick. The old man's name was Pettrus. Once, just like Wood, he'd been a Command Sergeant and the two had met at an old soldier's drinking evening, down at the *Soldiers' Arms*, a dockside tavern of ill repute. The night had been a long one, and when Wood stepped outside for a piss, shuffling down a narrow alley to avoid prying eyes, he'd spotted Pettrus standing by the dockside, staring down into the black, cold, lapping waters, the churned scum and detritus of a busy city port.

"Pettrus? What are you doing, man?"

"I want to die."

"Don't be insane! You're a Command Sergeant in the King's Army! You've got everything a man could want!"

Pettrus turned then, and it was the haunted look in his eyes, the pain, that made Wood realise he was about to jump. There was anguish in the lines of the man's face; pure anguish. He was in mental turmoil. A psychological hell.

"I have nothing!" he snarled, and went to jump... but Wood was there, powerful fist around the older man's bicep, straining to pull him back. They fought for a few moments, struggled and scuffled, and fell back onto the dockside in a slightly drunken heap. They started laughing, and Wood stood, hauling Pettrus up after him.

"I'll buy you an ale. You can tell me all about it."

Pettrus nodded, and they went into the *Soldier's Arms*, through the smoke and crowds to a quiet corner. Wood brought two jugs of frothing ale, brown, bitter and intoxicating.

"Why the hell did you want to do that?" said Wood, slamming his jug down, a creamy moustache atop his real one.

"My wife."

"What's wrong with your wife?"

"Nothing. That's the problem. She's perfect. She's beautiful, well proportioned, long silky black curls, a perfect physical female specimen."

"However?"

"She'll open her legs to any man willing. I caught her, last night, with a young soldier from my own platoon. You hear that? My own *fucking* platoon. I beat him, of course."

"Of course."

"He ran around that bedchamber, trews round his ankles, squawking like a chicken with each punch until I knocked him down the stairs. That shut the bastard up. Then I turned on Darina..."

"You didn't..."

"No, no." Pettrus waved his hand. "We argued. She told me about them. About her lovers. Every week, a different man. Every night I was on sentry duty, she'd come down here, to the taverns, drink her fill and find somebody for comfort. She said she didn't want to be lonely, but we both know that's horse shit."

"Yes."

They drank in silence for a while, then Pettrus looked up, intense, and grabbed Wood's arm. "Thank you. Thank you for saving me."

"Ahh shit, Pettrus. Don't be ridiculous. I did nothing."

"No. No. You saved my life. I owe you."

And from that day they had become good friends, talking often, and helping Pettrus overcome his destroyed marriage. Until the plague hit. Until Tahlan and Sazah died, weight dropping away, skin turning grey, huge sores forming under armpits and in groins, gums peeling back from teeth and forcing them to protrude like on a five-week corpse…

Wood stood on the banister, noose round his neck, looking down into the shocked eyes of Pettrus. The man was older now, retired from the army, powerful but stooped a little. Too much sentry duty, he used to joke. Too much manual work.

"Get down here," he growled.

"Leave me be!" said Wood, tears streaming down his face.

"I'll not let you!" snapped Pettrus. "I thought you were stronger than that!"

"Stronger than what?" screamed Wood, swaying dangerously on the banister which creaked in protest at his weight. "Stronger than a man who watched his family crumble and die, holding their trembling hands whilst they begged for life? Begged me to help them? Spewed blood and black bile and black tears? Stronger than a man cursed by the very Black Axeman of fucking Drennach to the pits of fucking Chaos? Only he's not dead, he's alive and having to live through the same shit day after day after day? Tell me, Pettrus, in all your fucking unholy wisdom, what should I do?"

"Don't jump, is what you should do. Taking your own life is not the answer, my friend."

Wood stared down into those dark brown eyes. He

saw a great sadness there, but it was not enough. Not enough to stop him… he went as if to step forward, but Pettrus held out a hand.

"The reason you are not to die, my friend, is because Tahlan would not want it so. She would want you to go on. To live. To be happy. And if you think about it, if you died, would you wish your wife and daughter to follow you to the Oil Lands? No. You know this in your heart, Wood. Trust me. Listen to me."

As he'd been speaking, Pettrus moved slowly up the creaking stairs, each board tuned so that intruders would alert Wood in the night; now, the noise got on his nerves, and he watched Pettrus reach him, and help him down from the banister, and he was covered in tears and snot, and sobbing, but as Pettrus' hand touched his, so the warmth of human contact felt good; it felt so very good.

They drank a bottle of rum, and talked about old times, talked about good times.

"Remember them, my friend."

And the next night, another bottle. And the next. And the next. Until Wood had a warm glow of memories, and of long companionship, and that nasty bite of wanting to die had gradually dissolved.

"Remember them always."


Now, Wood sat on the rooftop, eyes narrowed, watching the vampires. Over the past three nights he'd been making his way slowly, warily, across the Port of Gollothrim and towards the house of Pettrus. Hopefully, the old man would have locked himself in the attic and kept his temper in check. Wood needed to reach him. Needed to plan. Needed the bastard alive, for Pettrus was one of the best tacticians he'd ever met. But the going was slow for Wood, not just because of the rooftop scampers across ice-slippery slate, but because in *hours* he had watched the vampire filth spread, like an evil plague, a virus, oozing through the city like oil smoke. However, unlike the stories, the fireside myths whispered to frighten children in the dark, these creatures moved through the gloomy daylight; even more-so when thick fog rolled in off the Salarl Ocean, obscuring the winter sun. They weren't afraid of the light. And *that* worried Wood right down to his bones.

Now, down by the docks, Wood could hear a riot of activity. Carpenters were sawing and hammering, carving and sculpting, labourers carting huge planks of wood, and ship builders in their hundreds were at work. Wood stood a little, holding onto the chimney, aware that if he slipped and a piece of slate went tumbling to the ground the bastards would be over him like a swarm of insects. He shaded his eyes, trying to see the docks; he could catch glimpses, of bodies hard at work. And of course, their noises echoed through the light mist which had seemed, ridiculously, to have lingered for the past three days now. Or at least, since Bhu Vanesh and his vampire demons had invaded the Port of Gollothrim.

*Think. Think. What to do?*

*Reach Pettrus. But* then *what?*

He shook his head. After all, why were they building *ships* of all things? Wood moved off across the icy rooftop, lowering himself over a stone lintel and down to another. He eased tenderly across ridge tiles, hunched over and trying not to pose a large target, and below in the streets he caught peripheral glances of the creatures, the *vampires*, call them what you will, drifting like ghosts, almost regal in their lazy decadent dawdling.

After another few hours of subterfuge, of careful travel, Wood crouched by a stone gargoyle, glancing past ugly twisted features wearing a stubble of moss and hair-cream of seagull shit. There. He could see Pettrus' house, a narrow terraced stone building on a steep, cobbled road leading down to the southern docks. The door was open. Wood grimaced. *That was bad.* Even as he watched, he saw two vampires move to the doorway and pause, looking around. There came a subtle *crack* from inside, and the creatures moved in; vanished from sight.

"Bollocks." Wood leapt down to a lower roof, then scrambled to a pipe, swinging his legs over and dangling precariously for a moment, cold fingers clawing, nails dragging on stone, boots kicking uselessly until they found purchase. Wood half climbed, half slid down the iron water-channel pipework, and landed in a heap on the cobbles. He stood, drew his army-issue iron short sword, and approached the door...

Inside, darkness beckoned like a bad nightmare. Wood glanced behind him, licked his lips, and thought better of calling out for Pettrus. It would bring a city full of blood-sucking vermin to the door, that was for sure! But then, he did not need to call out – he heard Pettrus' voice, as grumpy and scratchy as ever.

"Get out, you filthy bastards!" he was snarling, and Wood heard the rasp of steel.

He ran, into the lower quarters where he'd spent many a happy evening drinking brandy and sherry and port, and recounting endless old war stories, tales of campaigns in Anvaresh and Drennach, Torragon and Ionia. Then Pettrus would break out the black bread and cheese, and they'd wash it down with more fine brandy and watch the sun come up over misty rooftops, hearing the call of gulls and distant cacophony of ships unloading their foreign wares at the docks.

Wood ran for the stairs. There came a thud, and a gurgle, and Wood stopped in his tracks. At the foot of the stairs was a dead vampire, chest awash with a flood of crimson, face a rictus mask, fangs gleaming, eyes blood-red and wide and dead. Through the heart. It had been stabbed straight through the heart.

Wood stepped gingerly over the corpse, and eased up the stairs. He heard Pettrus again.

"Come on, you blood-puking bastards! Let's see what you've got!"

"You will not be underestimated again," came a soft, feminine voice, followed by a crunch of wood, and a growl, and the sound of smashing glass.

Wood ran, reaching the landing and spinning into the modest bedroom. Pettrus' sword was on the floor, stained with blood, and he had been flung across the room, hitting the wall, one arm smashing through the window. Blood trickled over his wrist, and his face was slapped, stunned, dazed. Before him, back to Wood, stood a slim girl, no more than eighteen, with long blonde hair and hands focused into claws. She was hissing, a low oozing sound, and hunched ready to spring. To the right, there was another creature, crumpled in a foetal position, hands clasped to chest, panting fast like a heart-attack victim. Pettrus had not been taken easily. But even now, the slim girl was readying to pounce.

Wood leapt forward, shouting "Hah!" as his sword thrust out, but the girl moved fast, *too fast*, spinning as the blade struck, aiming for her heart but missing, and it scored a line under her arm, parting her flowered dress and opening a huge wound but she did not scream, did not moan or cry out in pain but simply took the blow, flesh parting like razored fish-flesh and no blood came out, just flapping bulging muscle revealing yellow ribs within. Wood's blade came back, and she leapt at him, and in reflex his sword shot up and she knocked it away, fist slamming out to thump his chest, the impact a crushing blow that threw him back against the wall, his head ramming back, stars fluttering and she leapt again, pursuing him, and Wood's head twitched sideways where the vampire's fist skimmed his cheek, punching a hole clean through the stone wall. Dust rose, Wood choked, the girl struggled for a moment with fist trapped and Wood side-stepped, glared at her in temper, pain pounding through his chest with hammer blows and realisation in his dark eyes that if her punch had connected, she would have crushed his head like a ripe fruit. His blade lifted, and he struck her a savage blow across the skull, which split her open revealing skull and brain within, a cross-section down halfway to her nose. She did not die. Wood stared with his mouth hung open at the large V of wound, the open skull, the struggling creature who should be dead as a corpse, but was still mouthing obscenities, flapping and fighting, and her fist came out of the wall grey with powdered stone and her fingers were twisted and mangled, snapped and bent in order to retrieve her fist and she turned on Wood, face a horrific open V, eyes split wide apart but still staring at him with recognition, understanding, *hatred*, and Pettrus against the far wall croaked, "Cut off its head!" and Wood's blade lifted wide, and slashed at the girl, and there was a thud as her decapitated split head hit the thick carpet. The headless corpse stood for a moment, and Wood watched it, wondering if the bastard thing would still attack him. What would he do then? Cut off the arms and legs? And what if each body part came after him? He felt an insane giggle welling in his chest and he forced it down with a grunt. *Focus! You've seen worse than this!* But when? When, *really?*

The corpse collapsed, and lay still. Wood gave a sigh, and glanced right to the fast-panting vampire. Its eyes were watching him, and blood was pooling under it.

"I winged it," said Pettrus, pushing himself to his feet and brushing broken glass from his dressing-gown sleeve. "Go on. Kill it, lad."

Wood moved to the thing, wary, sword gripped in a heavily sweating palm. He could feel droplets in his moustache, and on his shining pate. Damn his thinning hair! How would he woo the young ladies now?

His sword slammed down, separating the creature from its head, which rolled a short way and stared up at him, tongue protruding and purple like a great bloated worm.

Pettrus moved to Wood, and slapped him on the back. "Thanks, boy. I had it under control, but you arrived just in time, all right." He coughed, and grinned, and bent to retrieve his own sword.

"Why are you wandering around in your dressing gown?"

"I was asleep, wasn't I?"

"What, *here?* Didn't you have the bloody sense to hide, man?"

"Of course I hid, you buffoon!" chortled Pettrus, and rubbed at his sliced wrist. "I was in the attic! What did you think I'd be doing, painting my arse blue and parading it up and down the docks? I just needed a piss, is all."

"Why not piss in a bucket?" snapped Wood, as usual becoming irate at the old man's obstinacy.

"I'm not doing that, boy. It'd stink."

"You risked certain death because of a piss stench?"

"Not certain death. You turned up. Eh?" He slapped the younger Command Sergeant again, and grinned a mouthful of bad teeth.

"Stop calling me 'boy'. I'm fifty years old!"

"Still a boy to me," said Pettrus, then his mood turned a little sour, and he surveyed the corpses. "We need to do something about this outrage. We need to sort this shit out."

"I agree. They've taken over the whole damn city, and worse than that, it's spreading quicker than the Red Plague!"

"Yes." Pettrus rubbed his side-whiskers. "We need to get rid of them, because unless we do, all the good restaurants will remain closed. And how will I get my steak and port then, eh?"

Wood stared at the old man. There was a twinkle in his eye.

"You always liked a challenge, didn't you?"

"When the Gold Loop Tribes of Salakarr mounted a charge on elephants with spikes attached to their legs, and tigers straining on golden leashes, and with arrows which flamed and spears which had mechanisms to cut a man in two, well, me and the lads did not flinch! We stood our ground, shields high, spears and swords ready, jaws tight and with good hard Falanor steel, good old Falanor backbone, and a bit of Falanor spunk, we turned back those screaming hordes. We did that."

"And your point?"

Pettrus stood straight, as if to attention on a parade square. He held his sword, and ignored the blood, and with proud whiskers quivering, said, "I'm not going to let some dirty blood-sucking youngsters ruin *my city*. We need to get to the Black Barracks. That's where all the old soldiers know to go in times of crisis. The Black Barracks! And when we've got a few of the old boys together, well, Command Sergeant Wood…"

"Yes?"

"We'll give these damn vampires a bloody nose to remember," he grinned.


Graal sat in the high stone tower, head in his hands, mind pounding. It was the worst headache he'd ever had, a flowing river of thumping tribal drums that seemed linked to his clockwork, to his inner gears and cogs, a rhythm in tune with the *tick-tock* of his twisted clockwork heart.

Reaching out, Graal took a glass of brandy and drank deep. He had started to drink more and more, usually just before he was required to see Bhu Vanesh and give the Vampire Warlord an update on progress. Certainly, he drank *after* every meeting. Because, and he knew this to be true, General Graal was now little more than a slave. He had worked so hard to summon the Warlords, with the mistaken belief he would be in control… when in reality they were so powerful as to be beyond physical retribution.

Graal had tried to kill Bhu Vanesh. Just the once.

On the second night, he had crept to the darkened bedchambers where Bhu Vanesh slumbered. The room was filled with blacks, and purples, and crimson colours, candles burned stinking of human fat and corpses littered the floor at the bottom of the bed – evidence of Bhu Vanesh's supper.

Normally, Lorna and Division General Dekull would be standing in attendance; but Graal had witnessed them leave the chamber, and decided it was time to strike.

He drew his thin black sword, and with blue eyes glinting in his pale, white face, Graal stepped daintily over husked corpses, their flesh shrunken and shrivelled over grotesque twisted skeletons thinking all the time how this reminded him of the *Harvesters*, and the way they drained the blood for the Refineries... his mind snapped to the present. Bhu Vanesh reclined on black satin sheets, stained with pools of dark, dried blood. He slept, breathing rhythmical, body still coiling and twisting, each limb fashioned from dark smoke, red eyes closed in dreams of... what did a Vampire Warlord dream of? World domination? World slaughter? An end to fear of imprisonment? Graal had grinned, then, a slightly manic grin. Remove the head, and the body dies. Such was the vampire mantra.

He crept with all the agility and silence he knew he possessed. His sword lifted, so gentle a butterfly could have landed on its razor edge and not been disturbed by its fluid movement. Then, it slashed down, angle and force perfect for removing a head, and Graal watched in lazy-time slow-motion as if through a shimmering wall of treacle and the air felt suddenly *muzzy* with a discharge of magick and Graal realised too late the charms which surrounded this ancient creature. His blade struck Bhu Vanesh and simply stayed there, a hair's-breadth from severing his neck, and slowly Bhu

149

Vanesh rose from the bed in one rigid arc of movement and his red eyes opened and he stared down at General Graal as his sword thumped to the satin sheets.

"You had one chance," said Bhu Vanesh, his voice a portal to the Chaos Halls, smoke oozing from the terrible orifice as he spoke. "That is now gone. Betray me again, and I will suck your bones. Go now."

Graal turned, shaking, and walked past Lorna and Dekull who stood either side of the door, fangs gleaming, red eyes watching him with hunger. He returned to his tower with a panicked *tick tick tick* in his ears as he acknowledged he was vachine, and he was weak, and he was a slave, and he did not know what to do.

There came a knock at the door. Graal drank the brandy and placed the solid glass down with a *clack*.

"Enter."

The man was small, stocky, with thick black hair, shaggy eyebrows, frightened eyes. Once, Graal would have relished the terror in this little man, but not now, not today, not in this life; because Graal was subject to the same rules and the same slavery. He was shackled by fear. Strangled by power. Bhu Vanesh was Warlord. Graal was a worm.

"What is it?" snapped the General.

"I… I've been sent here, because of the ideas I had, I'm a designer, an engineer. I… I…"

"If you stutter again, I'll rip out your throat and eat your spine. Now. Continue."

Graal focused on the man, watched him swallow, could smell the ooze of piss in his pants, could hear the rumbling of his churning guts, smell the acid of his fear-filled reflux. That made Graal smile. To add a razor edge to any conversation always filled Graal with an almost sexual delight. To put the pressure of *death* on a simple exchange of words made Graal feel strong again, powerful, in control. Ha! But he knew it was a false feeling, the imitation of an imitation. So... the feeling of elation dropped like an avalanche from his soul.

"You are building new ships?"

"No, I have a thousand carpenters and riggers carving piss-pots. Of course we are building ships."

"I have a new design."

"I have hundreds of designs. They work well. We have corvettes, frigates, galleons and merchant hulks. We have everything we need, armed with the biggest damn crossbows I've ever seen and capable of punching a hole the size of my whole body through the side of an enemy vessel. What could you possibly offer me?" sneered Graal, and poured himself another large glass of brandy. Below, the shipwrights, caulkers and carpenters worked on, their noise adding to Graal's pounding head and rising temper. Who was this little man? Why did he plague Graal so? And what fucking idiot had sent him up? Graal would kill this fucker, then make sure whoever was responsible got to clean out the sewers for the next year.

"I can build you a metal ship," said the man.

"Ridiculous! It would sink."

The man watched Graal carefully, then shook his head. "No. I have designs, and I have made models. A metal ship will not burn, and is armoured by natural design; it will be smaller and more manoeuvrable than any war galleon you care to pitch against it."

Graal considered this. "What is your name?"

"Erallier, sir. Just think, if I can do this for you, if I and my family are looked after, and not turned into… " He shuddered. Then composed himself. "You will please your," he considered his words carefully, "your *master*, yes? You will have an incredible warship the like of which has never been seen."

Graal nodded. "Yes. You have a month to deliver plans and begin work. See Grannash below, he will issue you with coin and a… *mark*."

"A mark?"

"A ward. To protect you, like those out there," Graal waved a hand in the general direction of the thousands of workmen on the docks. "We can't be having all our workers *changed*, can we? How then would the ships be built? Now. Go. Please me, and I will personally guarantee your family's safety."

"Yes, General. Thank you, General."

Erallier departed, and Graal considered the proposal. A metal ship. The greatest warship ever! Enough to beat the Vampire Warlords? Graal shrugged, and stood, and stretched his back, and stared out at the Port of Gollothrim. Beyond the docks, the navy of Falanor was being gradually recalled. Now, four hundred vessels lay at anchor along the docks and for as far as the eye could see; and to the south in the city's shipyards, another two hundred skeleton vessels were in building progress. Graal had been given a year. One year to build up the navy. And then the Vampire Warlords would seek to… expand. They would travel. And they would conquer. They would take their plague to every corner of the modern world. They would build a new empire!

Graal smiled. And sighed. And pondered. And waited for news. And plotted against Bhu Vanesh. *One day, you fucker, I'm going to eat your heart and take your place. One day. One day!*

To the north of Falanor, where the Selenau River flowed through the Iron Forest and entered the vast realms of the Black Pike Mountains, there was a wall of rock, a half-league wide, jagged and black, sheer and vast. Impassable, and yet beyond there was a road, a black road, a wide road, built over a hundred years by the White Warriors, the soldiers of the vachine, the soldiers of the Harvesters, a secret road from whence the Army of Iron arrived at Falanor's northern borders and thence to the city of Jalder, and beyond.

This mammoth wall of towering rock was a barrier, a shield of sorts, between the world of men and the world of albino soldiers. Between men and Harvesters. Men and vachine.

Snow fell from a bruised sky. The wind howled mournfully from the edge of the Iron Forest, and whipped up in little dancing eddies, creating complex patterns in the snow before scattering and merging once more with undulating fields of white.

Everything was still, and calm – a perfect watercolour of serenity.

Then the black wall shimmered, each chimney and vertical ridge hung with rivers of ice sparkling for a moment as if hoarding a million trapped diamonds... And then the wall was not a wall, but a veil, like a shimmering black curtain. And beyond, a black road stretched away, edged with ice and snow, a blasted road, a desolate road. And as the mountain rock shimmered like insubstantial lace, so there came the stamp of marching boots, and the rattle of armour, and beyond the wall as if seen through mist came ranks of soldiers, their flesh pale and white, their armour matt black, carrying spears and wearing swords and maces at belts. They wore high-peaked battle helmets, and their shields bore silver insignia. The sign of the White Warriors. The sign of the Leski Worms, from whence they were once hatched.

The front battalion approached the wall, then stopped with a stamp of boots. Slowly, they walked forward, and *eased* through solid rock, out onto the snowy drifts. Rank after rank came, until the battalion was free of a rocky, blood-oil magick imprisonment, and they moved out across the snow in a square unit formation – to be followed immediately by a second battalion, another square group of four hundred soldiers, marching out into the cold crispness of Falanor from the black road beyond the Black Pike Mountains. More battalions came, until they made a brigade, and the brigade doubled into a division of four thousand eight hundred soldiers, and eventually, through churned snow and mud, the battalions finally formed into an albino army. The Army of Silver, the silver on their shields glinting with reflections from a low-slung winter sun.

The Army of Silver, led by General Zagreel, moved west from this secretive rock entrance, and they were trailed by a hundred Harvesters, bone-fingered hands still weaving the magick of *opening* and long white robes drifting through snow, tall thin bodies ignoring the bite of the Falanor wind.

Silence flowed for a while, followed by the stamp of more boots, and this time the approaching battalion held matt black shields decorated with insignia in brass, and they flowed from the mountain wall like a river of darkness, their pale faces impassive, their spears erect, swords gleaming black under winter sunlight, ignoring the whipping snow as more and more units and regiments filed out to stand before the mountain wall and then, with the tiniest of sighs, the mountain wall lost its sheen and became solid once more, leaving two full albino armies standing in the snow between the Black Pikes and the Iron Forest.

General Exkavar turned his eyes to the forest, the dark iron trunks twisted and threatening, and a cruel smile crept across his narrow, white lips. Blood eyes surveyed the snow, and he removed his helmet and ran a hand through thick, snow-white hair. He glanced back at his perfectly ordered Army of Brass, and then over the snow fields to the equally professional Army of Silver.

He turned to the bugler. "Sound the march," he said, and his eyes were distant, as if reliving a dream. "We head south."

## CHAPTER 7
### Black Pike Mines

Kell, Saark and Nienna moved as fast as they could down narrow trails which weaved like criss-crossing spider-webs through the Iron Forest. West they headed, constantly west, and eventually, on one dull morning with light snowflakes peppering the air, they broke free of the trees and looked out over a rugged, folded country, full of hills and rocks, stunted trees and deep hollows. Everything was white, and still, and calm. This was wild country filling in the gaps between Corleth Moor and the Cailleach Pass to the west of Jalder. They were past Jalder now, past the Great North Road; the Iron Forest had done its job, but as Myriam pointed out before her fight with Saark, and her sudden departure, the once outlaw-occupied forest had been curiously devoid of criminal activity. Dead, or just sleeping? Or fled to safer climates?

They stared out over the undulating folds of these raw wild lands. "Looks like rough travelling," said Saark, chewing on a piece of dried beef.

"We're going to need supplies," said Kell, ignoring Saark.

"I *said*, it looks like rough travelling," snapped Saark.

"I heard what you said, lad. But you're stating the obvious. We've had rough travelling ever since we left Jalder, through the tannery and down the Selenau River. What did you expect? A cushioned silk carriage waiting for you?"

"You're a grumpy old bastard, Kell, you know that?"

"Yeah. You keep mentioning it."

Saark bent down, rubbing at his legs. Ever since falling into the polluted lake in the Iron Forest, his skin had flared red, all over his body, stinging him with knives of fire. But Kell had come up with a theory why his flesh had not fallen from his bones, as certain rumours would have it. As a vachine, Saark had accelerated healing. Now, his flesh was being eaten by toxins, but healing just as fast as it was being destroyed.

"So I'll be like this, in a scratching agony, forever?" Saark had snapped, face twisted in annoyance.

"I thought you'd be used to a bit of scratching by now," Kell had smirked.

Now, it was irritating Saark again and he rubbed his legs, and chewed his beef.

"Won't they have food at these Black Pike Mines?"

"Maybe. We're not sure what we'll find, though. Maybe it'll be deserted? Maybe it was ransacked by the Army of Iron on their way through. It could be a burnt shell, smouldering timbers and blackened rocks."

"I assume that would end your wonderful and secret plan," muttered Saark, still scratching.

"It certainly would." Kell took a deep breath, staring up at the sky, then out across the wilderness. "By the gods, there are a thousand places out there for an ambush."

"Hark, the happy voice of pessimism," said Saark.

"Will you stop that damn scratching? It's like standing next to a fucking flea-bitten dog!"

"Hey, listen, I feel like I've got a plague of ants living under my skin. I can't stop bloody scratching. It's not like I have a choice."

"Well, if you'd not been so stupid and put the donkey first, you wouldn't have gone through the damn surface."

"There you go, blaming Mary again. Listen Kell, it's not Mary's fault and I resent the constant implication that she's holding up your weird and unspeakable mission that is so clever you have to keep it a secret!"

Kell leaned close. "The reason I keep it to myself, you horse cock, is so when, shall we say, certain priapic fools started sticking their child-maker into hot, sweaty and untrustworthy orifices, there's no possible chance of a blurted word at the wrong moment. You get me?"

"So…" he frowned, "you think I'd spout our plans during sex? Like some loose-brained dolt?"

"Of course you would, lad. You're a man! You think with your hot plums, not with your brain."

"Oh, and I suppose the great Kell–"

"There's a farmhouse."

The two men ceased their squabbling and followed Nienna's line of vision. Through swirls of snow, half-hidden by a hollow of rocks and heavily folded landscape, there was indeed a farmhouse.

"Any smoke?" squinted Kell.

"None I can see." Nienna clicked her tongue, and led Mary ahead. Ten paces away she stopped, and turned back. "Are you coming? Or shall I go searching for food alone?"

Kell and Saark followed at a distance.

"Stroppy girl, that one," said Saark.

"Yeah. Well. She's sad Myriam has gone, you know? They'd become friends. Been through a lot. Shame you had to start sticking your pork sausage where it didn't belong."

"If you're going to keep on at me, Kell, I'm going to walk with the fucking donkey."

"You do that, lad. No talk is better than your talk."

"I'll watch her arse," muttered Saark, marching away from Kell. "It's a damn sight prettier than your battered face."

The farmhouse was deserted, and had been left in a hurry – presumably when the Army of Iron had marched through this way, months earlier. The travellers hunted through various rooms, scavenging what they could. Fresh clothing, blankets and furs, boots for Saark, salt, sugar, coffee, some raw vegetables preserved by the winter, and some chunks of dried beef and goat from a small curing shed with a slanted, black-slate roof. They found hard loaves of bread, which would soften in soup, onions, and also a large round of cheese sealed in wax which was placed reverently in Mary's basket. It had been a long time since they'd eaten cheese. That would be a tasty reward on the hard, unforgiving trail.

Saark wanted to stay in the farmhouse to rest, but Kell shook his head, forcing them to push on. It was with great regret they left the sanctuary of the building, heading back out into the snow, into the folded wild lands. Soon it fell far behind, and only snow, and heather, and rocks were there to offer comfort.

• • • •

Kell pushed hard, and they travelled long into the night before collapsing into an exhausted sleep. He woke them at dawn, and they pushed on again, grumbling and cold, feet aching, joints aching, growing a little warm with travel but at least now with bellies full of meat and cheese instead of straggled weeds and unwholesome mushrooms from the forest.

The landscape here was warmer to travel, for the shape of the land, the folds and dips, cut down on many a crosswind. Once, Saark had been separated from a unit on military manoeuvres with King Leanoric, and had to walk ten leagues across Valantrium Moor. The wind-chill alone nearly killed him, and it took a week of hot baths, hot liquor and hot women to restore his good humour.

Now, however, there was no promise of hot baths, liquor or women; only a cold prison mine and the prospect of meeting prison guards. Would there be nubile young women included in that gathering? Would there be succulent wobbling flesh? Eager thighs? Clawed and painted nails? Saark doubted it.

For a week they travelled like this, Kell always ahead, his stamina a true thing to behold, especially for one so old. Saark and Nienna had taken to walking together, and for the first few days Nienna sulked with Saark, her lower lip out, face turned away, jealous no doubt of his frantic coupling with Myriam. But Saark worked on her relentlessly, with nothing else to do except talk to the donkey; and gradually, his charm began to break through her iron and ice resolve. On the third day after leaving the Iron Forest, there came a smile, quickly followed by a scowl. After four days, a chuckle. After five, a real bursting laugh of good humour. And by the sixth day she had started to talk again. Internally, he punched the air with joy; looking back through his long life of talking to, and fucking, women, he now realised Nienna had become the hardest challenge. Ironic, that only days earlier she'd been falling over herself to please him. To help him. To couple with him.

"This feels like a never-ending journey," said Nienna.

They had stopped at the top of a low rise, which fell away suddenly in a steep cliff. Kell had gone on ahead to find a safe path down. It gave them a good – if limited – view of the near distance. Anything further was blocked by occasional swathes of mist, or flurries of snow.

"Hard on the feet," said Saark, removing his boots. He scratched his legs, then rubbed at his toes.

"That's quite a stench," said Nienna, smiling to take the sting from her words.

"I think it would win me certain awards, back at the King's Royal Court," grinned Saark, and pulled a face as he rubbed between his toes. "By the Chaos Halls, the old gimlet pushes a fast pace."

"He is a great man," beamed Nienna.

"Yes, with a bad temper and a tongue fiercer than a dominatrix's whip," scowled Saark.

"You do goad him," said Nienna.

"Only to keep the old goat on his cheesy toes. Look at it this way, without me to take his mind off more serious matters, he'd be going crazy with grief! My talk of wine and wenches gives him a simple anchor-point for his short-term anger episodes."

Nienna considered this. "You have, er, enjoyed a lot of wine, then?" she said, carefully.

"And wenches, that's what you really mean, eh?" smiled Saark, easily, and pulled on his boot. He removed the other. "By all the gods, this one is worse! How can a man's feet smell so bad? I do believe I should cut them off and burn them on the fire!"

"I agree."

"Ask me, then."

"Ask you what?"

"Whatever's troubling you, little lady. There's always something troubling you, young... no, no, I take that back. You're no longer young, are you? So I'll begin again. There's always something troubling you, *Nienna*." He smiled kindly.

"Do you love Myriam?" she blurted out, then bit her tongue, aware she'd probably gone too far.

The smile froze on Saark's face like a rictus of ice-smoke magick. It was a question he hadn't anticipated, and Saark looked down at the frozen rocks, rubbing his chin thoughtfully. His mind swirled. Did he love Myriam? Despite the fights, and the betrayals, did he? Did he *really*? Despite her trying to kill him? To drown him like a flapping chicken?

And bizarrely, Saark realised that he did. But he recognised this was not the time to say such a thing, and especially not to Nienna, here, in this place. What harm her ignorance? What harm protecting her from herself?

"No," he said, finally. Then added, "I have a lot of affection for the girl, after all, ever since she stabbed me in the guts we've been through a lot together." Then a flash of inspiration bit him. "What you think you saw, you did not. We coupled, but it was nothing to do with love, or even lust – it was everything to do with the clockwork. Everything to do with the vachine."

Nienna frowned. "How does that work?"

"I was bitten by a Soul Stealer; her blood-oil infected me. But the vachine are different from the vampires of old, and the blood-oil they carry instead of vampire's blood is like a drug, a living cancer, and without the clockwork machines to control it, it will finally kill you. What me and Myriam did was to save my life. Nothing more."

Nienna looked into his eyes. And she heard it. The *tick tick tick* of the machine vampire. Saark tilted his head, and then gave a short nod. "Yes. It feels... odd. Almost like I carry a weight in my chest. But that is all. Otherwise, I think and breathe and fight and love, just like before."

"Love me," said Nienna.

"I can't do that," said Saark, stiffly. "Kell would cut off my balls, and you damn well know it!"

"You have to live your own life. Don't be scared of my grandfather. I am a grown woman now, you said so yourself." She had moved closer, a lot closer, and despite Saark's accelerated vachine skills he only now realised. He swallowed. He could smell the musk of her skin and something took hold of his mind in its fist and squeezed, gently, and he felt himself losing control. It was always the same. With women. With wine. The temptation would present itself and Saark could never, ever, say no. It was as if his brain was mis-wired, and didn't work like a normal person's brain. He had not the capacity to deprive himself of *any* earthly pleasure. Saark was a slave to hedonism, and had very little real control in his conscious decision making. It was a curse he carried deep.

Nienna was close. He stared at her lips, slick and wet. Her tongue darted out, a nervous gesture, and then

Saark was falling into a well of uncontrollable insanity and every trick and nuance and skill fell neatly into place, click click click, like a brass karinga puzzle being worked by an expert's flashing fingers. And she tasted good, tasted sweet, and he was inside her and they kissed, sat there on the rocks, and kissed.

Saark pulled away.

"Oh!" said Nienna, and smiled.

"Oh *no*," said Saark, and grinned. "But shit, Kell will rip off my balls! He'll rip off my head!"

"Rubbish! It was only a kiss." And she giggled, but he could see it in her eyes, she wanted more, she wanted much more, she wanted it all. Saark swallowed, as a hand thumped his shoulder.

"Not far now, lad."

"Kell." Saark's voice was a croak, and he did well to speak at all.

"Did you sneak up on us, grandfather?" said Nienna, turning her head and fixing him with a beady stare.

"Heh, just checking Saark here was being an honourable gentleman. Anyway, come on, there's a cottage up ahead. It's been lived in recently, but it's empty now; probably owned by a crofter. We can have a good rest, I think we've earned it, and approach the Black Pike Mine prison fresh tomorrow, eh?"

Saark stood, and took Mary's rope.

And as Kell led the way, he threw Nienna a look which she missed; she was gazing, distantly, a dreamy look on her face. *Shit. Shit shit and double horse and donkey shit!*

Less than an hour saw them inside the small and cosy cottage. It was little more than a living room and a side-larder, mostly empty except for a few flagons, old mouldy bread and three small sacks of grain. Saark made a nosebag for Mary, filling it with grain and placing a blanket over her back under a rickety lean-to on the south side of the cottage, where there was the least wind.

Nienna prepared a thick broth, and Kell chopped firewood. He got a good blaze burning, and they sat, warm for the first time in what felt like years, bellies full of hot broth and mugs of coffee in dirt-ingrained hands.

"I'd forgotten what it felt like to be a part of civilisation," said Saark, quietly, and sipped his sweet coffee, relishing the heat and the mixture of bitterness and sweetness all mixed in together. A contrast of pleasures.

Kell snorted a laugh.

"What's so funny?"

"Not long ago, lad, this would have been far from your idea of civilisation. Where's all your raw fish on silver platters now? Where are your buxom serving wenches with rouged lips and powdered wigs? I tell you, a curse on nobility."

"Spoken like a true working man," smiled Saark.

Kell stood, and stretched, and Saark eyed the old warrior thoughtfully. He was much leaner than when Saark first met him back in Jalder, hiding in a tannery from a hunting Harvester. The miles, the fights, the climbing of mountains, it had done much to return Kell to a lean, rugged, muscular figure, despite his advancing years. Then Saark's eyes slid sideways to Nienna; here, also there had been a vast change in physical appearance. Whereas she had been slightly plump, and soft, her face carrying the puppy-fat of childhood, now she was slimmer, stronger, more muscular; she carried herself erect and proud, like a fighter. The fat had gone, and there were creases in her face, hard edges around her eyes. A young woman who had seen too much hardship. Still, she was coping, mentally, as well as physically. Saark wasn't sure how long many young women from King Leanoric's court, with their white make-up and long, crafted fingernails, would have lasted in the mountains, or being hunted by Soul Stealers and cankers and rough soldiers from the Army of Iron. No. Not long, he'd wager.

Nienna saw the look, and gave him a dazzling smile. Saark licked his lips. He could still taste her there. It was most pleasant. His ruse about Myriam had worked. Nienna believed him.

Kell moved into the small storeroom, and came out with a pewter flagon. He sniffed it warily, and his face lit up. "It's whiskey," he said, in all innocence.

"Oh no," said Saark. "You know you shouldn't drink that. You *know* what it does to you!"

"Just a small one," said Kell, and smiled easily, and pulled up a chair with a scrape. "Saark, after all the shit scrapes we've been through, lad, after nearly dying on Skaringa Dak and falling through that mountain, the least I can do is have a drink."

"It makes you bad," said Saark.

"No. *Too much* makes me bad. But I know when to stop. I always know when to stop. It's just sometimes I choose not to." He lifted the flagon, and took a hefty drink, then lowered it and smacked his lips with the back of his hand, rubbing at his beard. "By all the gods, that's a rough drop, but it warms a man's belly after a trek through snow, so it does."

"Here." Saark took the flagon, and took a hefty drink himself. He nearly choked as the raw moonshine burned his throat, but Kell had been right, and it warmed him right through.

"It's good, right lad?"

"It's like drinking donkey piss, Kell."

"You should know, mate. You and that Mary lass have got way too close." He laughed, and winked, and offered the flagon but Nienna waved it away. He took another hefty swig, and this time held it there for a while. As he lowered it, Nienna looked concerned.

"No more, grandfather. Saark was right. It turns you bad."

"Ach, I'm a big man, I can take the whole flagon and it wouldn't touch the hole in my stomach!"

"Or indeed, the ego in your skull," said Saark.

"Ha!" He took another big drink, and passed it to Saark, who put the flagon carefully to one side.

"No more, Kell."

"You big girl!"

Saark smiled. "Maybe, but I having a feeling that where we are going tomorrow, the last thing you need is a drink; or even worse, a damn hangover!"

Kell shrugged, easily, and sat down. For a while they sat in amiable silence, watching the fire, then Kell stood again. "I'll go and chop some more wood. You know me. I like to keep active."

Saark nodded, and Kell stepped outside. The world seemed brighter, more whiter than white. He grinned to himself, and licked at the droplets in his beard. They tasted just grand. Snow was falling heavy now, obscuring the sky, obscuring the world. A fluffy silence filled every space. This cottage clearing felt small, safe and secure.

Kell strolled around to the small woodshed, and glancing back to make sure he went unobserved, pulled a hidden flagon from under a pile of logs. He unstoppered the flagon, took a deep breath, and followed it with a long, gulping drink.

"No good will come of this," he muttered, but by then – as it always was – it was far too late…

Night fell. The fire burned low. Kell snored heavily on one side of the room, and Saark lay with his back to the fire, eyes closed, unable to sleep. Inside of him he felt something *shift* and it made him feel nauseous, like he was going to puke. Tick, tick, tick went his steady clockwork-enhanced heart. By all the gods, he thought, it feels *too strange*.

Saark heard Nienna shift, and kneel up beside the fire. Saark turned himself, and looked at her long hair glowing. She moved to him, and lay beside him, and he threw a glance to Kell but the man had drank more whiskey later that evening, and was now sleeping like a baby – albeit a very drunk one.

"We shouldn't," he said, as Nienna kissed him; but not like before, this time it was urgent, and this time she pressed herself into him, eagerly, filled with lust, filled with desire.

"We should." She had waited a long time to get hold of Saark. She wasn't going to let him go now.

They kissed, and she straddled him, and their passion grew and Saark felt himself in that place again, that uncontrollable place and, as he always did, he gave in to it, surrendered unconditionally and kissed Nienna, kissed her hard, with passion, his hands running up and down her flanks, caressing her breasts and she writhed atop him, moaning, and Saark was hard and pressing against her and something intruded on his thoughts and there was a *click* as he realised his error. Something was wrong. Shit. Kell was no longer snoring…

"Up you get, girl."

Kell lifted Nienna bodily from Saark, and placed her to one side. His eyes were glowing embers in the gloom of the cottage, his fists were clenched, his beard glinted with droplets of whiskey, and the firelight gave him the air of a demon.

Maybe he is, thought Saark.

"You too. Up you get."

"We've been here before," laughed Saark.

"No we haven't. This time I'm going to break your fucking spine, I reckon."

Saark looked up into those merciless eyes, and swallowed hard. Kell was not a man to back down.

"I implore you, Kell, there are greater things at stake here than Nienna's honour! Think of Falanor! Think of the Vampire Warlords! And let's be honest, look, the girl is fully clothed, all I did was maul her a bit. Squeeze her tits. Get her hot and ready. No harm is done, really, Kell, I beseech you!"

Kell loomed close. "The harm, fucker, is that you never stop. Ever. And unless I teach you a lesson, you'll come back time and time again. And I can't have that. Now get up, or I'll kick you into a pulp like the fucking dog you are."

Kell's boot swung, and Saark rolled fast, avoiding the blow. He leapt up, wearing only his trews, and lifted his fists slowly, as did the pugilists he'd watched in the Shit Pits.

"I've got to warn you, Kell. I'm vachine now. Stronger. Faster. Harder." His own eyes glowed by the light of the fire.

"Show me," said Kell.

"Stop it!" screamed Nienna, both hands at the sides of her head. "Stop it, both of you!"

They ignored her.

Kell charged, roaring like a bear and throwing a fast combination of five punches. Saark dodged, left, right, ducked, then leapt back and his back slammed the wall of the cottage. But Kell followed him, a right straight thundering a hair's breadth from Saark's chin and implanting a dent in the plaster of the wall. Saark skipped away, and Kell followed again, a whirr of punches coming faster than any drunk should be able; Saark ducked, shifted his weight, then slammed a right hook to Kell's jaw that rocked the big warrior.

Kell halted, and stared hard at Saark.

"Have you come to your senses?" snapped Saark.

"Ha, no, well done boy," he rubbed his jaw, "a fine punch. Let's see some more." He launched at Saark, arms grappling around Saark's own and pinning them to his sides. Together, they crashed through the cottage door reducing it to tinder, and landed in the snow with "oofs" of exploded air. Saark wriggled, the dead weight of Kell atop him, and a stunning blow caught the side of his head, blinding him for a moment, then another cracked his nose and that made Saark good and angry and he felt his fangs ease free and talons slide from fingers and with a scream he heaved Kell aside and leapt up, talons slashing for Kell's throat, but Kell took a step back, swaying, and lifted his fists. "Yes lad! Come on! Show me what this pretty dandy's made of!"

They circled in the snow, Nienna hanging at the doorway, panting. Both men were wary now, eyes shining. Snow fell thick around them, and the whole scene was surreal to Nienna, muffled, silent, as if she was seeing it in a dream, or from the bottom of a frozen lake…

"*Stop*," she begged, wearily.

Again, they ignored her. Saark attacked, aiming punches for Kell who swayed, the punches missing him. Kell's boot lashed out, catching Saark in the stomach, but Saark turned the blow into a backward leap, and he flipped, somersaulting to land on his feet, fists raised.

"A pretty trick, boy-lover. You left a piss-trail of perfume droplets in your wake."

"Funny, because despite the perfume I can smell your stale whiskey and bad sweat from here."

Kell growled, and charged, and Saark leapt over him, flipping again to land in the snow.

"Damn you, stand still and be battered!"

"No, Kell, I don't want to fight you! Don't you understand? There are enough fucking enemies out there to last us a thousand lifetimes! And you want to play here in the snow like little kids?"

"Little kids, is it?" growled Kell, and charged again. Saark leapt high, but Kell was ready, jumping himself with a grunt and catching Saark's legs. He swung Saark like a slab of beef, and the dandy hit the snow hard, head slapping trampled ice, all air smashed from him. Kell put one knee on Saark's chest, and one great hand around his throat. With his free fist, he punched Saark with a crunch, and glared down with lips working soundlessly, anger his mistress.

Nienna ran inside the cottage, and curled her hands around Ilanna. The weapon was cool to the touch, and perfectly smooth, like ice. Nienna lifted the axe, the huge axe, with ease. It was surprisingly light.

*I have missed you*, came the words in her head, and Nienna jumped. She nearly let go of the weapon, but for Saark wriggling around under Kell and returning punches to the great man's head.

Saark grabbed Kell's balls and squeezed hard. Kell howled, rolling to one side, and Saark scrambled free across the snow, but Kell lunged, catching the vachine's ankle and dragging him back –

Claws hissed through the air.

Nienna blinked. *Am I dreaming?* she thought, mind in a swirl of severed lust, fear and now, wonder.

*No. I am Ilanna. I am Kell's axe. Do you remember, back in the Stone Lion Woods? I saved your life, but at the time thought you were too young to shock with my... thoughts. Now, I see, you are a much harder woman. I congratulate you.*

*If only everybody thought so,* dreamed Nienna. She took a step towards the door. Kell and Saark were exchanging punches once more. Saark's newly accelerated vachine status was proving a match even for Kell, and both wore bruised and battered faces like horror masks.

*I've missed you,* said Ilanna, voice soft and sweet.

*What does that mean?*

*We worked together. In the past. It was a good union. One day soon, we will speak again.*

Confused, Nienna stepped out into the snow. "Stop!" she screamed, and held the huge battleaxe above her head. Ilanna gleamed dull, matt black, an awesome sight to behold. "Stop this foolishness! I demand it!"

Kell and Saark paused. Blood dribbled from the edge of Saark's mouth, and one of his brass vachine fangs had snapped. Kell had a blackened eye and blood coming from his nose. He looked superbly pissed off.

Kell gave a sudden laugh, a bark, and lowered his fists. "Whatever you say, granddaughter. I think I gave this popinjay a pasting."

"You think so, old man?" scowled Saark. "I've had grandmothers give me harder blow jobs."

Kell lifted his fists again.

"STOP!" screamed Nienna. "What is wrong with you? Saark, you idiot, stop provoking him! And Kell, what's your problem? One sniff of whiskey and you turn into an uncontrollable beast."

That stopped Kell in his tracks, and he rubbed his beard, and lowered his head, a little in shame, a little in guilt. "Yes," he mumbled, and then looked up again. "Give me the axe."

"Why?"

"Because she is mine."

Nienna chewed her lip. She nearly spoke. Nearly said it – that Ilanna had *talked to her*. But part of her thought it was nothing more than a hallucination brought on by stress, or lack of sleep; part of her thought that maybe she was a little crazy.

Nienna stepped forward, and Kell took the huge weapon. He stared at it thoughtfully, then over at Saark. Saark slowly lowered his fists, paling. Kell wasn't called a *vachine hunter* for nothing.

"Now wait a minute, Big Man," he said.

"Ach, calm yourself, dickhead. If I wanted you dead, you'd be dead." He gestured with Ilanna, pointing towards Saark's chest with the blade tips. His voice lowered to a bestial rumble. "But I promise you this, lad. If you lay another finger on Nienna, I'll cut your dirty vachine head from your fucking vachine neck. Understand?"

"I understand."

"And this time, it's a fucking promise, lad."

"Acknowledged."

Kell lowered the weapon, strode to Saark, and threw his arm around the man's shoulders. "But by all the gods, you've got bloody handier with those clock-work fists, so you have! I haven't had a black eye in thirty years!"

"Wonderful," said Saark, mouth dry.

"This calls for a drink! Nienna, bring out the flagons."

"Over my dead body," said Nienna, scowling.

Kell shrugged. "Was only a suggestion, was all. Let's have some soup, then – and talk about happier times gone by!"

"I remember my father hanging himself," said Saark, voice cold, testing his broken brass fang with his thumb and wincing.

"You always know how to put a pisser on it, don't you lad?" He slapped him, hard. "Come on. I'll tell you about when I lost my first bout of single combat."

"You lost in single combat?" said Saark, raising his eyebrows.

"No lad, of course I didn't. I'm just trying to cheer you up."

"It's big," said Saark, lying on his belly and staring down into the valley. "No. I'll rephrase that. It's a *monster*."

The Black Pike Mines.

Originally built by King Searlan to house the worst and most violent criminals in Falanor, it also became a repository for the Blacklipper smugglers – who, by definition, had probably caused murder in order to get their casks of Karakan Red.

There was a gap in the mountains, and the Black Pike Mines had been built into the gap, the front wall merging seamlessly with near-vertical walls of jagged mountain rock. However, to simply call it a mine or a prison was misleading; this was a *fortress*. The staggered front walls were a sort of keep, and the prison stepped back into the V of an inaccessible, impregnable mountain valley. There was no back door, and only sheer smooth black granite walls for those who wanted to get in – or out. It would take an army to enter the prison mine, and that was the idea. When King Searlan built a prison, he intended his criminals to stay put.

Behind the defendable battlement walls were rows of cells carved into the mountain itself, fitted with black iron bars. Further back, where Saark and Nienna could not spy, Kell informed them, was the Hole. The Hole, or the mine itself, was the place where so many thousands of criminals had been worked to death in the name of rehabilitation.

"It looks like a prison," said Saark.

"It is."

"I know. I'm just saying."

"Searlan wanted his bastards to stay put. That's what they called themselves, back in the bad old days. Searlan's Bastards."

"I expect you put a few good men away there as well, did you?"

"No."

"No?"

"No good men. Only scum."

"How many?"

"What does it matter?" Kell's eyes gleamed. More snow was falling, and the gloom made him look eerie; a giant amongst men, bear-like, with his looming, threatening mass, his bearskin, his huge paws. It was easy to forget he was over sixty years old.

"I'm just contemplating, right, what happens if we get inside that place and a few of the old prisoners recognise you? You understand? Old fuckers carrying some twenty year pent-up grudge. After all, I've known you but a few sparse months, and I already want you dead."

"Thanks very much."

"I'm just being honest."

"Listen, Saark. I must have put over a hundred men in there. And if they cross me again, they'll have a short sharp conversation with Ilanna. You understand?"

"You can't *kill* a hundred men, Kell. Be reasonable."

"Fucking watch me," he growled. "Come on. Get your shit. I know the Governor, a man called Myrtax. He's a good man, a fair man. As long as he kept those gates shut, even the Army of Iron would have struggled to breach the defences; and I doubt very much this pipe in the arsehole of Hell was high on Graal's invasion agenda."

They moved down a narrow track which led to a wide open, bleak killing field. As they moved across barren rock and snow, Kell pointed to four high towers.

"Each tower can take fifty archers. That's two hundred arrow men raining down sudden death. And out here," he opened his arms wide, "there's nowhere to hide."

"You fill me with a happy confidence," said Saark, voice dry.

"I try, lad. I try."

They moved warily across the killing ground, heads lifted, eyes watching the towers for signs of archers, or indeed, any military activity. But they were bare. Silent. The whole place reeked of desertion.

They drew closer. A cold wind blew, whipping snow viciously and slapping it into exposed faces. Nienna gasped frequently, her breath snapped away, an ice shock sending shivers down her spine.

Eventually, they were in shouting distance and Kell halted, Ilanna *thunking* to the snow, Kell stroking his beard as he surveyed the formidable wall and massive gates before him.

"IS ANYBODY THERE?" he rumbled, deep voice rolling out across the bleak prison fortress. Echoes sang back at him from the walls, from the vertical mountain flanks, from the slick, ice-rimed rocks. The wind howled, an eerie, high-pitched ululation.

Silence followed. A long, haunting silence.

"There's nobody here, Kell."

"I don't understand. Why would Myrtax give up his castle? He was a brave man. Loyal to the King."

"The King is dead," said Saark, weary now, sighing.

"Hmm."

There came a *crack*, and a head appeared over the icy crenellations. "By all the gods, Kell, is that you?"

"Governor Myrtax?"

"It's been a long time. Wait there, I'll come down and open the gate."

"Where are the prisoners?" frowned Kell, hand on his axe.

"Gone, Kell. All gone. Wait there. I'll be but a few moments; I have warm stew, a fire, and hot blankets inside. You must have travelled far."

Kell nodded, and rubbed once more at his frosted beard.

"Wonderful!" beamed Saark. "A little bit of civilisation, at last! I'd wager he has some fine ale in there as well, and all we need to make the evening complete is a couple of buxom happy daughters, and..."

"Saark!" snapped Nienna.

"What?"

"Saark!" Her frown deepened.

"I am simply pointing out that a buxom wench could be considered a luxury in these parts." He shrugged. "You know how it is, with me and buxom wenches."

"I certainly do," said Nienna, her voice more icy than the frozen battlements.

Governor Myrtax opened the huge, thick door, which in turn was set in the fifty foot high gates which guarded the prison wall; he stood, a beaming smile on his face, a well-built man who had run to fat. His hair was shaved close to the scalp, and peppered with grey. He wore a full beard, a mix of black and ash, and his eyes were dark, intelligent, and friendly.

Myrtax opened his arms. "Kell! It's been too long! No happy prisoners for me this time?"

"No," snapped Kell, and stepped forward, hugging the man. "Sorry. Not this time. But give a few months and I'll have ten thousand heads on spikes for you!"

"Are things that bad, to the south?"

"King Searlan is dead."

"No!" Myrtax drew in a sharp breath, and his face went serious. "That is grave news indeed." He glanced around, up and down the snowy field where the wind blasted gusts of loose snow in rhythmical, vertical curtains. "Better come inside. We've had Blacklippers sniffing around, the dirty, oil-taking bastards."

Kell nodded, and ushered Nienna and Saark before him. They moved into a long, dark killing tunnel, high roofed and with balconies for archers and stone-throwers used in times of siege. They walked a short way along, and Saark glanced up nervously.

"Don't worry lad. We can trust Myrtax."

Myrtax had stopped next to the second portal. Beyond, they could see black cobbles and streaks of ice.

Myrtax turned, lifted his hands, and his eyes fixed on Kell and his eyes were haunted, filled with guilt, and with grief. "I'm sorry, Kell."

There came a rattle of activity and above the three travellers, on the high killing balconies, rose fifty men, convicts, murderers, dressed in rag-tag furs and armour and each sporting a powerful crossbow.

"Truly. I am sorry."

A tear ran down Myrtax's cheek. "They have my wife. They have my little ones. What could I do, man? What could I do?"

"Throw down your weapons," came a gruff bark.

"There's only fifty of you," snorted Kell, dark eyes moving across the ranks of men. But Saark's hand touched his shoulder, and he knew what the dandy meant. Nienna. There was always Nienna. Like a splinter in his side, removing his strength, castrating his fury. "Damn."

Saark tossed down his rapier, and Nienna threw down her short sword and knives.

Reluctantly, Kell rested his great, black axe against the wall. His shoulders sagged. They had him.

Three men pushed into the tunnel, and shoved Myrtax aside where he stumbled against the wall, going down on one knee. They arranged themselves before the travellers, and each wore a snarl as ugly as his features.

"I am Dandall," said the first, a tall, narrow-faced man in his fifties with slanted green eyes. He had scars on his cheeks, and long, bony fingers.

"I am Grey Tail," said the smaller of the three. He was a head shorter than Dandall, slim and wiry, his face round and almost trustworthy, if it wasn't for the black lips of imbibed blood-oil which tainted him with its curse. Kell saw the man's hands were shaking, probably withdrawal from his drug of choice. The veins stood out on the backs of his hands, on his throat, black, as if etched in ink through his pale white skin, a relief roadmap pointing straight towards Hell and damnation to come – for that was where he would soon travel. When a Blacklipper became so marked, he had only limited time on the face of the world. He carried a small black crossbow, which quivered even as his fingers quivered.

"And I am Jagor Mad, because I'm *mad*," rumbled the third, a huge bear of a man, a good head taller than Kell and rippling with muscle like an overstuffed canvas sack. His head was misshapen, and riddled with scars and dents. His nose was twisted, and stubble grew unevenly around wide scar tissue tracts. His fists were clenched, and he carried no weapon like the other two, who both wore short swords. His eyes were gleaming, and his gaze never left Kell.

"I remember you, Jagor Mad," said Kell, almost amiably, although his eyes gleamed in the gloom. "I put one of those big dents in your dumb head, if I remember it rightly. I reckon it should have knocked some sense into you, but I can see I'm fucking wrong."

Growling, Jagor Mad stepped forward, but Dandall's bony fingers spread out, his arm blocking the huge man's path.

"Let me kill him, Dandall, let me rip out his windpipe with my teeth!"

"Not yet," said Dandall, voice soft. He focused on Kell. "You put us all here, my large and wearisome friend. But now," and he laughed, a nasal whining like spent vachine gears, "*now* we three are the Governors of the Black Pike Mines. Behind these doors, we have three thousand *new* soldiers, our new model army! Once, they were convicts, and Blacklippers and *scum*, the freaks and the murderers, the outcast from pretty little Falanor, but now they're under *our* command and we rule these damn mountains, this mine and this fucking fortress!"

Dandall motioned, and Grey Tail stepped forward. The crossbow lifted, suddenly *hissed* and took Kell in the shoulder, punching the large man backwards. He stumbled, but righted himself. He grasped the bolt protruding from his flesh, and blood pumped out through his fingers. His eyes glowed. "Just like a coward," he growled, voice dripping liquid hate, as Jagor Mad stepped forward and with a devastating right hook knocked Kell to the ground. Jagor put one knee on Kell's chest, and grabbed the bolt. He applied weight, and Kell groaned like a dying wolf. Saark leapt forward, but a rattle of bolts from the balcony above clattered around him on the cobbles, and Saark did a crazy dance, hands over his head, trying his best not to get pierced.

"We got you now, Kell old boy," Jagor Mad spat, furious scarred face looming down at Kell as if from a toxin-induced nightmare. "And you know what?"

Kell was swimming, not because of the pain or the bolt – he'd been shot before. But because of the drugs coating the bolt's tip, which even now entered his system forcing him down into a realm of drifting unconsciousness. And as he swam deeper and deeper down down *down*, losing control, losing connection, down into the inky void of bitter lost dreams and terminal disappointments, so Jagor Mad's last words rattled in his thumping, crashing skull...

"Get the girl. We'll torture her first."

# CHAPTER 8
## Prison Steel

When Kell came round, he was lying in a dark cave, bright winter sunlight spilling in unwelcome and unholy, and thumping his already pounding head with big new fists. For a few moments he thought he'd been on the whiskey again, down that hole, locked in that dungeon, and a terrible dread stole over him and he rifled frantically through the pages of his fractured memory. But then, like the break of a new dawn, images slowly filtered back through the upper reaches of consciousness. Black Pike Mines. Dandall, Grey Tail and Jagor Mad. Crossbow bolt. Right hook... Kell clutched for the bolt, but it had been removed, his shoulder bound with a torn section of shirt which he recognised as Saark's fine lace frippery. *Great,* he thought. *Just what I need. Saved from death by a dandy idiot.*

"Don't worry. There's no badness in there. And if there was, I'll be damned if I was sucking on your foul necrotic flesh."

Kell groaned, clutching his head, and sat up like a bear emerging from hibernation. His dark shirt was torn and bloodstained. The world swam. Then, he thought of Nienna.

He rose, like a colossus, and strode *at* Saark. "Where's my granddaughter?" he roared.

"It's fine, Kell, don't panic," Saark held up his hands, "that Jagor Mad was just putting his fist up your arse. Giving you something big and hard to worry about. I can see her from here, she's tied up in one of the cells across the way. Over there." He pointed. Kell squinted.

Kell took a few moments to analyse his surroundings. To his right loomed the great wall of the Black Pike Mine fortress, containing hefty stone barricades replete with steps and towers on which soldiers could defend against any opposing force. The valley floor ran pretty straight, pretty flat, and was lined to either side by hundreds, no… *thousands* of cells, all carved into the natural rocky walls and fitted with sturdy iron bars. Kell and Saark had been locked in one of these. Nienna, in another.

"Why didn't they separate us two?" he grunted.

"They didn't want you dying; gave me a needle and thread, had me patch you up good."

"Why the hell would they do that? There's three hundred men out there must surely want my blood."

"I thought you said a hundred?" Saark shook his head. "Anyway, they, er, they said something about *sport*, and *entertainment*, words of that calibre, and then something about a trial. They don't want you dead. Not *yet*. Not before you suffered as, I assume, they feel they have suffered under your rough justice." Saark's eyes were gleaming, and he grinned at Kell without humour. "They want to play, Kell," he said.

Kell digested this information. He finally caught sight of Nienna across the valley floor, and gave her a wave, but she seemed lost in a half-sleep, staring at the roof of her cave cell. Kell's tongue probed his dry mouth, and he cursed these people, and cursed the drugs they'd used to incapacitate him. By the Bone Halls, he thought, they'd better finish him off next time or he'd crack a few skulls!

Kell's gaze swept left and right. He could see, perhaps, three hundred men. They were roughshod, most quite stocky from years working in the Black Pike Mines. These were Falanor's worst, most grim and nasty criminals. The murderers, rapists, smugglers, child-killers. Kell stared at them with uncontrolled disgust, and an even bigger disgust at what he must do. He sighed. It was the only choice he had.

"So, come on then," said Saark. He was looking sideways at Kell, eyes narrowed. "What's the big plan now, eh? You managed to get us caught pretty bad, with your so-called *ooh Governor Myrtax is totally trustworthy and we can go in and get something to eat* old horse shit. *And* they've gone and captured Mary. I tell you something, if they cook my donkey, there'll be hell to pay."

"Stop whining."

"Give me some answers then, damn you!"

"Listen to the demands of Saark, the wonderful, masterful, all-powerful vachine shagging vachine coward. I didn't see you doing much to help when they peppered me with fucking crossbow bolts!"

"It was one bolt, Kell. Hark at the power of a man's exaggeration!"

"You're a fine one to speak. If anybody believed your tales, you'd have impregnated half of Falanor by now!"

"Maybe I have! They do say I have a certain way with the women."

"Yeah, and I bet you carry enough pox to drop a battalion. Now shut your mouth, Saark, and tell me what they did with my axe."

Saark frowned, then rubbed his bruised face. He, too, had taken a beating at the hands of Jagor Mad. As the huge oaf declared, he was indeed, at least partially, *mad*. But then, Saark was getting used to taking a beating in the fiery orbit of Kell's legend. After all, that's what friends were for, no?

"They dumped it in one of the cells, I think. Along with Nienna and the rest of our weapons. It's got to be said, Kell, sometimes I wonder who you love the most: Nienna, or that damn axe?"

"The axe'll never let me down," growled Kell, face locked in a terrible anger. "Now listen to me, Saark. This is the plan."

"Wonderful!"

"Take the grin off your powdered mug before I damn well knock it clear. Things are about to get serious, and you need to know what to do."

"Go on, then. Stun me with the geometry of your tactician's mind."

"I'm going to win over the criminals here, and we'll form them into a fighting unit, into an army, and march on the Vampire Warlords! We will take the battle to the enemy. We will attack, first Jalder, then Gollothrim, then Vor. We will kill the Vampire Warlords. We will stop the vampire plague."

There was a long silence. Outside, somewhere high in the mountains, an avalanche boomed. Crashing echoes reverberated from on high, a deafening and terrifying sound which gradually faded into drifting echoes, like a scattering of loose snow.

"Kell, even for you that's madder than a mad dog's dinner."

"Meaning?"

"Well, where do I begin? For a start, all the bastards here hate you and want your blood and spleen. The Vampire Warlords are, er, indestructible. How can you train an army out of scum? What sorry fool will do the training? And even more importantly, even if, and this is a big *if*, you persuaded three thousand hardened criminals to join your cause, what would stop them being criminals the minute we set foot back in the real world? They'd be straight back to killing and raping, I'd wager."

"Yeah. But we have the upper hand."

"Which is?"

"They have no idea what's happening, out there, in Falanor. They saw the Army of Iron passing through, they rebelled against Governor Myrtax and took over the fortress. They have no idea about Jalder being overrun, or Vor or the gods only know how many other damn cities. They know nothing of King Leanoric dying in battle, or of the cankers or the destruction of Silva Valley."

Saark snorted. "And they don't *fucking care*, Kell! Don't you understand? We're dealing with criminal scum here, the freaks of the country, the bastards who are bastards to their own mother's bastards. They don't deserve to live, and they won't fucking help you, I'm fucking telling you, I am."

"Ha, that's so much horse shit," snapped Kell. "You, with your southern queer dandy ways, you have no fucking idea what these men are like." Kell moved close, his voice dropping a little. "You don't get how life works, do you, Saark? You've had silver platters and boiled eggs all your life. You've had your face in so many rich bouncing tits, licking the arse-crumbs from oh so many perfume-stinking nobles' cracks, that you have no *connection* with reality. Most of these men, they're not bad men, not evil men, there are shades of grey, Saark, and we all make mistakes. It's nice to see you're so fucking perfect! In a different world, you would have lost your head a long time ago!"

Saark snorted again. "What the hell am I hearing? You put hundreds of these bastards in here! Listen to the last of the great hypocrites! You hunted them down, Kell, you killed a lot, and you dragged many back to Vor for trial. And now you want them to fight for you? Now you want them to *die* for you? I've met some mad skunks in my time, heard some crazy bloody plans, but this takes the ridiculous plum straight from the mouth of the insane rich. They'll never follow you, Kell, *Legend* or no. They'd rather shit on your grave."

"You'll see," rumbled Kell.

"And what you going to do? Kill the new governors?" Saark laughed.

"That's the idea."

"What with? Your left thumb?"

"If I have to. Now stop your prattling, I'm trying to think and you're carping on like a fishwife on a fish stall selling buckets of fish to rank stinking fishermen."

"What? *What?* Is that an example of how you're going to win over the crowd? Ha ha, Kell, you've got some serious lessons to learn in life. You're about to throw yourself to the wolves."

"We'll see," said Kell, eyes glowing. "We'll just see."

As the day progressed, Kell and Saark watched a hundred or so men sawing wood and putting together some kind of framed structure. Kell brooded in silence, wincing occasionally at his damaged shoulder, and sat with his knees pulled up under his chin, arms wrapped around his legs, wondering how to get out of this mess. Nobody came to their cell, and they were given no food or water. Occasionally, they saw one of the new Black Pike Governors wandering around the frantic building work, and as a hefty softwood frame took shape, Saark put his head on one side.

"Looks like a stage," he said, at last. "Why are they building a stage? Are they going to treat us to a performance of *Dog's Treason*, or maybe a sequence of sonnet recitals based around the life of that great lover, *Cassiandra*? I know! I've got it! They're going to perform *The Saga of Kell's Legend* just for *your* bloody benefit!"

"It's a gallows, idiot. That's why the centre has extra vertical struts. There's going to be a hole through which somebody drops."

"Somebody?"

"I take a lot of killing," said Kell, voice low, eyes narrowed. "Look, there's Jagor Mad. He really is a big, dumb fool. I thought he would have learnt his lesson last time I brought him in. Evidently not."

"What did he do?"

"Aah," Kell shook his head, then lowered his face to stare at the rocky floor of the cave. He kicked his boot against one of the pitted iron bars. "Jagor came from a city called Gilrak, to the west of Vor. All those who wanted to live in Vor, but couldn't afford to live in the capital, well they lived in Gilrak, and what a sorry heap of shit it was. Like a scum overflow. A sewer outlet. Now, the thing about Gilrak was that it was a new city, with the old one, Old Gilrak, lying a half-league southwest. But what few people knew was that the two were connected by old tunnels. So Jagor and a few of his friends came up with a wonderful money-making scheme. They'd kidnap children, take them through the tunnels – so that when a search went out there was no chance of finding the bastards – take them through the tunnels to the deserted city of Old Gilrak, fast horses, down to the coast where bad men from across the sea were waiting on Crake's Beach with boats."

"So he took children and sold them?"

"Yes. Sold them to bad men, for a lot of gold, men who would use them for, shall we say, unspeakable acts. Things a child should never have to go through." Kell's eyes were gleaming.

"Not a happy end for a child?" ventured Saark.

"No. King Leanoric had three genius spies, who eventually uncovered what was going on. Then they passed the information over to me, and the King charged me with stopping the trade. He gave me limitless funds, and the pick of his men. Well. I work fast, and alone, but Jagor had forty men working his trade so I picked out five of Leanoric's best killers. Not swordsmen, mind, not *soldiers*, but *killers*. Men I'd seen in battle, men with real stomach for the job."

"And the job was?"

"Extermination," said Kell, glancing up at Saark. "I've seen the way the justice courts worked in Vor." He spat. "I've watched good men hang, and I watched bad men walk free. I wasn't about to let this little fish escape the pond."

"So what happened?"

"First, we found one of Jagor's scouts. We tortured him, broke his fingers and toes, cut off his balls, held him screaming in a cellar before cutting his throat. The vermin. Well, he told us where the next targets were; where the next children were. And Jagor's kidnappers were getting greedy; they were going to take ten children that night, all under the age of ten. One of my killers took the place of Jagor's scout, and we waited, let them sneak in and take the girl from her little town house in the poor part of the city, then we followed those fuckers back to their camp in the woods, and the place they'd dug down and smashed through into the old tunnel network leading to Old Gilrak."

"What happened next?"

Kell shrugged. "We came on them in the night. Fucking slaughtered them, six of us there were with rage in our eyes and blood on our swords and axes. We massacred them, men and women alike, no mercy. Five escaped into the tunnels, including Jagor Mad. I'd gone in for the kill, we fought and I hit him so hard I put a dent in his skull, broke three bones in my hand but it was worth it. But then somebody jumped on my back, I rammed back my head, ended up with half his teeth stuck in my scalp, but it gave Jagor time to flee. Down through the tunnels."

"You don't make friends easy, do you Kell?"

"Shut up. Well, my men took the kids back to Gilrak and I went down the tunnels after these rats. I followed them all night, caught up with two who were injured, killed them easy enough, then another two tried to spring a trap on me in the dark. Well, Kell doesn't die easy, and I gave them a few things to think about – delivered courtesy of the butterfly blades of Ilanna. Then I chased Jagor Mad all damn night, but the bastard got away. He might look like a big brute, but he ran faster than any frightened schoolgirl, I can tell you."

"How did he end up here?"

"Some of Leanoric's soldiers caught him a week later, north in Fawkrin, heading there with all his ill-gotten gains. I reckon he was going to set himself up as a bandit in Vorgeth Forest, live like a woodland lord. Anyway, because the soldiers had him, he was delivered to the Chief Lord Justice in Vor. Meant he got a trial. Hah! I had to stand there, and them bastards with their fancy words and stupid wigs, they tried to make it sound like I was some bloodthirsty killer, or something…"

"And of course, they'd be right."

"And I pointed out I wasn't the one selling children to dirty bastards from across the sea, and that's when we went into the woods, it was six of us and forty of them. Still."

Kell rubbed his chin. "They had to put him in prison. Too many families weeping and wailing in the courts. Would have looked bad on the Chief Lord Justice. Not even *he* could have stomached a mass public retribution for his bad comedy court system." Kell chuckled. "I'll never forget, all those judges giving me their dirty looks from under powdered wigs. Gods! Enough to make a man puke, it was."

"So… Jagor Mad came here?"

"Yeah. Scowling at me all the way through the court-room, mouth uttering threats. He was the lucky one; the others got a taste of my axe. And they fucking deserved it."

Saark looked out from behind bars. He tested them, tugging gently, as he had a hundred times that day. "And now they'll give you *your own* trial, to satisfy Jagor Mad's sense of revenge."

"Looks that way."

"What about the others? Dandall and Grey Tail? You put them both here?"

"Aye, lad."

"And what did they do?"

"Dandall killed people. Lots of people. Used to wait down on Port of Gollothrim docks for drunks, men, women, didn't matter to him. He used to use a long stiletto dagger, get them down a back alley and push it through their necks. I reckon he thought he was doing somebody a favour, although it was probably himself. He was lucky there were seargents with me when I brought him in. He'd just done a drunk prostitute, killed her then cut out her eyes. If I'd been on my own, well, he would have got Ilanna in the back of the head."

Saark considered this. "Is there anybody you *don't* try to kill?"

"Yeah. People who mind their own business."

"So Jagor Mad kidnapped children for the sex trade, Dandall was an out and out murderer, what lovely crime did Grey Tail commit? Don't tell me, he was arrested for stealing sugar?"

"No. He used to eat people. Before he was a Black-lipper. Must have picked up that dirty stinking vachine habit – no offence – when he came to this wonderful shit-hole. Grey Tail lived in Vor, our illustrious capital city, quite a rich man by all accounts. Worked as a physician, tending the wounded arses of those too rich to get off them. It took the authorities years to realise that occasionally his rich clients would vanish. He had a big house on a very well-to-do street in Merchant's Quarter. Four storeys it was, very nice stone, big cellar below street level. Used to take the odd client, one who wouldn't be missed too much, take them down there, strap 'em to a chair and then, well then he'd begin."

"There he is now," said Saark, and they stared out at the small, wiry man with the round face. He was directing a group of carpenters, who were hammering planks in place as a makeshift floor. If you looked past the evidence of him being a Blacklipper, he was a modest-looking man who could have quite easily, in the eye of the imagination, been a respectable surgeon. "What *exactly* did he do to his patients?"

"Used to cut them up, piece by piece, and cook them in a little pan. Used to eat their flesh first, he'd gag 'em, slice off a chunk, fry it, eat it. Keep them alive for a few weeks whilst he feasted on their flesh. It was the neighbours who complained; I reckon they got sick of the stench of frying human fat."

"We live in a decadent world," said Saark.

"Aye. Sometimes, laddie, it makes me wonder if the vachine have the right idea."

"Hey, I can always bite you?" He grinned. "You'd become *one* of *us*."

Kell stared at him. "The day you bite me, Saark, is the day I rip off your skull."

"As I said, is there anybody you've met who you didn't try and kill?"

"No. I don't have it in me."

"That's what I thought you'd say. Oh, look Kell, up go the gallows. Hurrah!" Ten men laboured to erect a huge post, which was then strapped into position and secured with cross-struts. The sound of hammering echoed across the flat ground. Kell's face was grim.

"No need to be so happy about it."

"Hey, I'm pretty sure it's designed for me as well, mate. You're not the only one with the honour of being an enemy of the new Black Pike Mine Governors."

"Yeah. Well. We should rest. Going to need all our strength, later, aren't we."

"You really think you can convince them?"

"I hope so," said Kell. "All our lives depend on it."


"Wake up, you fucking bastards." It was Jagor Mad, growling through the evening gloom and between the bars. Snow was falling. Both Kell and Saark awoke, weary, groggy, as if they had been drugged. "Come on, quick, before I call a man with a crossbow."

Kell stood, and stretched languorously, ignoring the pain in his shoulder. "Yeah. Well, lad, that would be your way now, wouldn't it? Shoot us through the bars, in the fucking back, just like the coward piece of sliced horse dick you really are. But look, out there. All your pussy lickers are waiting, watching you. And you know you have to play the game, or some bastard will stick you in your sleep. Not that you don't get that every night, eh Saark?" Kell nudged Saark, who gave a nervous laugh, eyes fixed on the pure hate and rage that filled the trembling Jagor Mad standing before them.

"You will eat those words, Axeman," spat Jagor.

"Show me!"

"Your time will come, soon enough! On the end of a fucking rope!"

"Like that'll stop me," snarled Kell, moving close. Suddenly, he grabbed Jagor through the bars and dragged the huge bear close. Jagor Mad struggled, but despite his prodigious strength Kell was his match. Jagor's face slammed the bars, and Kell pushed his nose against his enemy's as his hands flapped and slapped, and grappled for his sword. When Kell spoke, his words were a low growl, so only he, Jagor and Saark could hear. "I could kill you, Big Man, right here, right now, bite off your fucking nose, put out your fucking eyes and you'd be screaming and then you'd be dead, and you fucking know it, you worthless worm." He pushed Jagor roughly back, just as sword cleared scabbard. The blade rang against the bars, and Jagor was in an uncontrollable rage.

"Wise?" enquired Saark, backing away as Jagor Mad fumbled with the locks.

"Is anything in this world?" snapped Kell. "Or would you rather dance on the end of a rope?"

"Calm," said Dandall, and a hand appeared on Jagor Mad's shoulder, and there were muttered words and the huge Governor strode away, face scarlet. Dandall opened the locks, and behind him were ten crossbow men, all grinning.

"Give up the tricks now, Kell. You're going on trial for your crimes. Either that, or ten bolts in your belly. You decide."

"I'll come quiet," said Kell, "although it isn't my way."

"Oh yes. The Legend." Dandall gave a slick sneer. "Well, it won't get you far in these parts. Not with these men. They like a good hanging, y'see? They like a bit of entertainment to pass away the long, cold winter evenings."

Kell and Saark stepped from their cage. Wind caught them, chilled them, thrilled them. It ruffled Kell's hair and beard, and he flexed his powerful fingers and looked around, like a wild beast in its first few seconds of release. Then he looked down, to where three thousand convicts crowded at the front of the now finished stage and gallows. Kell gave a grim smile. Everybody knew this was a farce, a stage-show; there would be no real trial, just a performance and then some killing. Kell took a deep breath. So be it, he thought.

Kell and Saark were guided down the rocky path, and Kell glanced left. He could see Nienna, clutching the bars of her own cell and watching, face small, white, filled with fear. Kell tried to give her an encouraging smile, but a spear butt jabbed him in the back of the head and he stumbled. Kell stopped, and turned. The man stared at him.

"Do that again, and I'll make you eat it, point first," growled Kell.

The man swallowed, and took a step back.

Dandall laughed. "Don't let the old fool scare you. He knows he can't outrun or outfight crossbow bolts; and at the end of the day, we have his granddaughter. Nienna. And the fun we could have with that pretty sweet slab of meat." Dandall licked his lips. "After all, Kell knows how skilled I am with a variety of blades. And if we were to give Nienna over to Grey Tail there, well," he chuckled, and sniffed the air as if sniffing the aroma of a fine cooking stew, "mmmm, I'm sure there's bits that would taste sweeter than she looks!"

Kell made a guttural growling sound, but said no more. He marched forward, down the path to be swallowed between the jeering, shouting crowd of men. Many punched and kicked out as he passed, but Kell ignored the blows, and marched with head held high, reaching the stage and pausing just for a second to stare up the steps, at the huge thick beam supporting the gallows and a gently swinging noose. Kell gave a sickly, wry smile. He'd sent enough men to be hanged under the supervision of King Leanoric. How ironic, it had come to this!

Kell mounted the steps, and Saark was jabbed up after him. Their boots were hollow, echoing on the planks as they were pushed forward and made to kneel. To one side, ten thick, hand-carved chairs had been set in a semi-circle, and now another seven men approached and mounted a second set of steps, taking their places in the chairs with as much regal air as they could muster. They were old, most of them, and wearing rich clothes and thick gold jewellery. Their eyes were bleak and cold – except for one man, on the end, Governor Myrtax, who was trembling, and kept his head low, eyes studiously ignoring Kell. It was clear he was being co-erced, but Kell felt a twinge of disappointment that the man had no backbone. Kell sneered at him, and gazed out on the crowd.

Thousands of faces. Filled with hate. Shouting, and sneering, crying and bellowing. Fists were punching the air. Their hate rolled out and encompassed Kell and he absorbed it, and he used it. He revelled in it. He used it to *focus*. It reminded him of fighting in the *pit*.

Now, Grey Tail and Jagor Mad approached, and took their seats, leaving one final chair free for Dandall who stood, and raised his hands, and gradually the cacoph-onous roaring cheering noise subsided.

"Men and women of Black Pike Mines!" he cried, and another roar went up and Kell's fists clenched. He glanced over at Saark, who was visibly pale, and trem-bling. Saark licked his lips and gave Kell a worried smile. Vachine or no, Saark would die in this place. No extra strength or speed could aid him against such numbers. A crowd like this, they were a killing crowd, a lynching mob. They wanted blood, and wouldn't be happy until they had it – even if that meant each other's.

"Hang 'em!" shouted a man near the front, a man with a thick beard and small dark eyes.

"Yeah, we want to see them dance!" cried another.

Kell squared himself to the crowd, and allowed him-self to smile. "Why don't you come up here and do it yourself, fucker?" he snarled. "Or have you lost your balls in that face full of beard?"

A roar of laughter rippled through the crowd and Kell grinned. "You are all fools," he said, and the laughter stopped in an instant. "You sit here in the place that imprisoned you, frightened to move, frightened to leave, frightened to fucking *fart*, and you have no idea what's turning in the real world outside!"

"Shut up!" snapped Dandall. "You are here for trial. A trial to determine your death, so I advise you to be silent when I tell you."

"A trial?" roared Kell, and saw Jagor Mad surge from his seat, face red, fists clenched but Grey Tail held him back. "What petty nonsense. And to be honest, Dandall, I don't give a shit about your trial. I reckon you'll all be dead, soon enough."

"What do you mean?" rumbled the bearded man from the front of the audience.

"STOP!" roared Jagor Mad. "This is OUR day, the day when Kell the Legend, *defender of the rich, arse-kisser to nobility, fucker of Queens, the day when he DIES!*"

Kell laughed. His voice was low, but carried to every man in the audience. "If you want me dead so bad, Jagor Mad, why not come do it yourself? Here. Right now."

"I will!" thundered the huge man. "Who do you think will be dropping you on the end of that noose?"

Kell spat out laughter once more. "Just what I thought of you, Jagor. A coward and a lick-spittle, spineless, chicken, hiding behind the decisions of others, hiding behind a hangman's horse shit when out there in Jalder and Vor and Gollothrim the Vampire Warlords have returned, they're killing all your people, your friends, and families, infecting them with vampire poison, turning them into vampire slaves!"

A murmur ran through the audience, and Jagor strode forward and hit Kell with a mighty right hook. Kell did not go down, but instead stared hard at Jagor, blood at the corner of his mouth. "Go on!" he bellowed, "show them what you can do to a man with his hands tied! What a hero! What a warrior! A man to be feared – by chickens!"

Again, laughter ran through the crowd and Jagor went red with embarrassment and anger. "You want to fight me, old man? You want to fight, here and now, and the loser hangs? Then so fucking be it."

Silence reigned. The falling snow hissed gently in a diagonal sleet.

"That would be unfair," said Kell, voice rumbling out slow and measured, a performance as good as any Saark had ever seen. Kell turned to face the crowd. He acknowledged that *they* held the power in this comedy trial; they would demand what they wanted, and would get it through strength in numbers. Kell stared at three thousand faces, hard men, criminals, men who'd survived the mines for many years, the hard manual labour making them stronger, more brutal in a struggle for simple survival. Kell smiled. He glanced at Jagor Mad. "You, on your own, ha, you would be far too easy. I would fight you, Dandall and Grey Tail! All at once. And if I win, I get to speak to the crowd. I tell them of the Vampire Warlords, and the carnage sweeping the real world."

"They don't want to hear your bedtime stories, you old fuck," snarled Jagor Mad. "They want to see blood!"

"Let's show them," said Kell, and lifted his bound hands. "Untie me!"

"No!" snapped Dandall, striding forward with Grey Tail close at his heel. The three Governors of the Black Pike Mines scowled at Kell. Swiftly, he had changed the dynamic of the trial. The three men almost felt as though *they* were back before the noose. "Kell will hang. That will be an end to it."

"You scared of him, Dandall?" said the bearded man near the front.

"Of course I'm not scared of him!"

"Let him fight you, then. You telling me the three of you can't take one old man?" The crowd started to laugh, and the three Governors exchanged glances. Somehow, the tide had turned. There was hatred for Kell, yes, but it didn't outweigh a lust to watch a good fight. Entertainment, Saark had called it. And he'd been right.

At that moment, Saark started to make soft clucking chicken noises. More laughter burst out, and Jagor Mad pulled free a curved knife and pointed at Saark. "I'll deal with you later, dandy," then slashed the knife through Kell's ropes.

Kell moved back, boots pacing the stage as he rolled his shoulders, loosening muscles, wincing a little at the crossbow wound but grinding his teeth and knowing he must show no pain.

Kell reached the other side of the stage, and turned, and lifted his fists in a stance taken by Shit Pit fighters; a roar went up from the crowd and Dandall placed a hand on Jagor Mad's arm. The three Governors looked at one another, gave a nod, and spread out, eyes narrowed, wary. They knew who Kell was, knew him far too well, far too painfully, and despite appearances they knew what he could do. Kell was a killer, pure and simple. But they were experienced. They'd done this sort of thing before.

"Come on lads, let's see what you've got."

Jagor Mad rushed Kell, fists high, purple face filled with hate and rage and spittle flying from lips which thrashed, teeth grinding, and he swung a powerful right hook but Kell swayed back, Jagor's knuckles flashing past his nose, and he slammed his boot into Jagor's groin. As Jagor grunted, and stumbled forward, Kell powered a punch down onto the bridge of the large man's nose and there was a terrible crunch. Jagor hit the planks face first and Kell stepped over him, watching as Dandall and Grey Tail spread even wider apart. They rushed him at once, a concerted attack, and Kell ducked a punch from Dandall, dropping to one knee and ramming his fist into the Governor's stomach, folding him over with an explosion of sour air. In the same movement, his arm powered back and he turned, where Grey Tail had leapt into a kick. Both boots hit Kell in the face, and he grabbed the wiry man's legs and they both went backwards across the doubled-over figure of Dandall, crashing to the boards. Grey Tail slithered around, getting atop Kell and delivering four powerful punches straight to Kell's face before Kell grabbed the man's cock and balls in a single handful, jerking tight, and Grey Tail let out a high-pitched wail as Kell crushed him in one mighty fist, rising to one knee, then to his boots, with Grey Tail dancing and squealing on his tiptoes, "Let go, let go, let go." Kell let go, and slammed a head-butt to his face, dropping the small man and turning into... a punch, which glanced from his cheekbone, and another, which glanced from his temple. Jagor Mad loomed over him, eyes mad with rage, and Kell dodged a third blow and kicked out, boot crunching against Jagor's kneecap and knocking the big man back. Kell stood, and lifted his fists. "It's like fighting three little girls," he spat though saliva and blood. Laughter rippled.

Dandall leapt at him, but Kell side-stepped, ramming an elbow into the man's face as he swept past, lifting him almost horizontally before Dandall thumped to the boards. Then with a roar, Kell charged at Jagor and delivered six punches, which Jagor managed to block, stepping back and back and back until he reached the edge of the stage, stumbled, his questing boot found nothing but air and he fell, face slapping the edge of the stage before he tumbled back into the crowd, who let out a loud jeer. Kell whirled, into a plank wielded by Grey Tail. The wood slapped his face and Kell went down, coughing, stunned, as Grey Tail set about kicking the large axeman. Kell warded off the blows, rubbed blood out of his eyes, then lunged at Grey Tail, grabbing him by balls and throat, hoisting him into the air and launching him into the crowd, who parted, allowing Grey Tail to land heavily. There was savage *crunch*, and his leg twisted beneath him at a crazy angle. Bone poked through cloth. Blood pooled out. Grey Tail screamed for a few seconds, then passed into a no-doubt welcome realm of unconsciousness.

Dandall stood, stunned, as Jagor Mad grunted and heaved himself back onto the stage. His face was battered, a diagonal line of blood crossing from one eye to his jaw, and his eyes held murder.

"Fuck this horse shit," he said, and drew a small knife. Kell's eyes narrowed.

"You upping the stakes, boy?"

"Fuck the stakes, I'm going to gut you like a rancid fish."

"But what about your crowd? They want to see a fight."

"They want to see a killing."

"Never upset your audience, Jagor."

"Fuck the audience."

The large Governor advanced, and Dandall backed away, face pale, recognising a fight now entering a different league; something of which he wanted no part. Jagor lunged at Kell, who backed away, then again, and they circled warily.

"Not so tough without your axe, eh Kell?"

Jagor ran at Kell, who batted the knife to one side and slammed a fist into Jagor's head, then skipped away as the knife slashed for his belly. Now, Kell's back was to the thick wood column and its dangling noose. He could feel the gaping hole of the drop behind him, and glanced back. Seeing his chance, Jagor ran at him and Kell stepped aside, slammed three straight punches into Jagor's face, slapped the knife from the man's hand then took hold of his tattered, bloodstained shirt.

"Is this what you wanted?" growled Kell, and shoved Jagor to the noose, grabbing the rope and lowering it over Jagor's head. Stunned, and coming round an instant too late, Jagor's fists grappled at Kell's bearskin and his boots scrabbled at the edge of the drop.

"What are you doing?" he shrieked.

"You said they came here for a hanging!"

"Not me, for you, Kell, for you!" Jagor's voice was filled with terrible fear, and his knuckles were white where he clung to Kell's bearskin. "No, no, get the rope off!"

"You try to kill me, you up the stakes to *death*, then don't fucking complain when I return the favour!"

"No, Kell, I beseech you, don't do this! I don't want to die!"

"None of us want to die, son," said Kell, and slammed a heavy slow punch between Jagor Mad's eyes. His fingers released Kell's jerkin and he stepped back, and there was a *snap* as the rope went tight and Jagor dangled there, kicking, face purple, hands clawing at the rope but because he was such a hefty, large man, battered and bruised and tired from the fight, he could not take his weight. He kicked for a while, and a cheer went up from the army of convicts ranged about the stage.

Kell glanced over at Dandall, who was white with fear. Kell stooped, picking up Jagor's knife, and his eyes were glittering and Dandall held up his hands. "No, not me, spare me Kell, please."

"Get down on your knees and beg."

Dandall got down on his knees, and touching his trembling forehead to the planks, he begged.

"And these are your leaders?" roared Kell, facing the crowd as behind him Jagor Mad's head and shoulders could be seen, struggling, and below the stage his legs kicked and danced and he refused to let go of that most precious thing. *Life.*

"You would fight for these worms? You would kill, for these fucking maggots?"

"NO!" roared the men before Kell, and he grinned at them, and turned, and sawed through the rope. Jagor Mad fell through the hole and hit the ground with a thump. He lay still, wheezing, and Kell peered down at him, where he squirmed in the mud and snow-slush.

Kell lifted his arms wide, and addressed the convicts. "The Army of Iron came from the north, from beyond the Black Pike Mountains. They slaughtered thousands of people in Jalder, men, women, children, I saw this with my own eyes. King Leanoric's army was beaten, their bodies fed into huge machines, Blood Refineries, to feed the vampire monsters to the north. But then it got worse, gentlemen. The vachine summoned the ancient Vampire Warlords – and they are terrible indeed. They rampage through our land, through Falanor, and none can stand against them. They take your friends and families, your kinsmen and countrymen, they bite them, they convert them to vampires and the world out there will *never* be the same again unless you stand beside me and fight!"

"Why should we trust you?" shouted one man.

"Because I am Kell the Legend!" he boomed, "and when I fight the world trembles! I do not do this for money, or lust, or any petty base desire. I do this because it has to be done! It is the right thing to do! I know many of you here hate me, but that's good, lads, *hate* is a good thing – I'm not asking you to kiss my fucking arse," a few laughed at that, "I'm asking you to help me put the world back together. These vampire whoresons have broken it, and they need a damn good thrashing."

"You put many of us here! We're criminals to you, scum, why the fuck would you care?"

"No, you're wrong, you're men who made mistakes, and yeah a lot of you did bad things, but now's your chance to do the right thing. Falanor needs you. She needs your strength. She needs your trust. She needs your steel. Will you fight with me?"

A terrible silence washed across the gathered men. Behind him, Kell heard Saark's sharp intake of breath. Their future, their lives and deaths, and the lives and deaths of thousands of people, the future of Falanor, all hung here, and now, as if a delicate thread of silk lay threatened by the brute bulk horror of an axe-blade.

Kell folded his arms, as if in challenge to the three thousand men ranged before him.

"Well lads," came a voice from the front. It was the hefty bearded man who'd spoken earlier. "I don't know about youse lot, but I ain't having no vampires shitting blood and shit in *my* bloody country!" He drew a short sword, and waved the dull blade above his head. "I'm with you, Kell, even though it's your damn fault I'm here! I'll fight beside you, man. We'll send these fuckers home and down into the shit!"

"Good man!" boomed Kell. "What do they call you?"

"They call me Grak the Bastard."

"And are you?" roared Kell.

The large bearded man grinned. "You'd better believe it, you old goat!"

"Glad to have you with me, Grak. Now then, lads, are you going to let Grak head out there into Falanor alone? Or are you going to show some brotherly bonding, are you going to fight for your homeland, fight for the future of your children? After all, it's damn fucking unsporting to let me and Grak kill all those vampire bastards on our own! It'd be a shame to have all the hero songs to ourselves!"

"I'll come!" bellowed a short, powerful man with biceps as thick as Kell's.

"Me too! We'll show the vampire scum what the scum of Falanor can do!"

"Yeah, we'll do better than any King's damn army!"

Kell watched the men talking animatedly for a moment, and Saark appeared beside him. Using Jagor's knife, Kell sawed through Saark's bonds and the dandy grinned at him. "I don't believe what I just saw."

"Men are always looking for something to fight for," grimaced Kell.

"But you're the same!"

Kell stared at him "Of course I am." It was no criticism, just an observation. "Listen – go and get Ilanna. I'm missing my axe terribly."

Saark stared at the big man, with his battered face and bloodied knuckles. "And Nienna? I should release Nienna?"

"That goes without saying," smiled Kell, easily, and turned as Grak the Bastard climbed the steps and moved forward.

"You're smaller than you look, up close," said Grak.

Kell grinned. "Well met, Bastard." They clasped hands, wrist to wrist.

"Only my mother calls me that."

"I have a job for you, Grak, and I think you're the man for the job."

Grak pushed back his broad shoulders, and clenched his fists. "You name it, Kell. I'm yours to command."

"I'll be the General of this here little army. You can be one of my Command Sergeants."

Grak raised his eyebrows. "Promotion is quick in your new army, I see. I'll surely stick around now. Who knows where I'll be in a week? In a year, I'll surely be a god with a big fat arse!" He roared with laughter, slapping his thigh, and many men joined in.

"I want you to round up Grey Tail, Jagor and Dandall. Get them tied up and brought to me."

"You going to kill them?"

"No. They're just blinded by hatred; and to be honest, Grak, I need every good fighting man I can get. These Vampire Warlords – they're like nothing I've ever seen in this world."

"I'll get on it, Kell."

"And Grak?"

"Yes, General?"

"What did you do out in the real world? So that I dragged your arse to this chaotic shit-hole?"

Grak the Bastard grinned at Kell with a mouthful of broken teeth from too many bar brawls. "I killed my last General," he said, turned his back, and strode across the planks of the hangman's platform.

Kell stood on the battlements as night closed in. Snow fell on the plains beyond, and a harsh wind blew across the wilds. Kell shivered, and considered the enormity of what he was doing. Kell knew he was no general, but he was going to lead an army of convicts across Falanor and engage the vampires and the Army of Iron in bloody battle. And the Army of Iron *alone* had slaughtered King Leanoric's finest Eagle Divisions, more than ten thousand men. And here, Kell had a mere three.

"It's an impossible task," he muttered, but he knew, deep down in his heart, deep down in his soul, it was something he had to do. Something nobody else would, or could.

Kell sighed, and Ilanna sang out in a vertical slice as a shadow moved behind him.

"Hell, man, I nearly cut off your bloody head!"

"Sorry, Kell, sorry!" It was Myrtax, wearing a fresh robe and rubbing his hands together, eyes averted from Kell's cold steel gaze. "Listen. Kell. I came to apologise."

"Ach, forget it, man."

"No, no, what I did was cowardly."

"Horse shit. You were protecting your family. I would have done the same."

"Very noble of you to say so, Kell, but I know that isn't the case. You would have stood, and fought, and overcome your enemies. I stand before you a broken, humbled man."

"Yes. Well." Kell was uncomfortable. "We can't all be a…" he smiled sardonically, "a *Legend*."

Myrtax moved to the battlements and stared off into the distance. Snow landed lightly on his hair, making him look older than his advancing years. Then he glanced at Kell.

"We're getting old."

"Speak for yourself."

"What you up to, Kell? You want to fight off all the vampire hordes?"

"Aye. It's the only way I know."

"I was speaking with Nienna."

"Yes?" Kell looked sharply at Myrtax. "And?"

"She said you're tired. That you didn't want to come here. Didn't want to do this. You said Falanor would look after Herself."

"Aye, I said that. And it's true." He sighed. "You're right. We *are* getting old. This is a young man's war."

"You're wrong, Kell. This is a time when the world needs heroes. Heroes who are not afraid of the dark. Heroes who will," he smiled, looking back off into the snow-heavy distance, "walk into a fortress prison of three thousand enemies, and turn them to good deeds."

"They can only do what's in their hearts."

"They will fight for you, Kell. I can feel it. In the air. In the snow. They are excited; horrified, frightened, but excited. You have inspired them."

"Maybe. But they won't be inspired when the vampires rip out a few hundred throats and crows eat eyeballs on the blood-drenched battlefields."

Myrtax squinted into the snow. "Somebody comes."

Kell shaded his eyes, and through the haze of snow-fall they watched a cart slowly advancing, being pulled by two horses. More men walked beside the cart, which had a heavy tarpaulin thrown over the back.

"Let's go and see what they want. The hour is late, and men don't wander to prisons in the dead of night for naught."

Kell and Myrtax descended the steps, and were soon joined by Saark and Grak the Bastard. They marched to the gates and stepped out, the huge walls looming behind them and seeming to cast a deep, oppressive silence over the world.

"They look cut up," said Saark, voice grim. "Like they've been in the wars."

As they neared, they slowed, and each of the six men carried swords, unsheathed.

"If you've come for a fight, lads, better be on your way," said Kell, hefting Ilanna and taking a step forward.

"We don't want trouble," said one man.

"We've come for help," said another.

"What's your story, lad?" said Governor Myrtax, not unkindly.

"We're from Jalder. The city was overrun weeks back, but near fifty of us escaped through the sewers. Women and children as well. No soldiers were sent after us, and after a few days' travelling, running, we camped up in an old farmhouse."

"I think we should invite them in, hear their story over an ale and broth," said Myrtax.

"Wait," said Saark, holding out his hand. Then he shook his head. "What's under the tarpaulin, gentlemen?"

"It's *them*," snapped one. "Two of the bastards who came hunting us." He looked suddenly frightened, a terrible look on the face of such a big, brutal man.

"Let me guess? They came at you in the night, slaughtered most of you, but you six escaped?"

The man nodded, and Kell strode forward, lifting the edge of the tarpaulin with the corner of his axe. "Did you cut off their heads?"

"No. They're still alive."

"You did well capturing them. They usually fight to the death."

"Well, forty of us died trying. We thought we'd bring them here, to Governor Myrtax. My dad always said he was a good man. He could… put them on trial, or something. I haven't got it in me to kill women, no matter how vile."

Nienna had appeared at the gates, rubbing at tired eyes, yawning. She padded to Saark's side and touched his arm lightly. He smiled down at her, and said, "You not sleep?"

"What, with you all making a racket out here? What's going on?"

"They caught some vampires."

"Oh."

Kell glanced up at Nienna. "Stand way back. These are vicious, especially if they've been tied down for a while. You don't know what they might do."

"Are you sure you know what you're doing, Kell?" Myrtax had gone deathly pale. Saark had drawn his rapier, and Grak held a short stabbing sword in one meaty fist.

Kell shrugged, and threw back the tarpaulin. On the cart lay two beautiful women of middle-years, their hair glowing and glossy, their skin pale white and as richly carved as finest porcelain. They were tied up tight with rope and field-wire, and they moved lethargically as they glanced up, struggling to move. Kell saw the rope which bound them had been nailed to the cart. Their yellow, feral eyes fell on Kell and one hissed, but the other, the more elegant of the two, stared hard at him and rolled to her knees, elegant despite the bindings. She licked her lips and Kell swallowed, mouth suddenly dry, hands clammy on Ilanna. Fear sucked at him, sucked out his courage and almost his sanity.

"No," he whispered.

"You! Bastard!" hissed the vampire.

"What is it?" snapped Saark, running forward and clutching Kell's huge iron bicep, and he realised too late Nienna was with him, and her run was pulled up short by the clamp of Kell's fist.

The vampire laughed, eyes glittering, snow settling gently on her long dark hair and smooth black dress. She stood, and stared down at them, tugging gently at her bindings, and Nienna fell to her knees in the snow, weeping and staring up.

"What's *going on?*" snarled Saark, feeling the panic of the situation rising.

"Saark, meet Sara," growled Kell, grimly, his eyes never leaving the yellow slits of the tall vampire. "My daughter. Nienna's mother."

## CHAPTER 9
### *Song of the Ankarok*

For a while, Kuradek the Unholy spent his days recovering, basking like a lizard on a rock. The journey from the Chaos Halls had been a long, hard journey, fraught with peril and indeed, filled with violent bursts of fighting simply to survive… even for one as savage as Kuradek.

Kuradek turned several humans into *slaves* and they brought him meat, and fresh blood, the near-dead bodies of children and babes on which he could gorge until full, until bloated. He would lie, in the Blue Palace, on a couch of silk, his skin smoking and squirming with evil religion, and his hatred was palpable, like a haze of ocean fog, and his red eyes surveyed the *turned* and he smiled with crooked smoke fangs.

Slowly, Kuradek fed, and he recovered his strength, and thought long and hard. He brooded. He remembered a time, the time of the *vachine* and he spat out black lumps of smoking phlegm with rage. He reached down and tore off a baby's arm, ignoring the dead blue eyes which stared up from a bloodied pile of infant corpses. He chewed on the fingers for a while, and having gnawed to the bones, moved up to the wrist, sucking at the bone marrow and picking strips of flesh clean with his fangs.

*The vachine!*

*Bastards!*

He remembered like yesterday their magick, how they had taken control from the Vampire Warlords by their deceit, them, the slaves he had allowed to live! And even the sacrifice of Silva Valley did little to cheer Kuradek, even the death of so many vachine did little to satiate his lust for revenge. For Kuradek knew, *knew* they had expanded north, past the Black Pike Mountains, and there were hundreds of thousands still remaining, still breathing air, still breeding human cattle and mixing their blood with foul oil-magick. They were impure, the vachine; they were deviants of the vampire. They were an outcast race. They were a *clockwork* race, and Kuradek would not have it! His eyes glowed, and his long arms flexed, talons dropping to shriek against stone with an array of sparks. No.

Kuradek would make the vachine pay.

One day.

All of them...

Slowly, Kuradek rose from his bloated slumber and blinked lazily. He stepped up to the high window in the west tower of the Blue Palace, and stared out across the blackness of Jalder. No fires burned, now, and a cold ice wind blew across what appeared a deserted city. And yet... yet he could *smell* those who still lived, could smell the blood in their veins, hear the pumping of their hearts like discordant music, off-key notes, a poisoned orchestra. Kuradek breathed deep, and leapt from the high tower window, landing and cracking the ancient stone flags of the courtyard. A group of the *turned* scattered in shock, then fixed eyes on their master and returned slowly, smiles on pale faces lit by the moon.

Kuradek hissed, and gestured the slaves back, then he moved, running through the darkened streets, moving with awesome speed across snow and ice, talons gripping with surety, smoke-trailing head weaving from side to side as he sniffed, as he *hunted*… he reached a cottage, skidded on ice, kicked the door across the room in an explosion of splinters and stood in the centre of the space. One talon smashed down through floorboards, and the whole room seemed to erupt in violence as screams rent the air and Kuradek leapt down into the hidden cellar where eight people hid, and swords struck at him but seemed to slow through his smoke-filled, symbol-tattooed body then emerge from the other side without harming the Warlord. His talons lashed out, punching holes through men's chests. He grabbed a woman, and his long limbs pulled apart and both her arms came off at the shoulders spewing blood and leaving her screaming, her blood describing fountains across the walls. Kuradek loomed over a four year-old girl with curly brown hair, brown eyes looking up at him in awe and shock and wonderment. He reached down, and with a quick bite, removed her head, swallowing it whole.

Kuradek lifted his smoky muzzle and… howled, howled at the city, at the moon, at the stars, at his tortured past, at his escape from the Chaos Halls, at the bastard vachine and their curse and imprisonment, but most of all, Kuradek howled with enjoyment and hatred and rage and impotent fury and the *joy*, the pure acid *joy* of the hunt.

• • • •

Throughout Jalder, Kuradek's howls and screams seemed to stimulate the turned vampires into action. They rampaged through the streets, breaking into houses, searching through attics and cellars, finding more hidden humans and either drinking their blood and leaving drained corpses, or as they had been instructed, *turning* them into yet *more* vampires. Into Kuradek's Legion.

For Kuradek knew.

Falanor was full to the brim with human offal. And they would bring the fight to him. They always did. It was their nature. But he would crush them. Unlike a thousand years ago, when the vachine turned on their masters, this time Kuradek and the Vampire Warlords would be ready…

As the hours passed, and day turned to night turned to day, so Falanor fell under the spread of the *vampire*. And unlike the vachine before them, who had sought simple extermination for blood-oil magick, and for sacrifice, the Vampire Warlords sought slaves, sought an army of the impure. For that way, they could expand. That way, they could create Dominion.

In Vor, Meshwar the Violent uncurled like a snake and stood tall, stretching, smoke curling from the corners of his mouth. His blood eyes dropped to survey the slaves before him, and he strode down the once pure regal steps of King Leanoric's beautiful Rose Palace, and stared out through huge iron gates, out over the destruction and desolation of Vor, Falanor's capital city.

Smoke curled along midnight streets, swirling about the feet of many slave vampires bearing the *mark* of

Meshwar. He grinned, a smoke grin of tightly reined insanity, and surveyed his handiwork. He was not called *The Violent* for no reason...

In the City Square, a huge pile of corpses burned, their drained, angular figures like wooden stickmen seen through flames. Meshwar's eyes drifted impassively over the thousand or so unfortunates, their clothing, skin and bones turning to ash as fire roared and crackled like feeding demons, illuminating the palace with an orange glow.

What Graal had begun so many weeks earlier with his ice-smoke and blood-oil magick, with his invasion of Vor by the Army of Iron – well, now Meshwar was finishing the task.

The Army of Iron were camped out of the city. All vachine camped alongside them had been taken into the forest and executed. Some vachine had put up a fight, several bands even escaping into the woods; but Meshwar sent squads of vampire killers after them, hunting them down, ripping out throats and clockwork hearts, spilling gears and cogs to the forest undergrowth,

Now, though, now it was all *his*. And the *worm* Graal was the problem of Bhu Vanesh. Slowly, through Meshwar's mind eased a thought web, for he did not think like normal mortals. This multi-threaded strand held ideas of death and destruction for Graal, but also amusement for it would annoy Bhu Vanesh. It would not be long, decided Meshwar, until Graal died a horrible death, despite his misplaced loyalty in their Summoning. To Meshwar, Graal was an imposter. A twisted impure. A melding of that which they sought to stamp out...

Meshwar's eyes surveyed Vor once again, then again, and again, taking in the destruction, the rampage, the *violence*. There, the Five Pillars of Agrioth had been chained and pulled to the ground by teams of horses and cattle. Five thousand years of history destroyed, because it was the history of the Ancient, the history of the *Ankarok*, and they were a pestilence long dead and better ground into the dirt, into dust, even moreso than the vachine.

The Great Library had first been ransacked, the books burned, then the ancient building itself set alight. That had been a particularly pleasing night's work, Meshwar nodded, smoke-filled mouth forming a smile, skin changing and shifting like a chameleon, and the image of the violence flashed across his flesh like moving, animated tattoos on smoke. On Meshwar's skin, the other slaves could see the re-enactment of the Great Destruction, as it would come to be known. Even after fires had died in the Great Library, leaving the teetering blackened walls smoking and charred, stinking and unstable, so Meshwar had personally led a team of vampires in pulling down the remaining walls until only rubble remained.

"No man should read," emerged Meshwar's guttural voice, as around him his vampires bowed and nodded and wondered when they would be fed. "He does not have the ability to utilise any such knowledge with wisdom and clarity. The only use for a human, is that of a slave."

Now, Meshwar watched the Three Temples of Salamna-shar burn, huge shooting flames of orange and yellow roaring at the night sky illuminating the huge piles of rubble and snow throughout the city on all three sites. Fireflies danced over the once magnificent domes, towers and crystal spires. And Meshwar smiled again. Kuradek the Unholy would have liked this moment.

This utter destruction of Falanor religion. The annihilation of man's petty gods and their base vanities. After all, the only religion *now* would be of their own making... worship of the Vampire Warlords.

Meshwar moved to the high iron gates of the Rose Palace. He reached out, touching the ancient, pitted iron, and looked up at the incredible artistry thousands of years old. Then he glanced back to the Rose Palace, in all its glory, and violence flooded his brain but he calmed himself, with small breaths, as a man would calm himself before ejaculation. "No. Not yet." He would destroy the Rose Palace, but it was the single largest symbol of freedom and the Royal spirit of Falanor. It would have to die *last*. But die it would.

Meshwar pointed at a young vampire girl, and she padded over to him. His talons caressed her face, then he lifted her from her feet and clamped fangs over her throat, and bit, and fed, her arms and legs kicking spasmodically as he fast-drained her to a husk. He allowed her skin-filled bones to drop with clacks, and rattle off untidily down the steps.

Meshwar turned, fast, to see the Harvester watching him with a smile on his curious, blank face. Small black eyes were fixed on Meshwar and his own blood-red gaze narrowed.

"You want something, Vishniriak?"

"My clan master would speak with you, Meshwar, great Warlord. It is most urgent."

"I will speak with him when I am good and ready. Not now. Not tonight. I have much work to... attend."

Vishniriak nodded, but the Harvester did not break the connection. Despite looking odd, with his tall angular frame, pale oval face, small black eyes and perfectly white robes embroidered with fine gold wire – despite the filth, and smoke, and fire filling the city of Vor – Vishniriak still carried an air of power, and an air of authority. The Vampire Warlords considered themselves superior to the Harvesters; but the Harvesters did not share the same sentiment.

"It's about the cankers. They have gone."

"I thought they were destroyed? Like all vachine filth?"

"No. There was a leader amongst them. And, against all odds, he has rallied the cankers and they have fled together, north, it is believed."

Meshwar considered this. "I did not think they had it in them; their bestiality is too far removed from any logical thought. Who commands them?"

Vishniriak smiled, head tilting to one side. "He is one of General Graal's impromptu clockwork creations. A second-hand canker impurity with far too many slices of humanity remaining. His name is Elias, once the Sword Champion of King Leanoric. Now, ahh, a *much* altered beast."

"Send a hundred slaves. Hunt them down. Kill them all."

"Yes, Master." Vishniriak bowed his head, an inch away from actually showing respect, turned with a billowing of white robes and disappeared towards the Rose Palace.

Meshwar scowled, face swirling with images of rape and torture and murder in the smoke. Then he relaxed, and decided what violence to inflict on Vor that night.

It was past midnight. General Graal sat at the table, staring into the solitary flame of a candle and thinking of Bhu Vanesh, thinking of Helltop and the Summoning of the Vampire Warlords. So much effort. So much blood-oil magick. So many dead. And all for what?

Graal smiled a crooked smile, and mocked himself. He had harboured such plans! He had thought he, and Kradek-ka, could rule the Vampire Warlords, use them as puppets to build an army and take control of the world! And yet things had turned out different. Things had become… *distorted*. And now, they were as much slaves as those poor lost souls *turned* down on the streets below.

The door opened, and a draught drifted in like plague. Wood slammed with a rattle, and Kradek-ka sat down opposite Graal and glared at the man, at the albino, at the *vachine*.

"I cannot believe it's fucking *come to this!*" he snarled, and bit the top from the bottle with a crunch of breaking glass. "I sacrifice my own *fucking daughter*, I sacrifice the *vachine civilisation* of Silva Valley, and here we are, locked in a tower like two old men waiting to die."

Kradek-ka poured two generous glasses of brandy, taken from the looted and ravaged city below. Even now, at this late hour, they could hear the hammering of shipbuilders. Frantic work on the new navy continued. And the ships' skeletons were growing. Slowly, imperceptibly, but they were growing.

"We should kill Bhu Vanesh," said Graal, drinking the brandy. It glistened on his pale lips; glistened against his brass fangs. "We should kill him. It. Now. Tonight." He glanced up, and Kradek-ka was staring at him. "We should send the fucker back to the Chaos Halls."

"We tried. We failed."

"We should try again!"

"We only get one more chance." Kradek-ka smiled weakly. "You know how to do this, and not die in the process?"

"I have an idea."

"Blood-oil magick?"

General Graal nodded, and drank more. "When we opened the gate to the Halls they followed a path between that place and this; every path has a resonance. A bond, if you like. The Vampire Warlords were bound to the Chaos Halls; being here is an unnatural balance. All we need do is give them a *push*, and they'll be dragged back, kicking and screaming. I think. I believe a killing blow will do this."

"Bhu Vanesh is mighty indeed," said Kradek-ka, with fear etched into his face and voice.

"We must attack when he is at his weakest."

"Which is?"

"When he feeds," said Graal, eyes gleaming.

Bhu Vanesh stood and stretched, and stepped down from the dais, staring at the three chained girls. They were shivering in terror, eyes staring at the ground, huddling together like sheep. Bhu Vanesh smiled at that. For, like sheep, they were about to become *food*. He moved swiftly, grabbing the first girl by the throat and pulling her close, almost as if to kiss. Then his maw stretched wide and the girl screamed, a wavering long high note, and Bhu Vanesh's fangs sank into her throat and started to suck her dry as the other two girls vomited, and squirmed, and moaned and thrashed with horror.

Out of the shadows came Kradek-ka, moving fast, and the spear thrust into the Warlord's back with as much force as the old vachine could muster, born of fear and hatred; the spear rammed through the Vampire Warlord, through his heart and through the girl on which he fed, making her go rigid, puking blood as her limbs twitched spasmodically. Even as the spear thrust struck, so Graal leapt from the high beams of the roof, sword slashing down to open Bhu Vanesh's throat and the Vampire Warlord dropped, pinned to the girl, gurgling and Graal stood, his curved blade dripping blood and looked down with a sneer and spat at Bhu Vanesh, until he realised that the Vampire Warlord wasn't gurgling in his death throes, he was laughing and he slammed upright and rigid in a splinter of time, and fire seared the girl to which he was attached, crisping her instantly to ash. What remained of the spear Bhu Vanesh grasped, and pulled it smoothly through his smoke-riddled body, as the smoke-flesh of his throat ran together and Graal screamed, and attacked in a blistering display of sword skill but Bhu punched him in the chest, caving in his breastbone and ribs with one mighty blow and sending him slamming backwards to roll amongst scattered tables and chairs until he hit the wall, his clockwork pounding, several wheels rolling from the massive open wound. Kradek-ka attacked from behind, and Bhu Vanesh turned, grasped the old vachine's head between both sets of talons, and with a *wrench* twisted his head clean off. Kradek-ka looked surprised. His mouth worked soundlessly, as blood dripped from his severed neck stump. The body spewed blood and tiny brass cogs, then one knee folded, and Kradek-ka's corpse settled to the ground like a deflating balloon.

Bhu Vanesh sighed, and tossed away the head. He pointed at Graal, and grimaced. "I cannot stand traitors," he snapped, and from the shadows eased Lorna, petite and blonde and smiling, and the bulk of Division General Dekull. They lifted Graal with ease. He could not fight. He was slowly dying, with his chest caved in.

"Take him to the Black Tower," snapped Bhu Vanesh, eyes glowing, and he waved his talons to dismiss them and turned his attention back to the two moaning girls who remained. "I am still enjoying breakfast. I will deal with him later."

Graal, his clockwork whining, was dragged from the chamber and out, into the cold stairwell, and up narrow winding steps.

General Graal lay on the floor, panting, pain flooding him like nothing he'd felt in his long, long lifetime. Breathing was hard, with a caved-in chest, and he knew even with accelerated vachine healing powers, this *pulping* at the talons of Bhu Vanesh would take him months from which to recover. *If* he could recover. But then, in a few short hours he would be dead. Bhu Vanesh was toying with him.

So, it was all for naught? How many men, down through the ages of history, have taken great risks only to end up, condemned and dying, in a prison cell? He smiled at that, then winced and vomited blood.

Many. *Many...*

And Graal had *exterminated* most.

Pain rocked through him in waves, and it was so bad, so painful Graal went beyond pain and into comedy. He laughed, laughed because it hurt so damn fucking much. He lifted his head, looked down at the hole in his chest. He could see his own beating heart merged with clockwork. Cogs spun, and gears stepped, but many were twisted and misaligned. The only time Graal had seen that was in the cankers. That thought made him shiver. Sobered him with a slap.

Better death, than to turn canker.

He had seen what becoming a canker did to a man. After all, it had happened to his brother. The brother Kell had killed. Kell! That old bastard. Graal grimaced. *Now there's a fucker who needs his head on a spike! His balls chopped off! His throat opening like a second smile! Far too much testosterone. Far too much of the fucking hero factor, the dirty stinking piece of reprobate horse-shit! Him, and that damn axe… that axe…*

"I'm sorry to intrude," said the little boy, "but it would appear somebody left a door open."

Graal groaned, and his eyes moved to the boy. He was five or six years old, skinny and raggedy looking to the extent he would be taken for a vagrant in any of the fine cities of Falanor. Not that many existed, in the old sense of the word *city*. The boy wore rags, and had no shoes, and he was smiling and his teeth were black, like insect chitin.

"You!" gasped Graal, and struggled to rise, but groaned as pain swamped him and he passed back into a welcome deep honey pool of glorious unconsciousness.

When his eyes fluttered open, Skanda was sitting on the edge of Graal's bed, staring down at him where he lay on the stone flags, still with that disarming smile stuck on his face. "You do look rather ill," said Skanda. "Maybe some medicine is in order?"

"I want nothing from you!" Graal spat, and he would have screamed and attacked, but had not the strength, nor the energy. Instead, he glared with blue albino eyes at the boy.

"I disagree," said Skanda, and he hopped from the bed and Graal cringed, as if expecting some fearful weapon. Instead, Skanda knelt down by Graal and placed his hands on the vachine's belly. Inside him, Graal felt the clockwork slow to a rhythm that was normal, not discordant, not twisted. Pleasure ran through him, tingling every fingertip, and pain fled like rats before a flood.

Graal sighed. Then he blinked, slowly, and allowed himself to breathe.

"Thank... you," he managed, and stared hard at Skanda. "But I haven't forgotten Helltop. I haven't forgotten your part in the deaths of my daughters!"

"Ahh. The delightful Shanna and Tashmaniok. Yes. I am sorry about them. But we need Kell alive. We need the Legend to exist. Or all our plans would be for nothing."

"Our plans?" said Graal.

"The Ankarok," said Skanda, softly, his dark little insect eyes fixed on Graal. "That is why I am here. That is why I need your help."

"There is nothing I can do for you, boy," snapped Graal. "Nothing I can do for the Ankarok! Nothing I can even do for myself..."

"We are alive," hissed Skanda, "and if you help me, Graal, General Graal, Graal the Dispossessed, Graal the Dying, Graal the Fallen, Graal the Slave, Graal the Whipping Boy of the *fucking* Vampire Warlords... then I will help you. *We* will help you."

Graal swallowed, and he looked at the six year-old boy, but it was the eyes, the eyes were old, older than Time it seemed. They were portals, piss-holes straight back to the Chaos Halls.

"What is it you require?" said Graal, voice a little strangled.

"We want our Empire back," said the Ankarok.

"What do you need me to do?"

"We need your blood-oil magick. Ours is trapped. Trapped in the curse that is Old Skulkra. I broke free, broke free and was aided by Kell and Saark. But now,

now we are ready to return. General Graal – we will sweep aside these vampires. We will send the Warlords back to the Chaos Halls."

"But we'll have *you* instead," said Graal.

"You will not be a slave," said Skanda. "I guarantee you that. You will rule by my side. You will be a vassal of the Ankarok. You will be a *Prince* of the Ankarok!"

"How do I know I can trust you?"

"Because you have little choice. But also, I could leave you to die. There are others, Graal. But I *like* you." The boy grinned. "I like your tenacity. I like your lack of fear. I like your *will* to get the job done." His smile dissolved. "I like your ability to kill."

"So we would exchange one evil empire for another?"

"Evil is all about perspective," said Skanda. "But these Vampire Warlords thrive on destruction; and what use is that? If you kill all the slaves, who then will *be* the slaves? It is a base stupidity. A flaw in their strategy."

"What do you need me to do?"

"Follow me."

"What about the thousands of vampires in the city below?"

"Trust me," said Skanda, smiling with those gloss black teeth. "They will not be a problem for my power."

"I will come with you," said Graal. "But I have one request."

"Ask."

"When we find Kell, the Legend, I want to be the one who places his head on a spike."

"Agreed."

## CHAPTER 10
## *Valleys of the Moon*

Kell stared at his daughter, and slowly, without taking his eyes off the tall female vampire, he reached down and hoisted Nienna to her feet.

"Mother!" she gasped.

Sara stared at Kell, glanced at Nienna, sneered, and turned back to Kell. "You are looking old, Bastard Father. Soon, soon you will be dead. Sooner, if I have my way."

Kell glanced at Saark. "Go and get chains. And shackles." He stared hard at Sara. "Better make them strong ones."

Saark nodded, and eased through the fortress gates.

"You're looking well," said Kell, staring up at his *vampire* daughter. She rolled her neck, as if easing tension, and smoothed her hands down her black dress. Then she looked at the bonds restraining her hands. They were tight, and blood bubbled around the rope and thin wires, which bit into her flesh.

"I am weak. These fools put a pitchfork in my back. Right through me! The bastards. But soon, when I am strong, I will return the favour!" She turned and hissed at the men, who backed hurriedly away from the cart, lifting their weapons in a parody of defence.

Kell realised, then: Sara had been weakened during a fight in which she killed *forty* men and women. She had been restrained. But soon, *soon* she would snap the wires like cotton thread. She had let them take her; so she could rest. Recuperate. To sleep the sleep of the vampire – like an injured hound licking its wounds, waiting, *waiting*…

Suddenly Kell leapt atop the cart so he was inches from Sara, and Ilanna was between them and she hissed when she saw the axe, and scrambled back as far as the bindings would allow.

"You remember my axe?" said Kell, voice deep, eyes fixed on Sara. The second vampire started to rise, but Kell waved Ilanna at her. At *it*. "Stay down, or I'll cut off your pissing head, I swear! There's no healing a wound like that!" He returned to Sara. "Not even for you, daughter of mine."

"It is a shame it came to this," she said, and licked her lips, showing sharp fangs.

"Indeed," said Kell, gaze locked. "Because now I'm going to have to kill you."

"Please, no," and suddenly she was pleading, voice soft, aggression gone and she dropped to her knees. "I will pray to you, great Kell, Kell the Legend, and I will do your bidding."

Kell gave a mocking laugh. "Like you prayed to your god? And look what he did for you, Sara. He cursed you! He made you like this! The gods? Bah! A curse on all their hairy arses! And all for what? The pain you caused Nienna with your hard ways, your religious learning, your pious necessities. Well, now she is my ward." Kell dropped to his own knees, so they were once again facing each other. His words came out in a low growl. "And you will serve. Or you will die."

"I will serve," said Sara, head low. She glanced at Ilanna.

"Look well on the blades," said Kell, and then climbed down from the cart as Saark approached with shackles. "For vampire or no, they will tear out your soul and devour it. This, you know. This, you have seen."

Saark secured the shackles on ankles and feet, and using a small ratchet tool, cranked them tight until Sara gave a howl and glanced at him, sharply, as if imprinting his face in her mind for future reference.

Kell lifted Nienna to her feet. "Come on, girl. This place is too painful for you."

"What will you do to her?"

"I will not kill her, if that's what you think."

"I... I love her, Kell. She is my mother, no matter all her faults. No matter her poisonous gossip, her force-fed opinions, her casual hate. I *have* to love her. No matter what she's done. That's why she's my mother."

"I know that, love."

"How did she become like this? What happened?"

And as they passed through the gates, into the dark and brooding shadows, Kell whispered, "I don't know, girl. I just don't know."


Kell slept badly. His dreams were dark flashes of black, violet and blood red. In his last dream, he dreamt he awoke and it felt real, felt like it was *happening* and Sara was there, inches from his throat, and she laughed and hissed and her jaws dropped, fangs puncturing his skin and Kell screamed and thrashed but she pinned him down, her strength incredible and unreal as Kell kicked and kicked and kicked, and felt his lifeblood sucked from him, sucked from his gaping throat. Sara would rise above him, dripping blood and grinning in absolute madness – and Kell sat up with a shout, a snap of jaws, and then glared across at Saark lounging in a chair beside his bed.

"What the fuck are you doing here?"

"Good morning to you, Kell."

"What the fuck is that *smell?*"

"It's perfume. *Hint of Venison*."

"Hint of what, lad?"

"Er, venison." Saark suddenly looked a touch uncertain.

"So, you're telling me you're wearing a perfume that stinks like a charging, honking stag?"

"No, no, it's more a suggestion of an aura of power, over which all women will stumble erotically when they enter the room."

Kell stared at him. "Either that, or they're knocked down by the stench and buggered unconscious by a group of rampant drunk nobility! Ha, Saark, it smells like rancid bowels on a ten-week battlefield. So I hope you don't want a good morning kiss, 'cos I fear I've got kitten breath something chronic!"

"Not at all, my sweetness," he said between clenched teeth. "I just dropped by to check up on you. Brought you some coffee, and here," he lifted a plate from the floor. "Compliments of Myrtax."

Kell uncovered a large tin plate filled with bacon, sausage, four eggs and fried mushrooms. Kell gawped. "By all the gods, that's a breakfast fit for a King!"

"Or certainly a fat bastard, more like. But you eat it all up, Kell, get some strength in you, then we need to talk about what's to be done."

Kell lifted mushrooms on his fork, chewed, looked almost euphoric, then snapped, "What's to be done? Eh? What do you mean, laddie?"

"Well, I refer to the next stage of your thrilling plan. I am curious."

Kell stared at his friend, who had taken the entire previous evening, late though it was, to bathe, sprinkle himself with perfume and a light dusting of make-up from Myrtax's wife's quarters. The Chaos Hounds only knew which wardrobe he'd raided – *now* he wore a pink silk shirt, ruffed with lace at collar and cuffs, and bulbous green silk pantaloons the like of which Kell had never seen. He also wore yellow shoes, polished to a bright vomit shine.

"Listen. I'll have my breakfast," said Kell, uncertainly, still stunned by Saark's garish wardrobe. "You go and gather all the armourers and smithy labourers together. Meet me down the Smith House with them, in about... twenty minutes. That's if they haven't kicked your head in first."

"Meaning?"

"You look like a peacock."

"Yes. Well. 'Tis hardly a fair division of work, I feel," said Saark, pouting. "And I *did* bring you breakfast."

"Eh? Well, I tell you what, next time I'm up to my neck in gore from the killing, I'll make sure *you* get your fair share of the fight as well. Agreed, Saark?"

"Point taken. Twenty minutes, you say?"

"Good man! Go knock 'em out."

And for the first time in what felt like *years*, Kell focused on one thing and one thing only. Gorging himself on a fine fried breakfast. He tried hard to shut out the shouts, laughter and whistles as Saark moved gaily through the old prison grounds, but could not help himself. Kell grinned like a lunatic.

The armourers were a bunch of huge, heavily muscled men – numbering perhaps forty in total, with one single exception. A small, weedy looking man standing almost swallowed by the wall of blackened, bulging flesh. They wore the universal uniform of smithies the world over: colourless leather pants, heavy work boots, and most went bare-chested, a few with leather aprons. The small man was the only one smiling.

"Look at him," nodded Saark, and nudged Kell in the ribs with his elbow. "Stands out like a flower on a bucket of turds."

"I'd keep your voice down if I was you," said Kell. "Smithies are not known for their fine tempers and happy chatter. You liken them to horse-shit, next minute you'll be trampled in it, mate."

"Point taken. Point taken."

"Right, lads," said Kell, standing with huge hands on hips. "You all know what's happening here, so I reckon I'll cut to the shit. We'll be going into battle. All the men here will be fighting men, and they'll need weapons, light armour, and shields."

"Won't we move faster without armour and shields?"

"Ha. Maybe. But we certainly won't live as long against... *them*. Now, I know you have great stores of iron and steel here in the mines. Have you any gold?"

The small man lifted his hand. "I believe there are several bags of coin in Governor Myrtax's underground vault. He kept a certain mint for King Leanoric. We found some large lodes down in the mines, you see. Way deep down, in the dark, where fear of collapse is greatest."

"Good. Good." Kell scratched his chin. "We'll need that to pay the lads. But with regards warfare, this is what I need. Short stabbing swords for close combat. Maybe only," he parted his hands, "this long. I want round shields with rimmed edges, so they can be hooked together, *locked* together to repel a charge. I need long heavy spears, maybe twice as heavy as you'd normally make, and arrows – I want iron shafts with slim heads."

"They'll be heavy for the archers to fire," said a big man, with thunderous brows, shoulders like an ox, and a certain distinct look of eagles about him.

"Yes," nodded Kell, "but they'll also have a lot more *impact*. And believe me, we'll need that for these vampire bastards. They'll take some killing, if they're anything like their dirty, blood-sucking vachine brethren."

"Steady on, Kell," said Saark, sounding a little injured.

"Just telling it how it is."

"The men who came in last night," said the large smith. "They said three vampires wiped out near forty of their friends. They managed to kill one, and after a long struggle they captured the other two. That means these creatures are pretty brutal, if you ask me."

Kell nodded. "They're brutal, I reckon. But they also prey on naivety. If we know what we're fighting, and we know how to kill 'em, and we have some protection – I reckon we can take the fight to them. Another thing we need," he looked around to check he wasn't over-heard, "we need steel collars."

"Like a dog collar?"

"Aye. Only these stop the bastards getting their fangs in your throat. You understand?"

"How thick do you want them?"

"About half a thumb-length."

"They'll be uncomfortable. Chafing, like."

"Not as uncomfortable as having your throat torn out and strewn across Valantrium Moor."

"I take your point. Although I'm not sure the men will wear them."

"They will. And those that won't, when they see a friend spewing blood they'll soon change their minds."

"What's the best way to kill these vampires?" asked the small man.

Kell jabbed his thumb towards Saark. "Lads. This is Saark. He's an, er, an *expert* on the vachine, and indeed, that makes him more of an expert on the Vampire Warlords than any of us could ever be. Any more questions about killin' 'em, ask Saark here. I know he looks like an accident in a tart's parlour, but he knows his stuff. I'm off, I need to speak to my daughter."

"*Kell!*" snapped Saark, frowning.

"What is it, lad?"

"You're leaving me here? With *these?*"

"Hey, you chose to dress like a sweat-slippery whore in a disreputable tavern." Kell grinned, and slapped Saark on the back. "Don't worry, lad! If they bugger you rancid, I'll hear the screams and come running to your rescue!"

"Kell!"

"Just remember, some of these blokes have been locked up for *years* without a quim as tasty as yours."

"Kell, my entire sense of humour has gone!"

"Good. Because now is not the time for jokes; now is the time for killing. Tell them what you know, and tell them well. One day soon, our lives will rest on these men."

Saark swallowed, and turned, and looked at the forty hefty labourers with dark eyes under dark brows. A cold wind howled down from the mountains, and from the corner of his eye Saark observed Kell stride away. *What a bastard. A bastard's bastard.*

One of the smiths stepped forward. His two front teeth were missing, and his forearms were as wide as Saark's thighs. "Is that really a pink silk shirt you're wearing, boy?" he rumbled, voice so deep it was like an earthquake beneath the Black Pikes.

Saark drew his rapier. He smiled. "Gentlemen. Allow me to begin your education," he said.

As Kell strode across the rocky earth towards the cells built into the mountainside, Governor Myrtax joined him, jogging a little to keep up with Kell's warrior stride.

"They will work for you?"

"Aye," said Kell. He stopped, and looked across to the smaller man. "I want you to oversee production. I want as many labourers as possible helping make armour and weapons and shields. When we go into battle, each man must have the best, for the fight will be savage indeed."

"Do you think we can win?"

Kell looked Myrtax straight in the eye. "No," he said.

"Then why fight?"

"Why indeed."

"This is insane, Kell! Madness! You say these Vampire Warlords are all-powerful. I saw those vampires the men from Jalder brought in; and they killed forty people! We cannot stand against such odds."

"But it matters that we stand," said Kell, his voice low. "Now tell me, what did you do with Jagor Mad?"

Myrtax pointed. "He's in those cells over there. With the other bastard so-called Governors. Why? Are you going to kill him?" There was a strange gleam in Myrtax's eye that Kell did not like. Kell grimaced.

"No. I need his help."

"His... help?" Myrtax's voice had gone up several octaves. "He'll not help you, Kell, unless it's to throw you in the furnace. He hates you with every ounce of his flesh."

"We'll see. First, I'm going to see my daughter."

"I'll come with you."

Kell stopped again, and turned. "No, Governor. Go to Saark. Help him organise the smiths. Saark is a canny lad, but he's little experience with metallurgy – or indeed, the instruction of people. Especially men. He tends to rile them the wrong way, admittedly by trying to sleep with their wives and virgin daughters, but still. Go. Help me, Myrtax. I cannot do this alone."

The Governor nodded, and hurried off, one hand on his robust and well-fed belly.

Kell continued to walk, glancing up at the skies, a huge pastel canvas of white, ochre and deep slate. Distant, heavy clouds vied for sovereignty. They threatened more snow against the world of Men.

Reaching the cell, Kell saw Sara was alone. The two vampires had been separated through basic mistrust. A wise choice. She watched Kell approach, eyes yellow and narrow, but she did not move from where she lay on the floor, curled like a lizard on a rock in the sun.

Kell sat down an arm's length from the bars, and placed his chin on his fist.

"Sara. What am I going to do with you, eh girl?"

"Knowing you, you'll use that great axe to cut off my head!"

"You are vampire-kind now. Maybe that would be a kindness?"

"My master will find you!" she hissed, suddenly, and leapt at the bars, claws raking out. Kell stayed motionless, and the sharp points of her talons skimmed the end of his nose. For a few moments Sara thrashed and hissed, trying to get to him, to his throat, to his jugular, to spill his blood and drag him like torn offal into her cage where she could gorge and feed… but she could not reach. Kell had judged his distance well. Gradually, she subsided, glancing at him like a sulky child.

"Your master is Kuradek the Unholy?"

"Yes."

"And he has taken Jalder?"

"Go to Hell!"

"You're already there, girl. Help me!"

Kell and Sara stared at one another.

"You know nothing about how I feel," she snapped, eventually, and Kell sat back a little, listening. She eyed him warily. "You were a bad man, Kell. I know your secrets. My mother told me all about you, before she… died." Her eyes narrowed. "And even that event is shrouded by mystery, is it not, great Legend?"

"What happened during the Days of Blood, happened," said Kell, softly. "I am not proud of myself. Not proud of my actions. But I tell you now, there's no need to bring your mother into this. You have reason enough to hate me yourself."

"I can still feel the handprint," she hissed, jabbing a finger at Kell. "Here!" She placed a hand against her face. "It burns me, like a brand, making me a slave to the Great Man, the Great Hero, ha ha! If only the people of

Falanor knew the real Kell. The bastard. The wife-beater. The child-beater."

"It was not like that," said Kell, darkly.

"Oh, but it was! You see, it's all about perspective, it's all about purity, and you had neither, you fucking old bastard. You turned on us. All of us. And not just your family, your King and country! Don't you remember? Or has the whiskey rotted your mind as well as your fucking teeth?"

"It was not like that," growled Kell, and his fists clenched. He forced himself to stay calm. "That is in the past. Now, Sara, we must talk about the present."

"What? About how you'll beat my little girl? Nienna never did see past your mask, did she, the little fool. Dragged in by the stories of glory, dragged in by the myth but not the man. I'm surprised you haven't bruised her yet, Kell. Or maybe you have. I'm amazed she's still walking in a straight line. It was my leg you broke though, silly me for forgetting."

"Still the acid tongue, I see," snapped Kell. "Just like your mother! There are bigger things at stake here, now, in this time. Like Falanor! Like the world!"

"Pah! Like you give a damn about anything but your own horse-shit ego and petty desires. Can't you see, Kell, I am part of something *bigger*, now, part of something *powerful!* I am strong, Kell. I could take you, in battle, I could rip your arms from their sockets and piss on your face as you stumbled slipping in the mud." Her eyes were gleaming, cheeks flushed in triumph. "Go on Kell, let me out, let me show you! Or are you still the pathetic, weak, moaning coward you always were?"

"Tell me of Kuradek."

Sara laughed. "What would you like to know? He controls Jalder. We have turned, between us, many thousands into vampires! There is little of the resistance left."

"So they did resist you? That's good. Their spirits still live."

"No! It is foolish! Kuradek is Master, he is incredibly powerful and he knows you, Kell, oh yes he knows you, he remembers you from Helltop and he has sworn to hunt you down, to change you into one of us! Imagine it, Kell, imagine how powerful you would be! Increased strength, speed, and you could never die!"

"You die," snapped Kell. "You die just like everybody else. All we need do is cut off your head, or ram a sword through your necrotic heart."

Sara went quiet.

"You forget," said Kell. "I know your kind."

"You hunted vachine," sneered Sara. "They are weak, spineless, mechanised with their pathetic ticking clockwork! They are an aberration of the pure; they are the weak, the diseased, the freaks." She chuckled. "The vachine are a corruption."

"I hunted vachine," said Kell, and met Sara's gaze. "But I hunted your kind, too. Me. And Ilanna. Do not think I haven't killed true vampires. It was a long time ago, but I remember the taste like it was yesterday."

"Impossible! Vampires were extinct until the Vampire Warlords returned!"

Kell shook his head. "Oh no," he said, eyes glittering. "You are so wrong, with your little mind from little Falanor. You never did travel, did you Sara? Never saw the world and all its mysteries. Well I did. I saw enough to make any sane man crazy. And that's why I know... I know your Master, Kuradek, Kuradek the Unholy – if

241

I kill him, if I remove his head, then I may save all those he has tainted with his evil."

Sara remained silent, staring at him. Eventually, she said, "How could you know that?"

"I do," growled Kell. "Because I have seen things you people could never comprehend. I have walked the dark magick paths to the Chaos Halls. Do you think the Vampire Warlords are the only creatures touched by evil? Sara. I have done... many, sobering things. I believe I am touched by darkness. But I am trying to be good. Trying so hard."

"Well don't! Don't fight it! Come with me, come to Kuradek! He does not want you dead, Kell, he wants you as his General! He knows your power, he knows what you and he could do together! You could overthrow the other Vampire Warlords! You could rule the world! We could be together again... father. We could walk the roads again, father."

Kell had lowered his head. Now his eyes lifted, and there were tears on his bearded cheeks.

"You would take me back?" he said, voice a husky low growl. "After all that I did? To you and your mother?"

"Yes! We could be a family again."

Kell stood, and turned his back to Sara. She stood, in her cage of rock and iron, and stepped forward, grasping the bars. "Come with me, Kell. Come to Kuradek. He waits for you!"

Kell turned back. His knuckles were white around Ilanna. "I'll go to him all right. I'll cut his puking head from his shoulders!"

"No, Kell, no! Wait!" but Kell was striding away, across the rocks, to the cell which held Jagor Mad.

Behind, in her cell, Sara sat cross-legged on the floor. She closed her eyes, and breathed deeply, and the *feeling* of Kuradek filled her, filled every muscle and every atom. She seemed to float, and she breathed deeply, and the world took on a surreal quality, a haze of witch-light, clouds rushing across the skies, dark ghosts walking the rocks beyond her cell like jagged, black cut-outs, holes in the raw core of the Chaos Halls.

"You did well," hissed Kuradek.

"I failed you."

"No. You gave him something to think about."

"He will come for you."

"Yes. And I will be waiting."

"He will try and kill you."

"Yes. But I am all-powerful. He will crumble. Like dust between my claws."

"Are you sure?"

Hundreds of miles away, on his throne in the Blue Palace at Jalder, Kuradek opened his dark crimson eyes and smiled. "Yes, my sweet," he said, smoke oozing from his mouth, skin writhing with corrupt religious symbols that squirmed as if fighting to be free of his dark-smoke skin. "They always do."

Kell's mood could be described as a thunderous rage as he approached Jagor Mad's cell. The three men who had called themselves the new Governors of the Black Pike Mines were sat together, eyes sullen, faces lost to despair. They were awaiting execution. The atmosphere was sombre.

Kell stopped by the bars, and gestured to the two guards who held long spears and wore short stabbing swords over kilts of steel. "Open it."

"But… Governor Myrtax said…"

"Governor Myrtax does what *I tell him, laddie!*" barked Kell, employing a parade ground bellow that once made many a Command Sergeant piss his pants.

"Yes, yes sir," snapped one guard, shaking as he fumbled keys and unlocked a three bar gate, swinging it wide from its slot in the mountain wall.

"Jagor Mad. Step free."

"What do you want?" said the big man, voice husky and low, his face still battered and bruised from their fight. Jagor stepped from his confinement, squinting at the bright daylight, and he stretched his huge frame. His throat was heavily bruised, huge welts showing where the rope had savagely burned him.

"I want your help," said Kell, folding his arms.

"Why would I help you?"

Kell drew Ilanna from his back, glanced at the twin black blades, and hefted her against his chest. "You help me, or I execute you now. Right here. On this fucking spot."

Jagor Mad considered this, and a finger lifted, touching the marks at his throat. "Seems like a fair choice. I'll help you. But don't be asking me to fucking sing and dance."

Kell grinned. "No, I have something far more fun than that planned." He turned to the guard. "Give Jagor your sword."

"What?"

"Are you deaf, lad, or shall I unblock your ears with my axe?"

"No need to be rude," grumbled the guard, and handed Jagor Mad the sword. Jagor took the weapon, face showing a mixture of confusion and suspicion.

"What's happening here, Kell?" he murmured.

"Follow me."

"You wish to battle?"

"No, Jagor, you big dumb fool! These vampire bastards threaten the whole of Falanor! I want you alive, because you're a big hard bastard, and I'll not waste a man like you just because you were fighting for your freedom! I respect that. I respect your anger, your fire, and your fucking brutality! You were born to fight, Jagor, not be locked in a cage, not to hang from the gallows. Well, I'm giving you the chance to earn redemption."

"What do you want me to do?"

"There is a place. A hidden place. Where the last of the Blacklipper Kings reside, after their brother was killed by the vachine known as Vashell. Do you know what I'm talking about?"

"I know."

"Can you take me to this place?"

"It is a closely guarded secret amongst the Blacklippers," said Jagor Mad, carefully.

"We are all threatened here," said Kell, eyes glittering. "I need the help of the Blacklippers. I hunted them for decades, aye, and I am their sworn enemy. But now, I am like a brother compared to the nightmare in the dark."

Jagor stared hard into Kell's eyes. He lowered his sword. "I will take you. But they will kill you, old man. With no remorse."

Kell grinned. "I don't die easy," he said.

Kell strode up to Saark, who was sat on a stool eating a plate of sausages from his knees. He glanced up, then leapt up spilling his plate and knocking over his tankard as he saw Jagor Mad looming behind Kell. Saark grappled for his rapier, shouting, "Look out, Kell, he's behind you!"

Kell patted Saark on the arm. "I know, lad, I know. I brought him here."

"What? *What?*" snapped Saark, spitting and dribbling sausage everywhere.

"He's coming with me. To help me."

"Where are we going all of a sudden?" said Saark, lifting and picking his sausages from the snow with a curse and a dirty glance. "I thought you said we had an army to train?"

"Yes. *You* have an army to train. *I* have a problem to solve."

"What problem, what the hell are you talking about? And army? Me train an army? You have to be sky-high out of your fucking donkey skull if you think I'm capable of training a bloody army!"

"You were a soldier, weren't you?" said Kell, and nodded to Grak who appeared, carrying a newly forged steel collar in his powerful hands. Grak stopped, and put his hands on his hips, grinning.

"I was King Leanoric's Sword Champion," said Saark, looking injured, "if that's what you mean?"

"There you go. You were in the army. That's good enough for me. That's all settled then."

"Now wait a minute," said Saark, "I was a commissioned officer, I didn't rough it with the scum in the barracks," he glanced at Grak, and Jagor, and swallowed, "no offence meant, I was in the High Court watching the jesters and eating venison and lobster from silver platters! I was attending the buxom serving wenches and bestowing gifts of fine silver jewellery on nobility! I wasn't eating bloody beans from a pan and scrubbing my boots! I had servants for that sort of thing! Peasants! Like... well, like you..." He stopped.

Grak gave a cough, and slapped Saark on the back, a slap so hard he nearly pitched Saark to the ground. "Don't worry, lad. I'll help you! Grak the Bastard by name, Grak the Bastard by nature. I won't let no fancy big-titted silver-wearing venison-stuffed ladies get in the way of you training the lads. Right?"

"Er, right," said Saark, weakly, and seemed to physically slump.

"After all, if all our lives rest on your scrawny shoulders, I think you're going to need some help. Right?"

"Right."

"I mean, if we're going into battle to face a terrible foe, a foe who is savage and brutal, knows no remorse, is stronger than us, faster than us, more brutal than we could ever imagine – well, we'd be idiots to let a dandy moron train us without any experience or skills, wouldn't we?"

"Er. Yes."

They stared at each other. "Not that I'm saying you're a moron," explained Grak, helpfully, and roared with laughter.

Saark stared at the carrots stuck in Grak's beard, and shook his head. He threw Kell a nasty glance. "So, *Legend*, what wonderful little jaunt are you going to be enjoying whilst I get stuck here with three thousand condemned *convicts*, nary a beautiful woman in sight, and food so bad even Mary would turn up her muzzle in disgust?"

"I'm going to the Valleys of the Moon," said Kell, smiling and nodding.

"What?" said Saark, and placed a hand on one hip in what could only be described as an effeminate stance. "The Valleys of the Moon don't exist! Leanoric hunted for them, for thirty years, after his father had damn well given up!"

"It's said you have to be a mystic to enter," said Kell, cryptically.

"And I suppose you qualify, do you?"

Kell shrugged. "I have three thousand soldiers here. Or I will have, when you complete their training. I need more. It's not enough to take Jalder, or indeed, any of the other cities. The vampires are savage. And the Army of Iron is disciplined, that's for sure. They also rely on magick. We need the magick of the Blacklippers."

"Pah, what are you talking about? Have you been on the whiskey again?"

"It's true," rumbled Jagor, stepping forward. Saark looked again at the sword in his huge hands. It looked like a child's toy. Saark swallowed, for he was within striking distance and Kell seemed extremely laid back. As if he had nothing in the world to worry about.

"Which bit? The fact the Valleys of the Moon don't exist, or the fact that you have to be a village idiot invested with the dribbling liquid brain of a certifiable peasant to even *want* to look for such a mythical artefact?"

"No. It exists," said Jagor. "I have been there."

"And you're a mystic, are you?" scoffed Saark, examining the lace ruff of his sleeve.

"I surely am," rumbled Jagor, eyes flashing dangerously dark. "Watch. I can mystically transfer this short sword into the middle of your head."

"Point taken," prickled Saark, and turned his attention to Kell. "But seriously, Kell, think about it. You know I like to gamble, drink the finest wines, suckle the most succulent foods, dance like a peacock and fuck like a stallion. All the sensible things in life, my man. I've never trained an army in my life! You'd be *insane* to entrust me with such an important directive!"

Kell loosened his axe, and in a sudden movement swung the blade for Saark's head. Saark rolled back, fast, faster than any human had a right to move. His rapier was out, and he'd grabbed up the stool on which he was seated and hoisted it as a makeshift shield. He'd also moved, imperceptibly, so his back was against the wall of the fortress.

Kell grinned. "You see? Defence, stance, back to the wall, and you shifted so that you could attack all three of us, not knowing from whence the next strike would come." Kell sheathed Ilanna. Saark scowled. "It's all intuitive. You'll do just fine, lad. Just teach them about the strength of shield walls, the tactical advantage of a solid fighting square and how to respond in formation to commands. Get them practising. That's what I need. That's what you must do. Lives depend on it, Saark. All our lives."

"Bloody great," mumbled the dandy.

"As I said," roared Grak, "the bastard here will help. I've trained soldiers before. Just see yourself as the commissioned officer, and me as your finely honed tool."

"There's only one finely honed tool around here," mumbled Saark, but forced a smile. "Very well. If train men I must, then train men I must! We will turn back the tide of these evil vampires! Hurrah!" He flourished his rapier. Everybody stared at him.

"But don't think you can sit on your arse and do nothing," said Grak, amiably.

"Er. That's something like what I had in mind. You said yourself, you've trained men before."

"Aye, but I won't put up with slothful bastards. I put my foot down, I do."

"I take it by your story and demeanour, young Grak, that something untoward happened to your last Commanding Officer?"

"Aye. I cut off his hand."

"By accident?"

"Well, it was his accident to be damn disrespectful about the men whilst I was chopping wood."

"I thought you said you killed your General?" interjected Kell.

"Aye, him as well. Why do you think I'm here?"

Saark stared at Kell. "Please?" he mouthed, silently.

Kell turned his back on the dandy, and slapped Jagor Mad on the shoulder, having to stand on tiptoe to do so. "Come on, lad. Our horses are waiting."

"How long will you be?" said Saark, in what bordered on a useless puppy whine.

"A week, I reckon," said Kell, and glanced back. "Don't let me down on this, Saark. You understand?"

"Yes, Kell."

"And Saark?"

"Yeah?"

"Watch out for Sara. She's a wily bitch. I think she communes with Kuradek, so I'd limit what she can see, hear and do. She can spy bloody everything from that cell you put her in."

"Perhaps you'd like me to put a bag over her head?"

"A brilliant idea! Just don't get too close to her claws."

"Yes," said Saark, weakly.

"And Saark?"

"Go on." He sighed. "What now?"

"Don't touch Nienna."

"Like I would dream!"

"I know all about your fucking dreams, lad. If you do it again, the next fight we have, vampire invasion or no, you'll be wearing your feet as souvenirs round your pretty slit throat."

"Any other advice?"

"Keep the men well fed, but work them hard."

Saark put his hands on his hips. "Any *more* fucking advice? Why the *fuck* are you leaving? Maybe you should write me a, y'know, short manuscript on the art of running a fucking soldier-camp full of scumbag convicts – no offence meant –"

"None taken," smiled Grak menacingly.

"– or maybe you should *just do it yourself!*"

"See you in a week."

Saark scowled as Kell and Jagor moved to the horses, the finest war chargers from Governor Myrtax's stables. Huge beasts of nineteen hands, one was a sable brown gelding, the other charcoal black. Kell mounted the black beast, which reared for a moment and silhouetted Kell against the weak winter sun.

Saark stared in wonder.

Kell calmed the gelding, patting its neck and whispering into its ear, and ducking low over the horse's neck, galloped off through the gates of the Black Pike Mines and out onto the snowy fields beyond, closely followed by the hulking figure of Jagor Mad dressed in bulky furs and standing in his stirrups, giving a final, menacing, backward glance.

"I hope he knows what he's doing," said Saark.

"I hope you do," said Grak, staring at him.

The gates closed on well-oiled hinges, and Saark glared at Grak with open hatred. "I'm going for a bath," he said.

Grak nodded, and watched the peacock strut away, hand on scabbard, a stray sausage stuck to the back of his silk leggings. Grak sighed, and stared up at the sky.

"The gods do like to challenge," he said, and headed for the barracks.

Kell and Jagor rode in silence for a long time. West they travelled, along a low line of foothills before the rearing, dark, ominous Black Pike Mountains. Both horses carried generous packs of provisions, and for a while Kell brooded on his last conversation with Nienna.

"I'll miss you, grandfather."

"And I you, little Nienna."

"I am little no longer," she laughed.

"You will always be a child to me."

He sensed, more than saw, her shift in mood.

"That's the problem, isn't it? You control. I heard what mother said, heard some of the things she accused you of; and I have seen you raise your hand to me on several occasions! You need to learn, grandfather, you need to get in tune with the modern way of thinking! I am a little girl no longer! Understand?"

"When I was a boy," said Kell, "a woman could not... *meet* with a man until she was twenty-five summers! You hear that? Twenty-five years old! And you are seventeen, a suckling child barely weaned from her mother's tit and still lusting after the stink of hot milk."

"How dare you! I can have children! I can drink whiskey! I am a woman, and men find me attractive. Who the hell are *you* to lecture me on keeping myself to myself? I worked it out, Kell. I'm not stupid. You were *twenty* when you sired my mother; and she was eighteen. Barely older than me! And I bet that wasn't the first time your child-maker had a bit of fun with her…"

Kell glared, and lifted Ilanna threateningly. "You need to learn to hold your tongue."

"Or what? You'll cut it out?"

Kell frowned now, as a cold wind full of snow whipped down from the mountains and blasted him with more ferocity than his memories allowed for. Or had he simply been tougher, during his youth? As the years passed, had he simply grown weak? More pampered? Relying more on his *reputation* than any real skill in battle?

Kell was troubled by Nienna, but aware that events were overtaking him fast. He knew Saark would destroy any training he hoped to give his fledgling army. And anyway – an army of bloody convicts? Kell would laugh so hard he would puke, if he could summon the stamina.

And just to make his life more miserable, filled with hardship, filled with pain, the poison injected into him by *Myriam* was starting to make its presence felt once more. It was a tingling in his bones. Especially the joints of his ankles, knees, elbows and wrists. "Damn that vachine bitch," he muttered.

"Are you well, old man? You look fit and ready to topple from the bloody saddle!" Jagor was grinning, but there was menace behind that grin. A low-level hatred.

"I'll last longer than you," grunted Kell, staring sideways at Jagor. "And don't be getting any fancy ideas. I ain't as fucking weak, nor as old, as you think."

Jagor held up both hands, as his horse picked its way through snowy tufts of grass. "Hey, I'm not complaining,

Kell. Thing is, I wanted you dead so much – so bad. So bad it burned me like a horse-brand. Tasted like sour acid in my mouth. But when I was hanging by the throat, all I could see were bright lights and hear the voice of my little girl singing in the meadow. I knew I was going to die. I knew I would never see her again. And that hurt, Kell. Hurt more than any fucking noose. But then you cut me down, and saved me. And although that burned me in a different way, I have to concede you spared me. You kept me alive. And one day, if we're not massacred in the Valleys of the Moon, I might get to see that little girl again."

"I didn't know you had a little girl."

"Why would you?"

"I thought it might have come out at the trial."

Jagor Mad laughed. "I told them bastards *nothing*, you hear? *Nothing*. If they'd found out, they would have arrested Eilsha. The Bone Halls only know where my little one would have ended up. At least I spared them the pain of imprisonment."

Kell considered this, turning his head to the left as more snow whipped him, making him smart, and his eyes water. "I am confused, Jagor. You were part of a syndicate that used to kidnap children, and sell them into slavery? Yes? How could you do that, when you have your own little one?"

Jagor's face went hard. "We had to eat," he said, scowling.

"Would you have liked it, if another slaver took your girl?"

"That's different. I would have cut out his liver."

"And so now, you have the right to hang on to yours?"

"I didn't say what I did was right, Kell, and believe me as I lay in my cell night after night, week after week, year after bloody year, I cursed you for catching me, yes, but I cursed myself for my poor decisions in life. Once, I believe I was immoral. Above all those weak and petty emotions. Now, I have changed. At least a little." He gave a grim smile.

"I don't believe men change," said Kell, bitterly.

"So you're the same as during the Days of Blood?" Kell's head snapped up, eyes blazing. "Oh yes, Kell, I have heard of your slaughter. You are legend amongst the Blacklippers – for all the wrong reasons."

Kell sighed, his anger leaving him as fast as it came. "You are right. And by my own logic, I am still a bloodthirsty, murdering savage. Maybe I am. I don't know. You can be the judge of that when we head into battle; for believe me when I say we have many a fight to come."

The night was drawing close, and they made a rough camp in the lee of a huge collection of boulders at the foot of the Black Pikes. Kell stretched a tarpaulin over them as a makeshift roof, which was fortunate as thick snow fell in the night.

Kell lay in the dark, listening to Jagor snoring. Pain nagged him like an estranged ex-wife, and it seemed to take an age for him to fall into sleep. He stared at the stars, twinkling, impossibly cold and distant, and thought about his dreams and aspirations. Then he smiled a bitter smile. What do the stars care for the dreams of men?

He awoke, cold and stiff, to the smell of coffee. He shivered, and looked up to see Jagor crouched by a small fire, boiling water in a pan, staring at him. Kell gritted his teeth. He had allowed himself to fall into a deep and dreamless sleep; not an ideal situation when travelling with a certifiable killer.

"Coffee?" said Jagor, raising his eyebrows.

"Plenty of sugar," said Kell, and sat up, stretching. He was wrapped in a blanket, fully clothed, his boots by his side. Ilanna was by his thigh. She was never far from his grasp.

"You snore like a pig," said Jagor, pouring the brew.

Kell squinted. "Well, I ain't asking you to marry me."

Jagor laughed, and a little of their tension eased. "I like it that you snore, old man. Makes me think of you as human."

"Why, what *did* you think of me?"

"I thought you were a Chaos Hound," said Jagor, face serious, handing Kell the tin mug. "When you followed me down those tunnels to Old Gilrak, well, I knew then I was cursed, knew I was being pursued by something more than human. Hearing you fart in the night – well, old man, that's helping my mind heal."

"That's Saark's damn cooking, that is, the dandy bastard." Kell sipped his coffee. It was too sweet, but he didn't complain; rather too sweet than too bitter. Like life.

"He's a strange one, all right. What's with the pink silk, though? And green pants? And all that stink of a woman's perfume? Eh?"

"I think he thinks he's a noble."

"Is he?"

"Damned if I know," said Kell, and took the proffered oatcake.

"Do you mind if I ask you a question?"

Kell nodded, eating the oatcake and drinking more coffee. After a cold night under canvas, it was bringing him back to life; making him more human. "Go ahead."

"Why do you travel with him? You two seem... so different."

"Don't worry," growled Kell, "I'm not into that sort of thing."

"That's not what I meant," rumbled Jagor, reddening a little. "I mean, him with his long curly hair and fancy little rapier; you with your snoring and your axe. I wouldn't have thought you'd put up with him."

Kell considered this, finishing his coffee. "You're right, in a sense," he said. "Once was a time I couldn't have stood his stink, his talk, his letching after women or the sight of his tart's wardrobe. But we've been through some tough times together, me and Saark. I thought I saw him killed down near Old Skulkra, and I was ready to leave him for dead; but he showed me he was a tough, hardy and stubborn little bastard, despite appearances. I don't know. I like him. Maybe I'm just getting old. Maybe I've just killed one too many men, and like to talk and listen for a change, instead of charging in with the axe. Whatever. Saark's a friend, despite his odd ways. I ain't got many. And I'd kill for him, and I'd die for him."

Jagor nodded, and finished his coffee. "I think we should be moving."

"Aye. A long way to go, and already my arse feels like a fat man's been dancing on it."

"You never were a horseman, were you Kell?"

Kell grinned. "In my opinion, the only thing a horse is good for is eating."

Kell and Jagor Mad rode for another three days in more-or-less companionable silence. Jagor didn't speak about his capture all those years ago, or the recent incident with the noose; and Kell didn't mention the crossbow wound in his shoulder, nor the recent threat of murder. When they did talk, they spoke of old battles and the cities of Falanor, they talked of Kell's *Legend*, the saga poem, and how Kell hated his misrepresentation. As if he was a damned *hero*. Kell knew he was not.

Eventually, as they passed through folded foothills, past huge boulders and a random scattering of spruce and pine, Jagor stopped and looked to the right where the Black Peaks towered. His horse pawed the snow, and Kell's mount made several snorting sounds. The world seemed unnaturally silent. Eerie. Filled with ghosts.

"Easy, boy," said Kell, patting the horse's neck. Then to Jagor, "What is it?"

"We are close."

"To the Valleys of the Moon?"

"Aye."

Kell ran his gaze up and down the solid, looming walls of rock. "I see nothing."

"You have to know how to look. Follow me."

They rode on, and again Jagor reined his mount. He seemed to be counting. Then he pointed. "There."

Kell squinted. Snow was falling, creating a haze, but he made out a finger of smooth, polished granite no bigger than a man. "What is it?"

"A marker. Come on."

Jagor led the way; Kell followed and loosened Ilanna in her saddle-sheath. Then Jagor paused, and Kell saw another marker, and they veered right, between two huge boulders over rough ground; normally, Kell would have avoided the depression – it was a natural and instinctive thing to do whether on horseback or foot. It was too good a place for an ambush.

Jagor led the way between the boulders, and onto a flat path which led up, out of the tiny bowl. "Now look," he said.

Kell stared around, and Ilanna was in his hand as he glanced at Jagor. "I see nothing. Are you playing me for a fool?"

"Not at all, Kell. It's there." Jagor pointed, to the solid wall of jagged black granite.

"You're an idiot! That's impassable."

Jagor shook his head, and said, "Shift to the left. By one stride."

Kell shifted his mount, and as if by magick a narrow channel appeared before his eyes which led *into* the seemingly impassable rock face. Kell shifted his gelding again, and the passage slid neatly out of view, the rocky wall naturally disguising this narrow entrance. Kell stared hard. "By the Bone Halls, that plays tricks on a man's eyes."

"You have to know it's there. One footstep in either direction and the passage vanishes! As you say, like magick!"

"You lead the way."

"You still not trusting me?" Jagor Mad grinned, his brutal face looking odd with such an expression.

"I trust nobody," snapped Kell. "Take me to the Blacklippers. Take me to the Valleys of the Moon."

Saark stood in the snow and the churned mud, and his feet were freezing and he was scowling. The men had been divided into platoons of twenty, as he had watched King Leanoric do on so many occasions. Each platoon was commanded by a lieutenant, and five platoons made up a company ruled over by a captain.

They'd held a contest on the second day, in which crates, barrels and planks of wood had been assembled beside a pretend river. On the other side, behind upturned carts, archers with weak bows and blunt, flat-capped arrows were the enemy. Each platoon had to work together to "cross" the river and take the cart. The platoon which succeeded first would earn wine and gold.

Saark and Grak watched in dismay at first, as men squabbled and fought over planks and crates. But a young, handsome man, Vilias, imprisoned for his spectacular thieving career, gathered together several crates and got three of the platoons crouched behind them for protection from the archers as the other platoons continued to argue, or were shot by archers.

"We need to work together," said Vilias.

"But then the prize is shared between sixty, not twenty!"

"But we still win the prize," grinned the charismatic thief. "One bottle of wine is better than none, right mate?"

Vilias set several men to smashing up crates, and they fashioned several large, crude shields. Then, with five men at a time using the wide wooden shields they worked under protection to build a bridge, crossed the river and stormed into the cart fortress with swords raised and battle screams filling the air.

Afterwards, Saark and Grak called Vilias to them.

"You showed great courage," said Saark, smiling at the man.

Vilias saluted. "Thank you, sir. But it was just common sense."

"Common sense has got you promoted to Command Sergeant, lad. That's extra wine and coin for *all* the platoons under your new command."

"Thank you… sir!"

"You understand that an army is all about working together," said Saark, with his chin on his fist. With his dark curls and flashing eyes, with his charisma and natural beauty, he cut a striking figure now he no longer wore fancy silk shirts and bulging pantaloons. Grak had persuaded him to don something more fitting for the Division General of a new army.

"Yes, sir!"

Vilias returned to his men to share the good news, and Saark sagged, glancing over at Grak who grinned a toothless grin of approval.

"Well inspired!" boomed Grak. "Any army indeed works – and *wins* by all the gods – by the simple act of cooperation. Soldiers watching one another's backs; spearmen protecting shield-men, archers protecting infantry, cavalry protecting archers."

Saark chuckled. "I only *know* because you told me last night after a flagon of ale."

"Still," said Grak. "You *sounded* like you knew what you were talking about! And that's what matters, eh lad?"

"I'm not cut out for this," said Saark, displaying a weak grin. "Only yesterday the smiths came with technical questions about the shields; what the fuck do I know about shields? Succulent quims, yes! Breasts, I could talk all day about the size and texture and quality of many a buxom pair of tits. But shields? *Shields*, I ask you?"

"With things like that," said Grak, "just refer it to me. Say you're too busy to deal with it. Last thing we need," he bit a chunk from a hunk of black bread, "is a shield with the shape and functionality of a woman's flower."

Saark paused. "A what?" he said.

"A flower."

"You mean the slick warm place between her legs?"

"Don't be getting all rude with me," snapped Grak. "I won't take it, y'hear?"

Saark stood, and stretched. Then grinned, eyeing the ranks of men who were now practising with wooden swords as newly appointed Command Sergeants strolled up and down the lines, shouting encouragement and offering advice. Grak had appointed those with soldiering experience, he'd said.

"I suggest we go to the quartermaster," said Saark.

"Why?"

"I suggest we get two flagons of ale and retire to my quarters. You can teach me about warfare, about units and field manoeuvres, and I, well," Saark grinned, and ran a hand through his long dark curls, "darling, I will teach you about *women*."


Kell and Jagor rode into the narrow pass. It was quiet, eerie, and very, very gloomy. Kell eased his mount forward, and the beast whinnied. High above, there came a trickle of stones.

Jagor turned in the saddle, and motioned to Kell to halt. "This place," he said, speaking quietly, "they call the Corridor of Death. It is the only way to reach the Valleys of the Moon, and is always, I repeat *always* conducted in silence."

"Why?"

Jagor glanced up, fearful now. "Let us say the slopes and rocky faces are far from stable. I once witnessed a hundred men crushed by rockfall; it took us three days to dig them out. Most died. Most were trapped, and as we dug, and hauled rocks, and had our horses drag boulders in this narrow shitty confine, all the time we could hear them crying for help from down below under the pile. They cried for help, they screamed for mercy, and eventually they begged for death."

"That is a very sobering tale. I will keep it in mind," said Kell, and glanced upwards. The sheer walls and steeply slanted inclines were bulged and rocky, covered in snow and ice and fiery red winter heathers. Kell licked his lips and shivered. He had no desire to be imprisoned under a thousand tumbling rocks.

They moved on, in silence, whispering soothing words to the horses. Sometimes the trail widened so that three horses could walk side by side; sometimes it narrowed so the men had to dismount, walking ahead of their mounts to allow them to squeeze flanks through narrow rough rock apertures. It did nothing to improve Kell's mood.

Eventually, the passage started to widen and they emerged in a valley devoid of rocks. It was just a huge, long, sweeping channel and Kell instinctively glanced upwards where high above, on narrow ledges, he could spy the openings of small caves.

"I don't like this," said Kell.

"The Watchers live here," said Jagor. "This is where we will be challenged."

"And what do we do?"

"We do nothing," said Jagor, forcing a smile that looked wrong on his face. "If you draw your weapon, they will shoot you down. Let me do the talking. You have been warned."

They cantered horses across the snow, hooves echoing dully, and in the gloom of the valley where high mountain walls – perhaps two thousand feet in height

– towered over the two men and cast long dark shadows, so gradually Kell became aware of movement…

Jagor held up a hand and they halted, side by side. Along the ridges scurried small figures, and it was with surprise Kell realised they were children. But as the figures halted their scurrying, and lifted longbows and drew back bowstrings, so Kell realised with sinking horror that these were no normal children. These were Blacklipper children – which meant they had drunk, and continued to drink, the narcotic refined drug, blood-oil, the substance which the vachine needed to survive. But when it was imbibed by a human, it caused a drug *high* like nothing in Falanor, or even beyond the Three Oceans.

Kell watched carefully, making no move towards his weapons, his eyes gradually adjusting to the gloom. There were perhaps fifty children in all, and each was what he knew could be described as a Deep Blood. They had drunk so much of the powerful narcotic, were so entrenched in the liquid's power and dark magick, the essence of the refined blood-oil so necessary to vachine survival – and so condemning of human flesh – that their lips were stained black, and their veins stood out across pale flesh like strands of glossy spider webs on marble skin.

Soon, Kell knew, these children would die.

Soon, they would travel what Kell knew they called the Voyage of the Soul. To an afterlife all Blacklippers believed in. To an afterworld that justified narcotic slavery.

"Throw down your weapons!" shouted one girl, no more than thirteen years old. Her hair was long and black, braided in heavy strips. She was naked to the waist, and her veins stood out like a river-system viewed from mountain crags at night. She carried an adult longbow, a weapon Kell had seen punch an arrow through a hand-thick pine door. The arrow fletch touched her cheek. As far as Kell could tell, her hand did not shake.

Slowly, Jagor and Kell complied.

"Now get off the horses and speak your names, and nothing funny, or you'll have fifty arrows through you!"

"Nice place," muttered Kell.

"Wait till you meet the parents," said Jagor.

"What's that?" cried the girl. "What are you saying? Speak quickly now, or you will die!"

"You are the Watchers," said Jagor, his voice booming out, "and I am Jagor Mad. Your people know me well."

"Yes," said the girl. "Welcome home, Jagor Mad. You may take up your weapon. Who is the man alongside you?"

"His name is Kell."

"Kell, the Legend?" said the girl, her voice painfully neutral.

"Yes," said Jagor, and threw Kell such a strange look the large warrior was moving before he heard the sound of the arrows. Shafts slammed all around him, peppering the snow and thudding home into his horse which reared, suddenly screaming a high-pitched horse scream, and Kell leapt for his axe, leapt for Ilanna as the charcoal gelding staggered back on hind legs, front hooves pawing the air, blood pumping from ten wounds and arrows protruding like the spikes on a spinehog. There was a devastating *thump* as the gelding hit the snow, a huge pool of red spreading fast around the creature and Kell's head slammed up, eyes narrowed, fixed on Jagor as he realised *realised* the bastard had led him into a trap...

"What did you do?" screamed Kell, and leapt forward, Ilanna in his fists and Jagor stepped backwards fast, his own sword coming up with a hiss. Ilanna swung down, and Jagor deflected the powerful blow with a grunt and a squawk.

"Nothing, Kell! Nothing! I did nothing!"

"I'll fucking eat your heart, you whoreson!" he screamed.

"Drop the axe, Kell!" shouted the girl. An arrow slammed between his boots, and Kell stared at that arrow, stared at it hard. A moment earlier, his horse's bulk had protected him. Now, he had no such protection.

Kell glanced up. "What's to stop you peppering me like a fucking deer in the woods?" he snarled.

"I am," came a deep, bass rumble, and from a cave which blended into the gloom of the rocky wall stepped a man bigger than any Kell had ever seen in his life.

The figure walked forward, dwarfing Kell and even Jagor. His skin was pasty and white, the black web-traces of Deep Blood veins marking him out as an addict of blood-oil; but more, his eyes were black with the oil, his lips, his nostrils, even his fingernails had been polluted by the toxin of his chosen drug. He carried a huge flange mace, matt black and nearly the size of Kell's entire torso. To be struck by such a weapon…

"And you are?" snapped Kell, slowly lowering Ilanna but keeping the beloved axe close to his body; a barrier between himself and the unknown; a last resort between Kell walking the world and walking the infinity of the Chaos Halls.

"My name is Dekkar. I am one of the Kings of the Blacklippers."

Kell bowed his head a fraction, and lowered Ilanna. "I knew Preyshan. I knew him well."

"Yes. But still you must drop the axe and back away,"

said Dekkar, and flexed his mighty chest. Muscles writhed like dying eels. "I guarantee my children will not kill an unarmed man."

Kell nodded, and Ilanna *thunked* to the snow. He backed away. Dekkar watched, and Jagor Mad moved forward and with an evil grin, placed his short sword – the very short sword Kell had given him – against Kell's throat.

"What's this?" said Kell, softly.

Jagor looked at Dekkar, and his grin widened. "Do you want to tell him? Or shall I?"

Dekkar moved forward, looming over Kell. The huge flange mace lifted, and Kell saw himself reflected as smeared, dulled, featureless colours in its merciless grim finish.

"Jagor is my brother," said Dekkar, his voice laced with irony. "And here, Kell, your name is indeed a Legend – for all present in the Valleys of the Moon are instructed that the Prime Law is that you must die!"

# CHAPTER 11
## *Blood Temple*

Command Sergeant Wood was having a bad morning, it had to be said. He stood in the stone tunnel, Pettrus unconscious on the floor behind him, a cold breeze blowing through with the stink of old sewers, and he watched the two vampires picking their way towards him over the twisted corpses of their brethren.

One was a girl, young, beautiful, with slender limbs and high cheekbones and curly golden hair. But her eyes were narrowed in a look of hatred and bestiality that shouldn't have resided on such a pretty *child's* face. Blood rimed her lips and vampire fangs.

"Shit," muttered Wood. "Shit!"

The second vampire was an old man, crooked and bent and moving in a twisted way, as if something was wrong with his spine. He had a white, bowl haircut, ragged and uneven, that was, perhaps, one of the worst haircuts Wood had ever seen – on mortal *or* vampire. Then recognition hit Wood like a mallet between the eyes.

"Langforf!" he exclaimed, stepping back, his short sword wavering in his grasp. "Langforf, it's me, Wood!

Don't you recognise me, man? We fought together in five campaigns!"

Langforf, along with his very bad haircut, growled and leapt at Wood, claws slashing for his throat. Wood stepped back fast, stumbling over Pettrus' unconscious body and hitting the ground hard on his arse with an "oof" that would have been comedic, if it hadn't been for impending death looming over him. Langforf leapt at Wood, landing atop the soldier as if they were old lovers on a secret tryst and eager for sex. Foul breath swept over Wood, into his mouth and lungs making him choke. It was rotting meat combined with dried, old blood. Wood screamed. Claws scrabbled for him, and he grabbed Langforf's throat, bad haircut bobbing to tickle his own forehead, and they struggled for a few moments with Langforf hissing and spitting foul stuff into Wood's open maw.

"Get it off, get it off!" he shrieked, but of course there was nobody to help him *get it off* and he realised he would have to help himself. He got one hand free, and Langforf's fangs brushed his throat making him squirm. His strength was failing, and for an old bowl-cut, Langforf was surprisingly strong. Wood managed to get a dagger free from his belt and he rammed it between Langforf's ribs. No blood came out, and indeed Langforf continued to struggle with the same strength and determination. Again and again Wood plunged the dagger into Langforf's side, until there was a large squelching hole and something round and slick and evil slid out, nestling in a pool of slime in Wood's lap and making his life just that little bit more uncomfortable.

"Aie!" he screamed, and got the dagger high, between him and Langforf at throat level. Then Wood simply let

Langforf descend with his fangs, pushing his own throat onto the dagger and cutting his head nearly clean in half.

Wood scrambled out from under the twitching old revenant, and grabbed his short sword – just as the young girl leapt. Wood hit her, hard, breaking her clavicle and shearing his sword down into her lungs – where it wedged under her ribs and was wrenched from his grasp.

Wood stood there, feeling like an idiot, as the girl took a step back and prodded at the sword as if she'd never seen such a weapon before. She tried to tug it free as Wood looked frantically about for another blade, then skipped back, grabbing Pettrus' sword – too long and fanciful for Wood's normal liking – and leaping forward he slammed the blade through her neck. It jarred, cutting through her spine, and her head came away, lolling grotesquely to one side and held in place by skin and tendons. Her red eyes glared at him, accusingly, as she continued to tug at the embedded sword. Wood shuddered, and hacked again, detaching the head. Slowly, a black smoke escaped from her neck as if released from a clockwork pressure valve, and the vampire collapsed.

Wood rubbed his beard with the back of his hand, and crept forward, tugging free his own sword. Then he moved back to Pettrus, who was gradually coming round.

"Got the drop on us, the bastards," he said, surveying the carnage. "But you did well, my friend. Very well."

"I'm getting tired of this," said Wood, grimacing. "I just want my old life back."

Pettrus grabbed him by the shoulders, looked into his eyes. "You know that's never going to happen. Right?"

"I know. I know. I just *wish*. In a sane and normal world, beautiful young women shouldn't try to bite your throat. Or at least, not until they've had a few drinks."

Pettrus chuckled. "Glad to see you've still got that sense of humour," he muttered.

"Yeah, me and most of the city. Come on. We're not far now. And it's still safer travelling down here under the rock than across the rooftops."

"Until you meet bastards in the tunnels."

"Until you meet bastards in the tunnels," agreed Wood.

They moved on, warily now for they had grown lax and complacent in the past few hours, coming upon the previous gathering of vampires with their weapons sheathed and minds tired and blank and definitely switched *off*. It had been a short, hard, savage fight, and Wood and Pettrus both knew they were lucky to be alive. Luck, and combat instinct honed over decades was what saved them. Now, they did not want to run the risk of a second encounter; not when they were so close to the Black Barracks.

It took another hour of careful navigation and creeping through the darkness. Rounding a bend in the rock tunnel, Wood stopped and squinted. He could see a figure at the bottom of the steps leading up to the Black Barracks. To Wood's right, a heavy flow of slow sewage didn't so much move as *coagulate*. Pettrus squinted over Wood's shoulder.

"That's not a vampire."

"Why not?"

"It's Fat Bill."

"Maybe Fat Bill got bit? Maybe Fat Bill is *now* Fat Bill the vampire scourge?"

"Nah," said Pettrus, shaking his head. "He's got his sword drawn. Look. He's guarding the steps."

"*Maybe* he's a vampire guarding the steps from people like us?"

"I don't reckon," said Pettrus. "Vampires don't use swords."

"Of course they do! I've seen hundreds!"

"There's only one way to find out." Raising his voice, Pettrus shouted, "Hey, Fat Bill! Are you a vampire? Do we have to stick a blade through your heart and skull?"

Fat Bill, who must have weighed the same as three sacks of flower, lumbered around in a slow circle and squinted through the darkness. "Any man who tries that better be ready to have their own head crushed," he rumbled, and grinned in the gloom. "By all the gods, is that you, Pettrus? And who's that with you? That skinny gay goat, Wood? It's bloody good to see you both!"

Pettrus and Wood moved along the walkway, and looked up at Fat Bill. He wasn't just fat, he was tall, broad, and both soldiers knew he packed a punch greater than any kicking shire horse. The men shook hands, chuckling, and Fat Bill led them up the stone steps.

"The lads'll be glad to see you."

"Who's here?"

Bill stopped, and turned. He grinned, with most of his teeth missing from brawling. His hair, straggly and white, whispered around his head like cotton. "All of us, Wood. All of us."

They continued, passing a couple more guards whom Wood only vaguely knew; then they emerged into a long, low-ceilinged barracks room.

The Black Barracks squatted on the outskirts of Port of Gollothrim, in what used to be an old warehouse area used for the loading and unloading of cargo; when an industrial accident had destroyed the nearby quays, the area had been pretty much abandoned and left to rot. It was a quiet place, and more importantly for the old men who ran the Black Barracks, a *cheap* place. Whoever said growing old made you generous was a lying bastard. The old soldiers who attended the Black Barracks for weekly drinking sessions and to regale one another with exaggerated tales of valour in their youth, well, they were uniformly tighter than any mother-in-law's hidden purse.

Despite being located in a quiet area of the city, still the barracks had been kitted out as if under siege. All windows had been blacked out and boarded up, and the doors had been reinforced by heavy planks of steel. Lanterns were kept to a lit minimum, and the noise level was a dull mumble as Wood stepped through the door – as opposed to the normal drunken roar that greeted him.

"My God, it's good to see you old boys!" grinned Wood, and for the first time since the vampires had spread through Port of Gollothrim, his heart lifted in joy.

"Wood!" roared a few old soldiers, who stood and smiled in welcome at the two new men. "Glad to see a few bloodsuckers didn't manage to suck you dry!"

Wood strode forward, and slapped a man on the back. "Gods, who've we got here? There's Kelv Blades, never been a better man with a battleaxe or I'm not Command Sergeant Wood! And look! Well met, Nicholas. Who'd have thought The Miser would have left his Gold Vaults, even in times of vampire plague?"

"Got most of it stashed," winked Nicholas the Miser.

"And there's Old Man Connie, Sour Dog, Stickboy Pulp and Bulbo the Dull. Well met! And look, by all the gods, it's Weevil and Bad Socks! I thought you two were dead?"

"It'd take more than a rock on my head to kill me!" rumbled Bad Socks, who climbed ponderously to his feet. He was, as ever, without his boots and his socks did indeed smell bad. He was also nearly seventy years old, one-eyed and his face was so heavily criss-crossed with scars there was little original skin left. He hadn't so much retired from the army, as been forcibly ejected.

Pettrus grinned around as conversation and arguments broke out. "They're all here," he said, meeting Wood's gaze. "What's that? Two hundred of them? *Two hundred!* That's two hundred blades, Wood. Our own little army."

"And not a man here under the age of sixty-five, I believe," said Wood. He was still smiling though. It was good to see so many friendly old faces. Indeed, it was wonderful to realise he wasn't alone and unloved in a hostile world.

"Just think of the experience, though!" said Pettrus.

"Just think of the arthritis!" grinned Wood.

"If any man here hears you say that, you'll get a sword in the guts."

"Yeah, I know. But by the Granite Thrones, it's bloody good to see them all." He raised his voice. "I said, it's bloody grand to see you all! It's good to know I'm not alone!"

"Have you been fighting 'em?" rumbled Fat Bill. "The bloodsuckers, I mean?"

"Fighting and killing them," said Pettrus.

"Good. 'Cos we've got a plan." Fat Bill grinned, but Wood felt his heart sinking. To Wood, the word "plan" was usually synonymous with "trouble", "error" and in-evitably, "massacre". "We need some handy men to help carry it out."

"It's nothing to do with robbing the Gollothrim Bank again, is it?" scowled Pettrus. "You know what hap-pened *that time*."

"No," said Fat Bill, and Wood realised everybody was quiet in the Black Barracks, all eyes on Fat Bill, Wood and Pettrus. "This is something infinitely more *juicy*."

Graal was tired. Bone weary. He had never felt so tired before and attributed it to the wounds suffered at the claws of Bhu Vanesh. He reined in his horse at the top of a rocky, barren hill, a stolen black charger from the stables of the old Mayor of Gollothrim, and turned in his saddle. Skanda was close behind, riding side-saddle on a small, grey mare which constantly eyed Graal with nervous eyes, tosses of the head and snorts and stamps.

Skanda pulled alongside Graal, and smiled.

"You are weary?"

"Through to my bones."

"Bhu Vanesh did more than torture your flesh. I think he may have poisoned your soul."

Graal snorted. "My soul was destroyed long centuries ago." He gazed out, across a country scattered with long shadows from a low winter sun. Snow rimed the rocks and trees, frosted the long yellow grass, and clung like diamonds to huge, scattered boulders.

"It will be night soon."

"No time to camp," said Skanda, and dropped from the saddle, stretching his back. "We have too much ground to cover, and tick tock tick tock, the clockwork always moves when you wind it up."

"I'm not sure I agree with your choice of paths." Graal was still gazing into the far distance. His mouth was a narrow, bitter crease, his hands albino pale on the pommel of his saddle.

"The Gantarak Marshes? It is a straight line."

"It's a damn dangerous line. I've heard tales of whole armies lost in the murky, shitty depths. And even now winter insects will be waiting to bite and sting and feed."

"On blood?" Skanda laughed, light gleaming from his gloss black teeth. "How beautifully, deliciously ironic! A blood-sucker feeding from a blood-sucker! I am stunned that you find the concept so hateful. Surely you must empathise with the insect?"

"I despise insects," said Graal, voice a growl. "I find their lack of empathy disturbing."

"What, and you *vachine* are so much better?"

"We look after our own."

"Until you slaughter an entire civilisation to satiate a mammoth greed."

Graal shrugged. "I am what I am. I believe in self-preservation and building on one's triumphs. What other goal to seek other than total domination? Total dominion? *'If one does not strive to reach the pinnacle of vachine development, then one should stay in the ground with all the other worms.'"*

"As spoken by a true vampire prophet. But his logic, and yours, are flawed. For by turning against your own race in your desperate search for an ultimate kingship, you left your flank unprotected."

"Sacrificing the vachine of Silva Valley was a necessary evil! A move on the gameboard of life and conquest, a sacrifice that will lead eventually to ultimate victory!"

"I'm surprised you still feel that way after watching Bhu Vanesh twist Kradek-ka's head from his shoulders."

"There are always casualties in war," growled Graal.

"Indeed there are," said Skanda. "But normally one seeks to wipe out the enemy, not one's own nation."

"It was the only way," said Graal. Then shrugged. "Anyway, plenty more vachine survive to the north who know nothing of my betrayal; I can always go slithering back to them with my tail between my legs." He grinned, an almost boyish grin if it hadn't been for the evil gleam in his cold blue eyes.

"There are more?" Skanda's head snapped up, a little too sharp.

Graal stared at Skanda. "More vachine? Yes. Does that bother you?"

Skanda relaxed, and his words slid out, cool as chilled snakemeat. "Of course not. I know the vachine civilisation wasn't restricted to Silva Valley. How many more?"

"Thousands," said Graal, and grinned. "*Hundreds* of thousands. Far north, north of the Black Pike Mountains which are simply pimples on the arse of the World Beast. North, where the ice rules, where the vachine built their master civilisation, Garrenathon, with the help of Harvesters Pure."

"Indeed," said Skanda, voice still cold, eyes fixed on Graal. "Why, then, do you not reside there? In this *Garrenathon?* Surely you would be received as a great general? Surely you could satisfy your whims of wealth and power and dominion from such a seat?"

Graal shook his head. "Kradek-ka and I, we came here, to Silva. Oversaw the building. So you see? The vachine of Silva Valley were *our* puppets, *our* playthings, right from the start; nurtured, grown, crafted, awaiting the time when we could resurrect the Vampire Warlords. But we underestimated them. Bastards."

"Come. Time to move on," said Skanda, and hopped up onto the mare with incredible agility. His black eyes fixed, once, on Graal, then turned and stared off to the

277

far north. There, he imagined vast, vast cities of ice; a world of huge towers and temples and palaces, filled with a million clockwork vampires, a million *vachine*. "One day, I will find you," he whispered.

"What was that?"

"Nothing. I shall lead the way, Graal. We wouldn't want you falling in the marsh now, would we?"

After the biting and discomfort of two days in the Gantarak Marshes, Graal was relieved to break free onto the Great North Road. Snow fell occasionally, a light peppering that drifted in the wind and frosted the pines which lined the road. They rode north for a while, horses picking their way with ease, but Skanda grew increasingly agitated at this open route commonly used by armies, and now by association, possible *vampire* armies. After all, the Warlords were spreading their new rule, their new *plague*, with acumen. And the Great North Road was the easiest way to move troops up and down the flanks of Falanor...

They cut northeast from the Great North Road just south of Old Valantrium, and travelled east towards Moonlake but with no intention of entering the city – which would either be deserted, or maybe ravaged by vampires, Graal was sure. He had not been privy to all plans set in motion by the Vampire Warlords; but certainly, infesting every city of Falanor was an initial priority.

Graal and Skanda travelled in silence, mostly. Graal thought long and hard on his past actions, on the vachine, their betrayal, the blood-oil legacy, and Kell. Kell. The bastard who had helped his current tumbling downfall... or at least, that was one way Graal saw events. If Kell had not killed the Soul Stealers, then Graal might, *might just*, have had the strength necessary to overthrow the Vampire Warlords in their initial moment of weakness. Instead, Graal had been slapped aside like a naughty child.

Bastard, he thought. Bastard!

Another two days saw the ancient walls of Old Skulkra edging into view past the rolling snowy heather of Valantrium Moor. Those two days had been a desolation for Graal, two days of plodding across high, exposed moorland, a sharp nasty wind cutting from east to west and carrying ice and snow, no paths to follow in this deserted landscape and a cold sky wider than the world.

Now, as the frozen heather dropped down from the moorland plateau, so Skanda found them a sheltered place and they made camp before nightfall. The sky was the colour of topaz and stars lay strewn like sugar on velvet. Graal built a fire, and for a change Skanda came and sat with him, and both warmed hands over the flames.

"What's the plan when we arrive?" said Graal, eyeing the small boy with distaste. Skanda may look like a child, a young human boy, but Graal knew different; he still remembered his inhuman movements when Shanna and Tashmaniok tried to cut his head from his shoulders. He had danced between their silver swords like a ghost. Like one of the *Ankarok*. The Ancient Race.

"You will see."

"You need my blood, do you not?"

Skanda tilted his head back, and eyes older than the moon surveyed Graal. Skanda smiled, but there was no real humour there, just a mask held in place by necessity and discipline. "Yes. You are observant."

"Well, I didn't think you dragged me all the way out here for my cooking skills."

Skanda shrugged. "Your blood-oil runs thick with the souls of thousands. It is rich with death and slaughter. General Graal, I don't believe I could have found a more worthy and more potent specimen if I tried."

"You will perform magick?"

"I will."

"And what will happen?"

"You will see, General. You will see."

And despite the fire, despite the warmth of the flames, General Graal realised he was shivering.

Dawn broke, the sky filled with grey ice. Pink highlighted the edges of huge, thundering stormclouds. The world looked bleak. To Graal, the world *felt* bleak. A desolation. A world without hope.

They rode from their makeshift camp, and soon could make out the huge, crumbling walls which surrounded the once-majestic and truly ancient city of Old Skulkra. The walls were thick, collapsed in segments, battlements crumbling, and within the city buildings had become slaves to time. Houses were fragments, part collapsed, spires crumbled, domes smashed and deflated, towers detonated as if by some terrible explosion. Those buildings that were intact *were* sometimes skewed, twisted, walls leaning dangerously or gone altogether. Graal observed all this as they rode from Valantrium Moor, and it was exactly as he remembered it. Back when he'd sent the cankers to kill Kell and Saark...

Old Skulkra was haunted, it was said, and as Graal and Skanda grew closer they saw a thin mist creeping through the streets, passing over cracked and buckled paving slabs, ghostly fingers curling around the blackened figures of skeletal trees lining many an avenue. Graal reined in his horse and took a good, hard, long look at this ancient, threatening place.

It was rumoured the city had been built a thousand years ago, but Graal knew this was a misconception. It was probably closer to three thousand years old, maybe even four; it certainly pre-dated the Vampire Warlords and their First Empire of Carnage. It had been a derelict tombstone when Graal first walked the young plains and forests of Falanor. It was simply amazing to Graal that still the city stood, as if defying Nature, as if defying Time and the World.

The city was filled to the brim with a majestic and towering series of vast architectural wonders, immense towers and bridges, spires and temples, domes and parapets, many in black marble shipped from the far east over treacherous marshes. Old Skulkra had once been a fortified city with walls forty feet thick.

Huge, vast engine–houses and factories filled the northeast quarter, and had once been home to massive machines which, scholars claimed, were able to carry out complex tasks but were now silent, rusted iron hulks full of decadent oils and toxins.

A wide central avenue divided Old Skulkra, lined by blackened, twisted trees, arms skeletal and vast and frightening. Beyond this central avenue were enormous private palaces, now crumbled to half-ruins, and huge temples with walls cracked and jigged and displaced, offset and leaning and not entirely natural.

It was said Old Skulkra was haunted.

It was said the city carried plague at its core.

It was said to walk the ancient streets killed a man within days.

It was said dark, slithering, blood–oil creatures lived in the abandoned machinery of the factories, awaiting fresh flesh and pumping blood, and that ghosts walked the streets at dawn and dusk waiting to crawl into souls and disintegrate a person from the inside out...

It was said Old Skulkra, the city itself, was *alive*.

People did not go to Old Skulkra. Through fear, it was a place to be avoided.

Gradually, Graal and Skanda found their way to a breach in the massive walls. Gingerly, their mounts picked their way amongst ancient rubble, and then a coldness hit them and Graal shivered. The mist swirled about the hooves of his charger, and they walked the beasts down a broad, sweeping side-street lined with ancient shops, the fronts now open like gaping wounds, the interiors dark and sterile. They emerged onto the wide central avenue, and now they were closer Graal inspected the twisted and blackened trees – as if each one had been struck by lightning, petrified in an instant. Graal eased his mount closer, and touched the nearest trunk. He looked back at Skanda with a frown.

"It's stone," he said.

"Yes."

"Were they carved?"

"No. They were changed. There was bad magick here, once. Old magick. Come on, follow me."

Skanda led the way, and Graal gazed up at the massive buildings which lined the avenue. They were vast, many of the carvings stunning to behold even after all this time; even the ravages of nature could do nothing to take away their ancient splendour, their once-majesty, their foreboding and intimidating watchfulness.

*They are looking at me. Watching me through veils of stone. What is this place? What secrets do the rocks hold? What terrible legends do they hide and protect?*

At the far end of the avenue, distant but growing larger with every hoof-strike squatted a giant building of dulled black stone. It looked almost out of place amongst the majesty of every other building on the avenue, and strangely it seemed less worn, less ravaged; none of the walls leant or were broken, and the roof – a single, sloping slab of black – was unbroken. Pillars lined the front, along with huge steps which, Graal realised as he drew closer, were each as high as a man.

"Was this place populated by giants?" said Graal.

"We found it like this," said Skanda. "The Ankarok. It was our home, but we did not build it. Even we do not know how it was made; what incredible engines, what mighty clockwork must have been used in its untimely creation."

Graal craned his neck, gazing up and up and then across the mighty front facade. Skanda turned his horse to the right, and Graal followed, and there was a ramp, smooth and black. Skanda dismounted and tethered both horses. The beasts were skittish, wide-eyed, ears flat back against their skulls. Graal reached out to calm the beast, not out of any compassion but because he simply didn't want the horse bolting and leaving him stranded… *here.*

They walked up the ramp, Graal's boots echoing dully, Skanda's feet slapping a soft rhythm. They stopped at the apex, and Graal peered in. It was warm in there, uncomfortably warm, surprisingly warm, and for a horrible moment Graal had a feeling he was stepping *inside* a creature, a living entity, into an *orifice*. He cursed himself, and stepped forward into the temple, hand reaching out to steady himself against a smooth wall.

Behind him, Skanda smiled, and started to sing a soft, lilting lullaby, and he followed Graal into the darkness which soon shifted by degrees into a warm, ambient, orange glow. Graal moved down long ramps through a massive, vacant room. At the head there was an altar, and glancing back as if for confirmation, Graal continued down and along the black stone floor until he reached steps. He looked up then, and nearly jumped out of his skin. The high vaulted ceiling was alive with thick black tentacles, that moved ever-so-gently, almost imperceptibly, but they *did* move, and there were thousands of them, and Graal realised his mouth was dry and he felt a strange primal fear course through his blood-oil. He was here, and he felt sleepy, and he was way out of his depth, and he laughed easily, the noise a discordant clash of sound, for he reasoned he'd been duped once more, just like with the Vampire Warlords... only now he thought it might turn out a lot, lot worse. It would seem Kell was not the only pawn in these games...

"Climb the steps," sang Skanda, talking and singing the words at the same time and the small boy followed Graal upwards and the albino vachine stood on the altar and turned and looked out, as if an audience awaited his performance and for an instant, just an *instant*, the ground seemed to squirm as if alive with black maggots. But then the feeling, the *image*, the *essence*, was gone, and Graal tried to speak, but found he could not.

"Over here," said Skanda, and took Graal's hand, and in a bizarre scene led the tall, athletic killer, warrior, soldier, *vachine* to the centre of the stage. They stood there, in the warmth, and Graal felt sweat creeping down his forehead, down his cheeks, trickling under his dull black armour and making him *squirm*.

Skanda's song rose in pitch, and suddenly in intensity and Graal could feel it, feel the magick in the air and he realised the *magick was in the music* and Skanda's song was summoning something, something *bad,* and Graal felt a sudden urge to flee this place, get on his horse and ride for all he was worth. To hell with dominion and ruling the world; some dreams were best left dead.

Skanda's song was a beautiful wail, dropping low into the deepest depths of reverberation, then shrieking high and long like a pig impaled on a spear, but all the time the notes came tumbling and they were beautiful and surreal and they spoke of an ancient time, a time of blood and earth and song, a time before the vachine, a time before the vampires, when Falanor was young and fresh and the Ankarok were good and proud and strong. Graal fell to his knees, choking suddenly, and Skanda was standing above him and he seemed to *stretch* upwards, he was huge, and no longer a boy but savagely ugly, his face the black of carved scorched wood, twisted like the roots of a tree, his face thick with corded knots of muscles and tendon uneven and disjointed and disfigured and this huge face loomed down at Graal and thin tentacles grew from his eyes and his mouth elongated into a beak and his eyes shrunk, became round and circular and still the song went on and on and on and huge powerful hands took Graal, and held him tight, and two more hands moved round only they weren't hands they were *mandibles* and they clamped Graal with sudden ferocious pain and he screamed, screamed as he looked down at the tiny glass disc on the floor before him, glowing black, radiating power and some ancient stench that had nothing to do with even human or vampire; and one of the claws rose, clicking softly, and a smell invaded the place and it was the smell of *insect chitin*. Graal swallowed, an instant before the claw lashed out and cut Graal's throat. He felt his flesh peel apart like soft fruit under a paring knife. Blood vomited from the new hole, his flesh quivering, his body pumping, heart pumping, emptying his blood-oil, his sacred refined *blood-oil* into the glass disc where it bubbled and was sucked down, absorbed. Graal would have screamed, but he could not. He would have fought and thrashed and run; but he could not.

Graal's body twitched and pulsated, and emptied itself onto the altar of the Ankarok.

Still Skanda sang, and looking back he was a boy again and Graal's eyes met Skanda's and Skanda gave a single nod, smiling, and released Graal to slump to the floor where he lay, curled foetal, twitching spasmodically. His fingers lifted, and touched his throat. Touched the gaping wound from whence his blood-oil and blood-magick had been *sucked*...

"Come and watch," whispered Skanda, and without any control of his body Graal climbed to his feet and as he walked, boots thumping clumsily as if he were a puppet on strings, he followed Skanda and a cool breeze blew through the room and into the gaping wound at his throat but he was not dead *was not dead* and he walked across the stone and out into the weak grey daylight –

The city was *squirming*.

Old Skulkra was *alive*, every stone surface a maelstrom of movement as *things* seemed to shift, and move, and push under the surface of the stone, as if the very buildings themselves were fluid, vertical walls of thick oil trapping large desperate creatures within. The whole world seemed to shift and coalesce, and Graal wanted to heave and vomit, but had no control and his open throat was flapping and if he could, he would have screamed with two mouths...

Skanda stood, and watched, and on his hand squatted a tiny scorpion with two tails, two stings, and Graal dragged his unwilling gaze back to the city, back to Old Skulkra, and he watched.

The walls squirmed and pulsed, and now the ground was fluid, heaving and churning as if under the blades of some terrible plough. Paving stones cracked and shifted, and the whole world was alive with movement, with shifting, with coalescing images a blend of reality and the fluid, a mix of sanity and the insane, and Graal watched with lower jaw hung open and his slit throat *forgotten* as from under the earth and from inside the walls they came, they pushed, they heaved, they were *born*.

The Ankarok emerged, and they were children, and their skin was gloss black and shining as if smeared with oil, and their teeth were the black of insect incisors, and many had four arms and claws for feet, some had pincers and mandibles and one young boy crawled forward, and Graal could see he had a thorax. The Ankarok weren't simply children, they were blended with insects, with scorpions and cockroaches and ants and beetles, and they shifted and squirmed and scampered like insects and there were hundreds of them spilling from the walls like ants from a nest, and there were *thousands* of them, surging from under the earth like a flood of beetles from a dunghill, and

*we have been imprisoned for thousands of years*
and
*we have been waiting for this moment, biding our time*
and
*we were sent here, and trapped here, tricked here, lost here*
but
*now we are free, now we can work, and that's all we wanted, all we ever dreamed, the joy of the labour, the joy of the slave, the joy of the making, the joy of the killing –*

Old Skulkra squirmed and heaved beneath him, and Graal faded away into a realm of impossibility, into a plane of unexistence in which the world was ruled by the Ankarok, and they

were
all-powerful.

# CHAPTER 12
## *Vampire Scouts*

Saark was drunk. Saark was allowed to be drunk! After all, it'd been a hell of a day.

He staggered from Grak the Bastard's quarters, set high in the fortress walls and, in times of war or attack, doubling as a store-room and a place for archers. It also made a good vantage point looking out over the plain to see who approached Black Pike Mines.

Saark, in his drunken state, found another use for the archer's slit in Grak's bedroom wall, and as his urine arced far and long over the snowy field below, Grak patted him heartily on the shoulder and suggested it was time for bed.

Saark staggered across the frozen mud of what was now the "Training Yard", although in all honesty, Saark left most of the training to Grak. Grak was a capable man, and Saark had to admit that he himself was capable of drinking, and enjoying a roll with a woman, and hell even cards or betting on bear fights were high on his agenda; but training men? No sir!

As Saark mounted the steps to his room, he recounted the week's success stories. Kell would be proud, no doubt, when he returned. They (meaning Grak) had whittled the men into a raw but efficient set of fighting units. They weren't an army. Not yet. They (meaning Grak) would need to put in a lot more effort to make sure the men could fight now as a *whole*, that's what Grak kept saying, a bloody *whole* – or was it hole? Saark stopped, and scratched his balls.

Still, they could charge in several formations, and at shouted commands or blasts from a tinny bugle, they could change from square to line to wedge, they could lock shields, they could disengage shields, they could charge and retreat. Because most of the men had worked (and indeed *survived*) the Black Pike Mines for a long period of time, they had great upper body strength and impressive stamina and endurance. Greater than Saark, as today's humiliating race had contested. But then, Saark *had* been drunk the night before. And the night before that. And, what a surprise, the night before that!

He stumbled to his room, and as the world swayed he removed his clothes and stood, hands on hips, naked and proud and desperate for a tankard of water. He moved to a water barrel and dunked his head in, coming up with a splash and lick of his lips. Gods he was hungry! What did he have in the room? Bread, cheese, donkey-meat…

"Saark?"

She sounded sleepy, and sat up in the bed, her dark hair tousled and illuminated by the moonlight easing through a small square window. Saark could make out her upper torso, naked, and he licked his lips again only not, in this case, with the need for water.

"Hello there," he said, and moved towards the bed.

"Have you been drinking?"

"Only a drop, sweetie," he murmured, and crawled onto the bed.

"Good," said Nienna. "I warmed your blankets. I hope you don't mind?"

"Of course not," he said, and she knelt up before him, and her body was perfect, white and pale, gleaming in the moonlight, her small but firm breasts young and pert, her lips slightly parted as her head tilted, and she stared at his face.

"Do you want me to stay?" she said.

"Oh yes," said Saark, reaching out and caressing her breasts. Instantly her nipples hardened and reaching forward, gently, his tongue circled her areola. Nienna murmured, and shuffled closer, and Saark's arms encircled her, and now his hard cock pressed into her, and he kissed her, he kissed her lips and they were warm and sweet from honeycakes and wine, and he kissed her neck, which was warm and soft like silk, and his hands ran down her back and she shivered in anticipation and thrust herself painfully against him, in need, in lust, and his hands came to rest on her buttocks, firm and hard from so much travelling in the wilds. They kissed again, harder this time, with passion and a need that transcended threats and Saark's hand dipped, stroked between Nienna's legs and she squirmed, giggling a little, then moaning and sinking into his embrace as his hand entered her, and he bore her down to the bed, and Saark was lost in wine and lust and memories, and he remembered Alloria; she was his first love and she was his true love and she was before him now, on the soft silk sheets in King Leanoric's chambers, Alloria, with her mane of curled black hair, her flashing dangerous green eyes, her ruby red lips, tall, with her elegant long languorous limbs and her tongue stained from blue karissia, and she smiled up at Saark, and Alloria said, "Make love to me, Saark," and Nienna said, "Make love to me, Saark," and Saark pushed himself into her, all the way, to the hilt, and she groaned and he groaned and they fucked long and hard on the bed, their groans and thrusts rising rising rising to a climax of perfect joy and union, and Saark whispered, "Alloria," but Nienna was too far gone to hear the words and she gave herself to Saark, not caring, not caring about the world and Kell's threats and vachine imperfections… and slowly, they spiralled down into a cold place, a cold world of reality, facing war and mutilation and death.

And in the cold dark hours of the night, they clung tightly to each other like children.

Governor Myrtax could not sleep. He was too hot, sweating and feeling fevered, and so he stepped from his bed and pulled on low, soft-leather boots. His wife murmured in sleep and turned, one arm flinging out, but she did not wake. Myrtax crossed to the next room and looked in on his sleeping babes; he saw their dark shapes, breathing rhythmically in the ink, and he smiled; smiled the happy smile of fatherhood; smiled the smile of innate joy at what a man's child could invest without effort – just simply by *being*.

Too hot. Too damn hot!

Myrtax stepped from his quarters and looked across at the distant fortress walls. Fires burned in braziers on the battlements, and ten guards kept watch across the snowy plains. Damn, but he didn't want to leave this place. Didn't want to go to war. Why would he? His family was here. His wife, who he loved more than life; his children, who he'd die for!

Myrtax jogged down the steps and onto the frozen mud. He was surprised to find he had a knife in his hand, and he slipped it back into the oiled leather sheath. *Strange. I don't remember belting the knife on. Why would I need a knife in my own mine? But of course, after the Governors – the false Governors – took over and threatened my children; well, a man has to protect himself; a man has to look after his own interests.*

Governor Myrtax moved across the ground, seemingly with no destination, until he found himself outside the cell of Sara. Kell's daughter.

*How strange to come here. Why would I come here? Kell said she was dangerous, and not to trust her, but I know he's wrong because I have seen into her eyes, and she is a noble creature, a beautiful creature, and anything that stunning must be good...*

"Good evening, sir," said the guard, and gurgled and vomited blood as Governor Myrtax's dagger slid under his ribs and up, with a hard jabbing thrust, into his heart. The man sagged into Myrtax's arms, and he frowned, confused at why the man was so heavy, and why the man had been drinking on duty, and why he was now asleep in his arms like a dirty drunkard.

"I'll have you up on a charge," muttered Myrtax, lowering the twitching guard to the ground and taking the keys from his belt. He moved to the cell, the interior of which was a black pool of oil, impenetrable to the naked eye, and Myrtax inserted the key and opened the gate.

Myrtax stood back, his mind flushed with confusion, and he looked up and the stars were bright, bathing him in a surreal glow and he smiled, as he thought about his children. He had been blessed when they were born, and blessed more as they grew into two of the most beautiful things he had ever witnessed in creation –

"Myrtax. You have surpassed yourself," said Sara, stepping from her cage. She smiled, and leant forward, fangs extending towards the dazed Governor of the Black Pike Mines.

"Hey! Hey you!" It was an inner-wall patrol of guards, set up by Grak. Boots pounded stone, and three soldiers wearing new armour and carrying newly forged short swords sprinted forward, and a sword whistled for Sara but she leapt, straight up into the air, the sword slashing beneath her boots. She twisted in the air, back-flipping behind the men. She landed lightly, reached out, and snapped one man's neck. He crumpled instantly. A sword hammered down, and Sara swayed, arm slapping out to break the man's arm in half. His hand and wrist fell twitching to the stone, spewing blood, and he screamed – a scream silenced as Sara punched out, fist entering his mouth and breaking his teeth and exploding from the back of his head… and as it exited, her claws extended with a *flick*, putting out the third soldier's eyes.

Sara withdrew her hand with a squelch and shower of bloody mush, and leaving one soldier sobbing on the floor, holding his ruined face, she reached over and gently kissed Myrtax on the lips. "Until the next time, *lover*," she said, and was gone in a whisper of darkness.

More soldiers arrived, led by Grak, his sword out, his face grim. He stepped up to the man without eyes and only half a face remaining; with a savage downward stab, he put the writhing man out of his misery.

"Check the cell." Grak whirled on Governor Myrtax. "What the hell happened here?" Then he saw the keys still in Myrtax's hands, and the dazed look on the man's face even as he started to drift back into some semblance of understanding.

"What? What… where did all the blood come from? Oh, my…" said Myrtax.

The soldier returned. "Sir. One vampire is gone, the other is… well, it's a husk."

"What do you mean, a husk?"

"It's shrivelled up. Like all the blood has been sucked out."

Grak strode forward, and stared at the skin-bag of bones. "Shit," he snarled, then turned back to Myrtax. "The vampire must have fed from the other one; to keep strong." He pointed at the Governor. "Are you happy with yourself? Eh?" Then back to the soldier, in a tone of disgust. "Go and lock that bastard up, before he does any more damage."

Two soldiers grabbed Myrtax's arms and removed the dagger from his belt. They led him away, tears on his cheeks, protesting confusion and innocence.

Grak looked down at the dead soldiers, then up at the night sky. The stars twinkled. Grak had no time for their cold beauty. "You, lad!"

"Yes, sir?"

"Double the guards."

"Where, sir?"

"Everywhere!" he thundered. "Tell them we have a vampire loose in the fucking mine."

"Yes, sir!"

"And soldier?"

"Yes sir?"

"Go and wake Saark. He needs to know about this."

Kell stared around in disbelief. The Valleys of the Moon was massive, and bisected down the middle of the floor by a huge crevasse from which steam slowly rose, along with a sulphurous stench that made Kell's eyes weep.

His hands were bound tightly behind his back, and Dekkar carried Ilanna in one hand, his own flanged mace in the other. He was grinning madly, and Jagor Mad walked by his side, a kind of strutting arrogance in his step now he had the upper hand.

"I can't believe I trusted you," said Kell, his eyes moving along the rift in the valley floor to the distant huts beyond. They lined the walls, small and made from mud and stone, with slate roofs and hand-carved doors of oak.

"More the fool you," said Jagor, cocky now, too cocky, his eyes shining with a new light. Kell realised what it was. Hatred. It hadn't vanished, only been pushed deep down whilst Jagor brought him here. Kell had been played like a pawn. Like a court jester. And that burned him bad, worse than any poison force fed into his bones by Myriam's invading needle.

"You know the stakes here," said Kell, face filled with thunder. "This is about everybody! This is about Falanor, this is about us all working together to rid the world of a dangerous menace!"

"The only dangerous menace here is *you!*" hissed Jagor, and pressed his sword against Kell's throat. "I *will* have my revenge for all those years spent in that fucking mine! I will spill your blood! But not yet, oh no, not yet!"

"Be silent!" roared Dekkar suddenly, and as they moved across the jagged rocks, filled in places with snow and ice except around the rim of the valley rift, where all snow had melted revealing black rocks veined with red and grey minerals, so Blacklippers streamed from distant huts and moved like a tide to meet their King.

Dekkar.

King of the Blacklippers.

Behind, many of the children followed, bows still aimed at Kell. Nobody trusted him, and he smiled a sour smile. Here, it would appear, he was a dark myth. How now would he convince these people to fight for him? How would he convince them to go to war against the Vampire Warlords? If he attacked them, he would have no chance of convincing them – for he would simply reinforce his status as enemy. And with Jagor Mad ready to stab him in the back, it looked like his luck had come head-to-head with a mountain flank.

"Hear me!" roared Dekkar, halting by the edge of the hot stinking rift in the rocky floor. Fumes hung over the great tear in the earth, and over it, near the centre, Kell squinted. He could see a bridge, a narrow span of brass filled with huge clockwork wheels and gears. Kell frowned. He had never seen anything like it in his life, except in miniature in the workings of a clock. "Here, we have the prisoner Kell! Sworn enemy of the Blacklippers! *Hunter* of the Blacklippers! Raper of our women, murderer of our children, *despoiler* of Blacklipper flesh!"

A hush fell over the Blacklippers.

Kell met their gazes, the men, all armed with spears and swords, faces grim, shoulders stocky and proud. These were a warrior race. These were the outcasts, the criminals, the freaks and deviants of Falanor – who had taken blood-oil to relieve their pain and suffering, to find an inner peace from physical torment, instead finding social torment and a finality as outcasts; names to be revered as evil and unholy, cast away to the dark regions of the mountains where nobody would travel. Kell knew this. He had hunted enough Blacklippers in his time. *Some*, at least, of what they said was true.

He grinned, a sour grin.

Because that's what this came back to, that's what this came round to: his earlier escapades. As a Hunter. A Vachine Hunter, but also a killer of those who smuggled Karakan Red across the mountains; those who stole blood to feed the impure amongst the vachine.

"Shit," he muttered, as full realisation dawned. "They were going to kill him. There was no persuading these people. He had been a fool. An arrogant, trusting, naive fool.

"Kell! The Legend!" roared Dekkar, and an answering roar met him and Kell tried to shout over the noise but it rose like thunder and hundreds of Blacklippers swarmed at him, swamping him, and he went down under a barrage of blows, fists and sticks slamming his head and nose and cheeks and jaw. Kell hit the ground hard, and was kicked, and then the crowd surged back and Kell looked up at Dekkar, who stooped, and *lifted* Kell above his head.

"The Bridge!" somebody shouted.

"Yes! The Trial! The Bridge!"

"Bridge! Bridge! Bridge!" chanted the Blacklippers, and Kell, dazed, felt himself moving as if on a sea of hands and he realised he had been taken, was being carried by many, and Dekkar held Ilanna again and *if only Kell could reach his axe, these bastards, he'd show them who was a fucking Legend, he'd carve himself a path so fucking bloody his name would ring like Death through a thousand fucking years of their mangled fucking history!*

Kell was carried along the edge of the rift. He glanced down, and wished he hadn't.

Fumes welled up, making him choke, and his eyes were met by a pulsing deep glow of red and orange. The heat was incredible. It singed his beard and eyebrows. It made him cough and choke. For the first time in *years* Kell felt panic well in his chest like a striking viper. This was a bad place, an evil place; and he realised instinctively he had been condemned and he would die here. Kell gritted his teeth. If he was to die, then he would take oh so many with him...

As they grew close to the bridge so Kell realised its awesome scope and size. It was a mammoth brass contraption, not just a bridge but a machine. The whole length was a mass of cogs and wheels, gears and levers. In the centre, disappearing down into the glow, was a huge pendulum like Kell had seen in many a clock, only this was the length of twenty men and must have weighed something shocking.

They reached the point where the bridge met the rocky ground – only it didn't. There was a gap too large to jump, and Dekkar reached to a small brass pod and pulled a lever. There came a heavy *clunk*, a spin of cogs which transferred to others cogs and gears stepped up and down like pistons. There was a groan, and the pendulum swung and the bridge shifted, lifted, and eased onto the rocky ground with a crash and grinding of brass on rock. Kell was prodded on, hands tight behind his back, and with a grimace he realised Dekkar had used his own axe, his own damn *Ilanna!* Kell spat onto the brass grid beneath his boots. Dekkar would pay for that.

They moved across the brass bridge, which continually shifted and moved, rolling like a ship at anchor in a bay. Beneath his boots Kell could feel the spinning cogs, and the shift of gears. It felt like the bridge was *alive*.

Reaching the centre, his eyes streaming with tears from the chemical updraft, Kell saw the swing and the noose of woven brass rope. So, he was to be hanged. *Again*. "Horse shit," he muttered, and glanced back. Now, there was only Dekkar and Jagor Mad. They were both grinning at him, and Dekkar passed Ilanna to his brother.

"Do you want to kill him, brother, or shall I?"

"No, that's my job," said Jagor. "I owe him. Owe him bad."

"Jagor, listen to me!" hissed Kell. "You know the vampires are coming. You know this is insanity! We must all work together, must fight together to remove this menace! If you hang me, the Vampire Warlords – they will not vanish. And slowly, they will hunt down every living creature in Falanor. You might live another month; you might live a year. But they will come for you, and they'll either turn you into a vampire, or they'll burn your fucking soul, lad."

"The Vampire Warlords?" said Dekkar, raising his eyebrows. "I have heard of such creatures. They are part of Blacklipper Legend. Part of *vachine* folklore as scribed within the Oak Testament."

"General Graal of the vachine flooded Silva Valley from the Granite Thrones on Helltop," said Kell. "He sacrificed the vachine in a mass offering of blood, to open the Paths to the Chaos Halls. The Vampire Warlords came back. Now, they are in Jalder, and Gollothrim, and Vor! They will spread, Dekkar. They will kill your people."

Dekkar considered this. Then he smiled. "I care nothing for the people of Falanor. Kill him!"

Jagor prodded Kell with Ilanna, drawing blood across the old warrior's forearm. Kell growled, and stepped up onto the brass ramp. Jagor climbed up behind him, and placed the brass noose about Kell's neck.

"You will die for my suffering," he snarled.

"If you kill me," said Kell, voice perfectly quiet, perfectly calm, "then you condemn yourself. You condemn the people of Falanor to an eternity of slavery. You condemn your entire race of Blacklippers to vampire slavery."

"You think one old man is so important?"

"No. But I know that I can make a difference. If I can get close enough to the Vampire Warlords, I will kill them."

"Ha! I'll do it myself!" snapped Jagor Mad. "Now step off the ramp, old man, lest I use this pretty axe to open your skull!"

Kell turned his back on Jagor, and took a deep breath. A million thoughts rushed through his mind. His misplaced trust in this, a convicted killer. Saark's training of the army. Nienna, sweet Nienna. Sara, snarling and hissing, spitting and cursing. And then back, back through the days and weeks and months, back through Myriam and the Soul Stealers, the fights on Helltop, scrapping on the dangerous ridges of the Black Pike Mountains with snarling cankers and creatures of the dark, the vachine and the vampires, the cursed and the unholy. Back back back, and one face kept returning to his mind and if Kell had to blame one man, then that one man would be Graal. General Graal. He had it coming. He had a hard death coming. But Kell would not be the man to see it through.

Kell thought about Ehlana.

He remembered the Crooked Oak, the sunshine, the flowers in her hair and tears were in his eyes, on his cheeks, in his beard. "You are man and wife. You may kiss her." And he leant forward, and he kissed her, and it had been an incredible moment, a moment of unity and purity and perfection. But how had it gone so bad? How had it all gone wrong? *I'm coming to you, Ehlana, I'm coming just like I said I would, just like I promised. We'll walk the long dark roads together, and I'll bring you to paradise. I can do no more in this place. In this world. In this life.*

"Jump, fucker," snarled Jagor Mad, and Kell turned and smiled at the big man, and saw the shock in his face for to see Kell cry must have been such a rarity; and over the thumping of the bridge and the hiss of the smoke and churning furnace below, Kell heard another sound, like shouting, and Jagor Mad's eyes went wide and Ilanna started to lift in his great brutal fists as an arrow materialised in one eye socket with a savage slap, and Jagor Mad screamed stumbling backwards, falling to the ground, dropping Ilanna with a clatter and reaching up to touch the shaft in his skull – which made him scream again.

Kell squinted through the smoke. A figure was galloping a grey mare along the edge of the valley's rift. Another arrow slashed through the air, but Dekkar was already moving, launching himself sideways and grunting as he hit the bridge walkway.

Kell tugged at his bonds, but they were too tight. He struggled, and dropping his head down and back, got the noose from its promise. Dekkar was crawling across the bridge and he hit a panel against one rail. The clockwork bridge cranked and lifted, as a third arrow sailed over and clattered along the walkway a few feet from Dekkar.

Kell leapt down to Jagor, who was weeping, touching the shaft in his eye tenderly. "Help me!" he wailed at Kell, and Kell drove a knee into his face sending him rolling, embedded arrow slapping the brass bridge and making him scream and scream and scream, and to this backdrop of noise Kell found Ilanna, and sitting and shuffling backwards, he rubbed the bonds across her razor-sharp blades and they parted like simple cotton threads.

Kell took Ilanna, and rose to his feet.

He was Thunder. He was the Storm.

Dekkar was standing, staring at him, his face a fury, the black flanged mace steady in his huge hands.

Dekkar looked down at Jagor, who had passed into unconsciousness. "I am going to crush you for that, worm."

"Show me," snarled Kell through strings of saliva.

With a scream, Dekkar launched an attack. He was huge, mighty, and attacked with such a sudden violent speed it made Kell blink in shock and surprise, stepping back, Ilanna coming up to deflect the mace – which struck in a shower of sparks, and continued onwards forcing Kell down on one knee, teeth gritted, muscles straining and bulging. The mace stopped an inch from his eyes, which flickered up to Dekkar, or rather, Dekkar's boot. The blow sent Kell reeling back across the bridge, rolling, Ilanna gone from his fingers and Dekkar leapt forward, the mace whirring down again. Kell twitched to one side, and the blow left a dent in the brass bridge. It would have crushed Kell's head like a melon. Another blow sent sparks careering from the bridge's rails, and Kell got to his knees, streaked with sweat, panting, anger rising through him in a colossal insane wave. Dekkar was bigger, and stronger, and faster. But Kell was mean. Kell was *fucking* mean. He screamed, spittle lacing his beard, and as the mace whistled over his head in a mighty horizontal stroke he came up from the duck into a lunge, grabbing Dekkar around the midriff and punching the large man backwards, off

303

balance, to hit the ground. The mace flashed up, but Kell caught the shaft against his arm, and it slid from Dekkar's fingers. Kell slammed a right straight down into Dekkar's face, and again, and again, and felt teeth break under impact. Dekkar screamed, and his hand grabbed Kell's balls, the other Kell's throat, and the huge man scrabbled to his knees and hoisted Kell over his head. He threw Kell down the bridge, and Kell rolled over and over, and lay for a moment stunned, his throat and balls on fire and clubbing him with waves of impact pain. Dekkar roared, and ran at Kell who stumbled to his feet. A straight punch jabbed Kell back, a right hook shook him, rocking him on his heels, and Dekkar took Kell's head in his hands and head-butted him, once, twice, three times and let go, grinning, blood and smashed teeth filling his mouth.

Kell stared up at the huge man. "Is that all you've fucking got?" he screamed, groggy, staggering back.

"I'll kill you!" roared Dekkar, and slammed another hook which sent Kell reeling sideways, hitting the bridge's rail and rolling along it, slamming against the panel which controlled the movement of the brass bridge. There came a huge, metallic groan and clock-work started to spin, huge gears pumping, mammoth brass pistons hissing and thrusting. The bridge lurched and suddenly spun, leaving a huge gap to the rocky bank and safety. An arrow sailed through the steam, missing Dekkar by a few inches. He scowled, and Kell realised he had found his mace. Dekkar advanced down the bridge at Kell, who was touching his broken nose and gritting his teeth in anger and frustration.

"Come on!" screamed Kell, as Dekkar broke into a run, but the bridge lurched again, spinning around, a heavy metallic cranking sound echoing through the Valleys of the Moon. Steam hissed from the brass bridge. Along the banks Kell saw hundreds of faces flash past. It was the Blacklippers, and they were watching, motionless, many with mouths open in awe. Kell couldn't see the person who'd saved him. The bridge spun around again. Kell felt sick, and was pitched off balance, landing heavy with a grunt. The bridge tipped, and he was sent skidding down the rough brass ramp, arms and legs kicking, to crash into Dekkar who was pinned against a brass strut. Kell hit him with three straight punches, heavy leaden blows that cracked the man's cheekbone making him howl, then the bridge spun again, lurching and groaning, and Kell was thrown away like a toy doll, down the expanse to hit the rail with such force he thought for a moment he'd broken his back.

"You have to get off the bridge!" a woman was screaming, and Kell nodded at this immutable logic. He got to his knees, a drool of saliva and pain trailing from his beard, mingled with blood from his smashed nose. He ran along the rail, fighting gravity as the bridge rocked back on mammoth pistons and it was all Kell could do to grab a nearby strut and hold on for his life. The bridge rose, near vertical now, and Kell felt his boots and legs slip away from beneath him so he was hanging, gazing down into a distant inferno with clouds of steam and sulphur.

"Holy Mother," he whispered, eyes wide, all thoughts of battle forgotten. Ilanna skated along the metal with a scream, and wedged against a brass strut below. Dekkar was also kicking beneath him, and Kell watched Jagor Mad's unconscious body slip and slide, spinning with arms and legs akimbo, until he bounced from a strut, jigged off at an angle, then soared from the edge of the bridge to be lost in the raging inferno below.

"*Noooo!*" screamed Dekkar.

But Jagor Mad was gone. Gone, into the furnace.

Dekkar looked up at Kell. "This is your fault!" he roared.

Kell said nothing, but looked up, searching for a way to climb from the bridge. The bridge groaned. More clanking came from deep down in the clockwork machine's *bowels*, and then it gave a sudden jerk. Kell nearly lost his grip.

Then –

A noise rent the air, long and ululating, almost like a war cry but far too high-pitched and feminine. Kell stared off across the banks of the valley rift, across black rock and ice beyond. Riders were streaming across the snow, and Kell saw the Blacklippers running for their huts, many drawing weapons and Kell squinted through the fumes, and–

And blinked.

They were vampires. Twenty of them at least, wearing black cloaks and with hair tied back tight. They were riding horses that were… *red?* Kell focused. No, not red. Pure muscle. *Pure muscle*, without the skin. The beasts were panting, snorting, whinnying in pain and fear. Kell could see the heavy muscle fibres working and he suddenly felt very sick, despite his own problems.

"Kell, you've got to reach the control panel," a woman was shouting, and Kell turned back to the rocky embankment. He squinted again, and then shook his head. It was Myriam, bow in hand, face earnest.

"What the hell are *you* doing here?" he yelled.

"Rescuing you, old man! Reach the panel! I can see the core shafts of the bridge, and they're *bending*, you understand? The whole damn thing is tearing itself free! It's going to fall!" Kell felt the sickness in his stomach rise through him. If the bridge fell into the furnace, well, it was Goodnight Sweet Lady.

Kell started to climb down, hand over hand, the brass warm to his touch. He could see Dekkar struggling beneath him, and his gaze moved first to the control panel, then left, to Ilanna. Kell gritted his teeth, and struggled to the axe. He took her. He cradled her to his chest. She was warm to his touch. She was thankful.

"Kell!" screamed Myriam. He glanced up.

The charging vampires hit the massed Blacklippers in a tight wedge, and he saw, *saw* heads sail up into the air and heard the vampires' high-pitched keening, realising with rising gorge that they were laughing, fucking *laughing* as they slaughtered. The swords of battle rang across the Valleys of the Moon. Steel on steel. Steel biting flesh. Steel breaking bone.

Kell scrabbled across the brass strut. The bridge groaned and shuddered beneath him. He stared at the controls, but there were small dials and levers and he did not understand. He started to press and twist things at random, and the bridge groaned, gears clanked, and there came a horrible, booming tearing sound. The bridge shuddered, and dropped – then in an eerie silence, tilted to one side and began to fall.

Kell hung on for his life, wind and sour sulphur fumes blowing through his hair and bloodied beard, and the edge of the bridge clanged against the edge of the valley floor, but behind him it fell away and then snagged with various metallic tearing sounds. Kell looked up, into Myriam's concerned face. "Shit," he snarled. "I can't believe it's you!"

"Come on. We have only seconds!" She glanced behind herself, fearful of the charging vampires who were cutting a path through the Blacklippers. Men, women and children were slaughtered like diseased cattle. Heads were cut from shoulders, arms and legs from torsos. It was a massacre. It was an abattoir.

Kell scrambled up the brass planks and leapt, catching Myriam's outstretched hand. She was strong. She hauled him up onto the rocky ridge, and Kell whirled, eyes narrowed, staring at the vampires. The Blacklippers had retreated, forming themselves into a fighting square surrounded by the corpses of their friends. Those with shields had made a wall at the front, and the vampires coolly dismounted and watched with interest, smiles staining faces as they lifted bright, silver swords.

"Help me up," he croaked.

Kell jumped, and glared down into Dekkar's face. The huge man was in pain, face twisted and battered and streaked with grime. He had climbed as far as he could, but could not traverse the final leap.

"Why?"

"Because they're slaughtering my people!" screamed Dekkar, and held out his hand.

Kell stared at it. The bridge lurched again, dropping another foot. Great tearing sounds echoed through the rift, and the bridge was vibrating as if alive and fitting. Cogs could be seen, spinning slowly. A huge piston went *thunk*.

Kell glanced at Myriam. "Hold my belt." She grabbed him, hands like iron shackles, and he knelt, leaning forward, hand outstretched. His eyes met Dekkar's. "You'll have to jump."

"Can I trust you?"

"No. But you have little choice."

Dekkar growled an ancient curse, and leapt...

Kell leant, and the two men grabbed one another, wrist to wrist and stayed locked there for a moment, Kell staring down into Dekkar's wild eyes, muscles screaming as they took the weight. Then Kell hissed, and hauled Dekkar up the wall as behind him the huge brass bridge squealed like a woman in pain, and slowly tilted, sliding backwards with a *whoosh* to vanish into the abyss.

Kell looked down at his hand, and then up into Dekkar's eyes. He noted the big man carried his mace, and he swallowed. Kell always said he took a lot of killing; well, here was a man hewn from the same granite cast.

Dekkar turned, and stared at the vampires. They had dismounted, and were smiling as they advanced on the retreating Blacklippers. He released Kell's grip, and Kell hoisted Ilanna and glanced at Myriam, who drew her own sword.

"It's time for those bastards to die," said Kell.

"Let's fight," growled Dekkar.

They charged across the rocky ground, and the vampires smiled wider until eyes fell on Ilanna. One pointed, but Kell, Dekkar and Myriam crashed into them and Kell's axe lashed out, opening a throat, and on the return swing cutting a vampire's head free from its body. There was an explosion of flesh, and Kell grabbed the hair and hoisted the head up high. "See!" he screamed "They can fucking die! Die, I tell you!" Everything was chaos. The vampires seemed to suddenly shrink back, staring at Kell, and Ilanna, and the severed vampire head with fangs still gnashing and gnawing. Kell launched the head into the pit, and kicked over the body which spewed out foul stinking black blood. Kell waded into the mass, Ilanna hewing left and right, thumping into flesh, spattering him with gore. The vampires attacked him with their inhuman speed but Kell was a demon, moving smoothly, seeming to shift here, twitch there, and claws and swords sailed past him by a hair's breadth, but always by a hair's breadth, and he had some inhuman instinct, some natural grace as if he was in perfect tune with the killers and always slipping beyond their claws. Dekkar was close behind, feeding in Kell's wake. As Kell moved forward through the vampires, Ilanna slamming left and right, so anything that went past was crushed under Dekkar's mighty mace. Myriam, also, moved with incredible vachine speed, sword slamming out, cutting throats and piercing hearts. Some vampires shrivelled into decayed mush. Some crumbled into ash.

In what seemed an instant, Kell broke through their ranks and high-pitched keening rent the air. Five or six fled, leaping onto horses and galloping away only to find a wall of Blacklippers had gathered, and charged at the remaining vampires with swords and axes, cutting them to pieces. Screams pierced the air. Without mercy, the Blacklippers killed the skinless horses, and threw them into the sulphurous rift.

Kell stood for a moment, panting, then whirled on Dekkar. Ilanna came up. Kell's eyes were bright glowing coals without trust.

Dekkar placed his mace head against the ground, and leant heavily on the weapon. Suddenly he looked old, and tired; bone-weary. He smiled weakly at Kell, and rubbed his eyes.

"You did well. For an old man."

"As did you. For a fat bastard."

"Ha! Kell, I think we may have got off to a bad start."

Kell scratched his chin. "You reckon? Maybe I'd have to agree with that one. I came here to warn you about the vampires, about their *army* gathered at Jalder. I have gathered my own army, and I was coming here to ask you to join."

"What, you would have Blacklippers fight alongside the good men of Falanor?" There was a hint of a sneer to Dekkar. Long-held prejudices could not be erased with ease.

Kell shrugged, and gazed at Ilanna's bloodied blades. They were slick with vampire gore. "My army is made up of criminals, freaks, and convicts from the Black Pike Mines."

Dekkar smiled. "That is good, then. My sort of people."

"Will you come with me?" said Kell. "Will you fight with me?"

Dekkar stared hard at Kell, then past him, to the thousands of gathered Blacklippers. His people. His outcast race. Then he nodded, and lifted his mace into the air. "Gather your weapons!" he roared. "We are going to war!"

A cheer rang out, and Kell turned, face a dark sour hole. Myriam grasped his arm and they walked away from the cheering Blacklippers to stare out, past the destroyed bridge and the torn clockwork moorings that were all that remained.

"What is wrong?" she said.

"They cheer because they know they will kill the men and women of Falanor. It is sick."

"You got your army."

"Yes. I got it. But what worries me is once I've unleashed it, and if we win… how do I rein it back again?

But that's a problem for another day."

Myriam nodded, and peered down into the depths of the rift. "I'm sorry, Kell. About before. About Saark."

"I should have let you drown him longer. Would have done him good. Cooled him off a little." Kell grinned. "Have you learnt your lesson?"

"So you're not going to cut off my head?"

"You saved my life, didn't you? With that damn fine bow."

"Maybe I was trying to hit you?"

Kell roared with laughter, suddenly, and slapped Myriam on the back. He was battered, his nose broken, his face and clothing covered in gore, vampire blood, strings of flesh. He looked like an animal. He looked worse than an animal. He looked like a Vampire Killer.

Myriam shivered.

"Either way, lass, you saved my hide on that bridge. And in a roundabout way, you have helped save Falanor."

"How so?"

"I think you led the vampires here. They were a tracking unit. I reckon they were after killing themselves a vachine. They know your kind are a threat, and you must be a priority hunt for them."

"Oh," she said, deflating a little. Kell put his arm round her.

"Don't worry, Myriam. You're with me now. And me and Ilanna, we're starting to get quite fond of you vachine. You certainly have your uses in a scrap!"

"Yes, but we're hard to love," said Myriam, and smiled, and looked up at Kell, and he stared at her as if almost seeing her for the first time. When Kell had first met Myriam, back in Vorgeth Forest, and she had poisoned him; she had been a husk of a woman, riddled with cancer, eyes sunken, hair lifeless; now, thanks to her vachine change at the hands of the Soul Stealers, she was tall, powerful, skin pale but radiant, and her hair was long, gently curled, luscious like the glossy pelt of a panther. Her eyes were dark and glittering and intelligent, and if it hadn't been for the brass vachine fangs, she would have been, to Kell's eyes at least, strikingly beautiful.

He remembered her touch. He remembered glimpses of her, little snippets of naked flesh, bathing, dressing. And back in Vorgeth Forest, just before she had injected him with poison, she had pressed close against him, and even now he could remember the musk of her body, and he remembered the rising lust in his loins and cursed himself, now and then, for being weak, for being pitiful, for betraying the memory of his long lost Ehlana. Back in Vorgeth Myriam had kissed him, and it had felt good. It had felt more than good. But he pushed the memory away. Never again, old man, he had told himself. Not in this life.

Kell shuddered.

"No," he said.

"No what?" Myriam was looking at him strangely.

"Just *no*. Come on. Let's take these Blacklippers to Saark and the men. The fight is just beginning."

"Wait." Her hand was on his arm.

Kell stared at her fingers, then lifted his head to look into her face. Again, that curious smile. The tilt of the head. Kell shivered, for he thought he knew what that smile meant. Myriam was weak – she needed to be loved, to be cherished, and to be in control. And she was attracted to power. Attracted to Kell's ferocity, his savagery, his Legend.

"Go on."

"That thing. Back there. With Saark. I didn't mean it."

"What, trying to kill him? Don't worry about that. I love the man, but I, also, want to kill him regular."

"Not killing him, no. The... other thing."

"Ahh."

"It was just... a moment. I am free of him. You see?"

"I see," said Kell, voice low, eyes locked to Myriam. "Come on, lass. We should go."

"Yes."

Kell led the way, and Myriam followed, sheathing her sword.

Dekkar sent a fast rider with three horses within the hour. The mission was simple: to reach Saark at the Black Pike Mines with a letter from Kell. In it, were instructions to assemble the new army and to rendezvous on the plains south of the Black Pike Mines. Then they would take a direct course from the Black Pike Mines to the occupied city of Jalder.

Now Kell, Myriam and Dekkar, King of the Blacklippers, led two thousand armed male and female *Blacklippers* across the ice and snow, and out from the Valleys of the Moon. They moved mostly in silence, hair and furs ruffled by the cold wind from the mountains. It was a bleak day, grey and cold and threatening snow.

"Now, we go to war," said Myriam, voice gentle.

"Now, we fight for Falanor," agreed Kell.

# CHAPTER 13
## *The Battle for Jalder*

"It's grandfather!" grinned Nienna, shading her eyes from the glare of the snow. From the hilltop across the valley emerged a horde of soldiers, heavily armed, who descended into the valley floor with Kell marching alongside a huge man bearing a mace.

"Looks like a bunch of murderous cutthroats to me," muttered Saark, then gave a sly smile. "As you say. Your grandfather."

"Don't be like that! He's done it! He's brought more soldiers!"

Nienna ran off ahead, boots ploughing through fresh soft snow, an almost childish look on her face which made Saark blush as he remembered the past week and the things they'd done. Nothing fazed Nienna. Saark had to admit, she gave him a run for his money.

Saark watched as Nienna leapt at the old man, throwing her arms about him, and he laughed and hugged her tight, shifting Ilanna to one side out of the way where sunlight gleamed on the dark matt blades.

*If he finds out, I'm a dead man. No. More. If he finds out, he'll beat me, then he'll torture me, then he'll cut me up into little pieces! He'll tear off my arms and cut off my balls.* Saark clutched his balls with compassion. *And I don't ever want to lose my balls. I like my balls. After all…* He grimaced. *My balls are my best feature.*

Saark moved across the snow, signalling to Grak the Bastard to stand down the men. As Saark approached, Kell grinned at him and cracked his knuckles. "I see you, dandy."

"Somebody hit you?" Saark squinted at the damage.

"People always hit me," said Kell.

"I see somebody broke your nose. You look better for it."

"Yes," said Kell, and gestured to Dekkar, the Black-lipper King. "We had a few, shall we say, disagreements. But then the vampires attacked the Valleys of the Moon, and it all worked out right in the end."

Saark nodded, grinning. "Nice to meet you, Dekkar." Saark held out his hand. Dekkar simply stared at him, as a lion would if presented with a potato. "Ahh, I see, you employ the old school of ignorance just like our big stinking friend here."

Dekkar leaned close to Kell. "Shall I silence this yapping puppy?"

"No, no, he's all right. He's always like this. You get used to him."

"I do not think I will," said Dekkar, scowling and hefting his huge mace.

"Hey," said Saark, scowling, "I'm here, you know, right here in front of you, now I'm used to people talking about me behind my back but this just isn't on. You wouldn't get this sort of thing in the Court of King Leanoric, I can tell you!"

"Did he look after you?" said Kell, to Nienna.

"He looked after me," she said, voice small, but thankfully Kell was looking away, surveying the army of criminals as presented by Saark. So he missed the blush. He missed Nienna's subtle tone of voice. Saark scowled at her, then waved up the slope.

"We trained them. Just like you said. And although I'd like to take all the credit, in fact I *shall* take all the credit, but maybe a little of the credit must go to Grak. He's a bastard, but he knows a thing or two about formations, and training men, and getting the best out of them."

"Stop babbling," said Kell.

"But. We had, er, a couple of problems."

"Such as?"

They watched Grak striding down the slope, dragging with him the unwilling figure of Myrtax. The man was struggling, and his hands were bound before him.

"It wasn't my fault, Kell," said Myrtax, red and sweating.

"Explain."

"He let Sara go," said Saark, voice low. "Killed the guards. Released her into the night."

"Horse shit," snarled Kell, "now the fucking vampires will know what we plan! Why did you do it, Myrtax? Why?"

"I was… I lost control!"

With a snarl, Kell hefted Ilanna and in a sudden stroke cut off Myrtax's head. There came a stunned silence, a pattering of blood, and the body flopped to one side, the head rolling to a stop in crimson snow.

"Why did you do that?" cried Nienna, suddenly, stepping back from Kell, face twisted in horror.

"He was a traitor, with a direct bloody link to the Vampire Warlords," growled the old warrior, and stared hard at Nienna. "I'm sorry. I seem to have *lost control.*" He gave a grim smile, and pointed with a stubby, powerful finger. "Now stop asking damn fool questions and get back up the hill to Grak. We have a lot to do, and because of this offal," he spat, "we need to move fast. Saark!"

"Yes sir!" He snapped to attention, then slumped again. He pulled a pained face. "Did I really call you sir? Shit. Something bad must have got into me."

"And indeed," said Kell, voice low, temper now gone, mind drifting into a mood for battle, "something bad *will* get into you if you don't listen. She's called Ilanna, and she takes no prisoners. We will march east on Jalder. It's not a complex plan. You finished all the weapons? And collars?"

"All done," said Saark. "The smiths worked through many a night. Do you think they'll be effective?"

"If they don't, we'll soon be dead," said Kell. "Let's use what remains of the daylight and close down a few leagues; we can talk and plan tonight. GRAK!"

"Sir?" bellowed the bearded warrior.

"Let's move out."

"Yes, General!" bellowed Grak, and leading three thousand armoured convicts, now bearing swords and shields and helms of polished steel, they descended into the valley churning snow to mud.

Kell glanced down at Myrtax. He was touched by sorrow for a moment. The man had a wife. And little ones. But then Kell's heart went hard. For Myrtax would have sold them all out for his own safety. His cowardice had become his undoing... And a lesson had to be shown to the many fighting men around Kell: that traitors would not be tolerated. Dealt with swiftly. Harshly. Without mercy.

"Goodbye, old friend," he said.

Governor Myrtax continued to bleed into the snow.


The two new Divisions of Falanor men moved in discrete units. The Black Pike Mine men were grim, it had to be said; but not as grim as the Blacklippers, who considered themselves born to die.

Grak and Saark headed one column, and Kell and Dekkar the other. Nienna rode with Saark, and though this irked Kell, he accepted it. She was upset with him for killing Governor Myrtax, and one day, he knew, she would understand his act. Now was not a time to be planning. Now was a time for action.

After half a day's marching, when they stopped by the edge of a young forest to refill waterskins and eat hurried meals of oats and dried biscuits, Kell strode to Saark. "We'll be joined soon by an old friend," he said, and frowned, feeling like an intruder on Saark and Nienna's conversation. Saark grinned up at him, but Nienna's face remained set in a frown.

"What, old friend?" she said.

"Myriam."

"What?" spluttered Saark, spitting watery biscuit down his pink shirt, "I'll kill the bitch, I'll rip off her head and piss down her neck! The bitch! The back-stabbing *whore!*"

"No," said Kell, and squatted down beside his friend. "In the Valleys of the Moon, I was dead, lad. About to be slaughtered by that huge fucker," he gestured to the mighty figure of Dekkar, who was talking quietly with some of the most senior Blacklippers and examining a steel collar. "Myriam had been following me. She came to my rescue. Without her, Saark, Nienna, I would be *dead*."

"She betrayed us, grandfather," said Nienna, softly.

Kell shrugged. "Then she rescued me. She redeemed herself."

"Does that mean you'll cut off her head, like poor Myrtax?"

"*Poor* Myrtax stuck a knife through the ribs of a good soldier. That man had a family, Nienna. Little girls, by all accounts. Little girls who will grow up without their father thanks to the betrayal of Myrtax. And down to his big mouth and runny brain, we might all well be walking into a trap at Jalder. This game has not played out yet."

Nienna shrugged, blushing. "Well, why go, then?"

"Because we must!" snapped Kell, feeling his temper boiling once more. He struggled to control himself. "Listen. I'm sorry. I just… I have so many hundreds of things running through my brain! I am a warrior, not a general. A killer, not a damn tactician. I am out of my world, and trying my damn best. But the only thing I truly know is if we don't make a stand, if we leave the spread of this vampire plague unchecked, then one day, and one day soon, we will all be dead."

Nienna nodded, and Kell rose. He pointed at Saark. "When she arrives, lad, you behave. You hear me?"

"I hear you, Kell. And Kell?"

"Yeah lad?"

"Don't worry. About the battle. We have some good men here. Some tough, hardy, unbreakable warriors, that's for sure."

Kell sighed. "I know we do. The great irony is it's up to the condemned to save the innocent. Still. I'd rather this honour and task had gone to somebody else. I feel uncomfortable wearing a general's helm."

"You'll do grand, Kell. You always do."

Kell snorted, and moved off to talk to Dekkar and Grak.

"Nice to see he's grumpy as ever," laughed Nienna.

Saark smiled, but tension throbbed behind his eyes. Myriam! What a... complication. Now all he needed was a few irate ex-girlfriends to turn up as well, pregnant and waving invoices for food and lodging, and closely followed by their even more irate husbands bearing spears and torture implements.

"Bah," he spat, and rummaged for another biscuit.

Saark watched Myriam arrive at a distance, and she dismounted and walked with Kell for a while, chatting. Saark glanced at her a few times, and Grak slapped him on the back. "She's a looker, eh lad?" he rumbled. "Look at those long legs! Wouldn't mind them wrapped around my back, if you know what I mean."

"Yes, Saark," said Nienna, glancing up at him. "Wouldn't mind them wrapped around your back, eh?"

"You know what?" said Saark, scowling. "I'm starting to hit that point where I've had my fill of women – for a lifetime!"

"Nonsense," boomed Grak, pushing out his chest. "The day I tire of a woman's fine company is the day they bury my casket."

"Not long, then," smiled Nienna, sweetly.

"Little lady," scowled Grak, "that's not a very good thing to say to a man on his way to a battle."

"Well, you talk about women as if they're objects! As if we can't damn well think for ourselves! Let me tell you something, Grak, you bastard, maybe if you'd treated a woman as an equal instead of some cheap slab of meat for the night, *maybe* you'd have a fine warrior wench right here by your side now! As for me, I'm sure

I can get some more equitable talk back there with the rapists and killers. I take my leave."

Nienna stalked off.

"She's a lioness, that one, that's for sure," said Grak, grinning.

"Aye," muttered Saark, weakly.

"I pity the man who ends up with *her!*"

"*Aye,*" mumbled Saark.

"And just think, not only have you to get past the sharpened tip of that acid tongue, but if you put a bloody foot wrong, you get Kell's axe in the back of the head!" He roared with laughter. "Not only would you have to be a masochist, you'd have to be as dumb as that mule back there." He gestured with his thumb.

"She's a donkey."

"Eh? Whatever. As dumb as that donkey back there, is what I said. And by the gods, lad, she's a dumb beast if ever I saw one."

"I suggest you leave Mary out of this," said Saark, tetchily, and moved off to walk alone, throwing occasional glances to Myriam – who was laughing at some ribald jest Kell had made.

"Damn them all," he muttered from his psychological pit.


"Saark?"

Saark half-rose from the fire, but Myriam showed both hands as she crept from the darkness, and he slumped back down with a curse.

"What do you want? I thought you wanted me dead last time we met. I *seem* to remember your certain attempt to drown me."

"I'm sorry."

"It's not good enough, Myriam! You can't just roll back into camp, apologise, and get on with your plans for world domination! What is it this time? Take over our army and conquer the Vampire Warlords that way?"

"I'm sorry. Truly. I was... out of hand. I wasn't thinking clearly. It's just, I love you, Saark. I was thrilled by our union. You understand? We are both vachine, and there's not many left now after the devastation of Silva Valley. We have to stick together, you and me." She shuffled closer, and punched him on the arm.

"Ha. Yes. There is that."

"I'm *sorry*, Saark. All right? I promise I won't do it again."

"Which bit?"

"Which bit would you like me to promise?"

"Er, for a start, you can promise not to kill me."

"Sure. I promise not to kill you." She leant in a bit closer. Saark inhaled the musk of her skin. He groaned, as that familiar feeling washed over him and he tried to focus and tried to keep it clear... but could not. *I am cursed. I am deviant. I have a brain like a child and the lust of a platoon. What am I to do with myself? What is the world to do with any man like me?*

Myriam kissed him.

And in the shadows by the edge of the campfire, Nienna stood bearing two cups of honeyed mead, and cried in the darkness, her tears glowing with the colour of the flames.

It was dawn.

Jalder sat below them, sheathed in an early morning mist which made Kell twinge in panic. If the vampires knew they were coming... if they had Harvesters, and blood-oil magick, and ice-smoke... well, the battle would be over before it had begun.

"Thoughts?" said Grak, lifting the heavy sword he had chosen.

They had sat up long into the night, formulating a basic strategy and trying to consider every eventuality. They sought to draw the vampires out onto the plain before Jalder for an open, pitched battle. There, the heavy formation of soldiers with shields and long spears could possibly counteract the vampires' advantage of speed and agility. If their army was drawn into the city itself, however, they lost all the benefits of armed and armoured units.

Kell was convinced they could do it.

"It is their arrogance," he argued. "They *will* come, they'll drift out from the gates and they *will* fight. The stench of our blood will be an overwhelming factor for them! They must have hunted down most of the humans in Jalder now; that means no fresh meat, no fresh blood! And they need fresh blood like a drowning man needs oxygen. When we roll up, it'll be like a plate of succulent beef stuck under the nose of a starving man! Trust me on this."

"I'm not convinced," growled Dekkar. "I think they'll run and hide when faced with a superior force."

"Whatever happens," said Kell, "we must not be drawn into a running street battle. These bastards are cunning. They'll lay traps in the streets, in back-alleys, leap from the rooftops. No. We must get them out here. This is where the battle must be."

And now, the two Divisions descended from low hills. Jalder lay silent, its ancient dark stones steeped in history and lore, its streets and temples and houses and schools silent, slick with ice and mist, echoing with horror from the recent atrocities.

"So far, so good," said Saark; he looked sick.

Kell glanced at him. "You took your happy leaf?"

"I have decided to give up women!"

Kell snorted in laughter, as the five thousand men, ranged fifty men wide and ranked a hundred men deep, a tight fighting square with shields presented to all sides, moved slowly down from the hills.

"An easy claim to make as we head into battle!"

"I mean it! Do not mock me!"

"Well then. I give up whiskey!" grinned Kell.

"And I give up killing generals!" boomed Grak, slapping Kell on the back, and around him many men laughed, helping to ease the fear which was creeping stealthily through their ranks as fluid as any ice-smoke.

They made the plain below. Behind, on the hilltop, Myriam and Nienna sat with another fifty or so women from the Black Pike Mines who had travelled with the army in order to help feed the soldiers and repair clothing and armour. They also carried bows and knives, for none believed this would end well. They were hardy women, stout and tough, with ice in their eyes and fire in their bellies. They frightened Nienna.

"This is it, then," she said, voice almost a whisper as the soldiers spread out on the plain between the hills and Jalder's main western gates.

"Seemed more romantic, back then," agreed Myriam. "Save Falanor! Raise an army and attack the vampires!" She shivered, suddenly, and pointed. "Look. The gates are opening."

Kell halted the army, and the huge bristling mass of soldiers waited. Shields were held tight, and spears stood proud to attention. A cold wind howled across the plain as the gates squealed on rusting hinges. Snow whipped up in little eddies that danced across the bleak place.

A single figure stepped out. It was a man, tall and lean, his face angular and with the blood-red eyes of the vampire. He walked forward with a curious gait, trailing through the compact snow, his eyes fixed on the large body of fighting men without any fear whatsoever.

He halted. He waited.

Kell stepped forward from behind the wall of shields, and approached the tall vampire. And Kell hissed as recognition bit him. This was Xavanath, Principal of Jalder University. Kell had met him once... when the man had been *human*. He was an honourable and respected academic. Now, blood stained his claws, and strips of flesh trailed from his fangs. And... and he *stank*. He stank like a corpse. He stank of death. He stank of murder. The smell washed over Kell and made him want to vomit, and it was something he had never considered before; the *vampires* were trapped in their own filth, their blood coagulated, their flesh necrotic. The longer they remained vampires, the more they began to *rot*.

"You are the leader?" said Xavanath, with all the haughtiness of any true academic superior.

"By all the gods, lad, you stink like a fucking corpse. But then, excuse my manners. You are one."

A ripple of laughter shifted through the ranks, and Xavanath stared hard at Kell. He made a clicking sound, a show of annoyance...

As if dealing with a disobedient child.

As if dealing with a naughty student.

"Kuradek, the great Vampire Warlord, instructs you

to immediately lay down your weapons and accompany me into the city. He guarantees your safe passage. He would talk the terms of a truce." Xavanath's blood-red eyes ranged across the soldiers, with their new armour and shields and spears. "There is no need for slaughter on this day," he said, his words soft but carrying to every man on the plain. Then he smiled, and it was a sickly smile, like the smile on the face of a man dying from necrotising fasciitis. "Your slaughter, that is."

"Well, lads," boomed Kell, turning and surveying the five thousand hardened men behind him. "He's come out with fighting talk, that's for sure!" Kell launched himself at Xavanath in a sudden blur of speed, Ilanna slamming up and over, and cutting vertical down deep through the vampire's neck. Xavanath stumbled back, claws flashing up but Kell followed, dragging Ilanna out as the vampire hit the snow; the second blow cut the vampire's head from his shoulders, and the corpse slowly melted into a wide, black, oily puddle.

Kell's head came up, and he glared at Jalder – at the silent city. "Come on, you fucking whoresons!" he screamed. "Don't cower in the dark like little girls, come out and face us! Or is Kuradek truly a coward? Is Kuradek the Vampire Pukelord cowering and whimpering in the corner, sucking his own engorged dick and vomiting up his dinner in rank open fear!"

Kell strode back to the ranks and planted Ilanna's haft between his boots. He waited.

Saark sidled forward.

"I don't mean to be pedantic, old horse," said Saark, "but wasn't that a bit… rash?"

"The only rash here is on your crotch!" snapped Kell.

"Shouldn't we have at least *talked* to him?"

"No. We have to piss them off. We have to draw them out for a fight. If we head into the city now, where they are strong, we lose the advantage of armour and steel. We cannot let them hunt us down. We must do battle."

"Why won't they come?"

"They don't like the light," grinned Kell, his face filled with humour but eyes narrowed, evil almost in the gloom. He glanced up at the clouds, heavy, black and thunderous above. "But there's a storm coming. They'll like that. They like the cold, and they like the gloom. Pray for snow, Saark. That'll bring them to us…"

Even as Kell was speaking, the sky overhead darkened perceptibly. Clouds rushed across the sky and thunder rumbled, deep and ominous. Then the gates to Jalder opened fully to reveal – a woman.

It was Sara. Kell's daughter. And she was smiling.

Kell glanced at Saark. "Go back. I'll deal with this bitch."

"What are you going to do?" said Saark, voice trembling.

"What I have to."

"You *can't*," hissed Saark, grabbing Kell's arm. "Nienna's back there! She's watching!"

Kell took hold of Saark's shirt and dragged the dandy in close. His talk was fuelled with fire and spittle. "I *must!*" he hissed into Saark's face, then threw the ex-Sword Champion back, where he stumbled in the snow and glared at Kell.

Kell strode out to meet Sara. Her hair was dark, her eyes shrouded in gloom, her face beautiful. Kell swallowed. He loved her. Loved her so much. Losing her to bitter internal family feuding had been a hard pill to swallow. Something he tried to put right again, and again, and again. But Sara was a stubborn woman. One of the worst. Kell had laughed at the time; "She gets it from me," he would chuckle, but in reality there was no humour about their situation, and it had to be here, and now, all events spiralling down to this battlefield outside Jalder. Between the castoffs of Falanor, and the vampire converted.

"Father," said Sara, striding forward. She glanced down at the beheaded corpse of Xavanath without compassion. When she looked up, there were tears in her eyes, and this confused Kell. Why was a vampire *crying*?

"Go back to your whining master, girl," snapped Kell. "This is no place for women."

"Spoken like the true woman-hating bastard you are!" she hissed, but still tears trickled down her face and it was this contrast which slowed Kell. He knew he had to kill her. And fast. She was deadly, he could sense it, and the world suddenly went slow, honey treacle, and Ilanna was there in his mind like a ghost...

*Talk to her, Kell...*

*Listen to her, Kell...*

*You know you must.*

Sara leapt, suddenly, claws slashing for Kell's throat. He leaned back, but her fist struck his jaw, rocking him – his boot came up into her groin, and his free hand grabbed her hair and with a grunt, he planted her head against the snow. She struggled violently, but Kell lowered Ilanna so the arc of the left butterfly blade pinned her throat to the ground like a stationary, waiting guillotine.

"Go on!" she snarled, legs still kicking. "Do it, *father*, you always wanted to. You were ever the fucking hero. Well kill me. Kill your own daughter, just like you killed your own fucking *wife*!"

Kell's eyes went hard, and with Sara in place, he pulled free his Svian and rammed it down hard into her heart. She started to kick, and struggle, but Ilanna pinned her in place, held her there like a slaughtered lamb.

Her eyes locked to Kell. And she smiled. And blood bubbled from her mouth.

"You remember the south tunnel?" she said, her teeth crimson, her legs still kicking. Her eyes were locked to Kell now, locked in death, and his teeth were gritted, and tears were on her cheeks, and snow was falling, a gentle drift all around them as huge dark clouds unleashed. Kell gave a single nod. "It is open," she said, on a flood of black blood, "and Kuradek lies at the end."

Then she spasmed, and Sara, Kell's daughter, died.

Saark ran up beside Kell, and the huge old warrior stood, slowly, wearily, and began to clean his Svian whilst staring down at his dead daughter. He remembered holding her as a babe, her mewling sounds, and the incredible love and joy he'd felt surge through him. For the first time in his life, here had been something which truly *meant* something to him. A child. A child for whom he would kill... and for whom he would die. But it had gone wrong. Gone so terribly wrong.

"What happened?" snapped Saark.

"She sacrificed herself," said Kell, gently, his voice cracked.

"What do you mean?"

"She knew I had to kill her. She *allowed* me to kill her. Then she gave me information. On how to reach Kuradek."

"How?"

Kell looked at Saark, then, and the dandy saw the old man crying openly. Tears flowed down his cheeks, and into his beard, and Saark stepped in close, supporting the huge warrior, holding him.

"When she was a child, she came riding with me and King Leanoric. She was so proud, sat on the saddle of a little black pony. We'd found a tunnel, dug by Blacklippers for smuggling, way to the south of Jalder." He waved a hand vaguely. "It led deep into the city, coming up in a building near the Palace. Leanoric had it sealed. Sara has opened the tunnel for me. I know this. I *feel* this."

"To get you inside?"

"To get me to Kuradek," growled Kell.

"It could be a trap."

"This is no trap," said Kell. He took a deep breath, and stepped back. His sorrow passed, and he gazed up at the falling snow. He turned and addressed the army. "They're coming, lads! Be ready! And Saark?"

"Yes... Kell?"

"Thanks, lad."

Saark grinned. "Hey. I love you like a brother, but I still don't want to marry you. So don't get any bloody ideas, you old goat."

"Wouldn't dream of it," said Kell, and turned to face the gates.

And they came.

The vampires came...

In a wide, dark flood, pouring from the city of Jalder with screams and hisses and snarls, red eyes crazy with blood lust, many running, some crawling, some leaping in huge bounds, there were men and women and children, there were bakers and smiths, armourers and greengrocers, teachers and students, and all were snarling and spitting, fangs wide, jaws stretched back, and Kell felt the men behind waver as they realised the *scope* of the battle – for these were not just a few vampires, they *poured* from the gates which bottlenecked their charge. But outside the city they spread, spread wide into huge ranks a hundred across. There were thousands. Kell swallowed, hard. His military-trained eye swept the surging, seething ranks as they halted, and assembled, like rabid dogs pulling at an unseen leash. Kell swallowed again.

"There must be ten thousand!" snapped Grak, who had come up close behind him.

"Fuck," said Kell. "You're right." His hands were slippery on Ilanna. He turned swiftly on Grak. "You know what to do," he said.

Grak nodded, and ran back to the men. "Shield wall!" he screamed. "Long spears at the ready."

"Time for us to move, old horse," said Saark, and there was fear in his face, nestled in his eyes like golden tears.

"Yes. I know. I might be hard," said Kell, "but I ain't stupid."

They turned, and as the vampires let out a mammoth screeching roar that filled the plain from end to end with a terrible decaying sound, and charged at the army of convicts and Blacklippers, so Kell and Saark pounded back to their battle lines and the shield walls opened to allow them in. They took up their positions, each taking a long spear and bracing themselves.

"Hold steady now, lads," growled Grak, and his voice carried through the ranks, strong and steady. "Let 'em come to us! Let 'em fall on us!"

The shield wall held.

Fear washed through the men, like a plague.

Snow fell from winter skies, as dark as twilight.

• • • •

The vampires charged. The front ranks slammed the men of Falanor. Vampires hit the wall of shields, which opened at the last second at a scream from Grak the Bastard, and spears slammed through piercing flesh, throats and necks and groins and hearts and eyes, and the first rank of vampires went down thrashing and screaming, spewing blood and black oil vomit, and the spears withdrew and then struck out again, and again, and again, and waves of vampires went down falling over their brethren, but the wall was wide, too wide, and on both sides the vampire charge swung around like enveloping horns, attacking the men of Falanor from three sides now. The Blacklippers and convicts from the Black Pike Mines were strong, grim men, and although they were not soldiers, they held their ground, and they slaughtered the vampires, and the snow was slippery with blood in minutes, in seconds. A breach appeared to Kell's left, a vampire slashing a man's throat and squeezing into their fighting square of armour and spears, and Kell's Svian was out, slamming into the creature's eye and it fell with a gurgle. "Breach!" screamed Kell, as more vampires poured into the hole in the fighting wall. Short swords stabbed out, but the vampires were fast, and strong, their claws sharp, claws like razors. They fought with tooth and claw. They ripped out throats, and ripped off heads using incredible strength. Snarls echoed through the Falanor men. Screams wailed up from the mud, down amongst tramping boots and the fallen. Kell used his Svian, for Ilanna was strapped to his back, too big and hefty for close-quarters combat. He grabbed a short sword from a fallen man as a vampire leapt, an old woman with yellow eyes. He shoved the sword point into her mouth, and down into lungs and heart, ripping it out in a shower of bone and blood which covered him. Snarls sounded in his ear. Kell whirled about, but Saark skewered the vampire through the back, through its heart. Smoke came out of its ears, and it lay whining in the mud until Kell stabbed it through the spine at the base of its skull. A vampire hit Saark from behind, and Kell cut off its arm. Saark stabbed it through the eye, its punctured eyeball emerging from the back of its head. Blood bubbled and splattered across the struggling men. Kell saw their fighting square was faltering, and with sword and Svian, waded into the breach. A vampire hit him in the chest, and he head-butted it, his broken nose flaring in agony, and his Svian cut up into its groin. He felt a warm flush of blood cascade over his fist and he pushed, heaving deeper. Another two vampires leapt, and coolly Kell sliced a throat and stabbed one in the eye, but there were more, always more, and five had widened the gap, ripping off the heads of convicts with dull cracks and twists and splatters. Kell and Saark launched at them, boots slipping, screaming and shouting as snarls filled their ears, but *these* vampires had swords and metal on metal rang, the discordant clash of steel, a song of battle, a symphony of slaughter, and Kell hacked like mad and a blade whistled in front of his eyes making him step back, as a vampire landed on his shoulders and he reached up, dragging it to the floor and kneeling on its throat to stab out its eyes. Then Dekkar was beside him, had fought his way alongside Kell and there was a space around him and Kell saw why. Dekkar's huge flanged mace whirled with a sullen whine, and caved in the brains of a vampire, crushing its head down into a compact bone platter. Another blow killed a second, then a third, then a fourth and fifth and Kell leapt forward, Ilanna sliding free and together Kell and Dekkar reigned bloody slaughter on the vampires, forcing them back through the breach of the shield wall, back onto the snow-swirling plain. They stepped out beyond their comrades, Dekkar's mace whirling and crushing, Ilanna singing now, a high pitched song like the voice of a woman, a beautiful woman, a sorrowful woman, and Kell felt himself tumbling into that pit, into that dark blood pit and he was back, back there, back in that place, back in the fucking Days of Blood *and it feels good it feels right and they fall before the axe before Ilanna before her blades, and none can stand before me, not man, woman, beast, or fucking vampire* and Kell's axe slammed left, and right, twin decapitations, and heads spun up into the sky on geysers of blood. Ilanna cut one vampire in two from crown to crotch, body peeling apart like halved fruit, necrotic bowel sliding free like diseased oil snakes. She slammed left, smashing ribs and leaving a vampire writhing in the mud where Dekkar's mace crushed the woman's face. In the same swing, Ilanna drove right, removing a vampire's legs. The man floundered, walking for a moment on stumps before being consumed by mud and snow and blood. Dekkar and Kell fought on, oblivious now to the widening circle around them, and although the rest of the vampires fought on, attacking with raw screeching ferocity, they were thinning. A child leapt at Dekkar, and he swayed back but could not kill. It landed on the Blacklipper King's chest, fangs snapping forward for his throat. Ilanna caught the child vampire on one blade, tossing it back into the vampire horde. Dekkar flashed Kell a smile, and Kell, covered from head to boot in vampire blood and gore, gave a nod. There was no smile. In his head, he was in a different place. Then...

A cheer went up.

Kell staggered, and righted himself. He started to breathe, and realised he was panting, and the world slid back into focus and it was a grim place. The vampires retreated, and reformed their ranks, and their dead lay scattered in their *hundreds*, a semi-circle around the fighting square of Falanor men.

"Grak!" screamed Kell.

"I'm on it!"

Grak started reorganising the men, and from behind came stretcher-bearers, removing the wounded. Wails and screams echoed over the battlefield. The vampires watched in silence, like kicked dogs licking their wounds. Licking their balls.

Kell, a gore-coated demon, gathered Dekkar, Grak and Saark to him. "You know what must happen now."

Saark took Kell's hand, wrist to wrist in the warrior's grip. "Be swift, my friend."

Kell nodded, and moved back into the ranks, and re-moved his bearskin jerkin, handing it to a huge man named Mallabar. The man carried an axe, an axe that looked similar to Ilanna and which had been forged at the Black Pike Mines.

"Fight well," growled Kell.

"Be lucky," growled Mallabar.

"I don't believe in luck," said Kell, and thumped the large man on the arm. "I make my own."

And then Kell was gone, to the rear of the thousands of fighting men where several horses waited. He rode up the hill, towards the women and Myriam and Nienna.

He heeled his mount to a stop, and Nienna stared up at him, face hard and white, eyes like stones.

"I had to do it," said Kell.

"You could have taken her prisoner," snapped Nienna.

"One day, you will understand."

"Today, I understand."

"And what do you understand, girl?" growled Kell.

"I finally understand your *Legend*," said Nienna.

Cursing, Kell put heels to flank, and the horse sped away over the hill, and circled to the south, away from the battlefield. Snow fell thickly. Kell rode hard, the stallion snorting and protesting at his weight and abuse. Kell slammed along, knowing that time was of the essence. The army was terribly outnumbered, and although they were fighting bravely, they would only last so long against so many enemies...

Kell entered a snowy forest, and before long could hear the trickle of a frozen stream. Hooves cracked ice, and Kell was across and galloping hard once more. Steam rose from the stallion's flanks, and the beast was labouring hard as they reached the next rise and Kell dismounted. He crouched low, eyes scanning the southern wall of Jalder. His mind was sharp with memories of Sara, the little girl on the black pony, and the laughing face of King Leanoric. In older times. Happier times. Times now gone...

There!

Kell moved through the snow, thinking back to Saark, and Grak, and Dekkar, Nienna and Myriam. Even now, Grak should be organising the women, the archers, to advance to the rear of the fighting square. They had been training hard in previous weeks, and Kell was sure they would inflict a terrible damage on the vampires...

Kell grimaced. He hoped they could hold out.

Kell crouched in a ditch by the tunnel entrance, and scowled. There were thick steel bars, thicker than anything he could ever bend. They had been wrenched open, violently outwards, as if by some terrible, powerful blast. Of one thing Kell was sure: whatever slammed through those bars turning them into splayed-out spikes and giving him a secret opening into Jalder – well, whatever it was, it wasn't human.

Kell squinted into the darkness. "Shit," he muttered, and hefted the solid haft of Ilanna.

*I am with you*, she said.

"That's what I'm worried about," muttered the old warrior, and touched one of the bars. It felt warm, and warm air drifted from the tunnel. Would it have rats? Or… something more sinister. Kell shrugged, and grinned. "Fuck it." *Whatever's down here, it can't be more terrible than me!*

"Kell! Wait!"

Kell cursed, and turned slowly, glancing up the ice-covered slope. It was Myriam, on foot and holding her longbow in one hand. Kell's eyes dropped to her waist, where a Widowmaker was sheathed. Kell licked his lips. He'd forgotten Myriam used to carry such a weapon, a multi-loading hand-held crossbow, powered by clock-work and packing an awesome punch. It was with such a weapon Nienna's friend, Kat, had been murdered by one of Myriam's former *colleagues*. The memory was fresh in Kell's mind, like a bright stain of crimson against his soul. In some ways, he blamed Myriam. And that weapon. That *dirty* weapon. That *underhand* weapon. Kell hated it with every drop of acid in his soul.

"What do you want?"

"I've come to help."

"You'll get in my way."

"I *need* to help, Kell! All those men dying back there, and a lot of this shit, it's *my fault*."

"Then go and fight in the battle!" hissed Kell, whirling on her. His eyes were flashing like dark jewels. "You'll get in my way! I can carry no baggage."

"Baggage, is it?" she snapped, and was close to him, and her hand slid down his thigh and he groaned, and the blade pressed against Kell's throat. She grinned into his face. "This baggage got close enough to cut your fucking windpipe out."

"I could kill you, you know," said Kell, quietly.

"I know. But what a thrill, yes? It's damn good to be alive!"

Kell looked into her eyes. He saw madness there. He saw a lot of things there. He wasn't sure he fully understood Myriam. She wasn't just complex, but unpredictable and wild. It was this which attracted him to her. This which made him interested in women again… after so long. *One woman*, he corrected himself. One woman.

Once, in the marshes of the east, Kell had been attacked by a wild *kroug* cat, a stinking shaggy beast which roamed the marshes using secret paths. Kell was in the army at the time, and as his regulation short sword slid through its belly, up into lungs and heart, so their eyes had been inches apart, Kell punched onto his back, the dying, bleeding cat above him, foul breath caressing him, entering him, a kiss from the other side of sanity. Myriam's eyes reminded him of that wild cat. Untameable. Living on the edge, dangerous, truly a creature of chaos.

Kell grinned. "You can move your hand off my leg, now."

"Do you want me to?"

"No," sighed Kell, and relaxed, and Myriam stepped back and sheathed her blade. The Widowmaker hung at her belt, longbow on her back. She was tall and fit and athletic. Kell could still taste her breath on his tongue. "Later," he muttered.

"So I can come?"

"I don't believe I have any choice."

"No, old man. You do not. Lead the way!"

"You've not dragged bloody Nienna along as well, have you? Last bloody thing I need is half my family jumping out at inopportune moments. Makes it a bit difficult to hunt vampires."

"And Vampire Warlords."

"Indeed, yes."

They crouched, watching, then eased into the tunnel. The warm air was disconcerting after the cold of the snow and ice. It was quiet in the tunnel, dry as the desert. Kell touched the walls. "What was this place?"

"An escape tunnel for royalty," said Myriam, and when Kell looked at her, she shrugged. "I think it is, although these things are not really publicised. No?"

"I forgot. You fucked your way into all sorts of academic secrets back in Vor. In your quest to survive."

"That's all any of us want," she whispered.

They crept through long, dusty tunnels, thick with grime and smelling stale, with a tangy scent, like raw abused metal. The stonework was ancient, and carved into baroque curves and flutes which made Kell frown. Why make carvings down here? Where nobody could see and enjoy? He got a sense these tunnels had an ancient story to tell; something he would never discover.

After an hour Kell could smell fresh air. The tunnel abruptly ended at an ancient, iron ladder, leading up to far distant daylight. Snow fell down through the aperture, and Kell welcomed it, breathing deep after the confines of the tunnel. He hated tunnels. Hated enclosed spaces. It reminded him too much of the grave...

"Is it safe?" said Myriam.

Kell laughed.

"What?" she said.

"There's three Vampire Warlords on the loose converting thousands into vampires; there's a battle raging on the snowy plains outside Jalder. And you're worried about a ladder?"

"I just don't want to be entombed," she said, quietly.

"Hmm." Kell started to climb, and the ladder shook, but held under his considerable weight. Myriam followed, and they appeared on the roof of a warehouse, emerging and crouching by a low stone wall. Distantly, they could hear the sounds of battle. The vampires were once again assaulting the lines of the new Falanor army.

"Which way?" said Myriam.

Kell pointed. The Blue Palace reared, and in the diffused light of the gentle snowstorm, looked ugly, gothic, ancient and evil. Kell shivered, as if with premonition. Bad things were going to happen here. Very bad things.

"We can go over the rooftops, to... there." She pointed. Kell nodded. "Come on. This is my area of expertise."

They moved, climbing a sloped roof to a ridgeline and then halting. Kell glanced over the walls which surrounded Jalder. He could see the old garrison, once housing one of King Leanoric's Eagle Divisions; now deserted, the cobbles no doubt stained with the blood of the slain.

Kell glanced back, down the hill towards the river, and saw the tiny square of his old house. His heart skipped a beat. *You've come full circle, old man. You're back where you started. Back in Jalder. Back where the Army of Iron invaded. Where the ice-smoke drifted out and took so many lives, froze so many innocent people to be just cattle for the bloodthirsty vachine...*

He glanced at Myriam. Vachine.

He shook his head.

*We must go*, said Ilanna, her words soft and drifting through his skull. *Kuradek awaits.*

*And you want his blood?*

*I want him to taste the Chaos Halls. To go back to where he belongs...*

Kell stood, but Myriam touched his arm. "Wait. Look."

Kell glanced back to the distant battle. The vampires had pulled back. The men of Falanor, no doubt under instruction from Saark, Grak and Dekkar, were reorganising their lines. But then Kell saw something that made his heart leap into his mouth. By the gates of Jalder were Harvesters... a *line* of Harvesters, and their hands were above their heads, eyes fixed on the Falanor men... and around their feet swirled and billowed a huge globe of pulsing ice-smoke.

"Horse shit," snarled Kell, his eyes bleak. And as his gaze drifted, through the falling snow, as if by instinct he looked to the north and saw the army that appeared through the haze. They marched in unity, black armour gleaming under winter sunlight, black helms and black swords proud and Kell's mouth went terribly dry. He could see they were an albino army, very much like the Army of Iron which had first taken Jalder. And they, combined with the summoning ice-smoke at the feet of the Harvesters before Jalder's gates… well, it did not bode well for the men of Falanor.

"Come on!" hissed Myriam.

"Look," said Kell, voice bleak, tears in his eyes. How could they battle such magick? How could they go to war against such evil – and even hope to win?

"They will fight," snarled Myriam. "They will stand strong! Come! We have our own path. *Come on!*"

They hurried across the rooftops, and Myriam signalled a place to climb to the ground. The streets were deserted, most vampires obviously out on the plain already fighting the Blacklippers and criminals of Falanor. Kell stood on the cobbles, and felt foolish. He felt lost. He felt a cold flood of *desolation* through his soul.

*Kill Kuradek*, said Ilanna. *You must do it! Now!*

Kell grasped the axe, and ground his teeth. They moved to a high iron gate set in a stone wall and grown about with wild white roses. The gate was open. It was almost as if Sara had anticipated their route, and Kell smiled at that.

They moved down paths, and into the cool interior of the palace. High chambers were empty, but showed many signs of destruction. Polished wooden floors were scarred with hundreds of gouges from claws, and furniture lay in smashed heaps, vases shattered, bronze cups twisted and crushed and scattered; everything showed signs of decadence, of destruction, of disrespect.

"I have a bad feeling," said Kell, voice low. He hefted Ilanna, and Myriam cranked her Widowmaker. It gleamed dully in grey light from the high windows.

They moved through endless chambers, empty

feasting halls, long high corridors with stone arches, many lined with statues of past kings and queens.

"Where is the bastard?" snarled Kell, eventually, and they arrived at a sweeping set of stairs. They climbed, wary, weapons at the ready, and when they were halfway up there issued snarls...

The vampires leapt from on high, snarling and spitting, and landed lightly before Kell and Myriam. One was a small, narrow-faced man, slim and wiry, his clothing torn, his hands curled into talons, his eyes blood-red and insane. Kell blinked in recognition, and licked his lips. This was *Ferret*, renowned through Jalder as a fighter, a thief, part of the hazy criminal underworld. He had a *reputation*. He was a Syndicate Man. But they'd got to him... the bastard vampires had got to him...

The second vampire was a girl, maybe eleven or twelve years old. She was slim, with dark skin, her eyes shadowed, her face twisted into the bestial. On her fingers were expensive rings set with huge gems, a contrast to her pale vampire flesh, her yellow, crooked vampire claws...

They attacked, in a blur, Ferret launching at Kell who slammed his axe up in a vertical strike, catching Ferret in the chest and lifting him, carrying him, flinging him back down the marble steps and onto the smooth marble floor beyond, where he skidded on all fours like an animal, and came charging straight back at Kell...

"No!" hissed Myriam, but Rose was on her, spitting and snarling and there was a *slam* as the Widowmaker kicked in Myriam's hand, and Rose was lifted vertically into the air, arms and legs paddling, face snarling, blood and strings of flesh drooling from her fangs and Myriam took a step back, aimed, and sent a second bolt hammering into Rose's face. Rose catapulted backwards, her head caved in, face gone, and lay twitching on the steps. Myriam whirled, saw Ferret leap high but Kell ducked, a swift neat movement, Ilanna slamming overhead and hitting Ferret between the legs, cutting straight through his balls and up to wedge in his abdomen. Both Ferret and Ilanna continued the arc, hitting the steps and wrenching the axe from Kell's grasp. He cursed. Ferret squirmed, claws ringing against Ilanna's blades as he tried to drag the axe free from his trapped body. Kell drew his Svian, and moved to Ferret squirming on the steps. Kell smiled, a warm smile of sympathy, and of empathy, and there was compassion in his eyes. "I'm sorry, lad. Really I am," Kell whispered, voice low, and soothing, and he punched the Svian through Ferret's heart. The small man went still, muscles relaxing, and blood pooled under his body, rolling down the steps in a narrow stream, dripping from one to the next until it finally slowed, and all that could be heard in the huge hall was the tiny *drip drip drip*.

Myriam reclaimed her bolts, and reloaded the Widowmaker. She glanced over at Kell.

"You all right?"

"No."

"It's going to get worse."

"I know. Come on. Let's put this fucking Vampire Warlord out of his misery."

Saark was breathing deep, and he touched tenderly at his ribs where a vampire's claws had sliced him down to the bone. But damn, he thought, they were sharp. And fast! Too fast. Faster than him. Suddenly, his vachine status didn't feel so menacing...

"Come on, Kell, come on, Kell," he muttered, watching the vampires retreat. They were hard, and fast, but the stout men of Falanor were standing their ground well and inflicting punishing casualties on the vampires. Long spears for repelling charges, and short stabbing swords for close-quarters combat were a devastating combination. The battlefield was littered with hundreds, even thousands, of dead vampires. Those that didn't disintegrate into oily puddles or smoke.

"How you doing, lad?" said Grak, slapping Saark on the shoulder. Saark groaned. He felt like one huge bruise.

"I feel like a big fat whore sat on my face."

"I thought you would have enjoyed that?"

Saark eyed Grak. The man was oblivious to sarcasm. "Aye," he said. "I suppose I would, at that. How long before they come back?"

"Not long," snapped Grak, peering out from the shield wall. "Shit. What in the name of the Bone Halls are *those?*"

Saark stared, and his mouth went dry. From beyond the gates of Jalder emerged a line of Harvesters. They wore white robes patterned with gold thread. They were tall, with small black eyes and hissing maws, but it was those long fingers of bone which attracted Saark's attention. He had seen up close what they could do. And they frightened him, deep down in a primal place.

"They're Harvesters," said Saark.

"They look mean. Do they fight?"

"They use magick," whispered Saark, and even as he watched, the ground began to blossom with surges of summoned ice-smoke. "Bad magick. Magick that freezes a man, renders him unable to fight. We must retreat, Grak! We must run!"

"Are you crazy?" snapped Grak. "If we run, if we break ranks, the bastards will slaughter us from behind! They'll pick us off like children!"

Saark saw the white clouds starting to billow. The Harvesters became shrouded in ice-smoke.

"They'll freeze us, here, where we stand!" hissed Saark, eyes crazy. "Then suck out our blood. I've seen it done! I've seen this *before*…"

"Sir!" snapped a soldier, slamming to a halt.

"What is it?" frowned Grak.

"Soldiers, sir. Lots of soldiers."

"Where?"

"To the north."

Grak and Saark ran around the fighting square, and stopped, dumbfounded. There, on a low hill, stood at least five thousand albino warriors. They wore black armour, black helms, carried black swords, and their shields were emblazoned with a brass image.

"Holy Mother," said Grak, and drew his sword. "We cannot fight two armies! On two flanks! We will be crushed!"

"We must flee the battlefield," urged Saark.

"No! We must stand! We must fight!"

"We cannot!"

"Archers!" screamed Grak, and turned, glancing to the square of women with bows strung, arrows stuck in the snow by their boots. He glanced back to the Harvesters. Ice-smoke billowed, and started creeping across the ground towards the men of Falanor… and the vampires stood, smiling, watching, claws flexing, blood-red eyes fixed on their prey…

There came a shouted command from the hilltop, and Saark drew his own sword. His mind was blank, mouth dry, bladder full of piss. They were going to die. Frozen. Cut down. Smashed apart like ripe fruit. "Shit shit shit," he muttered. "HORSE SHIT!"

The Army of Brass, led by General Exkavar, drew their swords with eerie precision, with the rhythm of a single machine... and charged down the hill towards the Falanor army in ghostly, flowing silence...

The room was filled with incredible opulence. From carved cherrywood chests, brass and gold urns, rich oil paintings covering huge expanses of wall, thick velvet curtains and drapes, carpets as thick as a man's fist covering the floors; well, it was a room fit for royalty.

At the centre, before the heavy, oak four-poster bed, stood Kuradek.

Kuradek, the Unholy.

"You came," he said, smoke curling around his smoke lips. And he smiled.

Kell and Myriam, who had been in the act of creeping into the room thinking Kuradek was in some kind of fugue, froze. They had waited a good ten minutes, watching him, but the Vampire Warlord had ceased to move, to breathe, apparently, to *live*. But he was alive. Alive and waiting.

"Well, we didn't want to let you down, boy," growled Kell, pushing his shoulders back and hoisting Ilanna.

*Be calm*, she said.

*Until the... Time.*

Kell stepped forward, and breathed deeply, and stared up at the towering figure of Kuradek, last seen on Helltop after his summoning from the Chaos Halls by General Graal.

"I thought you'd be bigger," said Kell.

"I knew you would come," said Kuradek. "It is written."

"What, prophecies again?" mocked Kell. "Give it a rest, you smoke-filled bastard. Now then." He pointed. "You know what I want. You know why I'm here. If you don't *fuck off* back to the Chaos Halls, I'm going to give you a damn good spanking and send you home with your tail between your legs."

Kuradek chuckled. "You think to challenge me, mortal? How?" He was genuinely amused. It was a genuine question.

"With *this!*" said Kell, shaking Ilanna at the Vampire Warlord.

The huge figure was silent for some time, as if analysing Kell and his weapon. Myriam, by the door, was of no consequence. Forgotten. Worse than forgotten: dismissed.

"One of the Three," said Kuradek, finally. "Well done. Still, *She* will not be enough."

"She is blood-bond," said Kell, gently, head lowered, eyes glittering dark. "And you know what that means."

"Then show me!" snarled Kuradek, and his huge long arms shot out, claws reaching for Kell who stepped back, and Ilanna smashed out left, then right, striking Kuradek's arms away. But incredibly, as they were slapped away, Ilanna's fearsome blades failed to penetrate the smoke flesh. Kuradek stepped forward, stooping, and behind Kell Myriam's Widowmaker hummed with clockwork and a bolt struck Kuradek straight in the face. The bolt was swallowed. Kuradek laughed. He moved with a hiss, so swift Kell was slammed aside, crashing through vases and a finely carved dressing table, turning them to tinder, hitting the wall and then the floor, winded, mind a blank, stunned by the speed and ferocity of Kuradek. Of the Vampire Warlord. "*You think a fucking mortal could fight me?*" he snarled, and held Myriam by the throat, two feet from the ground, her legs dangling, her face turning purple. "*You think to challenge the might of the Vampire Warlords?*" he shrieked, and threw Myriam who disappeared through the doorway, tumbling and rolling, flapping and slapping stone flags until she came to rest in the distance, useless and broken.

Kell climbed to his feet. He felt like an old man.

He stared at the smoke fangs. He stared hard at those blood-red eyes, glowing like coals.

He tried to summon Ilanna, but she was silent.

He tried to summon the rage from the Days of Blood... but it would not come. It had gone, deserted him, left him here like a lamb to die. To be sucked dry. To be slaughtered...

Kell stood his ground, pushing against the terrible fear which invaded him. "I have killed your kind *before!*" he growled, but his voice came out like a mewl from a frightened kitten.

"Not like me," said Kuradek, and there was a flash, a blur, and he was beside Kell, towering over Kell, looking down with those red eyes and Kell was frozen, could do nothing, and he realised in horror he was *charmed* by the vampire. Charmed, using blood-oil magick, a dirty back-hand trick. Kell snarled, but it was as if he was manacled in prison irons.

Kuradek leaned forward. His eyes were an inch from Kell's.

"You see. I have you in my power. Such an easy thing. Such a simple thing to disable the great Kell. Kell, the Legend?" Kuradek laughed, a low mocking sound, and smoked curled from his mouth, and entered Kell's lungs, and made him choke.

"I would say your time is done."

Kuradek's head lowered, and his fangs sank into Kell's throat...

## CHAPTER 14
### *The Days of Blood*

Kell stood in the razed city. Around him, corpses burned. He was naked. He was smeared with the blood of a thousand people. Men. Women. Children. He laughed, and there was insanity in his mind, in his heart, in his soul. These were the Days of Blood. This was what Ilanna promised. *Do it*, said the voice, only this voice was not human, it was the voice of the axe, the primal voice of Ilanna – one of the Three. *We must be blood-bond. For the future. For survival.* Kell strode through the streets. When people ran before him, Ilanna cut out, chopping off legs and arms, lopping off heads. Bodies toppled at his feet, dead before they hit the ground. Gore splattered his legs. His toes squelched through pulped flesh. The gutters ran red. The cobbles were slick. Kell walked, and walked, and walked, and it took an eternity, and he wondered if sometimes he were dreaming, or in Hell, in the Bone Halls, in the Chaos Halls. He did not need food, or water, he wanted for nothing. Only constant slaughter. Only constant rampage. And the rage in him was terrible, all-consuming, and he was not human, he was not mortal. His blood flowed like lava. He had become an infection. A plague. A creature created to...

Fight.

The Impure.

*To kill the impure, you must become impure. To eradicate evil, you must absorb the essence of evil. You must dance with the devils, Kell, you must be consumed by the Days of Blood, for only that way can you truly understand your greatest enemies, only that way can you become the nemesis of clockwork, of vampire, of wolf, of dragon, of all those other dark dreams which will come to plague Falanor during the following years...*

*It is written, Kell.*

*In the Oak Testament.*

*It is written you will be a killer, and a saviour.*

*It is written you must be impure, and pure.*

*It is written you shall never have redemption.*

*It is written you shall be a slave for all eternity.*

Kell nodded, and walked, and accepted his fate, and reached the house and she was there, his sweet wife Ehlana, slim and naked, lying on the bed, and she glanced up and fear infused her eyes, fear and confusion and horror, and then she recognised him, and started to rise –

"Kell?"

"Shh," he said, and Ilanna slammed down, but the blades did not smash her apart as they would normal flesh and blood and bone, they cut into her spirit, and with a cry, a simple "No!" she was drawn from her body which shrivelled and died, sucked free of fluid, sucked free of fire, sucked free of her terrible dark *magick* and Ehlana, Kell's wife, Kell's love, was taken and *absorbed* into the axe. She melded with steel. Wasn't that the spell she cast? To make Kell immortal. To make Kell a Legend. She had seen the visions. She had seen the following darkness. And they needed a hero. They needed some-body who could fight the demons. But her pact with the *Grellorogan gods* needed *more*. They needed life. They needed blood. They need love. They needed *magick*. Her dark blood. Her dark magick. And so Ehlana, reading the prophecies, casting her spells, creating the ultimate killer, the ultimate champion for King Searlan of Falanor... so she gave her own life, and love, and magick.

Ehlana became a prisoner of Ilanna.

Ehlana became Ilanna.

Kell's eyes flared open, and he understood, and he re-membered, and bitterness flooded him and hatred flooded him, and he wanted to scream *Why, Ehlana? Why did you do this to us? I never asked for it? I never fucking asked for any of it!* But Kuradek's fangs were in his neck, biting, sucking his blood in great thirsty gulps and Kell laughed, and breathed deep, and drew his Svian and rammed it hard into Kuradek's groin. Kuradek squealed high and long like a stuck pig and Kell reached up, grasped the smoky skin of Kuradek's head, and dragged the Vampire Warlord's fangs from his flesh with trem-bling, smoke-stained fingers...

With a heave, Kell sent Kuradek hurtling across the room. He hit the bed, flipped over it, smashed through two of the supports with crashes of splintering timber. Kell rubbed his neck, where blood flowed from twin vampire bites, and the Days of Blood welled free and wild in his mind.

"*I am a pawn no more!*" he growled bitterly and found Ilanna and lifted her. She was cold in his hands. Cold as ice. Her shaft and blades glowed with a deep sable black – not a *real* black, not steel or iron, not burned flesh or the night sky. This black was a *portal*. This black was an absence. An absence of *matter*. A pathway.

"Welcome back, husband," said Ilanna, her voice a soft breeze through his mind.

"Why did you do it? I loved you. I worshipped you. And you left me, sitting here in bitterness, self-loathing, believing I destroyed you in a fit of bloody madness! When all the time it was your own dark magick which brought about your death."

"I am not dead, husband," said Ilanna, "I live on, in this axe, in this symbol of strength and freedom, and together we will send back the Vampire Warlords! Together, we will show them what the Legend can do…"

"I do not want this!" screamed Kell, falling to his knees.

"Want is immaterial," said Ilanna.

Kuradek had gained his feet, towering over Kell, and the Vampire Warlord leapt for the old warrior, huge claws closing around him, lifting him into the air.

"I will tear you apart like a worm!" screamed the Warlord.

Kell looked deep into those blood-red eyes. He smiled, showing his bloody teeth. "My name is Kell," he said, pulling free his arms with ease and lifting Ilanna high above his head. Her blades were a dull black hole in reality. "And it's time you went home, laddie."

Ilanna struck Kuradek between the smoke-filled eyes, splitting the Vampire Warlord's head in two. Smoke poured out, a thick black acrid smoke which filled the room in an instant. Kell stood very still as before him Kuradek stood, top half split wide open and wavering like petals on a stalk in a heavy wind. The world seemed to slow, and *groan*, and a smoke-filled corridor opened up behind Kuradek. It stretched away for a million years. Kell lowered Ilanna to the ground with a *thunk*, and cracked his knuckles, and stared down the pathway, and waited. The corridor led to a chamber of infinity, endlessly black, and from the sky fell corpses, tumbling down down down through nothingness and unto nothingness. Kuradek's glowing red eyes were fixed on Kell.

"What have you done?" snarled the Vampire Warlord, both halves of his severed, smoke-filled mouth working together from two feet apart. "What have you done to me?"

"I've sent you back," said Kell, almost gently, and there came a distant clanking of chains, and something dark and metal, like a huge hook, came easing along the million year corridor of smoke. Clockwork claws fashioned from old iron, pitted and rusted and huge and unbreakable, closed methodically around Kuradek the Unholy. They crushed him with ratchet clicks. Somewhere, there came a heavy, sombre ticking sound. Gears clicked and stepped. Kuradek screamed, and in the blink of an eye was dragged into acceleration down the corridor. Hot air rushed in, and the portal to the Chaos Halls imploded, all smoke being sucked to a tiny black dot, which flashed out with an almost imperceptible *tick*.

Kell breathed, and shivered, and rubbed at the bite marks in his neck. He fell to his knees, then used Ilanna to lever himself up once more. "What a bastard," he muttered, legs shaking, and hurried out into the corridor. Myriam was starting to come round, and the first thing her dazed eyes fixed on was Kell's neck.

"He bit you?"

"Don't worry."

"He bit you! You'll turn, you'll see…"

"He's gone," said Kell. "I can't turn into nothing."

"You killed him?"

"He cannot be killed," said Kell, and hefted Ilanna. "The Vampire Warlords are immortal. But I sent him back to the Chaos Halls. Back to the Keepers. I think *they* were pissed at his escape. I think *they* had a special present waiting for him."

"What about the rest of the vampires?"

"Let's go see."

Kell and Myriam rushed up steps and onto ice-rimed battlements. A cold wind snapped along, slapping them. Below, on the plain, they watched in stunned silence.

The men of Falanor stood in a tight unit behind their shields, spear points twinkling in the ghost light. By the gates stood a massive horde of vampires, waiting behind ten Harvesters engulfed in wreathes of ice-smoke. The ice-smoke was moving towards the Falanor men, creeping eerily across the churned snow, but at the same time an army of albino soldiers charged, in silence, like a dream, and veered at the last moment from the men of Falanor, slamming into the ranks of Harvesters and vampires, crushing the front lines which went down in a scything sea of descending swords...

"I don't understand," said Myriam.

The Army of Brass clove through the Harvesters and vampires, who started to scream and flee. Thousands of albino soldiers slammed through Kuradek's slaves, killing them mercilessly as they turned to run, swords cutting off heads, ramming through hearts. Within minutes, it became a slaughter.

Kell sat back on the battlements, pressing fingers to his punctured neck.

"What happened?" snapped Myriam. "I thought they would turn back? When you killed Kuradek?"

"But I *did not* kill him," explained Kell, patiently. He chuckled, and rested his head wearily against the wall. He closed his eyes. "The Vampire Warlords are immortal. Once they turn you into vampire kind, you stay that way. They are a parasite on all life. That's why they were summoned to the Chaos Halls. That's why the dark gods banished them there."

"What about you?" snapped Myriam. "Should I get my knife ready?"

"Me?" Kell opened his eyes. He laughed again, and shrugged. "Hell, woman, you do what you like. It would appear I am blessed. Dark magick. Or something. From back during the Days of Blood. It would appear I was fucking *made* to fight these creatures. Can you believe that?" He laughed again. A weary laugh. The laugh of the defeated. A laugh of desolation. "Only they did it thirty years too soon. Bloody prophecies. Should have them tattooed on my arse, for all the use they are."

"Prophecies? Blessed? What the hell are you talking about? Who *told you* all this?"

Kell grinned at Myriam. "The wife. Now be a good girl, go and fetch Saark and Grak, will you? They'll be wondering what happened."

"And I suppose you can tell me why the albinos turned on the vampires?"

Kell shrugged. "No idea, lass. I'm as surprised as you. But I do know one thing."

"What's that?"

"Our army is getting bigger," he said, eyes twinkling.


Kell faced General Exkavar from the Army of Brass, and General Zagreel from the Army of Silver. Both men were tall, thin, with long white hair, pale waxen flesh and the crimson eyes of the albino, although Kell knew after his adventures under the Black Pike Mountains, that these warriors were nothing as simple as humans with a difference in pigmentation. These were the White Warriors. These were another *race* entirely.

"Please, explain to me what just happened, gentlemen," said Kell, seating himself at the huge feasting table and placing his hands before him. The two generals removed helms and placed them on the scarred wood. The room had been tidied of destruction, and only these gouge marks from the claws of the vampires were evidence of recent vampire occupancy.

General Exkavar fixed Kell with a hard look. "I thought that was self-evident. We stopped your men from being slaughtered. We killed the Harvesters who brought us through the mountains, and turned on the damn vampires." He gave a glance at Saark, and curled his lip. "We will serve no more. Not vachine, not vampire, not Harvester. It is time the White Warriors took a stand."

"Why help us?" said Kell, softly.

"We share common enemies. For many years the vachine, and indeed vampires, have preyed on both our races. We should stand together. We should rid Falanor of this vermin."

"And then?" said Kell, eyes twinkling. He had twenty men just outside the chamber, swords drawn, waiting for his nod. If Exkavar or Zagreel proved to be a threat, then Kell would exterminate them, and then their men, when they slept that night. Kell could not risk another enemy rioting through his homeland.

"We will leave Falanor, head back to our lair under the Black Pike Mountains."

"Why come out in the first place?"

"We have come for our Army. The Army of Iron. They are currently *slaves* in Vor, under the command of Meshwar, the Violent. There is no way to get a message to them. So we decided a show of *strength* was the order of the day."

Kell nodded, and placed his chin on his fist. He stared at the two generals, and then over to Saark, and Myriam, Grak and Dekkar. All were now bathed, well-groomed, and fed.

After the battle on the previous day, the routing of the Harvesters and the vampires, the Army of Brass had spent the rest of the day hunting down vampires through the streets of Jalder – and putting them out of their misery. Then, slowly, the people had begun to emerge, from sewers and factories, from attics and cellars and hidden tunnels, from warehouses and cottages and holes in walls. They had assembled before the Palace, perhaps two thousand in all, a sorry mess of stamped-on humanity. Kell set Grak to feeding and watering these refugees; to finding them clothes and medicines. Grak happily organised the convicts from the Black Pike Mines, and the men had gone about their work. Only the Black-lippers, sullen and dark in mood, stayed outside the city gates. They said it would be hypocrisy to enter.

With so much organising to do, Kell and Nienna had seen little of each other. Myriam had tended the girl, and reported to Kell that she was angry and hurt about the death of her mother. Myriam tried to explain there was no reversion from the vampire; and that Kell had done her a great service. But Nienna had descended into a world of sullen brooding. Kell shrugged it off. He had more important matters to worry about than a sulking child.

"So you head for Vor," said Kell, and stroked his beard. "You are confident you can wipe out the menace of Meshwar? The Vampire Warlords are terrible indeed. Creatures of the Chaos Halls."

"We have magickers," said Exkavar. "If we cannot kill him, we can open the portal. Once open, believe me, the Keepers will come for Meshwar. They have failed in their duties, you see? They want the Vampire Warlords back as much as we want them gone."

Kell nodded. "I suggest, then, that we head for Port of Gollothrim," he said. "We must cleanse that place of vampires as well, find Bhu Vanesh, and send him home."

"He is the strongest of the three," said Myriam, looking up from a goblet of wine. "The strongest, Kell."

Kell nodded. "Still. We must fight on. Are you with me?"

"I am," rumbled Grak the Bastard, and thumped the table. "By the gods, I am."

"My people will see this through to the end," said Dekkar, and gave Kell a nod. "We are your warriors in this battle, now. We will stand by you. We will fight by you. And we will die by your side, if that is what it takes."

"Good," said Kell, and glanced back at the two albino generals. "How long will you stay?"

"We will head south at dawn. Do not worry yourself, Kell; we have no wish to rule Falanor lands. Once we have our men, and have disposed of Meshwar, we will be gone."

"Have you made an enemy of the Harvesters?" asked Kell.

"Yes. But that is a battle for another day. We have learnt much from their mastery. Now, it is time for the slaves to throw off their shackles, rise up, and smite their masters." Exkavar gave a cruel, brittle smile. "Too long have their injustices been served on us."

Again, Kell nodded, and the two generals stood, donning helms. Kell stood, and reached out to shake their hands. Both generals stared at him, but did not extend their own.

"I am sure we will meet again. One day soon," said Zagreel, his crimson eyes shining.

"Indeed," said Kell, with an easy smile, and watched the two generals leave the hall. He glanced at Grak. "I want triple guards, on every building, every gate, every fucking *latrine*, until they are gone. You understand?"

"Yes, Kell. Can you tell me something?"

"Ask."

"Tell me again why they helped us?"

"Because we have a common enemy. But what worries me, my murdering friend, is what happens when all our common enemies are *dead*. In my experience, many freed slaves are full of bitterness and hate. And that never leads to a pleasant aftermath."

"What about the men? How long do we rest?"

"Two days. They've earned it. Then we march on Gollothrim."

Kell was eating a shank of pork, juice running through his beard, as Saark tottered across the tiles before him. "Oh, such luxury again!" he beamed, and then frowned down at Kell. "What is this? A pig eating a pig?"

"I see you found the perfume again," growled Kell, dropping the shank to his plate and wiping his hands on a cloth.

"You can smell it? Does it smell fine?"

"Smell it, lad? I've smelt *sewers* with more sexual allure."

Saark moved over and seated himself nimbly at the table. Once again, he had managed to find crimson leggings, a pink silk shirt, and some heavy silver beads which were draped about his throat like the finest pearls. Saark leaned forward, and cut a small slice of cheese with his knife. "I say, Kell, one day I really should teach you to eat with a knife and fork."

"And I should teach you some manners."

"Yes, but, I mean, look at your lunch! It looks like… well, like an abortion!"

"Not really the sort of talk I want to hear at the dinner table."

"Well, it has to be better than Grak's boring drivel. Swords and helmets, the feeding of the refugees, talk of repairing the city. Gods, the vampires have only just left and they're talking about fucking *building*. Those who've survived should be out in the damn streets drinking and whoring, dancing and humping! I should say an orgy of some kind is called for."

"They've just survived a terrible ordeal," said Kell through gritted teeth.

"Exactly," smiled Saark, nibbling on his cheese.

Kell stared at him. "Listen lad, don't be thinking you're wearing that *shit* when we march on Gollothrim! Last thing we need is your early warning stench giving away any element of surprise."

"Hah! Really!"

Saark reclined, stretching, and his face was a platter of rapture. "I could always stay here, Kell. Oversee the rebuilding of Jalder. Insinuate myself into the nobility structure here; I'm sure they will have room for one with such refined etiquette as myself."

"You're coming with us, lad," snapped Kell, and continued to eat, gnawing at the joint.

Footsteps echoed, and Saark spun around. "Ah! And here is the most *beautiful* Nienna."

Kell watched the grand entrance, and he licked grease from his lips, and considered his words with care. She wore a long silk gown, silk slippers, and her lips were rouged in the manner he'd seen women employ at Royal Court. And she wore perfume almost as nauseating as Saark's.

"A couple of fine dandies you make together," he growled, at last, and grasped his tankard, drinking his ale and spilling a goodly amount down his jerkin and on the table.

"We're not… together," said Nienna, frowning, then smiled.

Kell placed his tankard down with care, and stared hard at Nienna. Then over to Saark, who grinned, and held his palms outwards in a flourish, shrugging his shoulders. "We're not," he said.

Kell returned to his meal. "Good," he said. And as Saark and Nienna, whispering and giggling, moved towards the arched opening leading from the hall, Kell snapped, "Go pack your stuff. We'll be leaving early in the morning."

"So, just one last night of civility?" said Saark.

Kell glared at him. "Looks that way," he muttered.

Nienna watched Saark undressing. He was a little drunk, but she didn't mind, because she was too. She slid deeper down under the covers luxuriating in their softness, and the firmness of the bed. She wasn't used to such opulent surroundings.

"You still want me, Little One?" whispered Saark, removing his trews in the shadows. Nienna felt a thrill course through her veins. It was like dying. No, it was like being *born*. Born into a different world, at least.

"I want you," she said, husky.

He came to her, sliding under the covers, his flesh warm, soft, and he touched her and she writhed, responding to the delicate caress of his fingers. He was gentle. He was caring. He was skilful. He was kind. He kissed her, and they lay like that for a while, lips connected, tongues darting, his hand between her legs teasing her.

Nienna pulled back.

"Do you love me, Saark?"

"I love you," he said, and the words slid from his mouth like honey from a spoon.

"I bet you say that to all the women," she said.

"Only the ones I love," he said. "And I love you."

"Did you say it to Myriam?"

"No."

"I bet you did."

"I did not. I loved another woman – she was betrothed to another. She was Queen Alloria. She betrayed me. She was Graal's puppet on a string. I felt like a fool, and so the words do not come easy."

"So... you mean it?"

"I mean it, angel."

Nienna drew her to him, and as he entered her she gasped. Her hands raked his hair, cut trenches down his back, grasped his buttocks and pulled him deeper, with lust, with urgency, with open raw desire. "Fuck me, Saark," she whispered in his ear, biting the lobe and feeling him work harder. He liked that, she'd discovered.

"I'm trying," he muttered, biting her neck and then – withdrawing, at the last moment. His brass fangs gleamed under stray strands of moonlight. Saark hissed, but Nienna was too lost to the moment to recognise the danger. Saark shook his head. *How long can I live between worlds? How long can I suppress my vachine instincts?*

*Blood. Blood-oil.*

*The desires increase…*

"How long will you love me?" said Nienna.

"Until the day I die," crooned Saark, and the silk under his hands felt fine, the woman beneath his flesh felt succulent, and his perfume filled both their nostrils with its charm and sophistication.

"That might not take very long," came a low, cold voice, and a figure was there and it filled the room, filled the sky and Saark squawked and scrambled from Nienna, falling onto his back and sliding from the silk scattered bed with a *thump.*

"Kell!" he breathed.

Kell filled the space. He was vast, a giant, a titan, a god. His face was bathed in shadows, gloom was his mistress, darkness his master, and Kell stood with Ilanna lifted against his chest and Saark felt fear, knew fear, for this was it, the end, his death come so soon and for what? For the simple pleasure of a girl? *There are worse ways to die… Shit!* The axe glinted, dull in the darkness, moonlight tracing tiny chips in the black iron butterfly blades. Saark could not take his eyes from that axe. It was bigger than Kell. Mightier. It filled the universe. It drank in stars. It *was a pathway to the Chaos Halls and now, NOW Saark understood and he felt the wonder and vast dread and cold hydrogen horror of the weapon, more ancient than time, an eternal devourer in the dark. That was how Kell*

*fought the Vampire Warlords. That was how Kell took on
cankers, and vachine, and vampires, and gods. For Ilanna* was
not just metal, not even demon-possessed metal. She
was a symbol. She was a pathway. She was dark magick
made whole. She was Chaos, pure Chaos, in the form
of a weapon wielded by Man. And she controlled Kell.
Saark felt it. *Knew* it. Here, and now, Kell was not his
own person and he always said it was the whiskey
which forced him into unreasonable violence. However.
It had never been the liquor. No. It had been the *axe*.

"Damn you, do it!" screamed Saark, hands clawing
at the thick Ionian rugs. "Get it over with! Cut my
bloody head off!"

There came a pause, a slice through the realms of
time, and the world ran slow on its shifting axis. Then
Kell leant forward, and his face was a writhing mass of
war, contorting, a raging inner battle. Through gritted
teeth, he growled, long and low and slow, "You've
earned it, by all the demon shit that roams the planet,
you've earned it, Saark."

"I'm sorry! Sorry, Kell! I love her!"

"He does, grandfather." Nienna was standing, naked,
skin pure and soft and white, her eyes glowing as if
filled with molten love. She moved to Saark, stood before him protectively, like some faerie creature from
dreams come to defend the weak and downtrodden. "I
will not let you do this."

Kell stood quivering, torn, huge muscles tense,
Ilanna lifted high and ready for combat and slaughter.
Then, slowly, he slumped back, seemed to fold in on
himself until he was simply a mortal once more. A simple old soldier with a bad back, arthritis, and in need of
a simple life.

"I'm sorry, Nienna," he said.

Nienna smiled, and reached out, and touched his arm.

"I'm sorry for being the village idiot. I'm sorry for being stubborn, and rude, and brash, for my bad temper and threats and worst of all, for treating you like a child. You are a woman. I can see that now."

"Yes," she said, voice a lilting rose. "I am a woman."

"Do you know how hard it was?" said Kell, and tears were running down his cheeks, through his beard, making it glisten. "To kill Sara? My own flesh and blood? My own little girl? Shit." Kell shook his head, half turned, then turned back. He glared down at Saark. "You're one lucky bastard's bastard," he said.

"You think I don't realise that?" snapped Saark.

Kell waved Ilanna casually at the popinjay. "Get some pants on. Walk with me."

"But it's freezing out there! It's the bloody middle of... the... fine, fine, I can do that, it's not a problem, if that's what you want, that's what we'll do."

Kell walked fast down the huge hallway. High above, dark towers and pillars glistened. Huge archways and the carvings of ancient demons were hidden in shadows. Saark slapped along, bare-foot beside the huge old warrior. He eyed the axe nervously, not totally convinced this wasn't some secret ruse to get him alone and decapitate him.

Kell halted. Saark stopped, also, but not too close. Never too close.

"You look like pampered donkey shit," said Kell, gesturing Saark's bedraggled appearance, silk shirt hanging out his trews, feet bare, toenails blackened from far too many weeks marching the mountains.

Saark smoothed back his long dark curls. "Hey. We've had a rough few weeks, haven't we, Kell?"

"So we have, lad. So we have."

There came a long pause.

"Is there a purpose to this little chat, Kell? I'm freezing my balls into orange pips and there's a good warm bed, er, waiting for me." He stopped. Kell was glaring. "Er..."

Kell waved his paw. "Don't fret. It's something I'm going to have to get used to. Isn't it?"

"I, er, I suppose so."

"You'll look after her, Saark, won't you?" Kell had turned away, but Saark read the anguish in his words. Here, the mighty Kell was at last relinquishing hold on his precious granddaughter. And, even more frightening, he was passing the mantle to Saark.

Now, it would be Saark's responsibility.

He shivered.

"Of course I will, old horse. I'd kill for her, and I'd die for her."

"I can ask no more than that."

Saark folded his arms, and smiled. A little of his cocky arrogance returned. "Thanks for being so understanding. At last, Kell, you've allowed the girl to flower into a woman! She deserves that, after everything she's been through. She deserves her own life, her own freedom, not your iron shackles."

Kell eyed Saark up and down, nodding. "Aye. I suppose she does. But just be warned." He pointed with one large, stubby finger. "If you disrespect her in any way, I can still come looking. I'll cut your fucking head down the middle with the same thought I'd give to squashing an ant."

Saark shivered and frowned. "Yes. Yes, I know that, old man. I'd not forgotten all our previous... discussions!"

• • • •

Kell sat on his own bed. The night was dark and cool outside the palace windows. Distantly, he could hear song, and smell woodsmoke. He sat, and thought about the past, about the things he had done, and brooded, long and hard. It was all wrong. All bad. This wasn't the way his life was supposed to turn out. Not the way it was supposed to be.

*I'm here for you, Kell.*

*Go to Hell! Ha, I forgot, you're already there! And by your own treacherous dark magick hand, I might add.*

*I was only trying to do what was right. What was best for Falanor; for the people. For the innocent and weak!*

*Damn the people*, snarled Kell internally. And he felt Ilanna, felt *Ehlana*, shrink back from his rage. It was pure and bright, like a new born star in his soul. *What about us? What about the life we had? The life we should have had? You condemned us, woman! And you condemned me to a life of violence, and here you are, filling the axe with black sorcery in order to help others. WHAT ABOUT US? US! YOU DESTROYED US!*

Ehlana faded, and Kell sat there staring at the weapon. Well, they were blood-bond now. But more. Ilanna contained the soul of the woman he loved, and who, in reality, he would always love...

Until the end of time.

Until the stars flickered out.

Kell curled up on the bed, and slept alone.


"Kell?"

Kell groaned, and sat up. "What is it?"

"It's me. Myriam."

"Ahh. Yes. I could never forget you! That poison sluicing round my veins makes my joints feel on fire *all the fucking time.* So nice of you to call in. Just what I need in the middle of the night. A chat with a riddling mad woman."

"Mad? Maybe I am," said Myriam, and moved in close, sat on the end of the bed, and Kell found himself lost for words. He stared at her, as she whispered, "I am here for you."

Eventually, he said, "What do you mean?"

"You know what I mean. I don't believe you're that fucking naive."

"Myriam, there's something you should know..."

She laughed, and took hold of Kell. She was amazingly strong. She had always been strong, but with her added vachine clockwork she was nearly a match for the mighty warrior...

"Don't tell me. You're married?"

Kell pulled a face. "Well..."

"Shh," she said, and placed a finger against his lips. Then she kissed him, and Kell sat there for a while and let her, and slowly, like a behemoth rising from a slick mud pit, Kell started to respond. They kissed, and Kell placed his large hands on Myriam's shoulders, and pushed her away.

"I cannot do this," he said.

"I think you should," she said.

"No."

"What, I didn't realise you were *that old?*" she mocked. "Old, yes, but not past it."

"I'm not," he said.

"Are your teeth still your own? Do you piss in a bag attached to your leg? Is that really your own hair and beard, or something pasted in place like they do in the decadent theatres of Vor?" She smiled sweetly. "I thought you were a hero. A *Legend*, damn it!"

"Curse all women with sharp tongues," said Kell.

"There's a simple way to make me quiet," she smiled.

Myriam took a step back, and quickly undressed. She stood naked before him, hips swaying a little, her eyes wide and a friendly smile painted on her face.

"Come to me," she said, and distant, like the steady lapping rhythm of the ocean, there came a muffled tick *tick tick tick tick*…

In silence, Kell complied.

The new Falanor army marched in two discrete columns. One column was led by Dekkar, a grim host of Blacklippers in three marching lines. They had lost four hundred men at Jalder to the vampire hordes, and this had made them yet more determined, more hate-filled, and resolute to expel the enemy from their world. The second column, the criminals from Black Pike Mines, had lost nearly six hundred men during the fighting – or at least, six hundred who would never fight again. This now gave Kell a fighting force of just over four thousand. Not exactly the Eagle Divisions of King Leanoric! But at least the Army of Brass and Army of Silver had gone on ahead, to Vor, leaving them a clear path, now, a clear goal: Port of Gollothrim. Where Bhu Vanesh ruled.

Kell marched with a soldier's stride, Ilanna slung across his back, breathing deeply and occasionally whistling an old battle tune, or singing a ribald verse from a battle hymn. He soon had many of the men smiling, and some even joined in, their rolling song echoing out across the valleys and frozen woodlands of Falanor.

Saark sidled up to him. "You're in good form," he said, glancing up at Kell with narrowed eyes. Suspicion riddled his face like a parasite.

Kell stared at the dandy. "What the *fuck* are you wearing now?"

"It's the height of fashion in Vor, I'll have you know."

"Vor is overrun by vampires!"

"Well, I'm pretty sure they'll have better sartorial elegance than *our* army. If nothing else, the vachine have ego. It's what separates men from beasts, you know? Anyway, I was wondering why you were in such a good mood. I thought you were going to chop my head from my shoulders in the night."

"There's still time," said Kell, gruffly.

"Don't be like that, Kell. We're marching to near-certain death! The gods only know how many vampires Meshwar and Bhu Vanesh have turned. The whole damn country might be crawling with the fanged bastards. The last thing we should be doing is squabbling amongst ourselves like buzzards over a corpse scrap."

"Well, they won't miss you, with an orange shirt like that. What a target! Every archer in bloody Falanor will be sighting on you. I thought they taught soldiers to be discreet. You were in the army, Saark, you should know these things."

"Yes, but I was not a common low-life low-ranker, was I? I was bloody commissioned! I was an officer, I was."

Kell shrugged. "Well, a soldier should bloody well know better! Just make sure you stand a good way from me during battle; I don't want to take an arrow destined for your peacock arse."

"You never answered my question, Kell."

"Which was?"

"You're a happy beaver. Why's that? It's not like you to be upbeat. In my experience, you have the happy and joyous nature of a widow mourning five dead sons."

"I'm marching into battle, aren't I?" said Kell, grinning sideways at Saark. "You know how it is. Prospect of a few heads on spikes, a few splintered spines. Brings me out in goosebumps of anticipation, I can tell you, lad. You know me! I'm Kell, nothing gets me hard like a good fight."

"No." Saark shook out his long, oiled curls. "There's something else."

"I'm also looking forward to carving my name on Graal's arse with Ilanna. That's something been a long time coming. After all, it's no good sending these bastard Warlords back to the Chaos Halls if Graal just goes and summons 'em again. Eh, lad?"

"You're quite right. But you forget, Kell, I am a creature of the night. Or more precisely, a creature who hunts in ladies' bedrooms, dances on mosaic ballroom floors, caresses flesh in sculpted flowery gardens, and generally behaves in a way fitting for any would-be member of nobility. You, Kell, you know weapons and warfare. Whereas *I*, well old man, *I* know sex, and you've had you some."

"Eh?"

"You've been playing hide the pickle, haven't you, old man? Well, you cunning, raunchy little squirrel, you. You secret stag, you closet pike, you rampant bull. Go on, who was it? One of the maids? Not that I'm suggesting your low-born lack of nobility excludes you from the finer and more succulent morsels of flesh on offer, I'm aware the city's been desecrated, thousands turned into vampires, and all that stuff. Leaves much leaner pickings for those on the prowl, so to speak." Saark winked. "Go on. Who was she?"

"You are mistaken," said Kell, woodenly.

"Nonsense! When I see fish, I smell fish. And when I see Kell behave like this… well, I can smell fish. Spill the beans old goat, after all, you've done enough laughing at my terrible sexual misfortunes over the last few months. Aye, and judgemental, you've been. About time I got some payback for all those quips about the donkey."

"I notice she's still here," said Kell through gritted teeth.

"Mary is well and fine and carrying a payload of shields. You, however, are changing the subject. Go on, which lucky lass got to play with Kell's Legend? It was that young woman clearing the table, wasn't it? You scamp! She must be thirty years your junior! Have you no shame?"

Saark punched Kell on the arm. Kell stared at the place Saark punched him, then scowled, and glared at the dandy.

"You've got a big mouth. You've got a runny brain. Like a bloody undercooked egg yolk, it is. You need to keep your nose out of other people's business. And *you* need to refine your character if you think you're a fit man to look after my granddaughter for the next thirty years without me hunting you down and crushing you like a beetle under my boot."

"So, it *was* the cook! A fine and stocky lass she turned out to be, and I'm always the first to admit, a woman with a goodly amount of weight and mass to her, a big lass with big bones like that – well, you can't go wrong, can you? I mean, you need a woman who can take a good, hard–"

"It was Myriam."

They walked for a while, in silence, and Saark looked

at Kell, opened his mouth to speak several times, then closed it again. He tried again, and again closed his mouth. Finally, he said, "She told me she loved me. She said we would live together, be strong together. That we would never die – thanks to our combined vachine energies. She said we were like royalty! We could achieve anything our hearts desired!"

Kell chuckled. "Just before she tried to drown you, if I remember it rightly?"

"Harsh, Kell, harsh."

"Well, what do you expect? You prance about, trying your amorous expertise on any woman who'll give you the barest sniff. That's what you are, Saark. A bloody sniffer dog. I've never seen a man so damn and permanently *erect!*"

"I thought we were talking about one of my true loves, and how you'd just had your way with her? You seem to have strayed away from our topic, and indeed, the prickly edges of my rapidly breaking heart."

"She seduced me," said Kell, primly.

"*What?* Ha! What arse-rot. I know Myriam, and she is a fine judge of character."

"Maybe *that's* why she tried to kill you?"

"Amusing, Kell. Can you see me laughing?"

Kell chuckled. "No, but I can see Mary laughing. At least your ass finds my comedy a damn sight more amusing than her owner!" The sound of Mary braying could be heard, and various shouts as men tried to stop the unpredictable donkey from kicking and bolting.

"This is hard for me, Kell. You've taken my woman!"

"No," said Kell. "I have taken nothing. She gave me plenty, though."

They walked again, in silence, for quite a while.

"Hey," said Kell, staring at Saark. "You know that little sound she makes?"

"What little sound?"

"Like a bird, chirping."

"I never heard no sound like a bird chirping. What are you talking about, you old fool?"

"Sure, Saark. You must have heard her. She makes it, when she orgasms..." Kell placed his hand over his mouth. "Oh, sorry, Saark. Maybe you didn't hear it after all." Kell's booming laughter ranged across the marching columns on the Great North Road, and Saark trailed along behind him, fists clenched, face like thunder, heart ticking with clockwork.


The albino soldiers from the Army of Brass moved slowly through the valley. It was ringed with trees, and steep rocky flanks led up to Valantrium Moor to the east.

General Exkavar held up his fist, and the army halted. His captains came to him, and he issued orders to set up camp. He ordered scouts out to scan the surrounding country, and various patrols to watch over the troops as they set up base-camp for the night.

After an hour, tents had been erected, fires lit, food was cooking and night descended. Exkavar knew that further south and west the Army of Silver were setting up a similar camp. He smiled to himself. The Army of Silver would check Fawkrin, and Gilrak further south. The Army of Brass would march through Valantrium, and Old Valantrium, and then both armies would convene at Vor and smash the vampires there. The remains of the Army of Iron would join, forming the closing claws of a perfect manoeuvre, and Vor – the capital city of Falanor

377

– would belong to *them*. To the *White Warriors*. And the *Harvesters* with whom they worked…

Exkavar moved to his tent, and slowly removed his armour. Servants brought a bowl of water warmed over the fire, and the old general washed his pale, white limbs, washed sweat and salt from his skin, from his face, from his stinging eyes. And then he sat, in a simple white robe, and ate dried meat and strips of dried fruit – the *el-dabarr* fruit, grown far to the north, far past the Black Pike Mountains. In the place where the vachine ruled.

Distant screams reached Exkavar's ears, and frowning, he stood and reached for his black sword. He ran from his tent – and the world smashed down into *chaos*. All around men were fighting, swords slashing, most of the albino soldiers in underwear or simple cotton leggings. There had been no early warning. Not one patrol had sounded a bugle alarm. And the enemy, the enemy were –

General Exkavar *blinked*, hand tightening on the hilt of his sword. They were children, and their skin was gloss black, and they moved fast, some too fast to see until they stopped, for a moment, to chop off a head or arms or legs. They glistened under the moonlight and Exkavar's stomach *churned*, not just with the simple disgust of seeing them, for they were horrible to behold, a blend of child and insect, teeth black and pointed, many with claws instead of hands, and four arms, and taloned feet. They ran and jumped and crawled and squirmed, and some had large pulsing thoraxes dangling between legs like deviant, distorted pregnant bellies. His stomach *churned* because he knew what they were, and fear ate through him as easily as the *Ankarok* ate through his soldiers. They were like a swarm, of locusts, or something more dark and terrible, and there were hundreds of them, *thousands* in fact. They slammed through the Army of Brass, and killed everyone, and all the time there was a background hissing, like a million insects buzzing and croaking and Exkavar stood, and waited to die, but he did not die, it was a miracle, until he saw a boy walking towards him and his eyes were glowing black and he was dressed in rags but Exkavar knew him, he *knew* this was The Skanda. The King.

Exkavar stood to attention as all around him men were decapitated and ground screaming into the snow. White blood splattered tent walls. Limbs flew through the air to impact with sickening crunches.

He could hear them…

*we have been imprisoned for thousands of years*
*we are free now to roam and kill and devour*
*we are free to take back the land*
*we are free to kill.*

The Skanda halted, and looked up at General Exkavar. "You were heading to Vor?" he said.

Exkavar nodded, and then blinked, for behind The Skanda walked General Graal. The man held his head high, and his blue eyes shone, but his face was riddled with patches of black insect chitin. As if he had started to *blend*. To become a part of the ancient race known as *Ankarok*.

"You have another army, south and west of here."

"I will never divulge military information," snarled Exkavar, and attacked in a blur, sword slamming at Skanda's head. The little boy did not move, but Graal's sword intervened – and slowly, Graal pushed Exkavar's weapon back. With a flick of the wrist, Graal disabled Exkavar, then his head snapped left as if awaiting instruction.

"We have no further need for him. Kill him," said Skanda.

Graal's sword cut Exkavar's head from his shoulders. Graal looked up, and all around the camp had descended into death, and now silence. The several thousand Ankarok warriors stood motionless, eyes glistening, skin glistening. They were perfectly immobile. As if controlled. As if turned to stone.

"Kell comes from the north," said Graal.

"We head south," said Skanda.

"Kell has an army, now," said Graal. "That's what the patrol told us. Maybe five thousand men. Maybe more."

"Our priority is Vor," said Skanda. "Meshwar will be driven back. We *need* that city."

"And what of Kell?"

Skanda smiled, black teeth glistening. He reached out, and patted Graal's arm. "Don't worry. You shall have your time. You shall have your chance. And you shall have revenge."

Skanda turned, and a high-pitched squeal reverberated throughout the valley. The Ankarok turned south, and like a buzzing plague of insects, headed through the forests... and towards the unsuspecting Army of Silver.

# CHAPTER 15
## *Bhu Vanesh*

It was night. Kell crawled through the snow, which froze his knees and made him wince. Damn, he hated it when his knees seized up. *Getting old,* he thought to himself bitterly. *Old, and weak, and tired, and weary. Weary of the world. Weary of the years. Weary of the fighting. Everything seems so complicated now, why can't it be simple like in the old days? In the old days, Saark would have been hanged from the nearest oak if he'd stepped outside in silk and perfume…*

*How decadent we've become.*

*How decadent…*

"It's quiet," said Saark, who was lying next to Kell in the snow. "Maybe too quiet?"

"They're out there," said Kell, and his eyes scanned the huge sprawl of Port of Gollothrim below. On the outskirts were massive yards and factories, silent now, still, motionless, a ghost town within a ghost town. Machines should be grinding and clanking, Kell knew. Gollothrim was a thriving anthill, even at night. But not tonight.

The vampires had taken control…

"You know we'll not get them out for combat," said Grak the Bastard, voice low, stroking his beard. He was a reassuring mass in the darkness. Grak had proved himself to be a more than able soldier. "We'll have to go in after them. I reckon those Warlords speak to each other, up here." He tapped his head. "They'll know right enough what happened to Kuradek. Know how Kell disposed of him. There'll be no sneaking in, this time."

Kell scratched his beard. "I need to get to Bhu Vanesh. I need to bury Ilanna in his skull, open the pathway back to the Chaos Halls. They want him back, that much is for sure."

"Who?" said Saark, looking sideways at Kell.

"The Keepers," said Kell, darkly.

"You know *way* too much for a fat old man," said Saark, and shivered. "And sometimes, you can have too much insight. Me, I'd rather have a plump serving wench sat on my face, ten flagons of ale and a plate of fried pork and eggs in the morning."

Kell stared at Saark. "I have a favour to ask."

"Yes?"

Kell looked down, and seemed to fidget for a moment. He gestured to the vast sprawl of Gollothrim. "It's going to be wild down there, you know that? It's going to be *bad*. Much worse than Jalder."

"You think?"

"I have a sixth sense about these things," said Kell, quietly. "What I wanted to ask you, what I wanted to... *request*, was a promise. Something sworn in blood and honour. Can you do that for me, Saark?"

Saark stared into Kell's dark eyes. There was a glint of desperation there. Saark nodded. "Kell. I fool around a lot. But you know, deep down, I was the Sword Champion of King Leanoric. And yes, I betrayed him, but I do have honour – I have honour for my friends, and for those whom I love. I may wear handsome silks and the finest perfumes – don't comment – but when it really matters, I will kill and die if needed. You *know* that, don't you?"

"I know, laddie." Kell chewed his lip. "If I die down there, Saark, I want you to promise me you'll take care of Nienna. I want you to *swear* on your lifeblood that you will not treat her bad. You will treat her with respect and honour and dignity, help her with the hard choices in life… hell, I don't know. Be like a *guardian* for her. She's a tough girl, I know – she's my granddaughter, after all. But she's still just a babe when held against the warped tapestry of the real world. Of history."

"I will do anything for her, Kell. And for you. So yes. I swear. By every ounce of honour in my blood. By every clockwork wheel that turns and gear that steps. You know this, Kell."

Kell turned his gaze back to Gollothrim, and allowed a long breath to hiss free. He gazed past the factories and yards; storage huts, barracks, houses, schools, temples, narrow twisting streets and broad thoroughfares for the moving of goods from the docks. He could see the dark silhouettes of the ships at anchor in the bay. He could see the skeletons of many more new ships, destined to take the vampires abroad, to spread their plague to other continents in search of global dominion. And Kell knew, this would be the hardest fight of his life. He knew death waited for him down there. It looked quiet, it looked safe, but soon the vampires would come drifting out to play. And Kell had to find his way through the maze. Find Bhu Vanesh, and kill the bastard.

"You know I'm coming with you," said Saark.

"No, laddie. You stay here and look after Nienna. That must be your priority. That must be your mission. If things start to turn bad, then you take her. You get away. You take her some place safe. You understand me?"

"I understand."

"I'm trusting you, Saark, with the greatest treasure of my life. Don't let me down."

"I won't, Kell."

Even as they watched, as Kell had predicted, the vampires started to emerge into the dark quarters of Port of Gollothrim. They wandered the streets mostly in packs, some alone. They howled at the moon like dogs. They laughed and squealed, danced and fought. Kell, and Saark, and Grak watched grimly. They watched, down by the wide yard as a group of vampires cornered a woman. She screamed, and ran. They pursued her cackling like demons, and grabbed her, pulling her apart. Her arms came away spewing blood and she fell over, weeping, still alive. The six vampires descended on her, drinking her blood, laughing and singing and masturbating.

"We must go in," growled Grak, pinching the bridge of his nose. "We must end this depravity."

Kell nodded. "I agree. Go get the men ready. I want archers at the front, and we'll descend real slow. Pick off those we can, then divide into small fighting squares. If we stick to the wide avenues, we'll bring the fuckers out onto our spears. You must warn the men – never chase them into narrow alleys. They'll fall on us from above, and our long spears will be useless."

"How many in each unit?"

"I'd say fighting squares of twenty-five. Shields all round. Couple of archers in the centre of each square. We'll quarter the city, work through it methodically."

"Why don't we wait for daylight?" said Saark. "Most of them sleep."

"We'll never bloody find them," snapped Kell. "We'll waste too much time hunting in sewers and bloody cellars. No. This way we can fight them on reasonably open ground; get some good slaughterin' done. Then in the daylight, we can pick out the rest. Gather those still normal around us, they'll know where some of these vampires are hiding. Sound like a plan?"

Grak stared at where the six vampires chewed on the dead woman. He realised, stomach churning, that she was actually still alive. She was making weak mewling sounds. It was the sickest thing Grak had ever seen.

"Sounds like a solid fucking plan to me. Let's get it done." Grak crawled back, then disappeared into the dark.

Saark looked down on the city. "Kell. There's an *awful* lot of them out, now. Thousands of them."

"Good. We'll have plenty of targets then, won't we?"

"Don't you think the odds are against us?"

"Lad, the odds are always against us. From birth to death, life is just one whole shit of a bitch."

"I meant here, and now."

"I know what you meant." Kell's eyes gleamed. "You remember what I said? About protecting Nienna?"

"In some ways I'm relieved I'm not coming with you," said Saark.

Kell's hand smashed out, and stroked Saark's cheek. He grinned, like a demon in the moonlight. "Look after her, vachine. You're strong, fast, deadly. Nobody else can keep her alive like you."

Saark nodded. "What about Myriam?"

"Myriam? Why, she's coming with me, lad."

• • • •

385

The outcast men of Falanor, the Blacklippers and thieves, rapists and murderers, extortionists and freaks, kidnappers and maniacs, the cast out and the depraved and the downright psychotic, assembled in tight military units, eyes gleaming, shields on arms, steel collars fixed around throats, swords oiled and sharpened, boot laces tightened and jaws grim with the prospect of death and mutilation as they considered the enemy – their numbers, and their ferocity.

"Let's move," said Grak, and they marched through the darkness, through the trees and over low hills, boots tramping snow and ice and mud. They found the main arterial route which ran from the Great North Road to Port of Gollothrim, and picked it up like casual syphilis, emerging from the trees like armed and armoured ghosts, eyes hot jewels, lips wet, anticipation and hatred building like a slow-boiled rage.

The armoured units approached Port of Gollothrim.

It began to snow, a heavy snow obscuring their vision.

Boots touched down on slick iced cobbles. Cold hands grasped weapons in readiness.

In the darkness, Kell and Myriam slipped away…

"Steady, lads," said Grak, voice a low rumble. The twenty-four men around him shifted uneasily in their steel cage. Behind, other units were ready. Then the fighting began…

From the gloom and snow the vampires attacked. With squeals of rage they launched at the armoured unit, and spears jabbed out, impaling vampires through hearts and throats. Grak caught a flash of fangs, and claws slid between shields. He slashed down with his sword, cutting off fingers which tumbled below pushing, tramping boots. A fanged face leered at him, hissing, spitting, and in what seemed like slow motion Grak slid his short sword into that mouth, watched the blade cut a wide smile and jab further in, into the brain, killing the vampire dead. Smoke hissed black from nostrils and it thrashed on his blade. Grak pulled back, and heard a clang from above. A vampire, on their roof of shields. He shoved his blade up, skewering a groin. More vampires slammed into the armoured unit, and swords and spears jabbed and slashed and it was chaos, but an organised chaos, madness, but controlled madness. It was a surreal world, a blood-red snow-filled insanity. All around men were fighting, grunting, pushing. Claws slashed through to Grak's left and tore off a man's face with a neat flick of the wrist. Grak saw eyes popping out on stalks, a horror of gristle and spasmodic working jaws. The man screamed blood. Grak cut the vampire's hand clean off with a short hack, then roared in anger and burst from the cage of shields and grabbed the creature, but it was strong, so fucking strong, and they wrestled and Grak was slammed backwards onto the cobbles, and the *thing* with only one hand squirmed like a thick eel above him. A spear suddenly appeared in an explosion of black blood, drenching Grak. The spear point was a hair's breadth from his face. The vampire corpse slid sideways, like an excised cancerous bowel. Dekkar grinned, and held out his hand.

"You fighting it, or fucking it, lad?" he growled.

Grak grinned, and glanced around. The wide street was empty, save for armoured units and vampire corpses. "We beat them off?"

"For now. For a minute."

The units reformed themselves. In Grak's square they had lost four men. Grak stared down at their bodies, mouth a grim line, eyes glittering jewels. He realised, with desolate horror, that they could not win this day. How many were there? How many? They couldn't kill them all.

"I know what you're thinking," rumbled the Black-lipper King, and slapped him on the back. "And the answer is – we must try."

Grak gave a nod.

"The bastards are coming back," snarled a soldier.

And through the darkness, and the falling snow, squeals and cries and giggles reverberated from walls. The noise built and built and built, until it seemed the whole world was full of vampires. Shadows cast across walls, from rooftops above, from alleyways and streets and the darkened interiors of tall regal town houses.

"Holy Mother," whispered Grak, as around him his unit looked up, around, back to back, weapons wavering uncertainly.

And they came, boots thumping in quick succession with a sound like thunder. They came, like a cancerous flood, hundreds and hundreds of vampires sprinting and leaping and cavorting from the darkness...

Command Sergeant Wood sat on the roof of the Green Church, down by the docks, and watched the old soldiers from the Black Barracks creeping into position. Old they might be, but they moved with skill and practice earned over a lifetime of fighting. They may be old, but each would hold his own in a barroom brawl. Each would fight to the death. And Wood could ask for no more.

Fat Bill crouched next to him on one side, and Pettrus on the other. Both men looked grim, faces sour like they were sucking lemons. Wood gripped his sword tight, and blinked. The old soldiers had *disappeared*. Their skills at hiding were second to none.

"There," said Fat Bill, pointing into the darkness. It had started to snow, and everything more than ten feet away was hazy and surreal. A perfect Holy Oak painting. A perfect festival, a time to relax, to put out holly on the doorstep and presents in wooden crates before the fire delivered by Old Crake and his Wraith Keepers. But not now. Not here. Those times were long gone. After all, children had little to laugh about in Port of Gollothrim now the vampires had taken over...

"What am I looking at?" said Wood, careful to keep his voice low.

"The docks."

"So?"

"What's most precious to the vampires? The ships, I reckon. They're beavering away like their lives depend on it. Building a fleet. Take their vermin plague to warmer climates, I reckon."

"But that's good for us," said Wood. "If they clear off and leave us in peace."

"We both know that will never happen," said Pettrus, darkly. "I agree with Fat Bill. We need to torch these bastards. Hit them where it hurts. We haven't enough men to take them on in battle; but by the Bone Lords, we can stick a knife in their ribs whenever we get the chance."

"Most of the lads are carrying oil flasks," said Fat Bill with a fat grin. "I think it's time we turned the night into day."

Wood gave a nod, mouth dry, and stood as Fat Bill and Pettrus stood. There came a *slap* on stone behind them, and Wood turned fast, past a blur which made him blink, stepping back, knocking into Fat Bill as his sword flickered up. The *blur* was a vampire, and her flying kick slammed into Pettrus' chest, making him grunt, stumble back, hit the Green Church's crenallated roof and flip over. There was a hiatus as the vampire hit the ground and rose smoothly.

Then a *slap* and *crack* as Pettrus hit the cobbles far below.

Wood wanted to scream, to rush to the edge and look, but a deep sickly feeling raged through his guts and he knew, knew his friend and mentor was dead and in a moment, he'd be dead too. The female vampire was smiling, and Wood felt a lurch of fear riot through him. It was Lorna, Bhu Vanesh's bitch, the vampire he'd thrown from the high tower roof, watched her break on the ground below, squirming and squealing like a kitten after a hammer blow. But she was here. Alive. And strong.

"Remember me?" she snarled, glossy crimson black eyes bright with hatred. She moved left, and Wood's blade wavered. Then right, and his sword slashed before her face by mere inches.

"I remember watching you break your pretty little spine," he said, eyes fixed on the petite blonde. She was pretty, slim, but she had changed from the woman he had once known. The skin of her face and hands looked stretched, almost fake, as if she wore a mask. Her hair, once a luscious blonde pelt, was now stringy like wire. She exuded death. To Wood, she looked no better than a rotting corpse. "And I knew you were coming. I could smell your dead stink from a hundred paces."

Lorna hissed, claws slashing, then rolled right under Wood's sword, and slashed her claws across Fat Bill's belly. She opened him like a bag of offal, and his bowels spooled out as if from a reel, his hands dropping his sword and paddling at his entrails with mad scooping motions as he tried to hold himself together.

Lorna leapt back as Wood's sword whistled past her throat, and she was smiling, and Fat Bill slammed to the floor of the roof and made panting noises as he slowly died. He waved a bloodied hand at Wood. "Kill her, kill her!" he groaned, "don't fucking bother about me!"

Wood ran at Lorna, her face showing surprise for a moment, but she back-flipped away. His sword slammed at her, cutting a line down her pale arm, and the flesh opened but no blood came out. She grabbed the wound, and the smile fell from her lips.

"You see, you cut like any other bitch," snarled Wood, and anger was firing him into the realms of hatred now. This wasn't just another vampire. This had become personal.

"You didn't kill me last time," taunted Lorna, and they circled. She darted forward, claws slashing for his throat, but his sword flashed up cutting her short. She leapt away, and back-flipped up onto the battlements. She turned, and let out a howl, and below vampires swarmed from still, silent, dark buildings. They began to climb up houses and factories and towers, towards the hidden old soldiers. Faces gleamed like pale ghosts in the moonlight. Snow melted on necrotic flesh, making them shine.

Wood ran at her, but she leapt over him in an amazing high arc, a back-flip but Wood anticipated the move and leapt at the same time, his sword ramming up in a hard vertical strike, entering her body at the core of her spine and emerging from under her breasts in a shower of black blood.

Wood landed, panting, and turned fast. Lorna had continued her somersault, landed, and cradled the point of the blade emerging from her chest. She stood, the sword straight through her to the hilt, and smiled at Wood. There was blood on her lips. On her fangs.

"Bastard," she said, and ran at him, and Wood's hands came up but she grabbed him, and she was awesomely strong, and she pulled him into a bear hug and Wood found the point of his own sword pressing into him, into his chest, and then driving in through flesh and bone, and he gasped and it burned and steel grated on bone. Lorna was close. Close enough to kiss. Her breath stunk like the grave, and her pretty dark eyes were fixed on Wood.

She leant forward. "How does it feel, Command Sergeant Wood? How does it feel, not only to die, *but to see all your old friends die?*"

Wood gasped, and pain swamped him for a moment, the world turning red and hot and unbearable. Then he caught himself from falling into the dark pit, and turned, and saw the vampires stood across the rooftops. There were several hundred. Out of the shadows rose the old soldiers of Falanor, Kelv the Axeman, Old Man Connie, Bulbo the Dull, Weevil and Bad Socks and so many more. So many men. So many soldiers. So many memories. They were surrounded, and outnumbered...

Lorna kissed Wood, first on the lips, then on his ear. Her fangs lowered towards his neck. She jerked him tighter, into her, a metal conjugation of the blade. A hard steel fuck. And her fangs caressed his neck, as she savoured the moment of the hunt. She seemed to sniff him, and taste him, and enjoy a lingering moment.

Below, on the rooftops, the vampires attacked...

• • • •

Kell and Myriam crept from house to house, from street to street. They kept to shadows and moved with an infinity of care. Their aim wasn't to take on the vampire army. Their aim was to slaughter its Warlord.

"You were right," whispered Myriam, close to Kell's ear, her words tickling. "He's in the tower. How did you know?"

Kell grinned a skeletal grin in the darkness. "Intuition. These vampires. They have some fucking ego, that's for sure. Come on." They moved on through gloom, through falling snow which smelt of a distant, frozen sea. They could hear the sounds of battle now, shouting, screams, the echoing, reverberating cries of attacking vampires and *slap* of steel on flesh. Kell and Myriam did not talk about it. There was nothing to talk about. They simply pushed on, forward, further into the realm of the vampire.

Ilanna was drawn. And ready.

Myriam carried her Widowmaker in one gloved hand, and her vachine fangs were out. They gleamed in the darkness. She was as ready for battle as she could ever be.

They drifted like ghosts. Somewhere, a building burned. Vampires were screaming in the flames, and the roasting of flesh smelled like cooked pig interlaced with something subtly... *human*. Kell nearly puked, so they pulled back, crept down a different alleyway. As they left the black smoke behind they could see the Warlord's Tower.

They crouched and watched it for a while. Around the base were perhaps a hundred vampires, lounging in the snow, some walking, none talking. They seemed lethargic, sleepy, without any focus.

"What's the matter with them?" hissed Kell.

"Lack of fresh blood. They grow tired. Soon, they'll turn on one another. You'll see."

"How do you know this?"

"I feel it in myself," said Myriam, smiling and showing brass fangs. "We're not so different, them and me. No matter what they say, no matter what they think. They believe we are a deviant offspring; the Soul Stealers told me *we* were the more ancient race. We have our clans far to the north, in the cold places where humans don't travel. Me and Saark; we are parts of those vachine clans, now. Part of a distant, clockwork world. Part of an ancient heritage. One day, they will call us. And we will not be able to resist."

Kell stared at her, then shrugged. He got a sudden feeling the vachine of Silva Valley nestled deep within the Black Pike Mountains had been just *a glimpse* of what the vachine really *were*. Of their size, their might, their ferocity. Images flashed dark in his mind. Of huge clockwork vampire armies. Vast, cold and mechanical. Thousands, tens of thousands, hundreds of thousands. And Silva Valley had been an offshoot, rebels almost. And the vampires thought they had birthed the vachine – when in reality, it had been the other way round.

Kell shivered. It was too much to comprehend. Not here. Not now.

"That's a battle for another day," he said, finally, and saw the curious look in Myriam's eye. He held up a finger. "No. Don't even consider trying to convert me to what you have become. You had a good reason for becoming vachine, Myriam. A damn good reason. But I'm happy to die like any other old man."

"You can live forever," she whispered, and kissed him on the cheek.

"Sometimes, I think it's better to die," he said, with an inherent wisdom he did not feel. Then he blinked, and shrugged off her vachine spell. He grinned. "Come on, lass. How do we get in?"

"Up there." She pointed to another tower, and between the two ran twin cables. "It's for passing messages, from the Warlord's Tower to servant quarters. We can climb across that."

Kell looked at the awesome height, with an equally awesome fall to iced cobbles below. "I can't bloody climb across a cable like that!" he scowled. "I'll fall! I'll die!"

"No," smiled Myriam. "You won't. You're Kell, the *Legend*."

"I wish people would stop saying that," muttered the old warrior, and sheathing Ilanna on his back, followed Myriam to the second, smaller tower. It was unguarded, and they entered through a doorway that looked like a broken mouth,

*Into the breach*, thought Kell, and chuckled. *Somebody up there has a fine sense of humour!*

They climbed a massive circular stone staircase for what seemed an age. Kell's knees complained. His back complained. *He* complained, but in an internal muttering monologue which had served him well for many a decade in the army. Years of running through mud, carrying logs, wading through rivers, staggering under heavy armour, fighting with a heavy shield on one arm, axe in hand, bodies falling before him, beneath him, carved like fine roast beef...

Kell blinked. A chilled wind scoured him.

The view from the tower ledge was incredible, spreading away through a fine haze of snow. Fire burned throughout the Port of Gollothrim. Vampires screamed and shrieked. Again, he could hear the sounds of battle, but could not determine the armoured units of Falanor men, of Blacklippers and criminals he had created. *Here to fight for you. Here to die for you. So get on with it! Kill the Warlord. Then we can go home.*

*Is it ever that easy?*

*It always begins with a small step.*

Kell moved to the edge of the precipice, and grabbed the cable. It seemed ridiculously thin, woven from slippery metal, and he scowled and looked down to the distant courtyard. The vampires still lounged. It felt wrong. Like Kell was stumbling easily into a trap like a courtroom jester. Would they *really* leave such an opening unguarded? Or were there vampires with crossbows waiting from him to swing out onto the wire?

"I can't do this," said Kell.

"Why not?" hissed Myriam, who was tying her weapons to herself. "Secure that bloody axe. If you drop anything, the bastards will hear us and they'll look up. Then we're dead."

"This is too easy."

"You call *that* easy?" snapped Myriam, gesturing to the expanse of swaying cable – perhaps five hundred strides in all, and a good height. Good enough to turn the vampires on the ground far below into stick-men.

"We'll be vulnerable."

Myriam shrugged. "That's how us normal mortals feel all the time." She saw Kell's look, and pressed at one of her vachine fangs. "Well. You know what I mean."

Myriam took hold of the cable, and it was cold to the touch. Freezing. She grimaced. "Come on, axe man. We have a job to do."

"One thing."

"Yes?"

Kell grinned. "I like you, Myriam."

Her eyes glinted. "I know you do. You showed me that in oh so many different ways. Just proves what an old man has still got left inside him, if he really tries."

"No. I mean, we've had our differences. And I still don't trust you for spit." He held up a finger to silence her complaint. "But you've come good, Myriam. You may be as unpredictable as a violent raging sea storm, but by the Chaos Halls, I think I like that in a woman."

"What you're saying is, despite what we've been through, if I betray you now, you'll still lop off my head with that bloody axe?"

"You know I will," said Kell. "Now let's move. Before I change my mind."

Myriam took hold of the cable and swung her legs up, crossing them. Then she began to haul herself along the icy length, hand over hand, with smooth effortless strokes.

Kell took hold, Ilanna strapped tight to his back, and hoisted his legs up. The whole cable sagged, and Kell bobbed, and he cursed, and his muscles ached already. It was one thing in battle to be a huge, stocky, iron-muscled warrior – but such mass did not lend itself well to supporting one's own weight from a high cable.

Kell started to haul himself along. Within minutes the tower fell away, and he was far across the expanse. A cold wind whipped him. His muscles screamed. His bones creaked. His knees and back pummelled him with pain. And worse, the worst thing of all, the cable was freezing, and his hands were frozen. They were rigid, like solid brittle steel cast wrong in the forge, and Kell was struggling to move his fingers, struggling to pull himself across the vast drop.

Kell paused for a moment, and glanced down, just like he knew he shouldn't, but perversely revelling in the danger. If he fell now, he'd make a mighty dent in the cobbles. He grinned. Bastard. Bastards! He wanted to scream into the wind, into the snow, but instead he gritied his teeth and forced iron resolve to tear through him and he continued onwards. Onwards.

Half way.

Kell paused. His hands were as numb as they'd ever been. As numb as ice. As numb as Saark's brain.

"Donkey shit."

He clamped his teeth shut, blinking fast. He realised the cold was now numbing his *brain*. He looked up. Myriam was getting close to the portal, and he watched her flip over the lip. She disappeared, and Kell searched for her to reappear with a smile, and an encouraging wave. However, she did not. Kell scowled.

*Shit.*

He moved, as fast as lethargic muscles would allow, as fast as frozen bear paws would grapple. But the ice was winning. The cold was beating him down, no question.

Three quarters of the way, and Kell could not go on. He could not move and he hung there on a cable, high above vampire hordes and a city at war, and he listened to the wind, and wondered what the hell he was going to do now. And then, worst of all, he heard the sounds of battle from inside the tower. Steel on steel. The clash of blades. Myriam was in trouble!

Kell struggled to move on. To drag himself on. He glanced down. The vampires below had heard the battle as well, and they were looking up at him. One pointed. Several pale faces seemed to be grinning. Some vampires emerged, and they carried bows and Kell groaned.

An arrow sailed up, missing him by inches. There came laughter, like a ripple of metal across ice.

Kell tried to force his fingers to move. They would not.

Kell was stuck...

Saark stared at Nienna as if she'd struck him.

"That's the single most incredibly stupid idea I've ever heard in my entire life."

"But you can't stop me," she said, voice low, and purring, and dangerous.

"I *can* stop you," snapped Saark, "and I bloody will!"

"No. You'd have to force me down, sit on me, pin my arms to the icy ground. Because I'm going after them, Saark. I'm going to help them. They need my help, I can feel it in my bones!"

"What a load of old rampant horse shit," snapped Saark, and grabbed Nienna's arm. Her hand flashed up, and it held a blade. The blade touched Saark's throat.

"See? I'm good enough to get past *your* guard."

Saark stepped back, hands out, and shook his head. "Kell told me to keep you here. In the forest. To make sure no harm came to you. He made me *promise*."

"This is unbelievable!" stormed Nienna. "Everybody has gone down to Gollothrim, even the women, to fight! And I'm expected to sit on my hands and play with myself? Well, I won't do it. I'm going after Kell and Myriam. The only way you'll stop me is by killing me."

"The women are trained archers!" wheedled Saark, and Nienna strode off down the forest trail. Saark ran after her. "Wait, wait! At least let me grab my rapier."

"So you're coming with me?"

"Aye, bloody looks like it, doesn't it?"

"Well, a woman should always get what she wants."

"In my experience, she always does. Only most of the time she learns to regret it."

Nienna shrugged. "You know I'm right, Saark. You know we need to be part of this. We can make a difference. We can help Kell."

"Have you heard yourself?" snapped Saark. "*Help* Kell? Have you bloody *seen* him fight? That rancid old lion needs no help from a little girl like you."

"Watch your tongue, lest I cut it out."

"Girl, if Kell learns I allowed you to follow him into *that hell hole*, then he'll cut out more than my damn tongue."

"Well let's make sure we make a difference, then," said Nienna, eyes hard, and by her stance Saark could see she meant trouble. She'd come a long way from the day he'd met her in the tannery in Jalder; then, she'd been soft like a puppy, her eyes gooey and lustful, her skin like virgin's silk. Now, she was hard, and lean, and her eyes were dark. She'd seen too much. Her innocence had been flayed from her, like skin strips under a cat o' nine.

Saark trotted after Nienna through the woods. There seemed little other option.

It did not take long to reach Gollothrim, and they stood in a darkened alley on the outskirts, listening to the sounds of horror reverberating through the streets. Many fights were erupting in the distance. Vampires screamed. Men screamed. Flames roared. The city had erupted into chaos.

"This is a *bad* idea," muttered Saark.

"To the tower, you said?"

"That's what Kell told me," muttered Saark, feeling like a down and dirty traitor, like his tongue would turn black and fall out of his burning mouth. He moved to

Nienna, touched her shoulder. "*Please*. Let's turn back. This is not the time for us. Not the place."

"I am a child no longer," said Nienna, eyes hard.

Footsteps padded at the end of the alleyway, and a figure stopped, and turned. It was a woman. A vampire. She hissed, eyes glowing red, and extended her claws.

"Great," muttered Saark, drawing his sword, and turning, watched a second vampire casually close off the end of the alleyway. Two women, two vampires, working together as a small unit. To trap the unwary. To slaughter. To drink fresh blood…

Nienna had drawn her own short sword, and backed towards Saark. "There's two of them," she muttered, glancing up along the rooftops to make sure no more dropped from above.

"You reckon?" he snapped, eyes flickering between the two. They were advancing. Fluid. Too fluid. Graceful, like cats. Saark had seen vampires move like that before. These were the true predators of the pack. Deadly and swift. "Remember," he hissed, "eyes, throat and heart. Strike hard and fast, and keep hitting till the fucker's down," but there was no more time for words as the vampires shifted into a sprint and ran fast down the alley to leap at Saark and Nienna, who stood grim, blades glittering…

Grak shoved his sword into a vampire's open mouth, snapping fangs as claws scrabbled against his breastplate and slashed viciously across the steel band around his throat. But it saved him. The steel saved him.

"There's too many!" screamed Dekkar through the fighting throng. Their units of twenty-five men had been decimated, carved up, and backed together in a disorganised mass. They stood, panting, as vampires circled them on the wide main thoroughfare of Gollothrim. Occasionally, one would dart out but a spear would jab, and it would retreat. Grak looked frantically about. There were maybe twenty of them left, out of fifty. Most had lost shields, now. Most barely carried weapons. Dead vampires surrounded their boots. What happened to the other units? Fighting in their own shit, Grak reckoned. Down streets and alleyways. In buildings. What had he said? Stick to the main wide road, where each unit could help defend the other units. And what had they gone and done? Gone bloody running off in every bloody direction like horny young virgins at the sniff of a brothel! Grak the Bastard hawked and spat. Bloody undisciplined soldiers, was what they were. Bloody untrained, that was their curse! But... of course they were. They were never born for a life in the army.

Dekkar backed to him, and Grak stood side by side next to the Blacklipper giant. Grak glanced up.

"It's been an honour to fight alongside you, brother," he said.

Dekkar looked down. "You too. It's a shame it takes something like *war* to unite us."

Grak nodded. "You see how many there are? You have a slight height advantage over me."

"I reckon three hundred," said Dekkar, voice bitter.

"So, it's time," said Grak, and thought back past all the bad things he'd done. Would he go to the Golden Halls? The Halls of Heroes? He hawked, and spat again. After all the bad things he'd done? This hardly counted. No. He'd go to the Chaos Halls. With the Keepers. But at least one thing was sure and damn well guaranteed... he'd take as many fucking vampires with him as humanly possible...

"COME ON, YOU WHORESONS!" he screamed, and waved his sword, beating it against his breastplate and chanting and snarling. The others around him did the same, and their noise rolled out over the snarling vampire hordes which jostled and shifted like some huge live thing, some organic vampire snake.

Then a high-pitched squeal rent the air, and the vampires screamed, their noise rising up in waves as their claws extended, their fangs gleamed in the darkness, and with a unity uncharacteristic of their unholy race, they charged the men of Falanor...

Command Sergeant Wood snarled, and his head smashed forward, forehead slamming Lorna's nose and making her squeal, and as her head slapped back so he sank his teeth into *her* throat in a beautiful, ironic reversal. He bit and he chewed, his head thrashing, his teeth gnashing, and he chewed out her windpipe and bit through her skin and muscle and tendon, and Lorna's claws raked at his back but they were pinned together by the sword, and he bit and he chewed, he ripped through her flesh as hard and as fast as he could, and black glistening blood ran down his throat and it tasted foul, like decay, like death, like eternity. They fell to the side, rolled onto the stone flags which lined the circumference of the Green Church roof, and Lorna went suddenly still. Wood, in a crazed panic, in a fit of hatred and loathing, continued to bite and chew, not believing she was dead until his teeth clacked against her *spine*. He had chewed out her entire throat. Wood squeezed his hands between them, and pushed himself from the sword point with a cry of pain which rent the night skies like a lightning strike. Then he lay there, shivering, and with gritted teeth he grabbed the stone crenellations and yanked himself to his feet, bleeding and ragged, pain his total mistress. He gazed out across the old soldiers, but they had out-thought the vampires. Whereas the vampires had surrounded the hidden men of the Black Barracks, so this had simply been a *decoy*… to draw them out, into the open. Hundreds had risen from secondary hiding places, and as the vampires attacked so hundreds of iron-tipped arrows slashed through the night, through the snow, piercing eyes and throats, hearts and groins. Wood watched, saw hundreds of arrows slashing through gloom and darkness, watched vampires pierced and screaming and punctured, rolling down slates and tiles, toppling from rooftops to pile like plague victims in the alleys below.

Then eyes turned, and looked up towards *him*. Wood gave a single wave of his hand as he swayed, wheezing, blood dribbling from his jaws with strings of vampire flesh, and he watched the old soldiers moving across the icy rooftops. Despite their age, they were iron. They were ruthless. They were unstoppable. It filled Wood with a little bit of shame at his own moaning. After all – he was still alive. He gritted his teeth, and ignored the hole in his chest, he regained his sword, tugging it from the vampire corpse. But as he turned to leave… he glanced down at Lorna's face. Her eyes were shining. She was watching him. She was *still alive*…

Her hand moved. Slow, like a white worm in the moonlight. At first Wood thought she was pointing at him, but she made a motion across the gaping hole where her throat had been. It was clear and simple. She wanted him to finish her.

"Not sure you deserve it, girl," he grunted, but lifted the short stout blade anyway. Their eyes met, and there was a curious moment of connection. Strangely, Wood felt like Lorna was thanking him. Thanking him – for removing the plague curse.

The sword slammed down, and cut her head from her torso.

Lorna's eyes closed, and she was at peace.

Wood checked Fat Bill, but he was a fast-cooling corpse on the snowy roof. Wood closed the man's eyes, and wincing like a man with a sword wound in his chest, limped from the roof to join the old soldiers in the alley below.

From there, they headed for the docks…

Saark's sword slammed down. The vampire dodged. "Help me, Saark!" squealed Nienna, and Saark speared his rapier through the vampire's eye and kicked off from her chest, somersaulting backwards to kick the second vampire in the back of the head. She went down on one knee, Saark going down with her and his hand came back – paused for a moment – then scooped out her throat with his *vachine* claws. She thrashed for a while on ice-slick cobbles, then lay still, eyes glassy, blood puke on her chin and soaking her chest and belly.

Saark's head came up. He glared at Nienna. "Now we turn back."

"No. Now we go on." She frowned at him, stubborn as ever.

"You will take us to our doom!"

"Then that's the path I choose," she snapped.

"By all the gods, I can see you carry Kell's blood."

"Better the blood of Kell than the blood of a whining coward!"

"Me? I just saved your life!"

"Yes, that's physical skill! What I'm talking about is *determination*. Now come on!"

Nienna stalked down the cobbles, stepping on a vampire corpse as she passed. Saark followed, head hung a little low, wishing he was back in the Royal Palace like it used to be, dancing to fine tunes, swigging fine wines, fucking fine succulent wenches. Saark had come from the gutters, worked his way swiftly to a place of eminence – and then the damn royal rug had been pulled from under his lacquered boots in an instant!

"I must have been a bad man, in a former life," he muttered.

*You've been a pretty lowly shit in this one, too*, replied his mocking conscience.

Nienna led the way, almost by intuition. Certainly she seemed linked to her grandfather. As if by a miracle they slid between groups of vampires, eased between units and squads. Many times they heard fighting, and saw glimpses of armoured units, the brave criminals and Blacklippers of Falanor, battling ferociously against groups of screeching vampires. Swords and spears slammed out, piercing hearts and throats. Swords hacked and cut. Men fell to the ice and mud, screaming and gurgling on blood and entrails.

At one point they spied Grak and Dekkar, back to back, from the confines of a narrow alley. Their sorrowful collection of remaining soldiers were surrounded. Saark tugged to move forward, but Nienna grabbed his arm, holding him back.

"No, Saark, *no!*" she hissed. "Kell may need us! We have to focus!"

Saark glared at her, but allowed himself to be drawn along, feeling like a back-stabber all the way but knowing, deep down, bedded in reality, that the greater mission was the destruction of the Vampire Warlords. And Bhu Vanesh, in particular... the leader. The *Prime*.

Through alleys they crept, in gutters filled with corpses. They moved through desecrated houses, across dead people's furniture and belongings, their flesh creeping, their breathing ragged. Closer and closer they got to the Warlord's Tower, and only as they came through a long, low house, and stopped by the smashed doorway filled with the splintered remnants of a battered door, did they peer out onto the courtyard and see the hundred-strong horde of vampires lounging around, lethargic, almost decadent in their casual manner.

"What now?" muttered Saark.

"We have to get past them."

"Using what blood-oil magick, I ask?"

"We must find Kell."

"Well he's not in there," snorted Saark. "He couldn't have got through this hornet's nest without stirring up a whole bucket full of maggot shit. No. He's somewhere close, though. He'll be looking for another way in, I'd wager, the canny old donkey."

Even as they watched, the vampires started to take interest in something above. Something beyond Saark and Nienna's field of vision; a couple fetched bows, and languorously began to fire arrows at some high target...

"That has to be Kell up there," said Nienna, almost desperate with a need to leave their safe confines. "Come on. We must stop them!"

Saark took hold of Nienna, and shook her. He shook her hard. "We die as easy as the next man," he growled. "You need to use your brain, girl, or you'll get us both killed. You hear me?" He let go of her, and caught a glimpse of hatred in her eyes. Saark licked his lips. Suddenly, he realised what was wrong – Nienna was skirting along a razor edge of sanity. She had lost her touch with reality. Maybe it had been losing her mother to the vampires, maybe it was simply the act of growing up way too fast; she'd been through enough horror to last any man or woman a lifetime. But the fact remained – she was fast becoming a danger. To Saark, to Kell, and to herself.

Distantly, there came a sudden, deafening roar. There were more bangs, and clatters, and an undercurrent of strange violent crackling sounds. Saark moved to another window in the ransacked town house and stared off across the wide courtyard. The edges of the city glowed orange. Fire was raging along the docks.

Outside, the vampires had seen the fire as well. Screeches and wails echoed through their ranks, language that was guttural, feral, and definitely inhuman. With Kell forgotten, they moved as a mass of figures, running, leaping, and within seconds were gone, a flood raging out through the night... and leaving the route to the tower entrance undefended.

"They did it!" hissed Saark. "Grak's men must have reached the docks! They've torched the ships!" he beamed, misunderstanding. "The vampires are starting to panic, they need..." He turned, but Nienna had gone. He peered out of the window, and saw her disappear into the tower across the courtyard. Saark frowned. "You silly, silly little girl," he snapped, and with rapier clasped tight in his sweating fist and vachine fangs gleaming under errant strands of moonlight, Saark surged across the iced cobbles after his entrusted ward.

• • • •

Wood and a group of old soldiers watched fire dance along the ships, from timber to rigging, from sails to masts. On the docks beside one vessel a store of oil had caught, a hundred barrels of flammable fish oil, and gone up with a terrible, mammoth explosion which Wood felt tremble beneath his boots like an earthquake. Flames shot out, destroying dockside buildings, smashing through four or five ships and spreading streamers of fire high into the night sky. Flames roared. Night turned to an orange, smoke-filled day. Embers fluttered on the wind, igniting yet more ships – many of which were soaked in lantern oil from casks hurled by the old soldiers of the Black Barracks. When the vampires arrived, in a pushing, heaving horde, it was too late to save their new navy, and indeed, their *old* navy. Even ships moored a good way out soon came under fire. Drifting sparks and glowing sections of sail, carried high on heated currents of air, drifted far and wide, igniting yet more sails which spread to masts and rigging, planks and timbers and barrels of oil in storage. More explosions rocked the ocean. The whole dockside became an inferno. After a while, even the ocean itself seemed to burn.

Wood could feel heat scorching his flesh as he leant against the wall. He, and the remainder of the old soldiers, had retreated here after a vicious final battle. But now the ships were burning, the vampires seemed to have more pressing matters on their hands, and the short savage skirmish had been temporarily forgotten. Vampires lined the rooftops in their thousands, eyes glowing in the reflected lights of their burning navy. They simply watched, perhaps too afraid to tackle the flames. But then, Command Sergeant Wood conceded, only the ocean could extinguish such an inferno. He'd never seen anything like it in his life.

Port of Gollothrim glowed like the Furnace in the Chaos Halls.

Slowly, Wood became aware of another group of vampires. There were perhaps a hundred of them, which didn't make Wood feel too good; after all, the old soldiers numbered only thirty or forty, now. Wood nudged his companion, the man's white beard turned black with soot and cinders. His eyes were glowing and wild.

"We fucked them hard, eh, lad?" He grinned at Wood. "It'll take 'em *years* to rebuild all them ships!"

Wood nodded, and gestured to this new unit of vampires taking an unhealthy interest in the old soldiers' predicament. "I think these bastards want a bit of payback," he said, and hefted his battered, chipped, blunted sword.

"Let's make them earn their fucking blood," snarled the old man beside him, rubbing his singed beard, eyes bright and *alive* with the fire-glow from the shipyard inferno.

The group of old men hefted their weapons, and despite being weary, drained, exhausted, they faced the vampires creeping towards them with chins held high, eyes bright, fists clenched, knowing they had done their bit in bringing down the cancerous plague, the fast-spread evil, the total *menace* of the Vampire Warlords...

The old soldiers had helped break their backs.

Now, it would be up to others to finish the story... the song...

The Legend.

With snarls and squeals the fire-singed vampires, their pale skin stained with smoke and soot, some bearing savage, bubbling burns and fire-scars, *launched* themselves at the old soldiers, claws slashing, fangs biting, voices ululating triumphant calls across the smoke-filled city...

Swords clashed and cried in the darkness.

And in a few minutes, it was all over.

Kell watched the vampires disappear from down below, taking bows and hateful arrows with them. He watched fire fill the horizon like a flood. He watched the ships burn, his aerial view perfect in witnessing the fast spread of raw destruction. Kell could not believe the fire spread so swiftly; but it did, aided by a good wind and plentiful casks of lantern oil.

Still, he heard sword blows. Then Myriam appeared at the portal. "Come on!" she cried. "I can't fight them on my own!" She disappeared, and Kell grimaced and struggled on, cursing his weight, cursing his age, and vowing never to touch a single drop of whiskey again.

He reached the ledge, panting, sweat dripping in his eyes, his hands like the hands of a cripple with slashed tendons and no *strength*. He jumped down, blinded by the gloomy interior. To his back, silhouetting him against a raging orange archway, the entire naval fleet – old and new – burned.

Myriam was fighting a losing battle against two vampires. She spun and danced, avoiding their slashing claws, her sword darting out and scoring hits – but nothing *fatal*. They were too fast for her.

Kell growled, and hefted Ilanna. Then his hands cramped, and he dropped the axe, almost severing his own toes. "By all the bastards in Chaos," he muttered, scrabbling for the axe as one vampire broke free and charged him. He lifted Ilanna just in time, sparks striking from her butterfly blades and he slashed a fast reverse cut, Ilanna chopping swiftly, neatly, messily into the vampire's face. The man fell with a cry from half-chopped lips, and Kell stood on the vampire's throat, hefted Ilanna, and did a proper job this time, cutting his head and brain in half, just below the nose. Blood splattered the flags. Myriam speared her adversary through the eye, and he fell in a limp heap.

Myriam turned back to Kell. "I thought you were going to fall off!" she snapped.

"Me too."

"Your arse would have made one mighty huge crack in the cobbles."

"I'll lay off the ale and puddings when this is over, that's for sure."

Myriam grinned, and released a long-drawn breath. "Another one's coming. It feels like they were waiting for us!"

"I didn't expect anything less," said Kell.

Division General Dekull stepped from the shadows, a large man with a bull-neck and a hefty scowl. He had thinning brown hair and large hands, each one bearing a sword. He was a formidable opponent, equalling Kell in size and weight, but carrying less fat.

Before Kell could speak, Myriam charged, light, graceful, sword slashing down. Dekull swayed slightly, a precise movement, and back-handed Myriam across the chamber where her head cracked against the wall. It was a sickening noise, and made Kell wince.

"At last, the mighty Kell," said Dekull, voice a rumble. "We've been... *waiting* for you. Let's say your reputation precedes you."

"I won't ask your name," said Kell. "And the only thing that precedes you is the foul, rotten-egg stench."

Dekull's face darkened. "You should learn some respect, feeble, petty, rancid *mortal*."

"Respect? For your kind? I'd rather show you my cock."

"I'm going to teach you a lesson you will never forget, *boy*..." snarled Dekull, vampire fangs ejecting, shoulders hunching, swords glittering.

Kell laughed, an open, genuine sound of humour. "My name is Kell," he rumbled. "Here, let me carve it on your arse, lest you forget."

Kell moved forward, wary, and Dekull charged with a roar which showed his vampire fangs in all their glory, glinting with reflected firelight from the orange glow outside.

Kell felt the killing rage come on him, and it was now and here and the time was *right*. He was no longer an old man. He was no longer a weary, aged, *retired* soldier. Now he was strong and fast and deadly; he was a creature born in the Days of Blood and he *revelled* in his might, prowess, superiority, and although he knew this was a splinter of blood-oil magick, a *dark* magick, a trick and a curse instilled from his dead wife trapped inside his mighty, possessed axe – he locked the information in a tiny cage and tossed away the key with a snort. Now, he needed this energy. No matter how dark. No matter how bad. No matter how inherently *evil*.

Now, he needed the Legend.

Kell needed the *Legend*...

Kell slapped the swords aside, left right, a fast figure-of-eight curving from Ilanna with intricate insane skill, and front-kicked Dekull in the chest. But Dekull came on, crashing into Kell, who grabbed Dekull's ear and with a growl wrenched it off. Dekull screamed, a shocking high-pitched noise as blood erupted, and Kell crashed his fist – still holding the flapping ear – into Dekull's nose, breaking it with a crunch. Then Ilanna lifted high, keening with promise, and slammed down, cutting Dekull from collarbone to mid-chest allowing the huge man to flap open. Dekull staggered back, almost cut in two, his arms a good eight feet apart. Swords clattered to the stone, useless, released by limp twitching fingers.

Kell rolled his shoulders, and stared into Division General Dekull's eyes. They were glazed in disbelief, but he was still alive, still *conscious*. "Damn," muttered Kell, clenching and unclenching his hands. "That cold out there, it spoiled my bloody stroke. Here, lad. Let's have another go, shall we?" The second blow started where the first had ended, cleaving Dekull clean in two. Entrails and internal organs slopped to the floor, along with fat and muscle and skin and neatly severed bones. Kell turned from the dead vampire and stared through the portal.

Myriam had regained her feet, swaying and holding onto the wall. She sensed a change in Kell, and kept well back. He was different. He wasn't just dangerous; he was *deadly*. Deadly to *everyone*. She licked her lips and his terrible raging eyes fell on her. There was insanity there, wriggling, like a corrupt worm at the heart of a corrupt apple.

"Kell?"

"Yes?"

"Bhu Vanesh. Through there." She pointed.

"Stay here," said Kell, with a torn, sickly grimace. "I wouldn't like you to get in the way."

Kell strode forward, through the archway, up several steps and into a huge circular chamber. It was devoid of furniture, but thick rugs covered the walls and windows keeping the room in perpetual darkness. The floor, also, was completely filled with thick embroidered rugs, each showing complex patterns of blood-oil magick invocation, or scenes of rape and mutilation from ancient battles.

Bhu Vanesh sat in the centre of the chamber, cross-legged, long limbs relaxed, his smoky skin squirming with half-formed, drifting scenes of his distilled depravity; the eating of flesh, the biting of throats, acts of decadent arching screaming deathrape, the joy of giggling child murder, the orgasm in the hunt of the innocent, the frail, the stupid...

Bhu Vanesh.

Greatest of the Vampire Warlords.

The *Prime*.

Bhu Vanesh...

The Eater in the Dark.

Kell halted, and Ilanna clunked to the carpeted stone. His eyes burned like molten ore. He smiled a grim smile that had nothing to do with humour, and glanced down at the pile of child corpses, a small pyramid of desolation nestling pitifully beside the Warlord. There were perhaps thirty or forty babes in all, drained to husks, nothing more than bones in mottled flesh sacks.

"Interrupt breakfast, did I, you corrupted deviant fuck?" snarled Kell. His voice was bleak, like breeze over leaden caskets. Like the solitary chime of a funeral bell.

"Welcome to my humble home, Kell, Legend," spoke Bhu Vanesh, and smoke curled from his mouth, around his grey vampire fangs, around his long long claws which reached out towards Kell, as if imploring the old man to lay down his axe.

"Well, I got to say it, this ain't your home, Vanesh. It's time for you to go back. Back to the Chaos Halls. Back to the Keepers. You know this. You know it's time you left my world."

Bhu Vanesh's eyes flashed dark, like jewelled obsidian in smoke pools. He stood, a long, languorous uncurling imbued with restrained *power*. He towered over Kell, and his long legs seemed to sag at knee joints which bent the wrong way, and his arms reached almost to the ground and ended in vicious-looking curved talons. And all the time his smoke skin curled and twisted, depicting scenes of murder and cruelty and evil sex and deathrape and the hunt. The hunting of women. The hunting of children. From Bhu Vanesh's past… His History. His Legacy. Faces flashed in quick succession across his smoke skin. All begging. Pleading. Screaming. Dying.

Darkness, desolation, fear, hate, all emanated from the Vampire Warlord like a bad drug. A stench of hate. An aroma of evil.

Kell swallowed.

Something grabbed him in its fist.

Fear, a rancid ball of fat, filled his belly and throat and mind.

It took him over. It rolled into him, and filled him like a jug to the brim.

Kell wanted to puke. He wanted to scream. He wanted to die…

It was all he could do to meet Bhu Vanesh's piercing gaze.

"You *dare* to come here and challenge me?" snarled the Vampire Warlord. "You, nothing but a smear of shit on the vastness of time and purity, nothing but a wriggling, deformed babe fresh from its mother's stinking syphilitic cunt, *nothing* but a smear of organic pus from the rancid quivering *arsehole* of Chaos?" His voice had risen to a roar. The walls seemed to shake. Brands flickered wild in their brackets, almost extinguishing with Bhu Vanesh's open raw wild fury. He took a step forward, head lowering to Kell's level, and his huge long arms lifted threateningly. "Turn around, you fucking pointlessness, and leave me in peace."

Bhu Vanesh began a slow turn, back to his pile of suckled corpses, his face and *demeanour* filled with disgust, and loathing, and revulsion, and raw pure abhorrence.

"A pointlessness, is it?" growled Kell, and leapt forward with a bestial growl, Ilanna singing a beautiful high song, a song from the dying of worlds, a song plucked from strands of strummed chaos, a song of purity, and Ilanna struck for Bhu Vanesh's head but the Warlord turned fast, long arm slamming out with piledriver force to strike Kell in the chest. The old warrior grunted, was punched backwards, and hit the wall several feet above the ground. He landed heavy, in a crouch, and his head came up. He rubbed at his chest, and with a wrench pulled out a battered steel breastplate – now a mangled mess of twisted armour. Kell coughed, a harsh hacking cough, and dropped the steel to the ground.

Kell spoke. His words were low, harsh, inhuman, barely more than guttural noises as a fire demon would make... and certainly not the voice of Kell. "Bhu Vanesh. Creature of the Chaos Halls. It is time to come back. The Keepers have decreed it so. I am here as your Guide."

Kell charged again, and Bhu Vanesh turned fast and claws raked against Ilanna's butterfly blades, only now they were not steel – and flames from brands in iron brackets did not reflect from Ilanna's blades but were sucked deep into them like trailing streamers, sucked and spooled and drawn into the eternal portal of the Chaos Halls. Bhu Vanesh fought, and as Myriam staggered to the door and leaned heavily against the frame, watching, it seemed to her that he struck with long, lazy strokes, like a pendulum, a clockwork machine, claws slamming Ilanna left, then right, and curling around Kell to lift him from the floor, accelerating him high up so he nearly touched the vaulted ceiling.

"Petty mortal, I will tear you in two!" he snarled, long smoking drools of saliva pooling from vampire fangs. "You cannot stand against me! I am Bhu Vanesh. The Eater in the Dark. I do not *obey* the Keepers! *I mock them!*"

Kell struck down with Ilanna, crashing her butterfly blades into Bhu Vanesh's skull. "Is that so, you baby-sucking bastard?" he roared. He slammed down again, Ilanna squealing, screaming, wailing like an animal in pain, and again, and again, and sounds of tortured metal reverberated around the chamber, "Well if you don't obey the Keepers, you can fucking obey me!"

Kell struck down a third time. Black light seemed to crackle around the room, igniting the carpets and tapestries, which all burned with black fire. A cold ice wind rushed through the chamber. Bhu Vanesh squealed, and tossed Kell like a piece of tinder. The old warrior hit the wall, clothes setting alight with black fire, and his huge hands patted frantically at his clothing as dark eyes watched the thrashing figure of Bhu Vanesh. But it wasn't enough, it still wasn't enough, and Kell charged back at the Vampire Warlord who was thrashing and squealing, claws flailing wide and flashing like scythes through the air, and a deep groaning chimed through the chamber, making the very stones vibrate. Through this chaos came Nienna, face pale, lips drawn back in horror, and Myriam grabbed for her, brushed against her arm, but Nienna slapped her away and stumbled into the chamber, sword held high, her eyes glowing triumphant as she faced *that* which she feared the most, Bhu Vanesh, the Eater in the Dark, and Haunter of Dreams, Desecrater of Flesh. "I defy you!" she screamed, "I banish you back to the Chaos Halls!" and Bhu Vanesh's laughter rolled out like terrible thunder, like the crushing of tectonic plates, and Kell was battling in fury in the midst of the storm, Ilanna rising and falling, the black fire inside him, his bearskin jerkin aflame, sparks dancing through his beard and grey hair, Ilanna slamming left, and right, and left and right, striking away the Warlord's claws, sinking into smoky flesh only to pull back and the flesh seal like hot wax as faces screamed at Kell from beneath the smoke surface. A claw struck Kell a mighty blow, sending him whirling through the chaos, Ilanna still singing, and his tumbling, spinning body careered into Nienna, crashing her to the ground, Ilanna's blades cleaving through her chest, straight down to bone, straight into her heart.

The storm ended, with a *click*.

The black fire died.

Kell, kneeling, his jerkin drifting smoke, an old man again, looked up slowly and in horror. Saliva pooled from his silently working jaws. His face and hands were lacerated. His blood dripped to the thick burnt carpets. Nienna was lying at his feet, gasping, a huge wound from her shoulder to ribs. Blood bubbled at her chin, on her tongue and lips. Blood pulsed easily from the wound. Her eyes were glazed, confused, tears lying on her cheeks like spilt mercury. Kell dropped to her side, threw Ilanna to the floor, and grabbed at the huge slice through Nienna's flesh. With trembling fingers he tried to hold Nienna together. With force of will, he tried to meld her body back into one piece. Blood pulsed up, ran over his hands with the beating of her damaged, irregular heart. "No," whispered Kell, staring down into his sweet granddaughter's face, "no, not here, not now, not this way..."

"Grandfather?" she said, although it was barely audible. "*Why?*"

And then her lips went pale, and her eyes closed, and she convulsed, and although Kell's hands tried to hold her back together, she died there on the floor at the bequest of the great Ilanna – at the command of the Vampire Warlord.

"NO!" screamed Kell, and shook Nienna, but she was dead, and gone, gone to another realm, and Kell stood and took up Ilanna, and he gazed at her butterfly blades where Nienna's blood, her life-force, her essence, her *soul* stained those portals into the Chaos Halls... and a wild wind slammed through the chamber, both hot, and cold, and bitter and sweet. Smoke poured out from Ilanna, a thick black acrid smoke which stank of Nienna's blood, her summoning, and which filled the room in an instant. The world went slow, filled with black sparks, and a *groan* rent the air, *the groan of the world torn asunder* as a smoke-filled corridor opened up behind Bhu Vanesh. It stretched away for a million years. It led to a chamber of infinity, endlessly black, and from the sky fell corpses tumbling down down

down through nothingness into lakes of blood and rivers of death and oceans of evil weeping souls. Kell hefted Ilanna, and glared at Bhu Vanesh, who lifted his hands in supplication, eyes glowing red, smoke curling from his slick wet mouth.

"Get thee back to Chaos," snarled Kell, and strode forward, and there came a deafening clanking of chains and deep within the vaults Kell could see figures, tall and thin, like grey skeletons, their eyes pools of liquid silver that *glowed*. They came forward, walking oddly, and Kell blinked for he was on the roadway, on the path to the Chaos Halls, and thick pitted iron chains slammed past him, wrapping around Bhu Vanesh who was weeping, smoke oozing from every orifice like drifting blood-mist, and Kell strode forward and slammed Ilanna between his eyes, splitting Bhu Vanesh's head in two but still the Vampire Warlord wept, and still the smoke spilled from his mouth, for Kell could not kill Bhu Vanesh. Nobody could kill Bhu Vanesh. He was *immortal*.

"That's for Nienna," he spat.

"Not the Halls," Bhu Vanesh wept. "Not the Halls!"

The chains rattled, and Bhu Vanesh hurtled off along the infinite road all the while chanting his mantra, and now Kell saw the roadway was made of bones, of skulls, a wide flowing road of skulls and Kell dropped to one knee and wept, and the tall bony figures strode towards him and stood, five of them, watching him with their silver eyes, in complete silence.

Finally, Kell ceased his crying. He stood, breathing deeply, and lifted Ilanna in both hands still stained with Nienna's blood. Only then did a chill breeze caress his soul. He turned, wind ruffling his scorched bearskin jerkin, but the portal to the World of Men was gone.

All that remained was that infinite roadway of skulls, an obsidian sky, and a world stretching off to a distant horizon of eternally falling corpses, of fallen souls…

Kell was trapped in the Chaos Halls.

Kell was lost to Chaos.

## CHAPTER 16
### *Kell's Legend*

Grak the Bastard knelt amidst a hundred vampire corpses, sword lashing out, and Dekkar was behind him, a few remaining men beside. As fires roared along the dockside, so other units from the new army of Falanor had found Grak, and they fought vicious short battles until they were together, clashed together, united, the last few hundred survivors. But still they were losing. Still they were being massacred...

Then, the vampires fell back.

The dawn was coming.

Still fires raged, flames crackling, and Grak couldn't tell where the snow ended and the ash began. The world was in chaos. A living nightmare madness. Grak watched the ring of vampires, their snarling faces, their blood-red eyes.

"What are they waiting for?" rumbled Dekkar.

"Beats me," said Grak, sword before him, eyes lost to *the horror*. There was no way out of this. If Kell had killed Bhu Vanesh, then it would have been done a long time ago. If Kell had killed the Vampire Warlord, then his creatures would have turned to dust, to slime, to oil. But here they stood. The dawn had come.

Kell was dead, Grak knew it in his heart, in his bones, in his soul. Kell wasn't coming back.

"Shit," he said, hawked, and spat.

"What are they waiting for?" snapped Vilias, words edged with pain. He had a long, ragged slash down his face, from one eye to his chin. He'd been moaning about how no woman would ever look at him again. Grak supposed it didn't really mattered any longer... soon, they would all be corrupt. Either that, or dead.

"Maybe they know they're outnumbered?" suggested Grak. "They know they're beaten! After all, we're what? Three hundred? And they've..." his eyes scanned the rooftops, the roadways, the distant rubble, the edges of inferno. "Three, four thousand bloodsucking scum? We can take 'em, eh lads? We'll give 'em a damn good kicking!" Chuckles ran up and down the ranks, and exhausted men, wounded men, hoisted their weapons and waited grimly for the end.

"Come on!" screamed Grak. "Show us what you're made of! Fucking cowards! FUCKING VAMPIRE PLAGUE COWARDS! COME ON!"

"Hey." Vilias nudged Grak in the ribs. "Somebody's coming."

"Who is it? Dake the Axeman?" He roared with laughter. "Shall I show him my arse?"

"Better than that," grinned Vilias. "It's Kell."

"No!"

"It is, I swear it!"

From the distance, and as the dawn broke like a soft ruptured egg, Kell strode. Beams of yellow winter sunlight traced lines over the horizon, and Kell was blocked for a moment by the huge edifice of the Warlord's Tower. Then he moved through the rubble, strode past corpses, past fallen shields and fallen men, and stopped before Grak with boots crunching. Eerily, the vampires had parted to let him through. Their snarling subsided. They stared at him.

Everything was focused on Kell.

On Kell, the Legend.

Kell hefted Ilanna, and Grak could see the old warrior had tears in his beard. He lifted Ilanna, and his mouth opened, and he looked out at the vampire horde.

When he spoke, his voice was soft. Gentle, almost. Like mist creeping over a battlefield of corpses.

"Time to go home," he said, and each vampire lifted its head and smoke poured from its mouth, and flowed like lines of silver into Ilanna, into Kell's axe, in the Portal of the Chaos Halls. Kell stood, shuddering as each vampire was cleansed, each vampire purified. And now, as people, they fell to their hands and knees weeping in horror as they remembered what they had done.

It seemed to take an age.

One, by one, by one, the vampires' corruption was drawn into Ilanna. Their evil exorcised.

A cold winter wind blew over the slain, bringing ice, and making those watching shiver.

When it was over, Kell sank to the ground, rolling gently to his side and closing his eyes. Vilias moved tenderly to the old warrior, the old man, the old soldier. No longer did he look like Kell the Legend. Now, he just looked old and withdrawn and lost.

"Well?" snapped Grak, frowning.

Vilias looked up. "Holy Mother! He's dead, Grak! Kell's dead!"

• • • •

Kell stood before the Keepers of the Chaos Halls. He scowled and clutched Ilanna tight, and looked from one, to the next, to the next, and they surveyed him with eyes of silver, unspeaking, unmoving, uncaring.

*Is this it, then? Is this where I die? Is this where the game ends? Is this my new eternity?*

*No.* It was Ilanna. Her voice was honey in his brain, and she was weaving her dark magick once more. *This is not punishment, Kell. This is reward. This is not where you die. This is where you choose to live!*

Choose to live?

So there's a bloody *choice*?

Kell braced himself, staring up at the five Keepers. They exuded a lack of emotion. A neutrality. They were neither good, nor evil. They simply *were*. Kell scowled.

"Can I do something for you sorry-looking fuckers? Eh, lads? Or maybe you'd like a good kick to get you started?"

"You are to be congratulated," said one of the Keepers. Its voice was low but musical, and without threat. "Without your help, we would not have all the Vampire Warlords back in our custody."

"What about Meshwar? He's in Vor..."

"He is with us, now," said the Keeper. "You are not the only creature with the power to open a portal to the Chaos Halls. Although, it would seem, you are the most... *efficient*."

Kell considered this, then gave a single nod. Then he seemed to deflate. He remembered Nienna. Bitterness washed through him like a fast-flood of liquid cancer.

"Why am I here?"

"We have one last task for you."

"And suppose I don't want to accept your task?

Suppose I'm sick of these games? Suppose I'm just a bitter and lonely old man, who wants nothing more than to die?"

The Keeper moved close, and bent down until its face was a finger's breadth from Kell's face. Those silver eyes drilled into him and in those swirling silver depths Kell saw something impossible, something eternal, something truly godlike. The voice was a gentle breath across his face, and he inhaled the words, sucked them straight down into his soul... "You are lost at the moment, Kell, lost to the sadness and for that I still grant you life for foolish words and foolish thoughts. But do not think to test us, for we are the Keepers and we hold the Key to All Life. The Vampire Warlords should never have broken free – and one day, there will a reckoning for that abomination. But still, in Gollothrim, the vampires roam, the spawn of Bhu Vanesh... you can go there, we will give you the tools to take it back. You can save thousands, Kell. Either that..." The Keeper pulled back, silver orbs still fixed on Kell who coughed, and dropped to one knee, choking as if on heavy woodsmoke. "Either that, or you can stay here and be our guest for an eternity."

The sky went dark, struck through with huge zig-zags of crimson. The falling corpses fell faster, and screams rent the sky, screams of pure anguish like nothing Kell had ever heard. Nor would want to hear again.

"There is always a reckoning," said the Keeper. "Nothing goes unseen. Nothing goes unpunished. Remember that, Kell, the Legend, when you finally seek our forgiveness."

Kell nodded, but could not speak. The world tilted, the Chaos Halls spun away into a tiny black dot and

Kell fell through light and opened his eyes, lying on his back, next to the fast-cooling corpse of Nienna.

Three horses picked their way across a pastel landscape of white, greys and subtle cold blues. The beasts entered a sprawling forest of pine, and it was half a day before they emerged again on the flanks of a hill, climbing, following old farmers' trails high into the hills east of the Gantarak Marshes. From here, the glittering, ancient sprawl of Vor could be spied far, far to the south, and Kell reined his mount and sat for a while, staring at the distant city; staring at the new home of the Ankarok.

Saark watched him for a while, then glanced at Myriam, who shrugged, pushing out her lower lip.

"You want to visit?" asked Saark, eventually.

"No."

"Do you trust Skanda?"

"No."

"He claims all the Ankarok want is that one, single city. He delivered Meshwar to the Vampire Warlords, turned the vampire slaves back into people, and set them gently outside the city gates. He did everything he promised. More. He gave them food, supplies, money. It's a small price to pay, I think, for saving so many lives."

Kell said nothing, continuing to scowl. Eventually he coughed, rubbed his beard, then his weary eyes, and said, "Only bad things will come of this, you mark my words. This is not the last we've heard of Skanda, nor the damned Ankarok. I have a bad feeling in my bones, Saark. A bad feeling that runs right down into the sour roots of Falanor."

"We could ride down," said Saark, eyes glittering. "Take the city! Single-handed! Just like the old days, eh, Myriam? Eh?"

Kell shook his head. "The battle for Vor. It is a battle for another day. I'm tired, Saark. Too tired. Too old. I saw my daughter die, and I saw my granddaughter die." He turned, and there were tears in the old soldier's eyes. "It shouldn't be like this. You should never outlive your children. Sometimes, Saark, I fear I will never laugh again."

"At least the scourge of the Vampire Warlords has ended, Kell. Nienna died defending the land she loved. She did it for the good of Falanor, for its people, its history, its honour."

"Doesn't make it any easier to swallow," growled Kell, still staring at the haze of Vor.

"We are free of oppression," said Saark, forcing a false brightness into his voice. As ever, he was dressed in silk; bright green, this time, in an attempt to "blend with forest hues".

"Yeah," snarled Kell, curling his lips into an evil grimace. "But for how long? The Keepers, down in the Chaos Halls, told me that a war is coming. The vachine from Silva Valley – they were just the beginning. There are more, many more, far to the north, far beyond the Black Pike Mountains where no man has trodden for ten thousand years. They have a vast, corrupt, vachine empire built in the ice. And they want revenge, for what happened to the vachine of Silva Valley."

"You think a war is coming?" said Saark, quietly.

"There is always a war coming," said Kell, impassively.

"What shall we do?"

"What can we do?" said Kell, voice and eyes bleak, tears running down his cheeks as he thought about

Nienna for the hundredth time, thought about the terrible axe blades of Ilanna and tried to persuade himself *tried to convince himself* that the axe had nothing to do with the young woman's death. After all, Ilanna was just steel. Cold black steel. Nothing more, nothing less.

"Time to leave," said Myriam, glancing up at the sky. "There's a storm coming."

Kell nodded, and dug heels to the flanks of his mount, cantering ahead of the small group.

Myriam glanced at Saark. "Do you think he'll be all right?" she said. "I mean. We thought he was dead, back there."

Saark gave a single nod. "Maybe he did die. A little bit. Lost a part of his soul."

"But will he be all right?"

"Of course he will. He's Kell. Kell, the Legend."

Spring was coming to Falanor. The cold winds from the north grew mild, and snow and ice began a long melt, gradually freeing up the Great North Road for easier passage; of both people and supplies.

Over the coming months, slowly, the cities of Falanor rebuilt themselves, and the thousands of people who'd fled the horrors, first of the albino Army of Iron, the Harvesters, and later the Vampire Warlords, the refugees, the outcasts, slowly they drifted back and populations began once again to grow, to build, to prosper.

As the first daffodils scattered brightness across the hills and valleys of Falanor, a new King was crowned. He had been found sheltered in the forest city of Vorgeth close to the Autumn Palace along with his brother, Oliver. His name was Alexander, son of Leanoric, and proud grandson of Searlan the Battle King. And although he was only just sixteen years old, he was wise, and stern, and honest, and promised to make a fine new leader. Immediately, he appointed a new General of his infant Eagle Divisions. The General's name was Grak, who earned his rank through sterling service to the Land of Falanor.

In time, Alexander's eyes turned south. South, to the city of Vor, once the capital of Falanor, once his *father's* city, his father's *pride*. And Alexander brooded on the secrecy of the occupying race known as the Ankarok.

Since Vor closed its great iron gates, nobody had entered nor left the much-altered city.

A year after the banishment of the Vampire Warlords to the Chaos Halls, Alexander, Oliver, Grak and twenty soldiers reined in their armoured mounts far to the west of Vor, and gazed with a mixture of wonder and horror at what had once been the oldest city in the country.

Whereas once huge white towers, temples and palaces dominated the skyline, and the city had been surrounded by white stone walls, now everything had been... *encompassed* by what looked, at first glance, like a giant, matt black beetle shell.

"Holy Mother," said Oliver, rubbing his chin and placing his hand on his sword hilt. "The city! It's gone!"

"Not gone," said Alexander, who now sported a small scar under one eye from duelling, from *training*, "but *buried*. What have those bastards done to our father's city? What have they done to *our heritage?*"

Grak kicked his horse forward, and placed a warning hand on Alexander's arm. "Majesty. I suggest caution. We must not approach the city. That was the pact made, the agreement between the leaders of Falanor and the... Ankarok."

Alexander nodded, but his eyes gleamed, and secretly he thought, *that was not my agreement*. Later, as he pored over maps in his tent, drinking watered wine from a gold goblet and eating cheese and black bread, so Alexander doodled a *hypothetical* retaking of the city of Vor.

For the honour of his father's memory, of course.

For the honour of Falanor.


A cold, fresh mountain wind blew.

Kell stood on a crag, exercising with slow, easy movements, swinging Ilanna left and right, running through manoeuvres so long used in battle they were now an instinct. He breathed deep, drinking in the vast pastel vision of mountains and hills and forests, valleys and rivers and lakes. It was a mammoth, natural vista, a painting more beautiful than anything ever captured on canvas. And it was there, there for Kell, there for his simple honest pleasure.

Kell finally ended his routine, and stood for a while, holding Ilanna to his chest, a violent internal war raging through his skull and heart. Part of him wanted to cast the axe away, far out from the mountain plateau, to be lost in the wilderness of crags and rocky slopes and scree below. But he did not. Could not. Even though he blamed Ilanna, to some extent, for the death of Nienna.

Nienna.

She haunted him.

Haunted him, with her innocence and the unfairness of it all.

"How are you feeling, old horse?" Saark grinned up at Kell, then deftly climbed up the ridge and sat, staring out over the early morning view. "By all the gods, this is a throne for a prince!"

"What are you doing here?"

"A simple *good morning* would have been a far more pleasant and agreeable salutation."

"Ha. I'm not here to be pleasant."

"I noticed. Here." Saark unwrapped a cloth sack and handed Kell a chunk of cheese and grain bread. Saark bit himself a lump of cheese and began to chew.

Kell, also, broke his fast, and the two men sat in companionable silence for a while. Until Kell winced, and clutched his stomach, tears springing to his eyes. He coughed, then rubbed at his head.

"The poison?"

"Aye, lad. It's gotten worse."

"You know what this means?"

Kell stared into Saark's eyes, and gave a nod. He sighed. "Aye. I must travel west. Find the antidote. Find the cure. I am reluctant to leave Falanor, but – well, I think after what happened with Nienna, maybe it would do me good. To see new countries, meet new people. To put my mark on a new place. A new world."

"'Different cultures, different customs'," quoted Saark, chewing on his bread. "You would of course need to travel far across the Salarl Ocean, my friend, out towards the lands of Kaydos. It is told the place is a vast, hot continent. Thousands and thousands of leagues of forest, hot, humid, damp, uncomfortable, where insects fight to make a merry meal of a man, and it is claimed in hushed whispers around strange fires that men and wolves walk together under the full yellow moon."

Kell eyed Saark thoughtfully. "Sounds like a harsh land, laddie."

"Only a fool would travel there," Saark agreed.

"I've already packed my things. I believe a ship leaves

from Garramandos in a week. It should not be hard to acquire passage. As I said, it would do me good. And of course, this damn poison still courses through my veins. Some days, I curse Myriam her lusts."

"And some days you thank her," grinned Saark.

"Aye. That I do."

They sat in silence for a while. Eventually, Saark said, "I, also, have taken the liberty of packing. It would, of course, be highly foolish to let such a moaning old goat as yourself travel alone. Imagine the trouble you would get yourself into, with your ignorant peasant ways, base stupidity and crude manners! Whereas I, I with my noble breeding, sense of natural etiquette, and *love* of everything honourable, well, I would surely keep one such as you out of terrible mischief."

Kell looked sideways at Saark. "I suppose you've packed a huge wardrobe? Silver goblets? Silk shirts? A perfume of subtly mingled horse shit?"

"Of course. But thankfully, I have Mary, my donkey, to help shoulder my burden."

Kell groaned. "You're *not* bringing that stinking and cantankerous beast."

Saark frowned. "But *Kell*, how else will I journey with an extensive wardrobe? Just because I travel with peasants, doesn't mean I have to look like one. I must protest…"

"Wait, wait." Kell held up a huge hand. "What do you mean, '*peasants*'? Plural? You told Myriam?"

"Well," Saark shifted uncomfortably, "I couldn't have you sneaking off in the night without her, could I? I couldn't allow you to do the dishonourable thing."

"*Dishonourable thing!*" spluttered Kell, turning bright red. "You! *You!* You dare to come out with that whining bloody gibberish? After all the things you've done to the poor women of Falanor! After all the hearts you broke? After all the children you sired? After all the chastity locks you picked?"

"Hey," frowned Saark. "I never said I was perfect. Only that you should show some morals."

"Morals?" screeched Kell, but they were rudely interrupted. Myriam appeared, climbing deftly up the rocky ridgeline. She was dressed for travel, and had her bow strapped to her back. She smiled at the two men.

"I'm ready," she said.

Kell scowled. "So I need to book passage for three travellers, do I?" he snapped.

"And a donkey," said Saark.

"And a donkey," growled Kell, through gritted teeth. "Well, we better be going, I reckon. It's a long trek to Garramandos, that's for sure. Over some treacherous terrain."

All three stared across the western flanks of the Black Pike Mountains, vast and black, towering and defiant, and their gazes drifted down towards the Salarl Ocean, which glittered like molten silver in the early morning sunlight.

"Men and wolves," said Kell, distantly.

Saark grinned and slapped him on the back. "Aye. Men and wolves. Come on."

Against a sparkling horizon of ocean and a rearing backdrop of savage mountains, the three travellers began a long, careful descent from the mountain plateau to the breathless, waiting world below.

# *Acknowledgments*

Thanks must go, as ever, to many people. To Sonia, Joe and Oliver for lots of laughs; to Dorothy for advice and critiques; to my ever-increasing circle of editors, you are all wonderful creatures and *always right…*; to my many filmmaking friends for enduring my abuse on either side of the camera; to Nick for all his Mac advice and weird Combat K machinations; to Jim for being such a good sport; to Kev for relighting an old friendship (and *I* won that old Monopoly tournament, by the way…); and seeing as this is the final Clockwork Vampire novel, a final big kiss to the Gemmell community for not savaging me *too much* in what is a genuine homage to my writing hero.

## About the Author

Andy Remic is a British writer with a love of ancient warfare, mountain climbing and sword fighting. Married with two children, he works as a writer in the fields of Fantasy and SF, and in his spare time is a smuggler of rare Dog Gems, a drinker of distilled liquor and hunter of rogue vachine. He also dabbles in filmmaking.

**www.andyremic.com**

## A Quick Q & A with the Man
## Behind the Clockwork

**Angry Robot:** So that brings us to the end of the Clockwork Vampire Chronicles. Prior to *Kell's Legend* you were known for your science fiction. How have you enjoyed your first foray into the realms of epic fantasy?

**Andy Remic:** I've absolutely LOVED writing in the fantasy genre. I really appreciate the opportunity given to me by Angry Robot, so lots of man-love should be squirted around the room. It's quite a different process writing in the fantasy genre compared to SF; I have a completely different mind-set, and enter a completely different world during creation. In some ways (many ways) when I write in the fantasy genre it's a lot more realistic for me – I think I used to be a warrior of Genghis Khan. Or something. I love riding ponies. And can smell the Prairie Steppes on a rainy day... even in London ;-).

**Angry Robot:** You've always acknowledged a debt to Gemmell, and have described Kell's adventures as a tribute to your hero. Did you accomplish everything you set out to do with the series?

**Andy Remic:** Kell was indeed a tribute to David, but an idea I actually had – oooh, gods, about 15 years ago now – when I was cycling on the Pennine Moors in the ice and snow. And of course, this was also when David was alive. It was intended that Kell was always going to be my "Druss", a no-nonsense axe man who took the world by the balls and gave it a good kicking, whilst "doing the right thing" in an ultimately moralistic sense. In my original mental planning, Druss was a retired warrior living in an abandoned lighthouse on a rugged coast, and when the albino soldiers invaded (I was reading *Elric* at the time, so hats off to Moorcock) Druss would have to take up his mighty axe. However, I never wrote the book at the time – I didn't feel I had enough original elements, and indeed, back then I was still a fledgling unpublished author. The original elements for *Kell's Legend* only came with the introduction of the Clockwork Vampires, a completely different and deviant mental direction. And then, when all the ideas gelled… whoosh! Yes. Those long winter bike rides through the ice on The Viking Route were superb planning time for what would transmogrify into *Kell's Legend*, *Soul Stealers* and *Vampire Warlords*. However, in terms of accomplishing everything… no no no. Oh no. Kell and Saark are not being let off the hook that easily! I have so much pain waiting for them, it's going to make *Evil Dead* look like a silly little film about puppies.

**Angry Robot:** The parallels between Kell and Gemmell's Druss have been discussed elsewhere. Why pay homage to Druss, in particular? What was it about this character that inspired your series?

**Andy Remic:** *Legend* by David Gemmell was the first fantasy novel which really made me sit up and think, Holy crap! This is GENIUS! when I was about 15 years old. Obviously, Druss was the driving force in *Legend* and you could completely identify and comprehend how much love Gemmell put into the old man. Druss became an icon of Gemmell's heroic fantasy worlds (for me and many, many others), and as such, I wanted to pay tribute – not just to the character whom I so admired, but to the author I so admired as well – and had sadly passed away. When David died, me and Ian Graham built a fire and toasted him to the Hall of Heroes with lots of whiskey. I hope his shade finds my story a worthy homage. If not, I'm sure Snaga will be teaching me a lesson in the Afterlife! *Checks over his shoulder in the dark shadows of the room.*

**Angry Robot:** Will we see Kell and Saark again?

**Andy Remic:** I have another six books of pain, agony and torment planned (in my head) for Kell and Saark, so yes, I definitely want to work with them again. They truly were a joy to write, and by the end of *Vampire Warlords* they didn't so much feel like characters I created, more like old friends and comrades I had been to Hell and back alongside. I lived through their squabblings and their battles, and enjoyed every damn second of it! First, however, I have another series to attend… but trust me, I will be back to Kell and Saark in the near future. There are plans, my friends, PLANS!

**Angry Robot:** You're an established SF author, and now fantasy. What's next – Andy Remic's paranormal romance series?

**Andy Remic:** It's funny you should mention that, I have plans for a series of romantic novels called, "Love's Loving Kissing Flame", "The Pink Rose of the Virgin's Nun" and "The Throbbing Clitoris of Ecstasy"... Or maybe I just dreamed that ;-).

On the fantasy front, I have a new series planned called tMachine Dragon Chronicles – *The Dragon Engine*, *Dragon's Ice* and *Twilight of the Dragons*, where the upper world of man has become a prison of vicious ice, thus men have been forced underground, slaves to the dwarves and their "dragon engine" used in the smelting of ore. The novels follows the machinations of religious maniac, poet and torturer Cardinald Skalg, and his plot to use three dark adventurers to free the dragon engine of its world chains. This is still in the planning stages, but it's going to be fast-paced, dark and dirty, a bastard deviation of everything Tolkien did.

That's the plan!

## your Robot overlords.

*Twitter @angryrobotbooks*

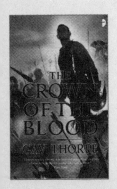